The
MX Book
of
New
Sherlock
Holmes
Stories

Part III: 1896-1929

THE MX BOOK OF NEW
SHERLOCK HOLMES
STORIES

PART III - 1896-1929

SOUTHAMPTON
STREET

359

EDITED
By
David
Marcum

OFFICES

TRADITIONAL HOLMES
ADVENTURES
COMPILED FOR THE
BENEFIT OF THE
RESTORATION OF
UNDERSHAW

ISBN 9781780928531 Hardback
ISBN 9781780928548 Paperback
ePub ISBN 9781780928555
PDF ISBN 9781780928562

Published in the UK by MX Publishing
335 Princess Park Manor, Royal Drive,
London, N11 3GX
www.mxpublishing.co.uk
Cover design by www.staunch.com

CONTENTS

PART III: 1896-1929

(Continued on the next page . . . .)

(Continued on the next page . . . .)

These additional adventures are contained in
The MX Book of New Sherlock Holmes Stories
PART I: 1881-1889

. . . and PART II: 1890-1895

(Continued on the next page . . . .)

COPYRIGHT INFORMATION

The following contributors appear in
The MX Book of New Sherlock Holmes Stories
Part I – 1881-1889 *and* Part II – 1890-1895

Editor's Introduction:
The Whole Art of Detection
by David Marcum

Part I: *The Great Watsonian Oversoul*

According to Merriam-Webster, a *pastiche* is defined as a literary or artistic work that imitates the style of a previous work. Almost from the time that the first Sherlock Holmes stories began to appear in print, there were Holmes pastiches as well, side by side with the official sixty tales that are known as *The Canon*. Some from that period are more properly defined as parodies, but a few were written to sincerely portray additional adventures featuring Our Heroes, Holmes and Dr. John H. Watson,

I personally discovered pastiches at around the same time that I found the original Holmes stories, and began reading them just as eagerly as I did the material found in The Canon. In my mind, a well-written pastiche, set in the same correct time period as the originals, was as legitimate as anything written by the first – but definitely *not* the only! – of Watson's literary agents, Sir Arthur Conan Doyle. In the past, I've described the whole vast combination of Canon and pastiche as *The Great Holmes Tapestry*, with each providing an important thread to the whole, some brighter or thicker than others perhaps, but all contributing to the big picture. Perhaps another comparison would be to say that the union of Canon and pastiche forms a *rope*, with the Canonical adventures serving as the solid wire core, while all the threads and fibers of the additional pastiches bound around it provide greater substance and strength, with the two being indivisible.

I believe that pastiches have contributed immensely to the ever-increasing popularity of Holmes and Watson throughout the years. Additional cases and adventures only serve to feed the Sherlockian Fire, and ideally refocus interest back to the original narratives. There are some Sherlockian scholars who want nothing at all to do pastiches, and there are others who don't even want to classify all of the original sixty stories as being authentic, stating in various essays and books that this or that Canonical tale is spurious. I cannot agree with them.

In my essay, "In Praise of the Pastiche" (*The Baker Street Journal,* Vol. 62, No. 3, Autumn 2012), I argue that just sixty original stories relating incidents from Holmes's career are simply not enough. There must be more *about* the world's greatest consulting detective to justify that he *is* the world's greatest consulting detective, rather than just a few dozen "official" stories that leave too much unanswered. Pastiches fill in the gaps and cracks.

In "The Adventure of the Abbey Grange", Holmes tells Watson that ". . . I propose to devote my declining years to the composition of a textbook, which shall focus the whole art of detection into one volume." The vast amount of stories that make up the combination of both Canon and pastiche may not be – in fact, it certainly isn't! – what Holmes had in mind, but it is the closest we'll get to seeing and observing that overall tapestry of his life and work, the *Whole Art of Detection.*

Over the years, an incredible number of people have added to the body of work initially introduced by Watson's first literary agent. Sometimes, people discover lost manuscripts, usually written by Watson, but occasionally narrated by someone else – a Baker Street Irregular perhaps, or a client, or Mycroft Holmes, or a passing acquaintance, or maybe even by Sherlock Holmes himself. On a regular basis, an adventure is discovered in one of Watson's Tin Dispatch Boxes – and there must have been several of those to hold so many tales! These stories may be narrated in first person, or they may have a third-person omniscient viewpoint. No matter how they are found or transcribed, I believe that each of the "editors" of these later discovered adventures has tapped into what I like to call *The Great Watsonian Oversoul.*

When I was in high school, my award-winning English teacher, (who sadly never ever taught anything at all about the literary efforts of one Dr. John H. Watson, leaving that joyful task for me to capably take care of for myself,) introduced us to the concept of an "oversoul" – she was using it in relation to how it influenced some poet. Essentially – and I am no doubt remembering this somewhat incorrectly – the idea is that we are all tiny pieces of a greater entity, split off for a time from it, out here in the darkness and trapped in our own heads, before returning at some later point to the protection, warmth, goodness, and omnipotence of the greater whole. I, however, appropriated the idea to describe the overall source of the Holmesian narratives.

To my way of thinking, all of the traditional Canonically-based Sherlock Holmes stories are linked back eventually to this same basis of inspiration, no matter how the later "author" accesses it. Since the mid-1970's, I've read and collected literally thousands of adventures concerning the activities of Mr. Sherlock Holmes, and since the mid-1990's, I've been organizing all of them – both Canon and pastiche – into an extremely detailed day-by-day chronology, now covering hundreds of pages and literally thousands of narratives. Among the things that have become apparent to me over the years are: 1) There can *never* be enough good Holmes stories, relating the activities of the *true, correct,* and *traditional* Holmes of the Victorian and Edwardian eras; and, 2) The people who bring these stories to the public, no matter how they go about it, or whether they even realize it, are all somehow channeling Watson.

So one way or another, the spark of imagination that sets these narratives in motion originates in the *Great Watsonian Oversoul.* That's not to say that a lot of authorial/editorial blood, sweat, and tears doesn't go into all of these "discovered" stories, and these efforts should not be negated at all. These works don't simply appear as finished products – even the ones that are found essentially complete in Tin Dispatch Boxes. It takes a lot of work to first make contact with the Watsonian Oversoul, and then to transcribe what is being relayed in such a way that the public can understand and enjoy it. Sometimes the person relaying the story might misunderstand a fact or two along the way, leading to an odd discrepancy, or the "editor" channeling the tale may weave some little thing from his or her own agenda onto Watson's original intentions that isn't quite consistent with the big tapestry. But if the writer listening for that still small Watson voice within is sincere, the overall sense of the Sherlockian events that are being revealed within the story remains true.

Part II: *The MX Book of New Sherlock Holmes Stories*

This collection of new Sherlock Holmes adventures came about by listening to that still small voice. One Saturday morning in late January 2015, I popped awake, several hours earlier than I had intended, having just had a full-fledged and vivid dream about a new Holmes anthology. Now, I've tapped into the Oversoul and "edited" a few of Watson's works myself, but I hadn't tried anything like this before. If I'd rolled over and gone back to sleep, the idea would probably have disappeared. But it had grabbed me by then, so I quietly got up and started making a wish list of "editors" of Watson's works that I already knew and admired, in order to see if they would be willing to go through the effort to come up with some more new adventures

I emailed Steve Emecz of MX Publishing, and he enthusiastically liked the idea. Early on, we agreed that the author royalties for the project would be used to support Undershaw, the home where Sir Arthur Conan Doyle was living when both *The Hound of the Baskervilles*, as well as some of the later Holmes adventures, were written. MX Publishing has supported this effort in the past, so this decision was an easy one.

The same morning that I had the idea, I began to email authors, and I immediately started receiving positive responses. I was then emboldened to start asking still more people, and quickly the whole thing escalated. I reached out to friends to help me track down some authors in England that could only be reached by the old-fashioned mail. People already participating suggested still more folks who might also want to tap into the Oversoul and contribute a story to the anthology. It quickly grew to the point where it obviously needed to be two volumes, and sometime after that, it became three. (If it hadn't been split into multiple books, the whole thing would have become so fat that the book spines would have cracked apart.) It was always important to me that this collection, although finally presented under three covers, be considered as *one unified anthology*. As such, it is the largest collection of new Sherlock Holmes stories assembled in the same place.

These volumes have contributors from around the world: the U.S. and Canada, all over Great Britain, India, New Zealand, and Sweden. There are a couple of British expatriates who were living in Asia at the time they made their contributions, and two American ex-pats in London and Kuwait as well. Early on, I let all of the participants know that, since we had contributors from all around the globe, the format and punctuation of the books would be uniformly consistent, but they could use either British or American spellings in their finished works. Therefore, if you see some stories with *color* and others with *colour*, for example, that's why.

The contributors to these anthologies come from a wide variety of backgrounds. Some are professional best-selling authors. Others, like me, write for fun, but have day jobs elsewhere. A few are noted fan-fiction authors, taking this opportunity to write for a wider and different kind of audience. (I've always felt that some of the best Holmes writing has appeared as fan-fiction, and that a great Holmes story doesn't have to be found in a published book.)

There are several here who are writing a Holmes story for the first time. In the case of a few of these, I specifically invited noted Sherlockians who have worked long and hard to promote the World of Holmes but haven't written a pastiche before, with the idea that someone – and I can't think of who – once said that every Sherlockian should write at least one pastiche in their lives. This was their chance, and they did a great job with it.

A number of our authors have not been previously associated with MX. Welcome to the MX family! I'm aware that a few of these authors have already caught the Holmes-adventure-writing bug and are working on additional stories for future MX books of their own. I can't wait to read them!

Early on, I decided to arrange the stories chronologically, extending from 1881, when Holmes and Watson first met, to 1929, the year of Watson's death. This allowed for a logical arrangement of the stories, covering the entire period of Holmes and Watson's friendship and professional partnership. I was greatly influenced by that wonderful volume edited by Mike Ashley, *The Mammoth Book of New Sherlock Holmes Adventures* (1997). He also arranged the stories within by date, and as a hard-core chronologist, I have a great appreciation for that method.

My conditions for participation in the project were very basic. First and most important, as the editor of this collection I was very firm that Holmes and Watson had to be treated with respect and sincerity, and as if all involved were playing that fine old Sherlockian tradition, *The Game.* For those unfamiliar with this idea, Holmes and Watson are treated as if they were living, breathing, historical figures, and as such they *cannot* be transplanted to other eras, or forced to do something that is completely ridiculous for the time period in which they existed, such as battling space aliens. The stories had to be set in the correct time periods, ideally from 1881 to 1929. There could be no parody, nothing where Holmes was being used as a vampire-fighting Van Helsing, and nothing where he was incorrectly modernized, as if he is some version of Doctor Who to be reincarnated as whatever version of hero the current generation needs him to be.

Additionally, the stories had to be approximately the same length as the original short stories, with no novellas, and no fragments, such as something along the lines of "The Return of the Field Bazaar" or "How Watson Learned Another Trick". Also, I initially stated that the submitted tales all had to be narrated by Watson. However, there were a few that showed up in my email (t)in-box that stepped away from the Watsonian viewpoint – specifically, a case narrated by Wiggins, a couple by Professor Moriarty, one by a passing acquaintance of Holmes during The Great Hiatus, and two about the Professor told in third person. These provided valuable insight, they were set within the correct Holmesian world, and they were simply too good to miss.

Another goal that I set was to make use of completely new stories for the collection, in one format or another. With this in mind, I was *almost* completely successful . . . but not quite, if you wish to be technical about it. I must admit that, by way of a tiny bit of Watsonian Obfuscation, a few of the items herein have appeared in other locations or in other mediums, although they have never been published in this format before. One story was previously in a rather obscure local publication, and I believe that it is almost completely unknown to the larger audience, and might not be read by a lot of people otherwise. (In fact, with all my pastiche collecting, this was one that I didn't know about until it was submitted for this anthology.) A couple of the submissions have previously been on the internet for a short time, and two of the submissions are in the form of scripts that were previously used for radio broadcasts in the U.S. and the U.K. This their first appearance as text in book form.

As a side note, mentioning the scripts reminds me to acknowledge this volume's unintended but happy association with Imagination Theatre, which broadcasts traditional radio dramas weekly throughout the U.S., and has recently passed 1,000 broadcasts. As part of their rotating line-up, they feature a series of original tales, *The Further Adventures of Sherlock Holmes* – as of this writing numbering 117 episodes – and they are also in the process of broadcasting adaptations of the original Holmes Canon as *The Classic Adventures of Sherlock Holmes.* Currently, they are close to completing radio dramatizations of all sixty original Holmes stories featuring the same actors as Holmes and Watson throughout, John Patrick Lowrie and Lawrence Albert respectively, and with all adaptations by the same scriptwriter, Matthew J. Elliott. One of the scripts in this collection, never before in print, is by Imagination Theatre founder Jim French. A number of other Imagination Theatre writers besides Mr. French have contributed to this collection, including Matthew Elliott, Matthew Booth, John Hall, Daniel McGachey, Iain McLaughlin and Claire Bartlett, Jeremy Holstein, J.R. Campbell, and me (David Marcum) – that's a sizeable chunk our authors!

Part III: *With many sincere thanks . . . .*

Throughout the process, everyone that I've contacted about writing a story has been more than gracious, either by immediately stepping up and offering to provide one, or – when he or she couldn't join the party due to other obligations – continuing to offer support in numerous other ways. As the editor, being able to read these new adventures straight out of the Tin Dispatch Box is an experience not to be missed. Having never before tried to put together such a diverse Sherlock Holmes anthology, I must say that the whole thing has quickly become addictive, and I cannot promise not to do another one, although one of this size and scope, which was truly jumping into the deep water and *then* learning to swim, is unlikely.

Of all the people I'd like to thank, I must first express my gratitude as a whole to the authors – or "editors", if you will – of these new adventures from the Great Watsonian Oversoul. You stepped up and provided some really great stories that didn't previously exist. You also put up with my reminders, nudges, and story suggestions when I had to don my Editing Deerstalker. Along the way, as I was able to read these fine stories, I also met some really nice new people.

More specifically, I'd like to thank the following:

- My wife Rebecca and my son Dan, who mean everything – and I mean *everything*! – to me. They constantly put up with my Sherlockian interest, my ever-increasing pastiche collection, and my tendency to wear a deerstalker as my only hat for three-quarters of the year.
- Steve Emecz, publisher extraordinaire and the hardest working man in show-biz. Thanks for the constant support and for always listening!
- Bob Gibson of *staunch.com* – an amazing graphic artist, who let me keep tinkering with the cover, which became two covers, and then three . . . .
- Joel and Carolyn Senter. Years ago, my family knew to start my birthday and Christmas shopping with Joel and Carolyn's "Classic Specialties" catalogs. Later, when the original version of my first Holmes book was published, they enthusiastically got behind it and were responsible for selling almost every copy that was sold. They've encouraged me at every step, and I'm so glad that they could be a part of this anthology.
- Roger Johnson, who is so gracious when my random emails arrive with Holmesian ideas and questions. Visiting with him and his wife, Jean, during my Holmes Pilgrimage to England in 2013 was a high point of my trip. More recently, he located some wonderful pictures of Holmes and Watson for use in these books. In so many ways, I thank you!
- Bob Byrne, whom I first "met" by emailing him a question about Solar Pons – if you don't know who Solar Pons is, go find out! – and then we ended up becoming friends.
- Derrick Belanger, who hadn't specifically channeled Watson before, and is now on his way to becoming one of the best. Thanks for the friendship, the back-and-forth discussions upon occasion, and the support.

- Marcia Wilson, an incredible author and friend who received my first fan letter, long before I ever started thinking about writing anything myself. I've always said that, with her complex tales of Lestrade and his associates, she's found *Scotland Yard's* Tin Dispatch Box.
- Denis O. Smith, who was at the top of my pastiche wish list. I'm so glad that I was able to track him down, and I've really enjoyed the ongoing e-discussions we've had along the way since then;
- Lyndsay Faye, who said yes the very first day that I invited her to submit a story, and who also educated me about contracts.
- Bert Coules, for his advice and contributions, and for helping put together the Holmes and Watson that I hear in my head, Clive Merrison and Michael Williams.
- Carole Nelson Douglas, who – among many things – gave me some invaluable advice about foreign editions.
- Les Klinger, who spent part of a Sunday afternoon in a cross-country phone call, giving me some really valuable advice.
- Otto Penzler, who helped me several times when I pestered him for advice, and who wisely told me that "editing anthologies isn't quite as easy as drawing up a wish list and signing up stories".
- Chris Redmond, who jumped in early, and for all that he does, and just for having that incredible website, *sherlockian.net.*
- Kim Krisco, whom I met (by email) along the way, and was a never-ending source of encouragement.
- Tim Symonds, also an email friend with a lot of great ideas and support. I look forward to catching up with you at Birling Gap someday.
- John Hall, whose books – both pastiches and scholarship – I've enjoyed for years.
- Andy Lane – Thanks for the clever back-and-forth emails. I'm sorry I couldn't make it to New York when you were over here. I'll catch you next time!
- James Lovegrove, who corresponded with me way-back-when about the *true* location of Holmes's retirement villa on the Sussex Downs. (You know where I mean.) I'm very jealous of where you live.
- Steven Rothman, editor of *The Baker Street Journal*, for always responding so nicely whenever one of my emails drops in from out of the blue.

- Matthew Elliott, for all that he's done, and also for helping with the description of what he's accomplishing at Imagination Theatre.
- Maxim Jakubowski, who introduced me to a great new set of people.
- Mark Gagen, who gave me permission to use that absolutely perfect picture of Holmes on the back cover.
- And last but certainly *not* least, Sir Arthur Conan Doyle: Author, doctor, adventurer, and the Founder of the Feast. Present in spirit, and honored by all of us here.

This collection has been a labor of love by both the participants and myself. Everyone did their sincerest best to produce an anthology that truly represents why Holmes and Watson have been so popular for so long. This is just another tiny piece of the Great Holmes Tapestry, which will continue to grow and grow, for there can never be enough stories about the man whom Watson described as "the best and wisest . . . whom I have ever known."

David Marcum
August 7th, 2015
163rd Birthday of Dr. John H. Watson

Questions or comments may be addressed to David Marcum at
thepapersofsherlockholmes@gmail.com

Study and Natural Talent
by Roger Johnson

Greenhough Smith, editor of *The Strand Magazine*, hailed Arthur Conan Doyle as "the greatest natural storyteller of his age". Over a century on, Conan Doyle's genius keeps us reading, and, because many of us feel that sixty adventures of Sherlock Holmes just aren't enough, we write as well. The original tales are exciting and often ingenious; they're intelligent without being patronising, and they're never pretentious. The characters of Holmes and Watson – the apparently contrary forces that actually complement each other like Yin and Yang – stimulate our imaginations. Surely every devotee believes that the world needs more stories of Sherlock Holmes, and as, barring a true miracle, there'll be no more from his creator's fondly wielded Parker Duofold pen, we should provide at least one or two ourselves. We know the originals inside-out, or we think we do; we have a grand idea for a plot, and the style seems to be – well – elementary. How hard can it be?

In fact it's a sight harder than most of us think. Believe me: I know! To set a story convincingly in late Victorian or Edwardian London can require a fair deal of research just to avoid simple anachronisms and similar errors of fact. There are aspects of personality that may need careful attention – not just Holmes and Watson, but other established characters such as Messrs Lestrade and Gregson, and Mrs. Hudson (who really *was* the landlady at 221B, and *not* the housekeeper). Vocabulary and speech-patterns are important . . . .

Some will say, of course, that it's impossible to replicate the Doyle-Watson style. Nevertheless, there are writers who have come acceptably close to the real thing. Edgar W. Smith declared that *The Exploits of Sherlock Holmes* by Adrian Conan Doyle and John Dickson Carr should be re-titled *Sherlock Holmes Exploited*, but it is actually a remarkably good collection. Nicholas Meyer, L. B. Greenwood, Barrie Roberts, and Michael Hardwick are other names that come to mind, of authors who have, as Holmes himself said in a different context, applied both study and natural talent to the writing of new Sherlock Holmes adventures. For the current monumental collection, conceived and published for the benefit of the house that saw the rebirth of the great detective, David Marcum has coaxed stories from the best of today's generation of Holmesian chroniclers. Some of the contributors are famous, and some perhaps are destined for fame, but all of them bring intelligence, knowledge, understanding and deep affection to the task – and we are the gainers.

Roger Johnson, BSI, ASH
Editor: *The Sherlock Holmes Journal*
August 2015

Foreword
By David Stuart Davies

The Sherlock Holmes Mystery

The real mystery about Sherlock Holmes is his universal appeal. What is it about this character created by a young Scottish doctor over a hundred years ago that has caught the imagination of readers worldwide? His stories have been translated into many languages; there are Holmes fan clubs all over the globe, in countries as diverse as Japan and India; and statues have been raised to this man who never lived in England, Scotland, Switzerland and Japan. His fans range from teenagers to pensioners, from labourers to aristocrats, from postmen to politicians. Why?

Well, the appeal of Sherlock is not new. Conan Doyle's tales about Holmes fascinated the Victorian reader and they became the mainstay of the *Strand* magazine – the sole reason why people purchased the publication. When the author tried to do away with his detective creation by casting him into the swirling waters of the Reichenbach Falls, the public mourned his loss, wearing black arm bands as a mark of respect. One outraged lady wrote to Doyle in protest, beginning her letter, "You brute!"

However, by this time the Sherlock bandwagon had begun rolling. After his supposed death at Reichenbach, Sherlock Holmes gradually grew into a media star. The first actor to portray the Great Detective in public was Charles Brookfield in a bit of comic nonsense called *Under the Clock* at the Royal Court Theatre in London in 1893. The piece made great fun of Holmes and his fawning companion, Watson. In 1894, Richard Morton and H. C. Barry penned a popular song, *The Ghost of Sherlock Holmes*, which did the rounds of the music halls. Both these ventures reveal how famous Holmes had already become so early in his career.

Holmes's fame received a boost when William Gillette appeared in the successful production of a play he had penned himself from an early draft written by Conan Doyle. *Sherlock Holmes*, a melodrama, with a plot largely drawn from "A Scandal in Bohemia" and "The Final Problem", opened in New York in 1899. While the critics sneered; the public cheered. It came to London in 1901 and ran for six months, playing to capacity houses at the Lyceum Theatre.

13

Then came the movies. As early as 1903, Holmes was up there on the silver screen. The first known film to feature the sleuth was *Sherlock Holmes Baffled*, made by the American Mutoscope and Bioscope Company in 1903. This humorous movie, which lasts less than one minute, is little more than an exercise in primitive trick photography but it appealed because the detective's name was in the title.

And so Sherlock Holmes began to have a parallel career: on the page and in the media. And it has remained so ever since. For over a hundred years Sherlock Holmes, along with his friend and biographer Dr John H. Watson, has appeared in numerous stories, films, plays, radio shows, television dramas, cartoons, musicals, etc., delighting a growing legion of fans. Doyle only wrote fifty-six short stories and four novels featuring his detective hero – but this Canon has been added to greatly by other hands. The desire for more Holmes continues to grow.

And yet, this still does not quite explain the appeal of the deer-stalkered one. Of course there are some rational explanations. There is the playing of the light-hearted academic game started by Ronald Knox, which involves investigating the anomalies and omissions in the Doyle Canon caused by Watson's slip of the pen: establishing the true date of certain cases, providing solutions and theories with respect to some obscure point – exactly how many times was Watson married, which university did Holmes attend, who was Mrs. Turner, and why were the Moriarty brothers both called James? The friendship between Holmes and Watson, one of the great literary bondings, is another vital and appealing aspect of the stories. We know that despite his cold aesthetic nature, Holmes is lost without his Boswell, and to Watson his friend is "the best and wisest man" he has ever known. Then there is the enjoyment of the period and the wonderful atmosphere evoked by the stories: it is a world where no matter what nefarious deeds were being planned, the world's more foremost champion of law and order was on hand to set things right – an England of thick, rolling fogs, where "gas lamps fail at twenty feet." In the company of Conan Doyle's mythical occupants of Baker Street, we return to a magic childhood. Sir Arthur himself indicated that the stories appealed to the boy who was half a man and the man who was half a boy. As we immerse ourselves in these wonderful tales, we shed the shackles of the present day and are free to thrill to the hansom cab ride through the darkened streets, knowing once more that the game is afoot.

All these reasons and more may be proffered in response to the question – why Sherlock Holmes? And in some way they are all applicable to solving the mystery. But there is something else. Something that lies in the heart and beggars description. We experience what it is.

We feel it. We all share it. But it is too intangible, too precious to verbalise. That is why there is no truly clear and appropriate answer to why Sherlock Holmes? Only a feeling – one that brings intense and enriching pleasure.

David Stuart Davies, BSI
August 2015

Undershaw
Circa 1900 *(Source: Wikipedia)*

Undershaw:
An Ongoing Legacy
for Sherlock Holmes
by Steve Emecz

The authors involved in this anthology are donating their royalties toward the restoration of Sir Arthur Conan Doyle's former home, Undershaw. This building was initially in terrible disrepair, and was saved from destruction by the *Undershaw Preservation Trust* (Patron: Mark Gatiss). Today, the building has been bought by Stepping Stones (a school for children with learning difficulties), and is being restored to its former glory.

Undershaw is where Sir Arthur Conan Doyle wrote many of the Sherlock Holmes stories, including *The Hound of The Baskervilles*. It's where Conan Doyle brought Sherlock Holmes back to life. This project will contribute to specific projects at the house, such as the restoration of Doyle's study, and will be opened up to fans outside term time.

You can find out more information about the new Stepping Stones school at *www.steppingstones.org.uk*

Sherlock Holmes (1854-1957) was born in Yorkshire, England, on 6 January, 1854. In the mid-1870's, he moved to 24 Montague Street, London, where he established himself as the world's first Consulting Detective. After meeting Dr. John H. Watson in early 1881, he and Watson moved to rooms at 221b Baker Street, where his reputation as the world's greatest detective grew for several decades. He was presumed to have died battling noted criminal Professor James Moriarty on 4 May, 1891, but he returned to London on 5 April, 1894, resuming his consulting practice in Baker Street. Retiring to the Sussex coast near Beachy Head in October 1903, he continued to be involved in various private and government investigations while giving the impression of being a reclusive apiarist. He was very involved in the events encompassing World War I, and to a lesser degree those of World War II. He passed away peacefully upon the cliffs above his Sussex home on his 103rd birthday, 6 January, 1957.

Dr. John Hamish Watson (1852-1929) was born in Stranraer, Scotland on 7 August, 1852. In 1878, he took his Doctor of Medicine Degree from the University of London, and later joined the army as a surgeon. Wounded at the Battle of Maiwand in Afghanistan (27 July, 1880), he returned to London late that same year. On New Year's Day, 1881, he was introduced to Sherlock Holmes in the chemical laboratory at Barts. Agreeing to share rooms with Holmes in Baker Street, Watson became invaluable to Holmes's consulting detective practice. Watson was married and widowed three times, and from the late 1880's onward, in addition to his participation in Holmes's investigations and his medical practice, he chronicled Holmes's adventures, with the assistance of a literary agent, Sir Arthur Conan Doyle, in a series of popular narratives, most of which were first published in *The Strand* magazine. Watson's later years were spent preparing a vast number of his notes of Holmes's cases for future publication. Following a final important investigation with Holmes, Watson contracted pneumonia and passed away on 24 July, 1929.

Photos of Sherlock Holmes and Dr. John H. Watson courtesy of Roger Johnson

PART III: 1896-1929

Holmes and Watson's friendship and professional partnership continued throughout the second half of the 1890's. During this period, cases were numerous, and Holmes was at the top of his game. Although he did not immediately allow Watson to resume publication of his adventures following his return to London in 1894 after "The Great Hiatus", Holmes's fame reached far and wide.

In mid-1902, Watson married for a third time, as mentioned by Holmes in "The Blanched Soldier". Watson and his wife set up residence in nearby Queen Anne Street, and as before, he continued to involve himself in Holmes's investigations.

In Autumn 1903, Holmes, only forty-nine years of age at the time, "retired" and moved to the South Downs of Sussex, residing at a farm near Beachy Head, very near the coast. Ostensibly there to keep bees, Holmes had, in reality, removed himself from his consulting practice, as he was finding it more and more necessary to help with his brother Mycroft's work in delaying or helping to prepare for the upcoming conflict with Germany – at that point a matter of when *rather than* if. *While giving the impression of being a recluse, Holmes actually stayed quite busy, with the aid of Watson, who was still residing with his wife in London. Holmes and Watson were extremely active and effective during World War I, and after that conflict was over, Holmes continued to conduct the occasional investigation. Watson, though less busy in the 1920's, was often of vital assistance to Holmes, right up to the time of his death in July 1929.*

Holmes continued to reside in Sussex, still participating in intermittent adventures, throughout the 1930's and 1940's. He was involved in the Allied efforts during World War II, and thereafter returned to his farm, continuing to keep bees and conduct research until his death on the morning of his birthday in 1957, while overlooking his home.

"Good old Watson!"

– Sherlock Holmes, "His Last Bow"

"I shall ever regard him as the best and wisest man whom I have ever known."

– Dr. John H. Watson, "The Final Problem"

Two Sonnets
by Bonnie MacBird

Out of the Fog

When electronic clutter clouds our minds
With trifles, and presentiments of doom
There's always a retreat we know to find
Up seventeen stairs to that gaslit room.

Perhaps a brandy, in our easy chair
We turn the pages of a well-worn book.
Now, there beside the fire, sit our pair.
Two gentlemen, a smile, a knowing look.

And so with pipe in hand, our man unmasks
With reason, knowledge and a touch of art,
A source of horror, which he takes to task
And sets the evil, from us, far apart.

The side of angels and the depths of hell
Emerge from fog; are dealt with. All is well.

The Art of Detection

The world is puzzling, that we know for sure
To tame its mysteries a worthy goal.
For this we turn to science, but the lure
Is to unmask the secrets of the soul.

For Sherlock Holmes, the boundaries are clear.
The facts are clay, and scientists need bricks
To build a solid construct, yet appear
To some like a magician playing tricks.

But inferential logic can go wrong
And fail to parse out motives or mistakes.
The mind of man is like a complex song
And a musician's ear is what it takes.

Holmes uses all – his knowledge, mind and heart,
Because to practice science . . . is an art.

Harbinger of Death
by Geri Schear

$\mathbf{M}$y friend Mr. Sherlock Holmes has often spoken with disdain of superstition and the supernatural. Anything that is not firmly founded in science and the natural world are anathema to his cold, analytical mind.

On occasion, I have challenged him, pointing out there is much in the world that remains a mystery to us and observing that new discoveries are being made almost daily.

"Bah!" he replies. "When science proves to me that ghosts exist or that one man can read another's mind, I shall be happy to explore the subject. However, until that unlikely day dawns, I must consider it utter twaddle."

I was reminded of these conversations on a rainy Tuesday morning in 1896 when Holmes handed me a letter he had just received.

"Well, Watson," said he. "One of these deluded believers in the supernatural wishes to consult with me on a case of premonition."

The letter he handed me was quite baffling. It read,

> *Dear Mr. Holmes,*
>
> *I hope you will forgive a complete stranger writing to you. I find myself in a situation so outré, so distressing, I do not know where else to seek advice.*
>
> *My great-aunt Catherine is very dear to me and I am afraid, I am very much afraid, that she will die this week. Indeed, if the predictions are true, it seems quite certain.*
>
> *She herself is convinced of it. "I have seen the harbinger of death," she says.*
>
> *I shall call upon you tomorrow at two o'clock in hopes that you can advise me.*
>
> *Sincerely,*
>
> *Jane Asquith*

"How very strange," I said. "A harbinger of death. Shall you meet with this Miss Asquith, Holmes?"

"This is a matter for clerics or carnival hucksters," he replied. "Still, I have had no case of real interest since I helped my brother recover the Bruce-Partington plans. I suppose I can spare Miss Asquith half an hour."

Despite this dismissive attitude, I had a feeling Holmes was rather more interested in the matter than he said. Several times over the course of that wet and windy evening, he picked up the letter and re-read it.

The following afternoon we sat by the fire in our sitting room while a sulphurous fog enveloped the city. Holmes added to the effect by puffing endlessly on his favourite briar pipe. The atmosphere inside was soon as poisonous as that beyond our windows.

Two o'clock came and passed with no sign of our visitor. Twice Holmes picked up the newspaper only to toss it aside moments later.

"She may have been delayed by the weather," I said.

"Bah! If she were not coming, she should have sent a telegram. I might have gone out instead of spending the day cooped up indoors."

Some twenty minutes after the hour, we heard a knock at the door below and moments later a handsome young woman was ushered into our rooms. She was slender, with the finely boned features of a true beauty. Her clothes were well made and becoming to her English rose complexion. At this moment, however, she seemed flustered.

"I do apologise," she said. "I am afraid my train was delayed because of the fog."

"Perfectly understandable, Miss Asquith," I said. "Please sit down. I shall ask Mrs. Hudson to bring some hot coffee."

Holmes was unamused by this further delay. However, he could see the girl was trembling with cold and he is not unkind.

"Please sit here by the fire," he said. "While Watson sees to the domestic matters."

"Thank you," our guest said. "I really dislike being late. I pride myself on my punctuality as a rule. It is so discourteous to be tardy. Besides, I know what a busy man you are, Mr. Holmes. Oh, it is good of you to see me on such short notice."

A few minutes later, her coffee cup warming her hands, Miss Asquith told us her tale. "In order for you to understand the strange situation in which I find myself," she said, "it is necessary I tell you a little of my background."

"Proceed," said Holmes. He sat back in his chair and made a tent with his fingers. His hawkish eyes were almost fully closed, and yet I knew he was paying the closest attention.

26

"I was unfortunate enough to lose both my parents before my third birthday. My mother died just a few months after I was born, and I lost my beloved father in the train derailment at Wigan in 1873. However, my father's aunt, my great-aunt Catherine, came to live with me and raised me as her own child. She has been so very good to me and I am sure no parent could love me more.

"Two years ago, I decided I wanted to see more of the world and taste some independence. I became governess for a family in Ireland. While there, I met a fine gentleman by the name of Lindley Mead and, in short, we are engaged to be married."

"What does your great-aunt make of this arrangement?" I asked. Holmes continued to sit silent in exactly the same pose.

"She is delighted. Lindley comes from a very fine family and I shall want for nothing."

For a moment Miss Asquith fell silent. She sipped her coffee and seemed at a loss as how to continue.

"When did you return to England?" Holmes said.

"In December. Aunt Catherine had an incident with her heart in November and her health has been in decline ever since. I was – am – dreadfully worried about her. Lindley would not see me distressed for worlds, and so he suggested we spend Christmas in Hertfordshire with my aunt and my father's brother Ambrose, who has just recently returned home after many years in India.

"We had a lovely holiday. Aunt Catherine and Lindley got on famously and everything seemed delightful. I had never met my uncle before; he moved to India before I was born. It was delightful to meet him and, I confess, to imagine that my father might have been a little like him."

"It sounds perfectly charming," I said.

"It was," she said. "Indeed, we would have been perfectly gay but for one thing.

"When Aunt Catherine became ill, my uncle hired a young woman to be her companion. Kate is a wild gypsy girl, dark skin, dark hair, and her English is sometimes inadequate. However, she seems quite devoted to Aunt Catherine, and my aunt, in turn, is fond of her.

"On Christmas Eve, when we had finished dinner, we gathered in the drawing room. My aunt's health generally keeps her confined to bed, but that night my uncle carried her into the room that she might join in all the revels. We were in the middle of exchanging gifts when Kate seemed to go into a strange sort of trance. She mumbled words that we could not understand. Only one made any sense, 'Billy'."

"Billy?" Holmes said. "Does your aunt know anyone of that name?"

"No one. My great-grandfather's name was William, but no one ever called him Billy."

"Could you make out any other words?"

"It was just a strange jumble of sounds. Then she shrieked the word 'Death!' We were all quite unnerved. Lindley tried to shake her out of it but the girl was in some sort of ecstasy. She then seemed to fall asleep. Her head was sunk onto her breast and she breathed heavily for several minutes. Then she said, quiet clearly, 'Death.'

"At that she seemed to waken and she began to weep hysterically. She said the Angel of Death had come and told her that my beloved aunt would die on Friday the Thirteenth. She was unable to explain the name Billy and seemed to have no recollection of saying it. She later told us that she has had visions ever since she was a young girl."

"What is the nature of these visions?" I asked, quickly covering up my friend's snort of derision.

"Death. Always death. She seems convinced that my aunt will die on Friday the Thirteenth. I should say that my fiancé and uncle were amused by this, but my aunt was not. She heard the girl's words with extraordinary seriousness."

"By your own account, Miss Asquith," Holmes said, "Your great-aunt is in poor health, she is elderly. She might die at any time. I do not wish to appear unsympathetic, but what do you expect me to do?"

"I have tried to dismiss the matter as idle superstition, Mr. Holmes," said the woman. "I was raised to believe in the concrete, and to trust only what I could see and touch. Aunt Catherine instilled these principles in me. Yet, oddly, despite her rational attitude in almost everything else, she has always been extremely superstitious. She bows to magpies and knocks on wood for luck. She always feared Friday the Thirteenth, and she has a horror of black cats. To see her reduced to such terror by these dire predictions is very upsetting. The matter has become even more distressing of late."

"Why so?" I asked.

"Surely it is obvious, Watson?" Holmes said. "The day after tomorrow is Friday the Thirteenth. It is the first one this year."

"That is it exactly, Mr. Holmes," said Miss Asquith. "My Great-Aunt's health cannot stand up to sudden shocks. As the thirteenth draws ever closer her anxiety increases. I beg her to refuse to allow Kate access to her, but she will not listen. The girl arrived, it seemed, knowing many secrets about my aunt. My aunt is convinced the girl has some strange power."

"You still have not explained what you want of me, Miss Asquith," Holmes said. "No crime has been committed. This is a matter for doctors and priests, not for a detective."

The woman seemed utterly crestfallen. "Oh, I do not know what I hoped," she cried. "You are known for your common sense and for your wisdom, Mr. Holmes. I thought you might advise me."

It is rare indeed when Holmes appears dumbfounded, but he did at that moment. "What can I tell you that you have not already determined for yourself?" he said. "If this girl, Kate, is a person of conscience, perhaps you could point out to her the harm she may be doing. Make her your ally, if you can. If she refuses to stop frightening your aunt then you may have to threaten her with dismissal. As to the rest of it, well, someone who believes one superstition may believe another. See if you can offer your great-aunt a talisman of some sort. Convince her it will protect her from every evil. I'm sure you can find some sort of gewgaw in London that will fit the bill."

He pondered a moment longer, then said, "Is your great-aunt wealthy?"

"No, not very. Her father left her five thousand pounds and some jewels when he died. My own father also left her an annual stipend. She had enough to live in some comfort, but I am not sure what, if anything, remains. I am afraid she probably squandered a great amount on so-called spiritualists. Her fiancé died a month before they were to be married, you see, and she is obsessed with trying to contact him in the afterlife."

"And the house and property?"

"They are mine. That is to say, Aunt Catherine is my guardian, but I come into my inheritance when I am married."

"And when will this happy event occur?"

"The first week in July."

"I see. So there is no reason why anyone would want to harm her?"

"Want to . . . ? Certainly not, Mr. Holmes. Besides, it is unlikely she will live more than another year or two in any case."

"Is that what her doctor says?" I asked. "She had a myocardial infarction, and it caused serious damage to her heart, I suppose."

"Yes, indeed. Her illness was quite sudden and left her an invalid. We had to move her from her bedroom to the morning room, for she can no longer manage the stairs. Christmas was the last time she was able to leave her bed."

Holmes seemed thoughtful but remained silent. Our visitor rose and said, "Thank you for taking the time to see me. I realise what foolishness it seems. Only I am so very fond of her."

"Of course," I said, shaking her hand. "But superstition cannot harm her."

Holmes, too, shook the woman's hand. "If there are further developments, Miss Asquith," he said, "I hope you will contact me immediately. In the meantime, I would suggest you spend as much time with your great-aunt as possible, particularly on Friday. On no account leave her alone. Not even at night."

"Do you really think she might be at risk?" the woman asked.

"She believes it," Holmes said. "Your presence may serve as a distraction. See if you can find some activity elsewhere to keep this gypsy girl busy on that day. You might also ask your great-aunt's physician to visit, just to put her mind at ease."

"Thank you, Mr. Holmes, you are every bit as kind as I had been told."

For several hours after Miss Asquith left, Holmes sat in silent contemplation. His head sunk down, his pipe dangling from his lips, and not a word did he speak. Then, a few minutes before five o'clock, he suddenly sprang to his feet and said, "I'm going out, Watson," and was gone before I could even reply.

I did not see Holmes again until late the following morning. He joined me at the breakfast table looking perplexed and uneasy.

"Where did you get to last night, Holmes?" I asked.

"I was researching the background of Miss Asquith's family," he replied and said no more. He sipped his coffee and made an indifferent job of his eggs.

"Anything of interest?" I urged. Clearly, there was more to this tale of superstition than I had fathomed.

"Miss Catherine Anne Asquith is as blameless as you, Watson. She has lived a quiet, indeed, an exemplary life. She is not wealthy but is fairly comfortable. She lives in a large house in Hadley Wood and employs four indoor servants, and two outdoor men. As our client told us, Miss Catherine Asquith is merely the guardian of the estate. Jane Asquith comes into her inheritance on her thirtieth birthday, or on the occasion of her marriage, whichever comes first.

"The house belonged to the late Stephen Asquith, our young client's father. He, in turn, inherited the property and a modest sum from his father, Major Clive Asquith of the 3rd Bengal Light Cavalry. The major was stationed in Karnaul and served with distinction in Delhi."

"A prestigious regiment, Holmes," I said. "I have heard many tales of their exploits."

"Do you know anyone who served in that illustrious company?"

"Yes, my old friend, Windy. That is, Teddy Windermere. He is considered something of a regiment historian. Do you want me to talk to him?"

"If you would. See if you can find out anything that is not part of the official record about the major."

"Certainly, I shall go after breakfast. But surely you do not think there is some sort of plot against the unfortunate maiden aunt of our young visitor?"

"Probably not. All the same, I should like to be sure."

My friend declared he had other business to attend, and so I set off to visit my former fellow-officer in Hampstead. Windermere had been a senior officer when I first enlisted in the Fifth Northumberland Fusiliers, and he was kind enough to take a young subaltern under his wing. Despite a twenty-year age difference, we had a great deal in common and took a similar approach to the care of the wounded soldiers in our care.

Windy was at home and happy to see me.

"Glad of the distraction, young Johnny," he said. He tapped his leg with his cane. "This wretched thing worries me no end in this weather. How are your wounds?"

"They flare up from time to time," I said. "The curse of getting older, I suppose."

"Well, others are much worse off, eh? So you still solving murders with that Holmes fellow? I must say, I enjoy your stories. You have a real talent for it."

I confess I was very pleased to hear this. I explained that a case had brought me to Hampstead, and my old colleague heard the details in silence.

"Clive Asquith, eh?" said Windy when I was done. "Yes, I remember him. That is to say, I heard of him. He was long before my time, of course, but he had a reputation."

"A bad reputation?"

"Well, no, not entirely. There was some sort of scandal." He frowned and pondered for a few moments and said, "There was a woman. Well, there is always a woman in India. It seems the major became thoroughly infatuated with some girl. I've forgotten her name, I'm afraid. Anyway, she had a child by him. She died in the delivery and the baby died too. I believe the major was distraught. Of course, many people saw it as divine justice. He was a married man, after all, and had a family."

"Do you know anything else?"

"Well, another scandal emerged not long after the girl and the baby died. Her father claimed the major had stolen some rubies. They were

31

absolutely priceless, he said. The major was outraged and insisted his property be searched. Nothing was found."

"Did people believe he was innocent?"

"Oh yes, it seemed beyond doubt. It was generally believed the dead girl's family blamed Asquith for her death and simply wanted a reason to make things difficult for him."

"Do you know anything else about the fellow?"

He pondered for a moment longer. "No, other than that he served with distinction, I believe. This is related to one of Mr. Holmes's cases, I take it?"

I dissembled as much as felt comfortable. Shortly afterwards, I left and returned to Baker Street.

Holmes returned later in the evening. I told him what I had learned from Windy.

"Interesting," he said. "A tawdry tale but hardly unusual. There was no further scandal attached to the major?"

"None at all, as far as Windy knows," I said.

"And what of the major's descendants?"

"Windy wouldn't know any recent history, I'm afraid. He was invalided out of the service around the same time as I. I could make further inquiries."

"Not necessary," said he. "I have not been idle. Our client's uncle, Major Ambrose Asquith, made something of a name for himself in India during the past twenty-five years."

"The way you say that, Holmes, leads me to believe that name is not a good one."

"It probably depends on who you ask," he said. "His military record is unblemished if undistinguished, but he has amassed some large debts and has an urgent need of funds."

"Surely he cannot expect to gain from his sister's death?"

"It does not appear so, but I have sent some queries by telegram. I shall know more when I receive a reply."

"Then there seems no reason for anyone to hurt the old woman," I said. "And given her rapid decline, it's likely she will be dead before the end of the year. Surely nothing can be gained by hastening her death."

"What you say is perfectly reasonable, Watson," my friend replied. "It is exactly what I have been telling myself. It is only superstition, after all. No need to fret. Unless . . . ." At that, he sank into a brooding silence and did not stir for the rest of the evening.

Early the following morning, I was roused from a deep sleep by my friend. "Come, Watson," he said. "I have had replies to my telegrams. We must away to Hertfordshire. Make haste. There is no time to lose."

We got the train at Moorgate, and some forty-five minutes later alighted at the Hadley Wood station. The air was damp and misty, but it had none of the acrid quality of our London fog. It was pleasant to breathe in the natural scents of the woods and the grasses.

We took a cab from the station and hurried the Asquith home. We alighted outside a large iron gate and walked up the elegant, curving driveway to the front door. Holmes rang the bell and we waited.

"Splendid to be out of the city, eh, Holmes?" I said as I gazed at the rolling expanse of Hertfordshire that lay before us serene and enchanting in the damp air.

Holmes's attention was elsewhere. "I pray we are in time," he said.

We waited a few moments longer. Holmes was about to ring again when the door was opened by a flustered looking man.

"Can I help you?" he said.

"I am Mr. Sherlock Holmes," said my friend. "This is my colleague, Doctor Watson. We would like to speak to Miss Jane Asquith."

"I am afraid that may not be possible, sir," said the man. "We have had a sudden death, and the house is all an uproar."

"We are too late!" Holmes cried. "When did Miss Catherine Asquith die?"

"No more than an hour ago, sir," said the man. "Please come in and I will see if Miss Asquith might be able to speak with you. I am afraid she is very distressed."

"Damnation!" Holmes exclaimed, after the man left us alone in the study. "This is my fault, Watson. I should have come last night."

"Forgive me, Holmes," I said. "But are you not breaking one of your own rules? You are theorising in advance of the facts. After all, the old woman's death may have been from natural causes. She has been in bad health for some time, after all."

Holmes looked chagrined. "Yes, you are quite right, Watson. A salutary reminder. I shall wait until we learn more."

The door opened and our young client came into the room. "Oh, Mr. Holmes," she said. "How good of you to come. But there is nothing you can do, nothing anyone can do now for my poor aunt."

"I am sorry, truly sorry, that we did not arrive in time," said my friend. "But if you would be so kind as to tell us everything that happened regarding her death, perhaps I may be of some use after all."

The woman looked surprised. "I will tell you everything, Mr. Holmes, of course I will. But I cannot see how you can help us. She suffered a fatal heart attack. Still, as you have come all this way . . . ."

She sat down and gathered her composure. After a moment she said, "I took your advice, Mr. Holmes, and I have not left my aunt alone since Wednesday, when I came to see you.

"Last night she was in very good spirits. We played cards in her room and talked about the wedding. She was feeling better and even talked about joining us at the table in a day or two.

"At around eleven o'clock I kissed her goodnight and retired."

"Excuse me, where is your bedroom?"

"I had Lindley set up a divan for me in the morning room so I would be near her. She told me it was a foolish notion, but she did not really try to discourage me. Her sleep has been very poor lately, and I think it comforted her to know I was near.

"Even after I lay down, we continued our conversation. Eventually we fell asleep but my slumber was fitful. Then something woke me in the early hours. Perhaps I had a presentiment that something was wrong. I found my aunt gasping for breath. She had such a look of terror on her face. 'The harbinger,' she gasped. 'The harbinger of death.'

"I called for help and my Uncle went to get the local doctor. Alas, there was nothing anyone could do. She fell into a coma and died just an hour ago."

"I am very sorry to hear it. What time did you waken?" Holmes said.

"Around five o'clock. It was still dark out, but something felt wrong. I cannot explain it."

"Would you be kind enough to let us see the room where this occurred? I assume your aunt's body is still *in situ*?"

"Yes, she is. Please, come this way."

The morning room was at the back of the house. All the curtains were drawn and the body was covered with a sheet.

The dead woman's bed faced the window. The divan that Miss Asquith had been using was against the wall beside the door, about twelve feet from her aunt's bed.

"With your permission, Miss Asquith, Doctor Watson will examine the body. You might prefer to wait elsewhere. We may be several minutes."

"Take as much time as you need, Mr. Holmes," she replied. "I have a great many things to do. Please join me in the drawing room when you are ready. Ring for Craddock, the butler, if you need anything."

As soon as our client left, Holmes drew back the curtains and paused to examine the small casement window. "What do you make of this, Watson?" he said.

"It doesn't open very far; no more than five inches," I said, looking at it. "Between that and the rose bush below, I think we can safely rule this out as an entryway for any killer." I looked around the room. "I can't see a killer coming through the door, either. He'd have to pass right by Miss Asquith's divan to get to the old woman's bed."

Holmes rubbed his hands together in glee. "Quite a puzzle. And yet I see possibilities . . . . Do you examine the body, Watson. I shall focus my attention on the room."

"What am I looking for, Holmes?" I said. "Surely you do not think this could be anything more than a natural death? The fact that today is Friday the Thirteenth is no more than a coincidence. Unless you are willing to concede to a supernatural explanation?"

"I cannot say what I believe, Watson," he replied, ignoring my gibe. "Just do your usual, thorough job and tell me if anything strikes you as odd."

As I worked, Holmes began his own exploration of the room. He sniffed the bedlinen and the carpet and crawled around on his belly, examining every surface. He inspected the door and the lock. Then he returned to the casement window and scrutinized every inch of the glass, the sill, and the carpet below with his glass. "Wet," he said. "This window was open for some time."

"It was shut when we came into the room," I said.

"Yes," he said, chuckling. "Indeed it was. Well, what is your diagnosis? Natural causes?"

"I am afraid so, Holmes," I said. "A myocardial infarction."

He rubbed his hands together with glee. "What a case this has been, Watson! I was a dullard indeed not to have seen the signs before." He bent down and examined the old woman with his glass, then chuckled.

"Natural causes, you say. What do you make of this, then, Watson?" He held up a short black hair with his tweezers.

"A hair? What does that prove?"

"Murder, my dear fellow. It is unassailable proof of murder."

A short while later, the room locked, and the butler instructed to allow no one to enter; we joined Miss Asquith in the drawing room. She was sitting on the divan, pale and her eyes red from tears, but she was perfectly composed. Her fiancé was in attendance. He was a slender, handsome young man with black curls and high cheekbones. He had the look of a poet, though I later discovered he was an architect. At that moment, he was sitting beside our client, holding her hand.

"Miss Asquith," said my friend gently. "I would like to ask you some questions, if I may."

35

"Do you feel up to it, my dear?" said Mead. "I'm sure Mr. Holmes would understand if you would rather wait."

My friend looked as if nothing would please him less. Fortunately, Miss Asquith said, "I want to help, if I can. Please sit down, Mr. Holmes, Doctor."

"Before we begin, may I ask where your uncle and the girl, Kate, are?"

"My uncle took the doctor home, and Kate is in her room, I suppose," said Miss Asquith.

"I'm afraid the girl has vanished," Mead said, reluctantly. "Mr. Ambrose Asquith went looking for her after Jane's aunt died. He thought she would want to pay her respects. However, she was not in her room and it looked as if her bed had not been slept in. As Jane says, Ambrose drove the doctor home, but he said he'd see if the girl had caught a train. He should be back soon."

"Very well. Now, Miss Asquith, you said something woke you in the early hours. I need you to try to remember as much detail as you can about the state of the room when you awoke."

Miss Asquith frowned then she said, "Well, nothing seemed out of the way. The room was in darkness but the curtains were drawn back."

"That was how you had left them before you went to sleep?"

"Yes. My poor aunt liked to be able to see the sky from her bed."

"And the window was open?"

"Oh, no. The weather has been very damp of late, and we have kept the window closed. I do not think we have opened it since last autumn."

"Did you hear anything?"

Again, a pause as she considered. "I heard a rustle outside."

"The trees, surely," said her fiancé.

"Perhaps," Holmes said, but again, from his air of suppressed excitement, I knew there was more here than I had fathomed.

"Did you smell anything?"

"Why, isn't that odd?" exclaimed Miss Asquith. "I had quite forgotten, but you are right, Mr. Holmes. There was a peculiar smell. Something familiar and strong, but I cannot identify it."

"Ha!" Holmes said. "Excellent. I wonder if I might examine the grounds? No, you need not come with me, Mr. Mead. Please stay here and look after your fiancée."

We walked the circumference of the building. Outside the morning room, Holmes stopped and examined the bushes closely.

"No man could get into the room this way," I said. "Even if he could get the window opened widely enough, he'd be torn to bits on those rose bushes."

"And yet a man stood here," Holmes replied. He pointed at the clear outline of a man's shoes in the ground. "And there is something else here too, you see?" He plucked a tuft of black hair from the bush and showed it to me.

"Holmes," I cried. "I begin to see. But who would do such a wicked thing? And why?"

"Why indeed. Ah, what is this . . . ? Fish!"

It was indeed a piece of trout that, curiously, had a long string tied around its tail. Like the hair, Holmes saved it in an envelope.

"I do hope you won't have to carry that around too long, Holmes," I said. "You'll have every cat in Hertfordshire after you."

"Not every cat, Watson," he said, chuckling. "Just one."

We then began to search the grounds. Holmes would not tell me what we were looking for; only that it was something unusual. "You will know it at once as soon as you see it."

Holmes examined the small garden shed and came out chuckling.

"Find something interesting?" I asked.

"Milk," he said.

"Milk? In a garden shed?"

He refused to say any more and I continued my search. In the nearby copse of trees, I found a small patch of recently dug earth. "Holmes," I cried, "I think I have found something."

He hurried to my side and knelt down at the side of the small grave. Using his gloved hands, he dug up the earth and after a moment discovered exactly what he was looking for: the remains of a black cat. It had been strangled.

"You see, Watson?" said he. "Who would say only guns and knives and poison can be instruments of murder is dull of wit indeed. See if you can find something to wrap this unfortunate creature in. I spotted some tarpaulin in the garden shed."

"I'll get it," I said.

Holmes and I wrapped up the wretched creature and carried it back to the house.

"What are we going to do with this thing?" I asked.

"We shall leave it in the dead woman's room. It will be needed as evidence."

The front door was opened by the butler and, though obviously bemused, he assisted us to hide the bundle in the room.

"Has Major Asquith returned yet?" Holmes asked. "I thought I heard a carriage."

"Yes, Mr. Holmes. He returned a few minutes ago. He is in the drawing room with the rest of the family."

"And the girl, Kate?"

"No, Mr. Holmes. She's vanished. It is very odd. See seemed devoted to Miss Catherine."

"May I see her room?"

"Certainly."

He led us through a series of hallways to a small room at the back of the house. It was unremarkable. The girl's clothes still hung in the wardrobe. The chest of drawers revealed a few pieces of reddish-gold jewellery, and a sheet of paper covered in strange, flowing writing.

"*Devanāgarī*," Holmes said. "The alphabet used to write Hindi. Alas, I do not know enough of the language to be able to read it."

"Why would a gypsy girl have a paper written in Hindi?" I said.

"What do we know of her?" Holmes replied. "That she is dark of complexion and speaks English with an accent. I suspected she might be of Indian birth."

"Then she has committed this terrible crime," I said. "How awful. I suppose she was related to the family of that girl Major Asquith was involved with. Do you think she came all the way to England to have revenge upon his descendants?"

Holmes shook his head. "These are deep waters, Watson," he said. "We should join the family. But first, Craddock, I need you to send for the police – "

Jane Asquith was sitting with her fiancé on the sofa in the drawing room. Ambrose Asquith had returned and was sitting in an armchair. He was around fifty years of age and had the deportment of a military man. He rose, pulled down his cuffs, and said, "Mr. Holmes, I have only just learned that my great-niece consulted with you regarding my poor late sister's obsessions. I am afraid your time was wasted."

"Do you think so?" said Holmes. "If so, it is my time to waste. Tell me, what has become of the girl you call Kate?"

"Wretched girl has quite vanished," he said. "I've been all over the wood and went so far as Barnet looking for her."

"Did you report her disappearance to the police?"

"No." The man lit a cigarette and stared at Holmes with a slightly amused expression. "Whatever for? She's a gypsy. Wandering is in her blood, I suppose. I say, you don't think she had anything to do with my aunt's demise?"

"Why do you ask that?" Holmes said.

The fellow laughed nervously. "I suppose your presence makes me think of strange and unfathomable things. You do have something of a reputation, you know, Mr. Holmes. But it's not possible, surely? I mean, the girl couldn't actually put a curse on poor Aunt Catherine."

"Did the girl strike you as dangerous or irresponsible?"

"No," Miss Asquith said. "She is passionate and rather foolish, perhaps, but she is devoted to my poor aunt."

"I agree," said Mead. "She is a lively girl and perhaps she would be better not saying some of the things that she does, but she is very kind and, as Jane says, devoted to the old woman."

"Tell me," Holmes said. "How did you come to engage her, Major Asquith?"

He frowned. "Well, my aunt had a bad episode several months ago, not long before Christmas. I thought she would benefit from a companion. I contacted a few agencies and asked them to send some candidates for me to interview."

"Who had the final say?"

"My aunt did. I selected three that I thought were best suited and Aunt Catherine chose Kate."

"I believe Kate claimed to know things about your aunt. Things she could not possibly have known."

"Yes, it was dashed remarkable. She knew about Michael, my sister's late fiancé, and some things about Catherine's health."

Holmes said, "Hardly as remarkable as all that. You told her what to say."

"I . . . what?" The fellow paled.

"Oh yes, you already knew the girl. She was no gypsy but came from India. You came back to England because you had amassed such debts that India was too hot for you. You met Kaia Patel in Karnaul, where she was earning a living as a fortune teller. You wooed her. Please do not insult my intelligence by denying it. I received a telegram this morning that confirmed my suspicions."

The fellow mopped his forehead with a handkerchief and said, "Yes, all right, what of it? I knew Kaia in India. I felt sorry for her; you cannot imagine the poverty she was living in."

"Another lie. The girl has gold jewellery, not very expensive pieces, perhaps, but enough to prove she was not impoverished."

"I thought she'd have a better life in England. There was no harm done."

"No harm?" Holmes said. "You told her what to say to capture Miss Catherine Asquith's attention. It was you who made her deliver that preposterous prediction of death."

"No," Miss Asquith exclaimed. "Please tell me Mr. Holmes is wrong. Why would you do such a thing?"

"He was desperate for money," Holmes said. "I received a second telegram this morning, Miss Asquith. This one from your solicitor. The terms of your father's will are quite clear. Your aunt had control of the house and land until you turn thirty or marry. She managed the estate with considerable acumen and integrity. You will be a wealthy woman. However, if she were to die before the estate becomes yours, its administration goes to your uncle."

"Only until my niece marries," said the man.

"Long enough for you to do considerable damage and swindle her out of most of her inheritance. Besides which, if Miss Asquith were to die before she marries, the estate becomes yours irrevocably."

"But, Jane is in excellent health – " Mead began. "Surely, you cannot mean . . . Good God!"

Holmes said, "I would not trust Ambrose Asquith with any living thing. Even animals do not escape his cruelty. Those marks on your wrist that you are trying to hide show where the cat scratched you when you strangled it. You needed Miss Catherine Asquith to die so you could take the property immediately. You literally frightened that poor woman to death."

"How? How could I do such a thing? Why, Jane slept in the room with her aunt. If I'd gone in there during the night, she would have woken."

"You did not need to go into the room. You knew of your aunt's horror of black cats. You found one and hid it in the garden shed. Then, last night, you cracked open the casement window of the morning room. The carpet around the window is wet from the rain. Your footprints are clearly visible beneath the bushes outside. You let the cat into the room. The unfortunate woman was a poor sleeper; you knew she must awaken. It happened just as you planned: she woke, saw the cat, and suffered a fatal attack.

"Miss Asquith, you said your aunt had a horror of cats?"

"Yes, indeed, she had a morbid fear of them. A black cat crossed her path the day she learned of her fiancé's death and she had a terror of them ever since. It's curious you should ask about cats, though. Twice in the past week my poor Aunt claimed she saw one outside her window. Each time she said it was a bad omen. Oh, that is what she meant by 'harbinger of death.'"

"Be that as it may," said the Major. "If there had been a cat it would surely still be in the room."

"You lured the cat back to the window with a piece of trout tied to a string. Both fish and string were caught in the bushes beneath the window."

He opened the envelope to reveal the items.

"There was fur on the branches and I found cat hair on the dead woman's pillow. We found the body of the unfortunate animal where you buried it."

The front door bell rang and Holmes said, "That will be the local constabulary. They have brought dogs to help us find the body of the girl you called Kate. You could not leave her alive to testify against you. I believe you buried her in the woods."

Asquith lunged at Holmes, but Mead knocked him to the ground with a single blow.

In less than an hour, the dogs found the body of the unfortunate Indian girl in a shallow grave in the woods. She had been strangled.

Ambrose Asquith was found guilty of two counts of murder. The case added even more lustre to my friend's already glittering reputation.

I was disappointed that Holmes refused to attend the wedding of Miss Asquith and Mr. Mead, but at least we had some wedding cake sent to us by our former client.

As we enjoyed the treat. I said, "One thing still puzzles me, Holmes. Who was this 'Billy' that Kate spoke of in her trance?"

"Ah, it was Billy that first made me wonder about the girl's origins," Holmes replied. "*Billī* is the Hindi word for 'cat'."

"But why say that in a trance? It meant nothing to the old woman. Unless Kate actually had a premonition."

Holmes has been curiously silent on the subject of the supernatural ever since.

The Adventure of the
Regular Passenger
by Paul D. Gilbert

". . . for he was immersed at the moment in a very abstuse and complicated problem concerning the peculiar persecution to which John Vincent Harden, the well known tobacco millionaire, had been subjected."
    – "The Solitary Cyclist" by Sir Arthur Conan Doyle

During the course of the weeks that had immediately followed our dramatic return from Egypt and Rome, I had noted with some amusement the voracious manner in which my friend, Sherlock Holmes, had attacked each example of Mrs. Hudson's limited cuisine.

This fact is only worthy of note because Holmes's meal time habits were normally far more ascetic than they had been of late. This was especially true when he was engaged on a difficult case and he could therefore ill afford to expend the energy that was required for his mental faculties on a matter as trifling as the digestion of food!

One morning, during the course of a particularly cold and windy period that had been plaguing the October of '96, Holmes looked up from his plate and observed my amusement through a suspicious eye. He had just devoured a substantial plate of devilled kidneys and eggs, and he was in the process of wiping up the residue with a slice of bread, when his observation caused him to toss his fork down onto his plate with some annoyance.

"Really, Watson, I am surprised that after all of these years in my association you have not yet learned the simple truth, that there is nothing more harmful to a logical thinking process than to make false assumptions before one is in possession of the facts!"

I was on the point of questioning the cause of his fractious outburst when I realised the futility of such an enquiry. Holmes obviously had every intention of expanding upon his initial assertion, for he promptly stood up, strode over to the window, and struck a match for his cigarette with unwarranted violence. The flame almost flared onto the drapes, and his next few words were clouded in a plume of smoke.

He moved away from the window and turned upon me while pointing with his cigarette.

"On more occasions than I care to remember, you have berated me for my abstinence during a long and arduous case, little realising how beneficial this can be to my faculties. Now you have formulated the notion that, because I am not gainfully employed at the moment, I am merely eating to compensate for my lack of activity." Holmes shook his head dismissively while putting his cigarette to his lips once more.

"It has not even occurred to you that our adventure abroad might have drained, even I, of every drop of the mental and physical energies that I might possess. Perhaps I am eating so ravenously of late merely because I am hungry. To assume that my dining habits have changed because I am being starved of work is to dismiss the thought that I might actually be glad of this temporary respite. However, as you will soon see, it is also a grave error! Hah!" With a broad smile Holmes suddenly held up a small sheet of paper tantalisingly in front of me.

"Now deduce, friend Watson, do not assume!"

"You have a client." I stated flatly.

"Indeed, a John Vincent Harden to be precise, and he is due to arrive to seek our consultation in precisely five minutes time! Mrs. Hudson!" Holmes called for our landlady to clear away our breakfast things with understandable urgency, and he soon hustled her from the room once she had done so.

"Our consultation?" I queried, for I had often remonstrated with Holmes at the way he took for granted my participation without prior invitation.

"Well, if you would be so kind, allowing, of course, for any previous engagement that might inhibit you." Holmes smiled, fully aware of my current status and therefore the nature of my final response.

"I would be honoured," I confirmed with a smile, "and I will fetch my note book at once!"

I returned in an instant, and there was even a moment or two for me to look over Harden's short note of introduction, prior to his arrival. There was little of significance within Harden's brief request, save for a hint of urgency in its tone. Inevitably, Holmes's appraisal was at total variance to my own.

"These few words certainly tell us much about the man who wrote them, would you not say, Doctor?"

I was, no doubt, exhibiting an expression of confusion, for Holmes continued without awaiting my non-plussed response.

"Look at the care than has gone into the formation of each of his letters. Each twist and curve is accurate and precise, and there is not a dot or a cross that misses its mark. It is reassuring at the commencement of any case, Watson, to realise that we are dealing with a person of a remarkable nature. You can be assured of the accuracy of John Vincent Harden's evidence!" Holmes pronounced.

"And of his punctuality!" I confirmed, for at the very moment of his appointed time, we could hear Mrs. Hudson greeting our new client at the door to 221b Baker Street. At that moment, I recalled where I had heard his name before, and I hurriedly pointed out to Holmes that Harden was one of the most powerful men in the tobacco industry.

Barely a second later, John Vincent Harden walked tentatively into our room, and Holmes leapt up to greet him with a broad and charming smile. At once, Holmes could sense the elderly gentleman's apprehension and hesitancy.

"Calm yourself, Mr. Harden!" Holmes declared. "Have no fear, for I can assure you that you are amongst friends here. Perhaps a cup of coffee will have the desired reassuring effect?"

I decided to save Mrs. Hudson from being subjected to one of Holmes's strident orders and I called down quietly for a tray of coffee.

By the time that I had returned to the room, Harden was already perched, somewhat uneasily, on the edge of our visitor's chair while Holmes was busy filling his cherrywood pipe. No one uttered a single word until after the coffee had been safely delivered and Holmes had ushered our landlady from the room, in a somewhat unceremonious fashion.

Once his pipe was fully alight, Holmes turned towards our guest and, with an ironic grin, he held the note of introduction immediately in front of Harden's face.

"Mr. Harden, your letter was somewhat scant of detail," Holmes stated in an accusing tone.

"I apologise for that, Mr. Holmes, but I was certain that if I betrayed even one word of the nature of this affair, you would immediately dismiss me as some kind of madman and then refuse to grant me this interview." Harden's words immediately fuelled Holmes's love of the unusual and bizarre, and his attitude visibly softened as a brief smile of satisfaction played upon his lips.

I took my notebook over to my chair and I observed how perfectly Harden's appearance mirrored the pedantic nature of his note. Despite his advanced years, for he was surely not a day younger than sixty-five years, Harden was impeccably turned out. His worsted suit had clearly been hand tailored, his tie and shoes were equally immaculate, and his neatly clipped moustache and grey thinning hair told of a very recent visit to the barber shop. When he spoke, each word was clipped and precise.

44

Holmes took to his chair, while his keen eyes did not leave our client's face for an instant.

"Now Mr. Harden, I implore you to recount, as exactly as you can, the events and circumstances that have led you to seek my advice upon this matter. You may also be assured that you can rely as much upon Dr. Watson's discretion as you can upon my own.

"Please bear in mind that, apart from the very obvious facts that you smoke a very expensive brand of Havana cigar without a holder, that you have recently retired from the tobacco industry, and that you travel extensively upon the Metropolitan Underground line, I know nothing about you whatsoever!"

Upon completing this astonishing statement, Holmes turned his face away from our client, ostensibly to light his pipe but also, no doubt, so that he might evade the inevitable looks of admiration and amazement upon our faces, that he often found to be so tiresome.

His precaution was certainly warranted, for the reaction of both Harden and myself was precisely the one that he had sought to avoid. Harden added voice to his astonishment.

"Mr. Holmes!" he exclaimed. "Thanks to Dr. Watson here, I have read so many accounts of your remarkable talents that I did not expect to be so dumfounded by anything that I might have heard here today. I beseech you to explain yourself sir, for it is almost as if you knew of me already."

Holmes was barely able to subdue a smile of self satisfaction upon hearing Harden's words of veneration, although he was also clearly irritated by this slight delay to the proceedings. Consequently, his response was as curt as it was brief. He turned abruptly towards our client and demonstrated his explanation by pointing towards the tips of Harden's fingers

"The browning of your finger tips betrays the fact that you despise the prevailing trend for the use of cigar holders, while the light dusting of ash on your shoulder indicates the brand. As Watson will assure you, I have made an extensive study of cigar and cigarette ash and its use in the detection of crime, and Havanas are very distinctive. Your hat bears a thin layer of a type of soot that is unique to the Metropolitan line, and your gold watch and chain show of your very recent retirement."

In answer to our questioning glances, Holmes then added:

"The initials on the back of your watch, *HTI*, surely stand for *Harden Tobacco Industries*?"

At this juncture, Harden threw himself back into his chair and clapped his hands joyously.

"Mr. Holmes, I see now that there is nothing within Dr. Watson's accounts of your work that exaggerates your powers. You are correct on every count, although I cannot, for the life of me, understand how you could possibly have identified the name of my company merely from a set of initials."

No doubt fuelled by the enthusiasm of our client, Holmes was now clearly warming to his task. He suppressed a mischievous smile and lowered his voice, as if he was about to divulge a most singular secret.

"Mr. Harden, I must inform you that my friend, Dr. Watson, read of you in a recent morning paper, and he passed this information on to me, but a moment before your arrival!" Harden appeared to be both surprised and disappointed by Holmes's confession, a fact that did not go unnoticed by my friend.

He clapped his hands repeatedly and laughed uproariously, although Harden and I were somewhat slower in reacting in this way.

"I fear that if I continue to betray my secrets in this way, any reputation that I might have accrued will disappear in a thrice!" Holmes's amusement slowly subsided, and he soon turned towards Harden with a steely intent.

"Mr. Harden, as gratifying as this brief interlude has been, we have surely wasted enough valuable time by examining this commonplace trivia!"

Harden drained the remains from his coffee cup before clearing his throat. He looked anxiously towards me, for affirmation that he should now begin to recount his problem to us. I raised my pencil and smiled at him reassuringly.

"Thank you. I assure you, gentlemen, that I shall put this matter before you both, with as much brevity and accuracy as I can." Holmes smiled gratefully at Harden when he heard this declaration.

"As Dr. Watson so correctly pointed out, I am indeed John Vincent Harden, and I have been, until very recently, the most successful tobacco tycoon that this country has ever produced.

"Despite my success and the inevitable wealth that this has produced, I have always lived a most frugal and abstemious existence. My wife, Claudia, and I remain childless to this day, and we have lived in a modest town house in Chester Square these past twenty years, with barely a handful of servants"

"A most humble existence, indeed." Holmes stated quietly, with an understandable sarcasm, for the fine town houses of Chester Square are among the most sought after residences in one of the better parts of Belgravia.

Harden chose to ignore Holmes's irony and pulled out his cigar case, which he proceeded to offer around. Holmes and I declined in turn.

"Although they are undoubtedly most fine, I find my cherrywood pipe to be more conducive at the outset of a case." Holmes explained.

Harden removed the tip from a huge Havana and smiled long and indulgently while he slowly brought it to light. He waved a huge cloud of smoke away from his face before continuing.

"Throughout that time, my daily routine barely altered. My company had its main office in the City, and we kept our accounting department in somewhat smaller premises at West Hampstead. I liked to visit both of them on a regular basis, and often travelled from my club, which is situated just behind Gower Street, to West Hampstead via the Metropolitan. As you so correctly deduced, Mr. Holmes, I became a most regular passenger, and barely a day went by that did not find me within one of its carriages."

"Excuse me Mr. Harden, but surely, for a man in your position, a carriage would unquestionably prove to be a more agreeable proposition?" I found myself asking.

"We do keep a small brougham, Dr. Watson, but I find the running costs to be prohibitive and I reserve it for those rare occasions when I escort my wife to a social engagement and the like."

Just then, I noticed Holmes eyeing our guest a good deal more quizzically, and he ran his finger around the rim of the old man's hat.

"This layer of soot on your hat is still quite fresh!" Holmes stated with some emphasis.

Harden drew on his cigar and viewed my friend with some confusion.

"You appear to be making a point, Mr. Holmes, but I fail to see what it might be."

"Surely, now that you have retired, there is no real need for you to travel to West Hampstead and subject yourself to the grime and discomfort of the Underground?"

"Although I am retired, the company is still in full operation, and the accountant has requested my assistance in executing the transition of ownership. The work is almost complete and in any event, it only occupies two or three hours of my time each day. Once everything has been signed over, Claudia and I intend to travel extensively, for the first time in twenty years!" Harden declared joyfully.

"Mr. Harden, with your life seemingly in such fine order, I fail to see what prompted you to seek my consultation with such urgency." Inexplicably, Holmes was taking an obvious dislike to the elderly tobacco baron and he seemed intent on drawing matters towards a speedy conclusion. He tapped out his pipe against the side of the fireplace, lit a cigarette in its place, and turned away from Harden to face the window.

"Oh, Mr. Holmes, do not turn away from me at such a time, for I am being hounded and persecuted to the point where I am at my wits end!" Harden suddenly exclaimed while clambering back up to his feet.

"Steady your nerves, Mr. Harden, steady your nerves, persecution is a most unusual turn of phrase. You do not appear to be maltreated, so explain to me in what manner you have been interfered with," Holmes suggested, while striding back towards the centre of the room.

"It began harmlessly enough. Indeed, the unusual incidents were so slight and commonplace that individually they were hardly worthy of note, and might have even be put down to my own ineptness. Accumulatively, however, they became quite tiresome, and over a period of time, a cause of great concern."

"To what type of incident are you referring, and over what period of time?" Holmes asked grudgingly.

Harden returned to his seat and appeared to be most put out when Holmes applied more concentration to the task of scraping out his pipe than he did to Harden's unusual problem.

"Initially, when various items that I use on a regular basis, such as my umbrella for example, began to disappear, I put it down to an oversight on my part. However, I soon realised that another hand was at play, especially when these items suddenly turned up again, but in the most unexpected of places. A silver plated trophy, which I had won for playing golf many years ago, suddenly reappeared in the coal cellar!

"The first incident occurred over four months ago, but it has only been over the past fortnight that I have been plagued beyond the four walls of my house." It was only now that Holmes ceased his incessant scraping and turned his attention towards our visitor once more.

"As I explained earlier, for reasons of prudence and convenience, I have become a regular user of the Metropolitan Underground line. I travel between Gower Street and West Hampstead stations during the course of the same schedule every day. Consequently, I have become used to seeing some very familiar faces occupying the seats very close to my own, every time that I step upon the train.

"It has only been of late, however, that I have found myself drawing some undesirable and intimidating attention. I am constantly being stared at, sometimes in a most threatening manner, but my stalkers never seem to be the same person. They occupy the same seat as each other, they even present an identical pose and menacing demeanour. However, I have never seen any of them more than once. It is almost as if I have somehow become the victim of a gigantic and inexplicable conspiracy!"

At this juncture Harden became understandably agitated and he reached into his jacket pocket for his Vesta box.

"Although they now appear to be different to each other, do you recognise any of these conspirators as being amongst your fellow passengers from the time before your persecution began?" Holmes asked.

Harden thought long and hard before shaking his head and answering in the negative.

"Are there any obvious visual similarities between any of them, say their age or size, for example?"

"No, not at all, and that is the thing that is most damnably strange about the whole business! One day it might be a middle aged lady, the next a dapper business man and the next a pretty young nanny. The only thing that they all share is an unwarranted and disturbing obsession with me."

"Yet you still persist in making this journey, despite the discomfort that this strange behaviour is causing you?" I decided to ask.

"Yes, Doctor. I did not see why my daily routine should alter, just because a disparate group of characters have decided that I make an interesting subject of their scrutiny."

"However, that situation has now changed for the worse and quite recently, I think," Holmes proposed. Then he added, in answer to our questioning glances: "Why else would you come to me, after all of this time, unless you now feel that you have come under some kind of threat?"

"You are quite correct, Mr. Holmes, events have certainly moved in another direction of late. My stalkers are now no longer content to merely stare intently towards me; they have started to talk to me, from under their breath, and making contact of quite an aggressive nature. A whispered threat to my life, a clumsy elbow to my rib cage, these are just two of the most recent examples of their outrageous behaviour.

"As you might suppose, I took the matter up with the police, but as no crime has actually been committed, there is very little action that they can take. So I now turn to you, Mr. Holmes, in the hope that you might explain to me what this strange persecution can possibly mean. Do you think that my life might actually be in jeopardy?"

Holmes thought long and hard before making his pronouncement and he pursed his lips with pressure from his right forefinger. He cast Harden an oblique and anxious glance before slowly replying.

"You must be strong, Mr. Harden, but I think it to be not unlikely. Do you believe that the most singular occurrences in your home are in some way connected to the more threatening behaviour of your fellow passengers? After all, the disappearance of your personal possessions could only be attributed to your servants and family, and you would surely be able to identify them were they to suddenly join you on the Metropolitan."

"Our servants have been with us for many years, Mr. Holmes, and I cannot, for one minute, believe that they would collude with those scoundrels on the train. I have recognised nobody from my household during my journeys, of that I am certain."

"In that case, I suppose it has not occurred to you that your wife might be behind the temporary misplacement of your cherished objects, as some form of practical joke perhaps?" Holmes suggested mischievously.

"Absolutely not, Mr. Holmes. Indeed, I find the very idea totally preposterous and not a little insulting!" Harden protested while rising to his feet again. Undaunted, however, Holmes persisted with this line of questioning.

"Mr. Harden, what other reasonable conclusion is one to draw? Given that you trust your servants so implicitly, no one from outside of your household is likely to have run the risk of breaking and entering merely to move a golf trophy from one place to the next! If you cannot see that, perhaps you have formulated a theory that might explain your persecution on the trains?"

"Mr. Holmes, that is precisely why I have come here today, to seek your advice. Is there none that you can give me?" Harden asked pleadingly.

"Only that it would be in your best interest were you to start telling me the truth!" With that, Holmes turned away from him once more and disdainfully waved him away and in the direction of the door.

Harden stamped down his foot in his rage, and made for the door.

"Well, I never, Mr. Holmes. I am not used to being spoken to in such a fashion. If you are not able to help me, then I am certain that I shall find someone, of similar ilk, who is able to." Harden turned on his heels and he slammed our door behind him with a resounding crash. The door onto Baker Street was dealt with in a similar fashion a moment later.

"Well, I must say, Holmes, your dismissal of a potentially intriguing case, in such a cavalier fashion, goes somewhat against the pale! Are you so certain that Harden has been withholding the truth from you deliberately?"

"Of that, Watson, I am in no doubt. While I am not suggesting for an instant that Harden's story is a complete fabrication, there are certain aspects of his statement that simply do not hold water. The fact that he is so reluctant to reveal them to me suggests that he has been guilty of an indiscretion so shameful that he cannot bring himself to declare it to me.

"Nevertheless, there are certain aspects of this case that are unique in my experience, and Mr. John Vincent Harden has nowhere else to turn. He will return before too long, of that you may be assured. In the meantime, Watson, there is nothing to prevent us from making a few inquiries of our own, in the hope that we can put together the pieces of this puzzle before the next stage of Harden's persecution is revealed."

"Why are you so convinced that Harden has been withholding the truth? I did not see anything in his manner that would have suggested that to you."

"I am familiar with West Hampstead and I can assure you, Watson, that there is no accountancy in that vicinity capable of handling a client as considerable as Harden Tobacco Industries. Furthermore, a company on the scale of Harden Tobacco Industries would undoubtedly incorporate an accounts department within its own head office, so I rejected that notion from the outset.

"I was equally dismissive of the suggestion that Harden would subject himself to the tribulations of the underground merely to save a few pounds, when he had already confessed to having a perfectly good brougham at home, at his constant beck and call. I would suggest that there lies a far more tempting reason that would induce Harden into making that journey."

"Well, for one thing, there is far less chance of his own household discovering his whereabouts, by his using the underground service. After all, if he is perpetrating an indiscretion, there is little point in his advertising that fact to his driver and footman!" I suggested.

"Excellent, Watson, they were my thoughts exactly! Although, of course, I had the added advantage of having noticed the corner of a lady's handkerchief protruding from Harden's inside pocket, when he reached inside for his cigar case. It had been badly stained with makeup and bore the initials *S S,* not *C H* as one would expect." With that, Holmes dashed into his room and reappeared a moment later wearing his coat, a muffler and bearing his small bag and cane.

"Holmes, are we to assume that the next phase of Harden's persecution might involve a threat to his life?" I asked before Holmes had reached the door.

"As you surely know by now, Watson, I never assume. However, it would be a grave folly were we to exclude all possibilities, no matter how unlikely they might seem to be. There is not a moment to lose!"

"Where are you off to?" I asked, while remaining firmly rooted to the spot.

51

"Why, to Gower Street, of course, in the hope that Dave 'Gunner' King and his cohorts might aid me in ascertaining the true course of Harden's daily routines, and perhaps the identity of the mysterious lady who is now down one handkerchief."

I should point out that King was, without a doubt, the finest cabbie in London, and his vast knowledge and fortitude had proved to be invaluable to Holmes on many such occasions.

"Holmes, would you like me to travel to West Hampstead? Who knows, Harden's final destination might prove to be every bit as important as his starting point?"

Holmes appeared to be genuinely appreciative of my suggestion.

"Oh, Watson, if you would not mind. Ultimately it might prove to be a thankless task, but the time that it would save me could prove to be of immeasurable assistance." With that, Holmes was through the door, and he departed from 221b with a cursory call to Mrs. Hudson as he slammed the front door behind him.

My own departure was no less urgent than that of Holmes. I hurtled towards Baker Street Station while still fastening my heavy overcoat. I decided to forsake the relative speed and comfort of a cab in favour of taking the very same journey as had our beleaguered former client.

During the course of that long and uncomfortable journey, I inquired of the guard to see if he could recognise my description of Harden, but I was greeted with a look of bewilderment and a deliberate shaking of the head. Consequently, I arrived upon the cold, windswept platform of West Hampstead Station, with only the ticket clerk to turn to for a clue.

The worthy in question proved to be a genial old man, whose speech and deportment told of better times, long since past. Fortunately, his small office proved to be the warmest part of the station, and I gratefully accepted his invitation to step inside. Like a good many in his position, the clerk seemed grateful of the opportunity to strike up a conversation, and I had to endure a tepid cup of tea and a series of mind numbing anecdotes before he finally responded to my initial inquiry.

My patience and endurance were finally to be rewarded. As it turned out, the locals were rather proud of the fact that they had, from amongst their midst, something of a celebrity, an aspiring young actress who went by the stage name of Sophie Sinclair. I did not need reminding of the significance of her initials, but my enthusiasm was dampened by the fact that the clerk had only seen Miss. Sinclair in the company of an elderly gentlemen but once. I apologised for leaving my tea cup three-quarter full, and with a grateful hand shake, I took my leave.

I stepped outside to light a cigarette and gazed up at the front of the station. It was a surprisingly small and innocuous façade, fashioned from red brick with only a single arch, and it was cradled within a small clutch of run-down shops. At that moment, a thin veil of sleet was suddenly whipped into a frenetic dance by the remorseless Autumnal wind. I pulled up my collar, pulled down my hat, and made my way towards a small ale house on the opposite side of the road.

On more than one occasion, Holmes had gained valuable information from the loosened tongues of the clients of a public house, and so I decided to act upon his example and I stepped inside. In all honesty, it was also an act of self preservation!

Once I had purchased a large whisky from the bar keep, I immediately made my way towards a small fire that was struggling, in vain, to warm that small and dismal hostelry. I stood with my back to the flame so that I could survey my fellow clients and decide who I should best approach for information. I must confess that my brief appraisal proved to be a disappointment.

I was one of only six who had ventured over the threshold that day, and two of these had clearly sampled the landlord's wares to a point beyond all reason! The remainder comprised of two elderly gentlemen engaged upon a heated political debate, a young artisan fallen upon hard times, and a bucolic ruffian who was mumbling to himself while he drained his tankard of its last drop of ale.

Although he was the closest to me, I forsook the pleasure of conversing with the ruffian and instead made my way towards the artisan. To my dismay, as I turned away from him, I felt the ruffian's hand land upon my shoulder with vigorous intent.

"I say, sir!" I protested while I removed myself from his grasp. His straggly grey hair was as overgrown as his beer-stained moustache, and his overcoat was worn beyond the point of redemption. When he spoke, the stench of beer and tobacco was overwhelming, and each word was framed by bronchial phlegm.

"'Ere guv, I meant no 'arm, but I am short of the price of tobacco. Could a gent like yourself spare me that?" Each word seemed to be punctuated by a cough so severe that I was forced to cover my mouth with a handkerchief.

"Sir, from the sound of it, more tobacco is the very last thing that you require!" I was on the point of vacating that ghastly place when the fellow's voice suddenly modulated and dropped to a whisper. I was staggered by this dramatic alteration and stopped dead in my tracks! I turned back and immediately recognised a familiar smile breaking through the bedraggled hair.

"Watson, do not betray a single indication of recognition, I beseech you. Now give me one of your cigarettes and I shall meet you outside in five minutes." Even from within this startling disguise, Holmes's instructions had their usual compliant effect upon me. I handed over the cigarette without hesitation and stepped out onto the windswept street once more.

I paced back and forth in agitation for a minute or two until Holmes's ruffian, as good as his word, shuffled through the ale house door and lurched towards me aggressively. Holmes remained in character until we had turned a corner and he was certain that we could not be spied upon. He led me towards the cab of "Gunner" King, and it was only once we safely on board and moving towards town once more that Holmes slowly began to remove his disguise.

By the time that he had removed the last tuft of hair and straightened his frock coat, Holmes's ruffian had all but drifted from memory, and I was left with my old friend once more and a string of questions. Holmes could not help but laugh at my nonplussed demeanour, but he allayed my interrogation by raising his hand up while he lit the cigarette and took down the soothing smoke. He ran his fingers through his hair and bore the expression of a boy who had just been presented with his most sought after gift.

"Oh, Watson, before you ask, I must tell you that I arrived here ahead of you because King tore up the streets of London while you were meandering along on the train. As commendable as your choice of transport undoubtedly was, you were sadly ignorant of the need for speed. As soon as King had confirmed my worst fears, I donned the persona that you have just witnessed and rushed to meet you here before it was too late."

Holmes's breathless explanation had done little to make the thing clear to me, so I shook my head slowly and told him so.

"In truth, Watson, for once I would have been surprised had you been able to grasp the situation. Events have unfolded at such a rate, that even I am not clear on one or two details! However, we have a little time before we arrive back at Baker Street, so it would only be right were I to pass on my limited knowledge of the matter to you.

"No sooner had I mentioned the address in Chester Square than King and his colleagues were able to put together a schedule of Harden's movements in a very short space of time. To avoid detection, Harden hailed his cabs from nearby Eaton Square. Although he did indeed visit his company's offices in the City, he rarely remained there for any length of time, and he spent the majority of his days within his club in Pall Mall.

"I knew that my knowledge of London had not become so shabby that I could not recognise Harden's assertion that his club was near Gower Street as anything other than a lie! There is no such establishment, I assure you, Watson. Quite often, he would divert his journey to Gower Street via the Garrick Theatre, where his vehicle would await the arrival of a vivacious young actress who goes under the name of – "

"Sophie Sinclair!" I declared triumphantly. For once I had truly stopped Sherlock Holmes in his tracks. He sat there dumbstruck before turning towards me, smiling proudly.

"How could you possibly have known that?" he asked incredulously.

I explained to Holmes the outcome of my visit with the ticket clerk and the reasons for my subsequent visit to the ale house.

"Well, well, well, it would seem that our two diverse journeys have culminated in the same location, having reached the same conclusions," Holmes stated, just as we had turned the corner into Baker Street. "Well done, King!" Holmes called up to the driver as we pulled up outside 221b.

As we let ourselves in, I asked, "I still do not see how you also ended up in that same ghastly place, moreover in that astounding disguise."

"I discovered that on those days when Harden forsook the pleasures of the theatre, he and Miss Sinclair would use that dubious establishment as their point of rendezvous. Obviously I could not visit that place in my own person, for fear of detection. Harden would have recognised me in a thrice."

"Of course, but are you any closer to discovering the source of Harden's persecution?" I asked as we reached the top landing.

"I will only be able to determine that once I have discovered the true nature of Harden's relationship with Sophie Sinclair. That information I expect to receive from Harden himself when he returns here tomorrow. After all, by then he will have had all night during which to cool his heels. Good night, old fellow"

I was grateful for an early night and I made way up a further flight of steps to my room with a slow determination.

To my surprise, Holmes was still in his room when I came downstairs the following morning. Although he was prone to keeping the most bohemian of hours at times, he was normally highly energised when active upon a case, and I had expected to see him at his first cup of coffee. I took advantage of his absence by having the first read of the morning papers. The lead headline of the *Times* sent me scurrying towards Holmes's room in a state of great agitation!

When he did not respond to my hammering upon his door, I took the unprecedented step of entering without invitation and I began to shake him by the shoulder. This was a treatment that I had received at Holmes's hand, on many similar occasions down the years. However, now that the roles were being reversed, I did so with much trepidation, as I could not be sure of his reaction. I decided to present him with the headline as soon as his eyes were focussed, in the certain knowledge that its contents would deflect any anger that he might otherwise have felt.

Holmes was clearly shaken to the core by the awful news and he was out of his bed and at his toilet in an instant.

Tobacco Baron Has Fatal Fall

While Holmes completed his preparations, I looked back over this dramatic headline and studied the scant details of the death of John Vincent Harden, which were printed below. According to the initial reports, Harden was seen being backed up towards the edge of the platform at West Hampstead Station by the aggressive behaviour of two women, who were clearly much disturbed. One of these women seemed to push him in the chest and as a consequence, Harden fell headlong on to the track in front of an oncoming train. His death had been gruesome and instantaneous!

At such an early stage of the inquiry, neither of the women had been identified as yet, and the younger of the two had disappeared prior to the arrival of the authorities. Our old friend, Inspector Lestrade of Scotland Yard, was in charge of the investigation, and he had held the older woman for questioning.

Holmes was ready in a thrice, and, while our cab was speeding towards West Hampstead, I read out the brief report. Holmes sat silently and thoughtfully for a moment or two before peering at me with remorse set deep within his troubled eyes.

"Oh, Watson, I fear that I am guilty of having seriously misjudged the gravity of the next stage of Harden's persecution," he said quietly.

"Or perhaps Harden's death was a direct result of nothing more than misadventure?" I suggested in the hope of alleviating my friend's dark regret.

Holmes slowly nodded his head with a weak but hopeful smile.

We smoked in silence for the remainder of the journey, and we were met at the station entrance by the sight of the brazen and weasel-like features of our old friend, Inspector Lestrade, who appeared to be in a most animated disposition.

"Well, well, Mr. Holmes, I had not expected to see you here today and that is for sure. I suppose that you already have some knowledge of the matter, which you have absolutely no intention of withholding from me?" Lestrade sarcastically suggested.

"I have become acquainted with certain facts that may help to clarify this tragic situation, and I will gladly share with you any data that might prove to be relevant. Firstly, however, we must learn what we may from the trackside, if the area has not been too heavily trafficked in the meantime."

"I assure you, Mr. Holmes, that there is very little to show you there. The decimated and grisly remains of Mr. Harden have long since been removed and his wife, whom I strongly suspect to be his murderer, is safely within my custody for further questioning," Lestrade responded, with understandable apprehension. All too often in the past, the enthusiastic Inspector had believed himself to be upon the right path to solving a case, only to find that my friend was already one step ahead of him.

"Nevertheless, I would like to judge that for myself, with your kind permission." Holmes's smile was anything but engaging, and Lestrade waved him towards the site of the tragedy with an air of resignation. Before he began his examination of the area indicated, Holmes gave me his permission to explain every aspect of our involvement to the bewildered detective.

While I was making my report, I noticed Holmes hurl himself down upon his stomach, on an area of the platform that appeared to be dangerously close to the track. He pulled out his glass and examined the spot where Harden had evidently lost his balance, for it was marked with a small white cross of chalk. He then wriggled away from the edge of the platform, no doubt tracing Harden's progress in reverse.

Holmes stood up sharply and dusted himself down thoroughly before asking Lestrade to briefly explain the facts that had led him to his conclusions. Lestrade was only too happy to oblige.

As it transpired, he was able to add very little to the brief accounts that we had seen in the morning papers. Lestrade had obtained three eye witness accounts that seemed to verify his suspicions, including that of my old friend the ticket clerk. They all confirmed that two women began to berate the hapless Harden in unison, and he edged away from them in a state of some alarm. The older of the two women seemed to reach out towards him, and it was at that moment that Harden stumbled in front of the train, resulting in those ghastly consequences.

"Although the younger of the women made away long before we could reach the scene, Mrs. Harden was evidently too shaken and stunned by the results of her actions to do likewise, and she awaited our arrival in the ticket office, as if resigned to her fate. Naturally, it did not take me long to put two and two together, and Mrs. Harden seemed to confess to her crime while she was being led away by my constables." Lestrade crossed his arms smugly and his knowing smile indicated that he now believed Holmes's intervention to be redundant.

"She seemed to confess to her crimes, Inspector? That is certainly an unusual turn of phrase. Is it not just as likely that her state of mind prevented her from putting any cohesive thoughts together?" Holmes suggested.

"That is mere speculation on your part, Mr. Holmes, but even were it to be true, that still would not negate the testimony of those witnesses." Lestrade seemed to be determined to stand his ground on this occasion.

"Ah, but I am sure that you would not be adverse to me demonstrating an alternative explanation, were it to lead us to the truth. Eye witnesses can only account for what they believe that they have seen.

"We all want to arrive at the truth, Mr. Holmes, but I can assure you of the witnesses' reliability."

Holmes chose to ignore Lestrade's last remark, and instead he strode over to the unsheltered section of the platform where the sleet was still hitting the ground. He shuffled his feet around in the puddles until he seemed satisfied that his heels and soles were thoroughly dampened, and then returned to where Lestrade and I were awaiting his return. We were both amused and perplexed by Holmes's inexplicable actions, and when he began to slowly count out a few steps while moving backwards, we were no less confused.

Finally when he pulled up at a safe distance from the edge of the platform, he beckoned me over to him.

"Now, push me in the chest, Watson, but please make allowance for the strength of an elderly lady."

Naturally I carried out Holmes's bidding, and then looked on helplessly as he stumbled back slightly and then he took to the floor again with his glass. When he appeared to be satisfied with his examination, he invited Lestrade and me to join him.

"Obviously this first line of muddied prints belonged to Mr. Harden and they were formed while he backed away from his persecutors. As you can see, they are spaced out equally, but more significantly, they continue right up to the very edge of the platform. My prints, on the other hand, although following a parallel line to those of Harden, suddenly break off at the point when Watson pushed me in the chest. See how that slight but sudden movement caused my shoes to create skid marks both here and here.

"You know, it never ceases to amaze me, Inspector, how skeptical and confused you appear to be at some of my more unpredictable actions. Have I not assured you, on numerous occasions, that there is a perfectly sound and logical reason behind everything that I do?"

"That is all very well, Mr. Holmes, but I am still not convinced that your very fine demonstration devalues the testimony that I have already taken," Lestrade protested, but without any real conviction.

"In that case, perhaps you might be persuaded, were I to produce an alternative witness who might be willing to confirm my findings?"

"I am not aware of any outstanding witness. To whom might you be referring?"

"Why I am referring to none other than Sophie Sinclair, who happens to be the second lady to have harangued Harden on the platform. I am certain that a local celebrity such as she will not be too difficult to locate in such a small community."

"Oh no, Mr. Holmes, I am afraid that you have missed the mark this time. She was seen bolting from the station at the very moment of Harden's fatal fall. She will be long gone by now!"

"Indulge me for ten minutes, Inspector, and I shall produce her for you."

Holmes was as good as his word, and before long we three found ourselves outside the front door to a small suite of rooms above the local hardware shop.

The door was opened by an absolutely charming young woman who greeted us with a resigned and philosophical smile. She was tall and slim, and her long dark hair was curled luxuriantly. She did not pause to ask us for either our identities or our reasons for coming to her door, but moved inside and invited us into her small but artistic sitting room. Lestrade and I produced our note books and pencils, while Holmes paced around upon the extremely limited floor space. Miss. Sinclair allowed us no chance to speak.

"Gentlemen, I know precisely why you are here and at the outset. Please allow me to ask you not to prejudge me."

"That is not our intention, Miss Sinclair; we merely wish to discover the truth," I replied gently.

"That is no easy thing to do, Dr. Watson." She smiled exquisitely.

"So you know me then?" I asked.

"I know of both you and Mr. Sherlock Holmes, from the most vivid descriptions that are contained within your accounts."

Holmes grunted impatiently during our exchange of pleasantries and he lit a cigarette by the open window. Therefore, Miss. Sinclair hurriedly began her story.

"I have asked you not to judge me because in the very recent past, ladies who took to the stage accrued a certain kind of reputation, if you take my meaning." We all nodded our confirmation, although with an air of embarrassment.

"I assure you, gentleman that I received a decent education and I was, therefore, resolved to making my living in serious theatre. In recent months, I have been fortunate enough to have been offered minor roles in works by Shakespeare, Shaw, and the like, and gradually I am accruing a most positive reputation.

"I first met John Harden when he came backstage to congratulate me after a performance of 'The Merry Wives of Windsor'. He presented me with a magnificent bouquet of roses and dramatically extolled the virtues of my performance. Despite his age, he had retained a winning charm, and I found myself being quite swept off my feet by his compliments and enthusiasm. I allowed him to escort me to the very finest restaurants, and before too long our trysts become quite a regular occurrence."

Holmes turned towards her suddenly and addressed her in a tone that I considered to be quite unwarranted.

"Did you not find the clandestine nature of your rendezvous in any way suspicious? After all, to arrange meetings at a disreputable public house or to forsake a fine carriage for the underground was hardly the behaviour of a man of honour."

Miss Sinclair appeared to have been undaunted by Holmes's judgemental attitude, and I was strangely proud of her for refusing to lower her eyes from his.

"Mr. Holmes, I am not a naïve young girl, nor am I a fool! I had no doubt that he was a married man, but for so long as his intentions and behaviour towards me remained honourable, I did not feel as if we were doing any real harm. He assured me that his wife had ceased to have any interest in his comings and goings a long time ago, and that I was the only person who had ever captivated him in such a way.

"However, it soon became apparent that every word of his had been a complete lie. I had a chance encounter with an old friend of mine from my early years upon the stage who recoiled in horror when I told her of my relationship with Mr. Harden. She had had a similar experience with him, but a few months previously, and she told me how he had forced himself upon her on many occasions, something she had to use considerable force to rebuff!

"At once, I was resolved to bringing things to an immediate conclusion. After all, if he had lied about one thing or the other, how was I to know the immeasurable grief that our trysts may have been causing his wife? When I told him of my decision, his rage was something that I would hope never to have to experience again. He turned bright red, yelled obscenities at me at the top of his voice, and threatened to destroy my career by using unspeakable methods."

"The absolute blackguard!" I exclaimed. I noticed that her recollections were causing Miss, Sinclair considerable grief, and I immediately offered her my handkerchief, which she accepted with a gracious smile. After a moment's pause, she continued.

"He stormed out of my rooms and left me with his threats still echoing around my head, and I shuddered at the thought of having had a creature such as he within my home. I was resolved to informing his wife of his infamous behaviour, in the hope that we both might have our revenge. I donned a disguise, which I was well able to obtain from the theatre's wardrobe and makeup departments and arrived at Chester Square once I was certain of Harden's absence for the day.

"To my surprise and immense relief, Mrs. Harden was well aware of her husband's dalliances and rather than unleashing her wrath upon me, she even agreed to contribute to my conspiracy! It was agreed that she would do everything she could to unsettle him at home while colleagues of mine would confound him every time he boarded his train. He was so resolved to winning me back that he bombarded me with gifts and messages from every angle.

"I am certain that this was to satisfy his ego, rather than an expression of any real affection that he professed to have for me. I rebuffed every effort of his, and each visit to my rooms was met with a closed and bolted door. The encounters that were distressing him on the train were intensified by design, and he was clearly becoming affected by our persecution.

"Finally, before matters got out of hand, I agreed to meet him upon the platform at West Hampstead Station. I informed Mrs. Harden of my intention, and she agreed to meet me there so that the three of us might reach a resolution. Sadly, that was never meant to be. He extended his rage and insults to the two of us, and we moved towards him to silence him in such a public place. You know the tragic outcome of our efforts, and Mrs. Harden even tried to pull him back before he reached his sorry end."

"So he was not pushed?" Unbelievably, there was a trace of regret in Lestrade's voice when he asked this redundant question.

"Mrs. Claudia Harden is a kind and gentle soul who deserved someone far better than John Vincent Harden!"

Holmes was already making his way towards the front door, and Sophie Sinclair graciously showed us out.

"Once again, Mr. Holmes, you have saved a potential victim of my own ineptitude from the direst of consequences! Mrs. Harden and I have much to be grateful to you for," Lestrade admitted while we went in search of a cab.

"No, not at all, Inspector. You are merely guilty of reaching your conclusions far too quickly and easily. A simple adjustment to your report will show that Mrs. Harden was retained in your custody to allow her time to recover from the shock of seeing her beloved husband's tragic death, away from the public gaze."

Lestrade nodded his gratitude, and while we travelled back to Baker Street, I was left to speculate upon the effect that the Harden affair would have upon my friend's misogynistic tendencies.

I was also resolved to attending a performance at the Garrick Theatre in the not to distant future!

The Perfect Spy
by Stuart Douglas

My friend Sherlock Holmes was a voracious reader, though rarely of the acknowledged literary canon. Rather, he would frequently arrive in our rooms laden down with an accumulation of penny dreadfuls, true crime magazines, and police journals, spreading them around the floor in a giant paper fan comprised of murder, assault, and theft, with little regard for my own preferences or comfort. At such times, he could happily spend an entire day armed only with scissors and glue pot, snipping out articles of particular interest and affixing them to a page in his ever expanding archive of criminality. On such occasions, I would make my apologies and leave him to his endeavours, knowing as I did that – save for those times when he was intimately involved with an interesting case – he was rarely so happy as when cataloguing the crimes of the Empire.

Occasionally, however, Holmes would express his dissatisfaction with the contents of the various periodicals, lamenting their lack of criminal cunning as though it were a personal insult. So it proved one wet afternoon in 1896, as Holmes and I relaxed in Baker Street, following the conclusion of a somewhat protracted case.

"Diplomatic negotiations, secret weapons, and speeches by politicians! Is this the level to which the popular press have sunk, Watson!" he stormed as he cast the newspaper in his hand to the floor in disgust. "This nation is forever making preparation for war, yet that fact is constantly reported as though it were the freshest and most unexpected of news! Meanwhile, there is nothing in any of these pusillanimous rags regarding the activities of the fiend currently terrorising the populace of Streatham, or of the spate of city robberies which have so baffled Inspector Gregson, and only a passing mention of the execution of Dyer, the child killer. Really, it is not good enough!"

I was by this point more than used to the peculiarities of Holmes's opinions, but even so there was little I could think to say in response to so perverse a view. Consequently, I satisfied myself with a non-committal nod and was on the verge of taking up my own newspaper, when Mrs. Hudson appeared in our doorway clutching a plain brown envelope.

"A boy just this minute delivered this telegram for Mr. Holmes," that good lady said as she handed it over. "He waits downstairs for a reply. Shall I tell him anything?"

Holmes had already opened and read the missive, and shook his head in response. "No, no, Mrs. Hudson, there is no reply. Give the boy a penny and send him on his way." He turned to me with something akin to real excitement on his face. "We have a new case, Watson!" he exclaimed. "A man is discovered, dead but without a slip of identification upon him and possessing some *thing* – Lestrade (for it is he who writes) is no more specific than that – of a peculiarly mysterious nature. What more could one ask for on so dull a morning as this?"

He leapt to his feet and strode across to hat and coat. "Come along, Watson!" he chided. "We must make haste if we are not to arrive after Lestrade and his minions have trampled across each and every piece of evidence."

It being simpler to follow him than to make enquiry as to further details of the case upon which we now embarked, I did so, with alacrity.

Confounding Holmes's fears, Lestrade had made secure the entire street in which the body lay, positioning uniformed constables at every point of ingress and standing guard himself over the deceased. Holmes took one look at the wealth of policemen on display and jumped from our hansom while it was still moving, evidently of the opinion that there was no time to be lost. I paid the driver and followed at a more sedate pace, arriving at the scene several minutes after my friend.

So it was that I made my entry just in time to witness Holmes lambast Lestrade in no uncertain terms – and to the obvious amusement of nearby constables – regarding the waste of his time occasioned by the Inspector's foolish over-reactions. Of course, I knew of old that Holmes had little respect for even the more senior of Scotland Yard's officers, but it was rare to find him engaged in quite such a public display of that lack of respect.

"A suicide, Inspector Lestrade, nothing more than that!" he raged as I pushed my way past the ring of uniformed men. "All identification abandoned and no sign of violence, you say? I do not need to examine the body to know that self-murder is certainly the cause of death. Bereft in love or some similar foolishness, this man throws his wallet into the river, then takes himself to a quiet place and anonymously ends his own life. Some little interest may be gained from the manner of his death which, as you say, is not immediately plain – but otherwise it is utterly banal and commonplace. I would hazard, indeed, that there is nothing

64

here which might confuse even someone with the limited intellectual capacity of a Scotland Yard Inspector!"

With that he turned smartly round and would certainly have left the street entirely, had not Lestrade, with a smug smile, called him back. "There is more, Mr. Holmes, much more than meets the eye."

Holmes faltered for a moment as curiosity over-matched irritation, and Lestrade took his opportunity. "There was a paper found on his person, Mr. Holmes, hidden in a secret place. A paper which might well have led this man to the noose, had he not ended up face down in the gutter here."

Amidst the noise of this argument, I had not taken a second to examine the dead man, but I did so now. He lay on his back on the pavement, but the dirt on his face and shirt front confirmed what Lestrade had said, that he had been found otherwise. I looked over at the Inspector for permission to look more closely, which he gave with a wave of his hand and a muttered "Be my guest, Doctor."

On closer inspection, the man proved to be in the region of twenty-five years old, about five foot eight and of good, strong build, with fair hair, worn slightly longer, in the current fashion. His eyes were closed, but his mouth lay half open, exposing a full set of healthy, white teeth. It was clear that, whatever else he might have been, his past contained respectability and reasonable fortune. His face and hands were entirely unmarked, and a cursory check suggested no obvious cause of death.

I cast an eye around the surrounding ground, as Holmes always did, but besides the common detritus of any London street, there was nothing to be seen. I rose to my feet and brushed myself down. Holmes, however, had spotted something and crouched down by the body in my stead, removing his gloves as he did so.

Carefully, taking care to disturb nothing, he folded back the man's jacket and inspected the inner pockets for a moment. Apparently satisfied, he forced his hands beneath and, with a heave, flipped the unfortunate man round, restoring him to the position in which he was found, face down. Lestrade raised a quizzical eyebrow in my direction, but I was as much in the dark as the little detective, and could only offer a shrug in reply to his unspoken question.

Our confusion only increased as Holmes proceeded to pull back the waistband of the man's trousers, exposing a row of discoloured metal studs, and nothing else which I could imagine might be of significance. Holmes, however, had seen something else, and now rose to his feet.

"You noted the studs, and that the tailor's tags have been removed from both jacket and trousering, Lestrade?"

The frown which crossed the Inspector's face was answer enough.

"This, perhaps, casts a different light on matters, or at least a more confounding one," Holmes continued after a pause. "A self-murderer may desire to remain anonymous and so save his family shame. In such a case, the disposal of a wallet is sensible, in order that identification may be hampered and, perhaps, eventually abandoned altogether. But to cut from your clothes every scrap which might lead an investigator even to so remote a connection as a tailor's premises? That is more effort than a sane man would contemplate."

"A self-murderer is not a sane man, Holmes, by definition," I offered.

"There is something in that, of course, Watson, but even so there is also . . . ."

Lestrade had stood silently during this exchange, but now he spoke up.

"Very interesting, Mr. Holmes, but as I mentioned a moment ago, I have some additional information which would appear to lend weight to the idea that this man did not take his own life." He beckoned to a waiting constable to step forward. "Apprise the gentleman of what it said on the note which was discovered on the deceased, Drake," he said, prompting the uniformed man to pull a Police notebook from the pocket of his jacket.

"A scrap of lined note paper was found in the dead man's outer breast pocket, crushed at the very bottom of said pocket. Both sides had been written on, sir, with but a single word on one side, and a few words in a foreign language of dubious provenance on the other."

"Specifics, man!" barked Lestrade. "Mr. Holmes needs specifics!"

Drake reddened and cleared his throat before continuing his interrupted recital. "Sorry, sir. I have a note further on . . . yes, the word on one side of the paper was the name 'Chapmans', while the reverse contained the name of a town in Southern Africa and several lines in German." Eager to be of assistance, he closed his book and, in a less formal tone, continued, "I don't have a record of the original words, Mr. Holmes, but one of the lads at the station had a school teacher came from Berlin or somesuch, and so he knows a bit of the lingo. He wasn't sure, but he said that 'flowing blood' was mentioned, and something about smashing our fetters. That means irons, sir," he concluded helpfully.

"Thank you, Constable," Holmes replied, drily. "I was aware."

Lestrade's impatience during this exchange was unmistakable. "As you no doubt realise, Mr. Holmes, the name on that paper is one whose significance is known only to you and one or two other private citizens. A name, the very whispering of which is of concern to all of Her Majesty's servants." He coughed. "It is that name which leads you to be roused from your morning pipe and slippers and brought here, Mr. Holmes, at the request, I should add, of my superiors and not of myself. Whether this man has murdered himself or been dispatched by persons unknown, Scotland Yard would know what interest he had in Chapmans – and quickly!"

Holmes seemed distracted, nodding his assent without looking at Lestrade. "The original missive is not to hand?" he asked eventually.

Lestrade smile was sympathetic but unhelpful. "No, Mr. Holmes. My superiors felt it safer to have the original returned to the Yard. Is that a problem?"

Holmes shook his head. "Not at present, but I would be obliged if I could examine the original. Perhaps Dr. Watson could make his way to Scotland Yard and collect it? It will be entirely safe in his hands, I assure you."

Seizing the opportunity to be more than a dumb – and largely uninformed – observer, I hastily agreed to Holmes's request. Lestrade, after a moment's thought, also assented. I was pleased to have a more active role in the investigation to come, having been largely supernumerary until that point, but still, I preferred to armour myself with a little knowledge before I went any further.

"But what does this all mean?" I asked. "Who is this Chapman, and why is his name of such fascination that its very mention has us roused by the police and rushed to inspect the body currently lying before us?"

Before Lestrade could reply, Holmes interjected. "Chapman is not the name of a person, but that of a company. A chemical works, primarily, though with significant investments in explosives, armaments, and engineering."

"And the government's interest in them?"

Before Holmes could reply, Lestrade intervened, ordering everyone to step away then lowering his voice before speaking. "I know that you have, in the past, been privy to certain secrets of a political nature," he murmured. "Indeed, I am certain you have been made aware of many things, regarding which a humble Police Inspector like myself is kept unaware, but even so, I must stress upon the you the vital importance of what I am about to tell you."

"Chapmans are working on a new weapon which, they claim, will revolutionise warfare and guarantee Britain a suzerain role in world affairs, as well as a head start should recent unpleasantness in Africa escalate further. Really, Lestrade, we have no time for this music hall melodrama!"

Holmes's intervention rendered the Inspector mute with fury. His small eyes were almost forced close as he struggled to retain his temper and not cause a public scene in front of his men. There was no doubting, however, the degree of his unhappiness with Holmes.

"Mr. Holmes," he hissed, "I would be obliged if you would modulate your voice before every man from here to Norwich is made aware of Her Majesty's government's future plans!"

Sensing that Holmes was unlikely to react positively to a rebuke from Lestrade, I quickly interposed myself, suggesting that, if we had seen all we could in the street, we now go our separate ways, the better to speedily conclude this important case.

"That is a capital suggestion, Watson," Holmes agreed. "If you would accompany the Inspector back to Scotland Yard, there to collect the missing note, I have an idea that my own time might be best spent in speaking to one of his colleagues."

"One of my colleagues, Mr. Holmes?" Lestrade enquired quickly, a readiness to take offence evident on his face. "I can assure you that you will receive no more information than I have already supplied from any other Inspector at the Yard!"

"Calm yourself, Lestrade," Holmes snapped. "I mean no disrespect to your own position. But there are branches of the force other than your own. It is to one of them that I now turn."

Lestrade was immediately mollified. "You refer to the Special Branch, Mr. Holmes?"

"I do. Perhaps they may shed some much needed light on Chapmans, and on this fellow before us." He pulled on the gloves he held in his hand and turned to leave. "If you will meet me at Baker Street in two hours, Watson, that would admirable."

"Of course." I motioned to Lestrade that I was ready to leave. "Time would seem to be of the essence, so shall we return to your offices, Inspector, while Holmes makes his enquiries?"

Holmes's reference to Special Branch had obviously satisfied the detective that sufficient serious attention was being paid to his wider concerns, and he was quick to acquiesce to my suggestion. With a brisk farewell to Holmes, he led the way to his carriage. I looked back as I entered, and saw Holmes bent once more over the body where it lay. For a moment, I also thought I saw a figure in the shadows of a nearby doorway observing my friend, but then the carriage door closed and when next I looked the figure, whoever it had been, was gone.

Two hours later I made my way back to Baker Street, only to find Holmes already present. He sat in his favourite chair by the fire, wreathed in pipe smoke, his eyes closed as though in sleep. I had taken no more than a step inside the room, however, when his eyelids opened and he regarded me with a baleful expression.

"I hope that you have had a greater degree of success in your mission than I, in mine."

"That remains to be seen, Holmes. But let me hear your news first. Was Special Branch able to shed any fresh light on the issue at hand?"

Holmes allowed himself a thin, humourless smile. "They were much as I expected. A group of men who habitually maintain a cloak of utter secrecy around their every action are not easily convinced of the need for transparency, even in a situation such as this. Had it not been for my own small fame – and, I would conjecture, the intervention of certain figures in government – I would have gone no further than the front door and would, even now, be standing there, awaiting an audience. As it was, a polite, if largely unhelpful, junior detective was able to spare me half an hour of his valuable time and provide me with a modicum of somewhat general intelligence."

"Somewhat general?"

"Indeed. Detective Johnson was able to confirm that no gentleman matching the description of the dead man is known to them, either as an agent himself or a spy for a foreign power. He did, however, allude to an operation currently underway, in which several detectives, working out of uniform and in disguise, have infiltrated a collective of enemy operators. He could not be certain, he said, but it was possible that our man belonged to this collective."

"Only possible?" I asked. "How is it that he could not be certain?"

"I cannot say, only that one of the Branch's agents might be in a position to shed much-needed light on our anonymous victim."

"Victim? You now believe the man killed by other than this own hand?"

"Perhaps."

Holmes would say no more on the topic, but instead reminded me of my own recent mission. I pulled the scrap of paper I had been given at the Yard from my pocket and handed it to him. I had, of course, already made my own inspection, but confessed myself baffled as to its import. Physically, it was an unprepossessing remnant of a larger sheet, four inches across and approximately three deep, where it ended in an uneven tear. Both sides were lined for writing, though only one had been so used, the other bearing only the stamp of a company name, "Chapmans". On the reverse, as the young constable had intimated, were written three lines in the German language with, just below them and only partially visible due to the tear in the paper, most of the name of a town – Johannesburg – which was, at the time, gaining a degree of notoriety for its swift growth from a gold mining hovel to a heavily populated centre of Boer strength.

Holmes took the paper and examined it in silence for several minutes, holding it up to the light at one point, before laying it on the table beside him.

"Trust the police to remain blind to the obvious, while seeing treachery in the most innocent of actions," he said finally. "You do not have any German, if I recall correctly, Watson? No? You at least may then be forgiven for failing to recognise the words of a Teutonic love poem when you see it."

He crossed to the bookcase and pulled from it a thick, leather bound volume, which he opened at the index, before turning to a page within and reading a passage aloud.

> *Brechen Sie Ihre Fesseln*
> *und lassen Sie Ihre Blut freien Lauf*
> *Wir müssen vereint sein oder sterben*

"Penned by a German poet of the eighteenth century for his aristocratic lover, and most assuredly a poem of passionate regard, not of revolution and anarchy. Roughly translated, it reads:

> *Break your fetters*
> *and let your blood run free*
> *We must be united or die*

"It may still be a code, of course, or a call to arms, but if so, it is cunningly disguised." He frowned and tilted the page in the light. "And it seems that you are not the only one whose German is less than perfect, Watson. These lines are almost correct, but not quite. See here, and here? The tense is wrong and the final word mis-spelled."

"Could it be a code? The incorrect vocabulary deliberate and containing a secret meaning, known only to the Boer recipient?"

"Possibly, though if so, it is a code whose key eludes me. Besides, the errors are commonplace ones, which any non-native might make."

"Copied in haste perhaps, then?"

"More likely written down by someone with a less than complete grasp of the language."

"A student?"

"Exactly, Watson. And there cannot be too many German language schools in London. I wonder if any of them are missing a student?"

Energised by this breakthrough, as was his wont, Holmes leapt to his feet and would, I think, have rushed away, had not the door to our rooms opened at the exact same time, revealing a gaudily-dressed young man of about twenty-five, fair haired, with a small moustache and neatly trimmed beard, which complemented the yellow checked suit he wore.

"Sherlock Holmes?" he asked, stepping inside as he did so, and closing the door softly behind him. I thought of my revolver, lying in a drawer in my room, but if this man meant us harm there was little chance of my reaching it in time.

Holmes, however, appeared unperturbed.

"You must be the colleague of whom Detective Johnson spoke," he said, calmly. "Will you take a seat and dry yourself by the fire? I see that you have wet the bottom of your trousers when leaving the dockside public house in which you were engaged earlier this morning. I am obliged that you have come directly from there to here, signifying as it does a comprehension of the urgency with which Scotland Yard views this case. Were you successful in infiltrating the socialists, might I ask?"

Familiar as I was with Holmes's methods, I still marvelled at the inferences he was able to make from often miniscule clues, but the effect on our visitor was striking, even so.

He strode towards Holmes and stood only an inch or so away, so that their faces almost touched. "Explain yourself, Mr. Holmes, or the next conversation we have will be far less pleasant than the current one. Have you followed me, sir, to know so much about my doings today? Come," he raged, "I will have an explanation!"

Holmes was unruffled and resumed his seat and took up his pipe before speaking further. "I have no need to follow you, when the story of your day is written so plainly on your person. I simply deduce from the facts displayed clearly before me." He filled the pipe bowl and lit it with a splinter from the fire, taking his time to get the flame going properly, while the detective fumed in front of him. Only when he was satisfied did he reveal the path down which his thinking had taken him.

"There is a spillage of cheap gin on the right-hand cuff of your shirt, but little or none on your breath, which suggests that you were in a public house but only pretended to drink. That variety of gin is only sold in the dockland area, favoured as it is by sailors. This, plus the fact that a detective such as yourself would not normally be drinking low quality spirits first thing in the morning, suggests to me that you were on an assignment for Special Branch. That you have not changed your soiled garments indicates that you came directly from there to here."

"And the socialists?" asked the Special Branch man, his suspicions as yet not entirely answered. "How do you come to *deduce* that they, and no other, were the subject of my work today?"

"A section of a socialist pamphlet projects from your jacket pocket, detective. Consequently, I would hesitate to claim that as a deduction at all."

To his credit, the detective took Holmes's amusement in good stead and, placated by the demonstration of my friend's professional competence, took a seat beside us. He explained that, though he had been working that morning amongst the socialists who congregated in the pubs near the docks, generally he was employed in work of more immediate utility, seeking out spies and enemy agents working in England. Recently, such work had taken him to Birmingham, and Chapmans' main factory there.

"Word had reached us that certain suspected foreign agents had been seen in the city, asking questions in the local hostelries, and making friendly overtures towards workers from the Chapmans' factory. Fortunately, the Midlands breeds patriotic men, and the agents received short shrift for their troubles, one at least barely escaping with his life. Even so, we were unable to infiltrate the gang, nor were we able to bring any man into custody. Buying drinks for factory workers is no crime, and every foreign agent and spy knows it."

"But you think that perhaps the nameless corpse we examined this morning is one of your foreigners?" I could not readily envisage a way in which a spy in Birmingham should end up dead and bereft of identification on the streets of London, but the reason for Special Branch's precipitous arrival on our doorstep was, at least, made clear. I could hear the frustration in his voice as he spoke of these agents who thumbed their noses at the English police force and hid behind England's sense of justice and law. Any possible advantage would, therefore, be taken up assiduously and promptly. Who knew what secrets our dead man might give up to someone experienced in the shadowy world of international espionage?

"All I know, Doctor Watson, is that any man found dead with the imprint of Chapman's on a document in his pocket is of interest to Special Branch. Especially now."

"Now?" I asked.

Holmes cut in quickly. "Presumably the reference is to Chapmans ongoing negotiations with the German firm of Baumgartner and Sons. A merger has been in the air for several months, and yesterday's *Times* reported that a deal might very soon be struck."

The detective nodded his agreement. "Exactly so, Mr. Holmes. A merger between the two companies is viewed in Westminster as very advantageous for British interests, and much to be encouraged." He examined his pocket watch. "But I'm afraid my time is extremely limited, so perhaps we could take a trip down to the Yard and take a look at the unfortunate soul?"

There being nothing to argue against such an eminently sensible suggestion, Holmes and I took hold of our coats and hats and followed the detective out into the cold evening air.

The mortuary was dark when we arrived, with only the light of a single lantern low on the far wall ameliorating the gloom. A central aisle bisected the room, separating two sets of metal beds, each covered with a white sheet. The rough form of a body could be made out on those nearest us, but those further away were all but lost in the dim light and seemed more like the outline of mist shrouded hills than the remains of once living souls.

In spite of this, Holmes led us down the aisle and directly to a specific bed.

Without preamble, he pulled back the sheet, exposing a familiar face beneath which he illuminated with the lantern he held. The Special Branch detective, whose name I realised I still did not know, leaned in close and examined the man closely, then shook his head firmly.

"This isn't my man."

The disappointment in his voice was clear, and matched by Holmes own. "That is a pity. It would have been a tidy solution." He straightened, and smoothed out his waistcoat where it had become crumpled. "Still, the facts are what they are, and if this man is not known to you then we must look elsewhere." He restored the sheet and indicated the exit. "Perhaps we should leave now, gentlemen? I confess I feel this man and his lack of a name as a rebuke to me."

In down-hearted mood, we made our way outside and into the light London drizzle. Holmes uttered no word during the entirety of our return to Baker Street, and I found myself glad of our earlier thought regarding German language students, else I could not say what we should do next. Lestrade had made it clear that a quick resolution was vital – and thus far we had made little concrete progress.

The following day was one of those rare autumnal days when the weather makes one final effort and the sun beats down warmly all day. Holmes and I breakfasted early and were already in a hansom by the time the clock struck eight. London, it turned out, had a surprisingly large number of foreign language schools, all of which taught German, and we hoped to visit each one in short order.

With a large part of the city to cover and a limited time to do so, we split up as we reached the first school, a crumbling three storey building in one of the shabbier, but still genteel, areas of London. Holmes went inside, leaving me with a brief journey to the next address on our list, off Westcott Road.

The weather being particularly fine, I left our carriage for Holmes and walked the short distance, revelling in the early autumn sunlight. London can be a dirty city at times, but seen in this golden light, there was something magical about it, which I have never seen replicated elsewhere. So pleasant was it, in fact, that in spite of the urgency of my mission, I was not as swift in my footsteps as I might have been.

Fortunately so, for had I been rushing pell-mell, I might not have been aware of steps echoing my own in the quiet morning air. Even then, I might not have noticed my shadow at all, had I not stumbled on a loose stone in the road and heard someone come to a similar halt a small distance behind me. I quickened my pace briefly, then slowed again, repeating the pattern until I reached Walcott Road, at which point I walked briskly round the corner, laid my hand on my revolver (which Holmes had fortuitously suggested I bring,) and waited to confront whoever followed me. The man had obviously become suspicious of my staggering movements, however, for he did not appear, and when I carefully looked back the way I had come, there was nobody to be seen.

I told myself that my imagination had become inflamed by recent events, but whether that were true or merely a happy fiction, I had no choice but to continue my errand. The language school had at one point been a residential address, but some enterprising soul had thought to divide the space up into individual apartments, which several small businesses now occupied. Miss Sharp's Language Emporium was on the first floor.

The lady who answered my knock was dainty in every way. No longer in the first flush of youth, and with her grey hair tied in bun, she beckoned me to enter with tiny hands, like those of a china doll, and smiled a greeting from a face likewise diminished in size from the commonplace. The remainder of her person was similar in proportion. Not so small as to draw remark, but sufficiently so for it to be noticed, Miss Sharp quickly belied her size, with a wit and intellect to match her name.

"A missing student, you say, Doctor?" she asked in response to my enquiry. "Studying German, you say? You mean William, I'm sure.

William Simon Edwards, to give him his Sunday name. Not, perhaps, the greatest linguist the world has ever known, but enthusiastic and with real ambition."

"He has not been seen recently?"

"Not a sign for a week or more. He has missed four classes so far, after missing none in the first six months of the course."

"You did not worry about him, or report his absence, Miss Sharp?"

"Doctor Watson, you may think me a terrible old cynic, but do you imagine that the over-worked police force of this city would stop for a second to investigate a man reported missing for a week by someone who is not even a relation, but merely his German teacher? Especially one of my stature?" She frowned to herself. "Besides, it had only been a week," she ended, uncertainly.

"Could you describe Mr. Edwards, by any chance?"

"I can do better than that, Doctor. At the start of every year, I commission a photograph of the class, as a memento, a keepsake for myself. This year's image is hanging on the wall behind you."

The photograph was a little dark, rendering the faces slightly indistinct, but there was no mistaking the face of our, until now nameless, corpse. William Simon Edwards it was, as clear as day.

"This chap here?" I asked Miss Sharp, keen that there should be no confusion when I reported back to Holmes.

"The very same, Doctor Watson, the very same. William is a fine man, kind-hearted but also clever and diligent at his work. He is expected to go far, I believe."

"His work?"

"He is a chemist, working with a firm from the Midlands, if I am not mis-remembering."

Suddenly in a great hurry, I asked if I might borrow the photograph and, having gained the lady's assent and assuring her that I would return when I had news of her missing student, I thanked Miss Sharp for her time and assistance, and made my way back to Holmes, with this new evidence to share.

In spite of my haste, Holmes's carriage was moving away from the pavement as I arrived back in Westcott Road, and it was only through a last minute sprint that I was able to rap on the side and so bring the vehicle to a halt. As a result, I was out of breath when I eventually managed to take my seat inside, and barely managed to gasp out my findings to Holmes.

He took the photograph from me, agreeing that one of the gentleman pictured therein and the mysterious man found dead that morning were the same. "So, William Simon Edwards is our man," he said. "And far from spying on Chapmans, he may well be an employee." He knocked on the roof of the carriage, bringing it to a stop. "Do you know the offices of Chapmans the chemists?" he shouted up to the driver. Having received confirmation that that worthy soul did indeed know the London offices of the firm, we set off in a new direction, with Holmes's eyes seldom straying far from the photograph he held in his hand.

Chapmans' London office was anonymous enough; one of many similarly grand façades in a street lined with them, each button-holed with a small but highly polished gold plaque, on which was inscribed the name of the firm resident within. Chapmans was the third such door along, and no more or less grand than any of the others.

Entering the building via a set of tall glass doors, directly ahead of us lay a reception desk, manned by a thin, pale young man, whose sparse hair was combed straight across from just above his left ear to just above his right, in one solid, completely flat masse. As he turned to greet us, I was disconcertingly aware of this raft of hair moving and shifting in its imperfect mooring, but tried to avoid staring as Holmes enquired after William Edwards.

"Mr. Edwards is in Germany at present, gents," the office boy replied, and I am sure that Holmes felt the same thrill of discovery that I did on mention of that country.

"On business?" asked Holmes, confidently then, without waiting for a reply, went on, "You surprise me. My name is Oswald Furnell, and I am lately down from Manchester to meet with Mr. Edwards, who I understood to be resident in Birmingham but currently on secondment to the London office of Chapmans."

"On secondment, yes, sir. But to Hamburg in Germany, not here, I'm afraid. Mr. Edwards is part of the team from Chapmans who hope to come to agreement over a merger with Baumgartners, the main chemical manufacturers of that city."

"Ah, I see my mistake," said Holmes with a small smile of understanding. He reached into his pocket, then withdrew his hand with a shake of the head. "I have left my cards in the hotel, but never mind for now. Might I leave a message with you to pass to Mr. Edwards? I, too, am a chemist and hoped that Mr. Edwards and I might work together on a little project of my own devising. Perhaps you could let him know that I called, and was disappointed to find him out of the country. I will be in town until Friday . . . he will not have returned by then? No? That is a pity." He made to leave then, as though suddenly struck by a thought, turned back to the receptionist.

"I wonder if I might have a word with one of his superiors, actually? It may be that they can provide me with the same information, vital to my work, that I hoped to gain from Mr. Edwards."

The receptionist appeared doubtful. "I don't think so, sir. Only Sir Peter is actually on the premises today, and he is busy with meetings all day."

"Sir Peter Warburton?" Holmes asked with every sign of enthusiasm. "Why, he and I were at University together." He looked round and quickly spotted a door with the words "Managing Director" on a plaque on it. Before he could be stopped, he strode over and threw the door open, revealing an expensively decorated office. "Come along, Watson," he shouted as he entered, "let's go and visit old Peter Warburton!"

With a sheepish shrug in the direction of the receptionist I did as he asked and followed him through the door.

The little receptionist, of course, hurried along in our footsteps, protesting that we could not enter Sir Peter's office, that he would be forced to call the police and other, similar protestations, of a sort I had become immune to during my years of acquaintance with Sherlock Holmes. He stood in the doorway, as indecisive as I was sure he would be, shuffling from one foot to the other, while Holmes took a seat and I stood behind him.

"I'm sorry, Sir Peter," he said, "but these gentlemen just barged – "

"It's quite alright, Jones, I heard. I will see them." The figure seated behind the desk was every inch the English patrician. Tall and slender, with short grey hair and moustache, he dressed conservatively but well, and to my surprise regarded us with some amusement, rather the nervousness one might expect in a man suddenly confronted by two strangers in his own office.

"Now gentlemen, what can I do for you?" he asked, giving every impression of a man asking two treasured guests what they would like to drink.

"You do not care to know who we are, Sir Peter?" Holmes asked.

The man shook his head. "Well, I know that you did not go to University with me, but other than that, no – I can't say I care particularly who you are, specifically. Nor which newspaper you represent." He laughed and waved a finger at Holmes. "I shall tell you exactly what I have told every other hack who has attempted to inveigle himself into my confidences. Chapmans has no comment to make on the rumours that we are conducting work for the Government. Now, I mean you no hard feeling, but I am a busy man and my time is precious, so if you will excuse me . . . ."

Curiously, throughout this extraordinary speech, I had felt myself redden, almost as though I were exactly the sort of scandal chasing newspaperman of his accusation. As he finished and indicated the door with one hand, I actually began to bid him good-day, so powerful was the sensation.

Holmes, however, was unperturbed, and even happy to play his role to the full. "Very well, Sir Peter, but one question before we go, if I may?"

Warburton smile widened at Holmes's cheek, but he waved a lazy hand in assent. "One question then, as repayment for the bravado of pretending to have gone to Oxford with me."

"Where is William Edwards, Sir Peter?" my friend asked quietly.

All good humour vanished from Warburton's face in an instant. He rose from his chair, knocking a selection of papers to the floor in his haste to speak, but once he was on his feet, his voice appeared to desert him and he stood, staring at Holmes and myself in silence. He walked across to a tantalus on a nearby side table and poured himself a whisky before he spoke. "That fool!" he snarled finally, "That ridiculous, ungrateful idiot! I've no conception of why anyone would trouble himself with such a worthless individual, but if you must know, I received word a day or two back that he had been caught behaving in a drunken and ungentlemanly manner while in Germany and, following a series of foul-mouthed attacks on senior members of the merger team, had been dismissed. I believe that he intended to make his own way back to England, and may well already be here somewhere, though I cannot tell you where exactly." He frowned, though I felt there was something unnatural about the gesture. "Now, I have told you what I know of the man. It is your turn to tell me why you seek him, and how that might impact upon Chapmans. You may quote me about his drunkenness and lack of a gentleman's manners, incidentally," he concluded, now almost restored to his former humour.

Holmes was equally calm. "No particular reason, Sir Peter. Word has reached *The News of* . . . well, let us leave my employers unnamed, shall we, that this Edwards was a rising star in the chemical manufacture industry, and we hoped to use him as a form of human interest story." Holmes held out a hand, "But if he has ruined himself in the manner you describe, our readers would have no interest in him."

With that, Holmes shook Warburton's hand and we left the office before he could say anything further. For a moment, I thought he had sent the receptionist Jones to follow us, but whoever it was I glimpsed from the corner of my eye as we walked down the stairs outside the Chapmans' office was gone by the time I turned to look properly.

If I expected Holmes to be abashed by our failure at Chapmans, I was to be disappointed. No sooner had we rounded the corner of the road than he called for the hansom driver to stop. He opened his jacket and pulled from it a collection of crumpled papers which he sat and read, without deigning to explain his actions to me. I knew where the papers had come from, of course. Sir Peter had knocked them to the floor as he raged at us, and Holmes had slipped some of them into his coat as the distressed knight of the realm had poured himself a drink. I reflected that while I could admire Holmes's ability at sleight of hand, I could not necessarily evince a similar degree of admiration for his personal morality.

As Holmes scanned each page, he discarded it on the floor of the hansom, until finally he came to a page which interested him. "Aha!" he cried with delight, "This is the one!" He stabbed a long finger at the page, indicating one small section. "See here," he crowed, "this paragraph. *'The company is presently engaged in the development of new weaponry for the army, in case of war. The most promising of these experiments involves W.S Edwards' work on an odourless and colourless form of poison gas, based on Hydrogen Sulfide'*."

"Perhaps Lestrade is in the right then, Holmes?" I queried. "Edwards dismissed with no reference and a definite blot on his character, and the company working on a secret gas weapon to which he might well have had access. Is it so much of a jump to have him sell his secrets to a foreign power, and then be killed by agents of that power, eager to leave no loose ends?" A sudden thought occurred to me. "By God, Holmes, don't some of those Boer types speak German?"

"A west Germanic language, certainly, but rooted in Dutch rather than classical German."

"Even so," I insisted.

"Perhaps," said Holmes, though a look of doubt crossed his face as he spoke. "We shall learn nothing more here though. Let's pick up an evening paper and return home. A pipe or two and a browse through the reports of the Criminal Court may serve to loosen something useful from my brain."

With that, he lapsed into that blind concentrative state which marked portions of so many of his cases, leaving me to stare out of the carriage window at the London streets flying by.

We has been at home for no more than five minutes when Holmes gave a great cry and dashed his newspaper to the floor.

"I have been a fool, Watson! Remind me of this moment when next I lord it over the likes of Lestrade and Gregson." He struck the arm of his chair a great blow in his annoyance with himself, then snapped out a request for the original letter found on Edwards' body. I handed it to him and watched as he re-read it, then did the same to the discarded newspaper. "So simple a solution, and yet I allowed myself to wander in entirely the wrong direction." He handed me both letter and 'paper. "See for yourself, Watson!" he groaned.

The letter was short enough that I had no need to reacquaint myself with its contents, but I read the article indicated by Holmes with great interest, and greater confusion. It was merely a standard announcement of the engagement of two young people – the Hon. Michael Warburton and Johanna Baumgartner. The future marriage of the son of the Managing Director of Chapmans and, I assumed, a member of the family of German chemists, was something which Holmes was bound to find interesting, but I could see no other reason for his behaviour, and no link whatever to the lines of poetry. I said as much to Holmes, who was already taking up his coat and scarf, preparatory to going out.

"Not the poetry, Watson!" he barked as he threw my own coat to me. "Come though, there is no time to explain, or lose. Put that on, and let us make our way to Scotland Yard, stopping only at the telegraph office, where I must send an urgent wire to Germany."

I have often had cause to complain that Holmes could be as fond of the melodramatic revelation as the most humble of stage conjurers, but in this case it was clear that haste alone prevented his explaining further. He all but ran to the corner of Baker Street to flag down a growler, and leapt from it and into the telegraph office when we pulled up outside that establishment. I had scarcely had time to re-read the marriage announcement, which I still held, when Holmes re-appeared in the door once more.

To my surprise, he was followed into the carriage by another man. The newcomer's face was hidden by a heavy scarf, but his eyes were hard and cold, and the gun he held was steady and pointed directly at my own midriff. I had seen enough killers in the army and in my time with Holmes to know that I was in the presence of another who would not baulk at murder, if he felt it needful.

"Tell the driver to take you back to Baker Street," he ordered, in a heavy accent. "We have need to talk, Sherlock Holmes."

"In which case, I must apologise in advance, for I have no intention of speaking to you at all, beyond this current exchange."

"That is a great shame, Mr. Holmes, for if you will not tell me what I wish to know, I will be forced to fire a bullet directly into your companion's stomach." He smiled, without warmth. "That is not a good way for any man to die."

"No, I believe it is not." Holmes banged on the roof of the carriage and directed the driver to return us to Baker Street, then sat back, his fingers steepled before him, and observed the interloper. "You are a Boer?" he asked.

"I am."

"And what do you seek from me?"

"Come now, do not play the fool. You know what I want. Details of the weapon being constructed to use against my people."

"I know nothing of any such weapon, I assure you." Holmes was calm and gave no indication of nerves, but the Boer was unwilling to accept anything less than the information he desired. He leaned forward in his seat and jammed the barrel of his gun into my ribs, cocking the hammer as he did so.

"As I said, that would be a shame, Mr. Holmes. Perhaps you would care to re-consider?"

Holmes looked up at me, and I did my utmost to communicate to him that he should say nothing. I have never thought of myself as a particularly brave man, but a choice between death and betrayal is no choice at all. Holmes, though, either did not recognise the message I was trying so hard to convey, or chose to ignore it.

"Very well," he said, waving away my by now vocal attempts to prevent him from speaking. "If you will remove your gun from the vicinity of my friend, I will tell you what I know."

I should have had more faith in my old friend. For the next ten minutes, Holmes told a long, convoluted and entirely fictitious tale of a factory near Edinburgh which had, for several years, been working on a motorised flying machine, from which the British intended to drop bombs on enemy troops. Recent progress, he said, had been more than encouraging, with successful live testing having taken place within the previous month.

As he spoke, the Boer agent's face fell further and further, as he digested what to him must have been the most terrible of news. For myself, it was only the immediate danger of our situation which prevented me from laughing aloud as Holmes's fancy took him to ever greater levels of imagination. He described specially modified Maxim machine guns able to fire from the air onto lines of marching soldiers, and troops being carried for miles behind enemy lines, safe above the clouds and out of sight. He spoke of war being carried hundreds of mile inland, without the necessity of land-based assault, and of assassins being dropped from flying machines into noblemen's palaces and politicians' country homes. By the end, his picture of escalating destruction and chaos was so real, even to me who knew it to be false, that I had no desire to laugh anymore, and instead found myself pondering the fate of Europe should such innovations ever move from imagination to reality.

Still, I silently applauded Holmes's ingenuity, even though I knew that, while his story would prevent immeasurable harm being visited on Great Britain, it would do little to save us, once it had ended.

As the carriage drew up outside our Baker Street home, Holmes trailed to a stop, and sat back in his seat, seemingly entirely composed.

The white faced Boer, conversely, was anything but calm as he railed against the barbarism of the English. He thudded into Holmes's back as he pushed us both out of the carriage and directed us towards our front door. "Do nothing to arouse suspicion and I may just tie you up in your sitting room, rather than dispensing the justice which you English pigs deserve," he muttered under his breath as the carriage drove away.

"We shall do nothing whatsoever, I assure you," Holmes murmured, and opened the door and then, in an instant, threw himself to one side, pulling me to the ground with him. Before I could protest, the reason for his action became clear, as the swinging door revealed a half dozen armed police officers, all pointing their weapons directly at the Boer. For a moment I thought he would try to shoot his way free, but discretion immediately overcame any such consideration, and he lowered his gun and allowed it to drop to the street. Policemen swarmed over him and he was quickly led away in handcuffs.

Holmes and I rose and dusted ourselves down as Inspector Lestrade approached.

"Can we offer you tea, Inspector?" Holmes asked politely, and I was finally able to laugh.

Settled in comfortable chairs, with something stronger than tea in our hands, Holmes explained everything which had occurred in the past few hours.

"I really have no excuse for my failure to realise what had happened for so long," he began. "It was not until I read the announcement in *The Times* that the vital cog was inserted into the machinery of my thinking, and every other thing fell into place. You see, though I was never convinced that Mr. Edwards had committed self-murder, I allowed myself to be distracted by the mention of Johannesburg – and the fact that the victim worked on the very secret weapons Scotland Yard feared compromised merely made that distraction stronger.

"It was only when I saw the name of the young lady in the newspaper that I realised my mistake – the note found on Mr. Edwards was not intended for delivery to Johannesburg but to Johanna Baumgartner. The jagged tearing of the note left us only *Johann* and a closing *g* if you recall. Natural to assume the name of a city in a country already under discussion, but I should have considered the alternative, especially given the amorous – if martially expressed – nature of the poem underneath. I believe that Mr. Edwards and Miss Baumgartner met while Edwards was working in Germany on behalf of Chapmans, and fell in love. I cannot say who discovered this unwelcome news first, but whoever it was, whether in Germany or England, it cannot have been welcome news, with a financially lucrative merger in the offing, to be cemented by a similar merger of the families of two industrial giants."

Lestrade has not moved a muscle while Holmes spoke, so intent was he, but now he asked a question which had evidently been playing on his mind. "It is your contention, Mr. Holmes, that one or both of these industrial giants, as you term them, then decided that murder was the most effective way to keep the merger progressing smoothly?"

"Both, I should say, Inspector," replied Holmes smoothly. "It is too much of a stretch to believe that a German industrialist had instant access to assassins in London, but at the same time, what need had any of the English group to ensure that Edwards died nameless and unknown? A simple 'accident' in the lab could far more easily have disposed of an unwanted suitor, but Baumgartner, I suspect, wished his daughter to believe herself abandoned by the man she loved, and so more pliable and willing to marry the man her father had chosen for her."

He held out a hand to the rat-faced detective. "If Inspector Lestrade has with him the reply to the second telegraph I sent earlier today – the first being to Scotland Yard of course – then we should be able to confirm my suspicions."

Lestrade fumbled in his pocket and pulled out a telegraph, which he passed to Holmes, who read it quickly and with but a single nod of appreciation. "Read for yourselves, gentlemen. My telegraph was short and to the point, alerting Miss Baumgartner to the terrible news that her fiancé, Mr. William Edwards, had been found, dead of poison, in a London street. Her more wordy reply confirms both that she once hoped to be his wife, and that she had been told by her father that he had proven unfaithful and had fled in the middle of the night. If that is not enough to begin investigations into the two companies and you require further evidence, Inspector, I suggest you test the body for the presence of Hydrogen Sulfide. As Doctor Watson will confirm, in a concentrated dose it kills in moments and leaves no trace bar an unpleasant odour.

And ironically that odour was removed by Mr. Edwards' genius. One other thing the chemical does: its presence causes metals to become discoloured. It was for this reason that all money was removed from Edwards' body, but I believe the killers missed the studs which are found on a gentleman's trousers for the fastening of suspenders. You would do well therefore to examine such items more closely."

"So the African agent was nothing to do with the death of Edwards?" I asked in the silence which followed Holmes's speech.

"None, Watson. The purest coincidence, but a happy one, nonetheless."

"Happy – ?"

"The Inspector will, I think, agree with me that the most likely fate for our recent kidnapper is to be swapped with an agent of our own, currently a prisoner of the Boers. In such an event, imagine the furore on the African veldt when he reports that the English have flying machines, ready to rain death and destruction from the sky!"

Holmes's laughter as he concluded was so loud that Mrs. Hudson came upstairs to make certain everyone was unharmed, but that served only to make him laugh all the louder.

After a moment, Lestrade and I joined in.

A Mistress – Missing
by Lyn McConchie

It had been an irritating month. It had done nothing but drizzle, and in London the wet streets, the over-flowing gutters, and the angry shouts of drivers had been a constant theme. Inside, Holmes had been bored and made no bones about it. He had concluded an unpleasant case only the previous month, and was officially resting, save that resting – at least to his mind – is not Holmes's usual condition.

"Nothing in the newspaper again, Watson."

His lack of interesting cases had translated into boredom for him, but for me it had added to the irritations of remaining inside because of the wet weather, as he paced, smoked, and commented sourly each morning on the mundane and dreary round of ordinary criminal activity. I scanned the paper hastily.

"What about 'Strange Events in Pimlico'?" I offered. "A woman left her home in the early hours wearing only a nightgown and slippers. Fears are held for her safety."

Holmes snorted. "Her husband is well aware that she has fled to her lover."

"How can you possibly know that?" I asked in surprise.

"Because of his equivocations. See, he is reported as claiming that she took nothing, he knows of no reason for her disappearance, and is desperate for her return. But look at this excellent sketch of him, Watson."

I looked and belatedly realised his point. "Oh, you mean that he is well dressed?"

"Hair brushed back, a clean shirt, neat suit and tie, polished shoes. The artist did not observe, but he drew what he saw. No husband fearing the worst would appear so calm. His clothes would convey the disorder of his mental state. No, his wife fled and he knows to whom she has gone."

I rustled the pages again. "Well, what about . . . ."

"It's no use, Watson. I have already read anything you may offer and I have no interest in any of it." He sat back, his eyes heavy-lidded, and his face set in a slight scowl. "More and more commonplace cases abound, and – what is that?" The 'that' to which he referred was the front door slamming, thumps in the hall, and a howl. I walked across, opened the door, and a cat shot past me. Mrs. Hudson appeared in the doorway.

"Forgive me, I went to bring in the milk and it came past me. I'll put it out directly."

Holmes held up a hand. "Leave it, Mrs. Hudson. I presume it is drizzling again?"

"Yes, it is."

"Then let us not deny sanctuary to a fellow creature."

That, I thought, was my old friend all over. For all that he could be severe with people, he had yet a soft spot for the young or helpless. I shut the door again, sat and poured myself another cup of tea, and waited. After several minutes the cat came out, sat on the rug by the fire and stared at us. We stared back.

It was a solid animal of an odd shade of brown, wearing a light plaited leather collar. It was obviously a stray. It was rather dirty, and the wary look suggested knowledge of people who threw things at cats. I felt sorry for it, and, pouring milk into a saucer, I placed that near it on the rug. The cat walked over as one that is finally given its due, drank the milk, meowed at me and waited. I refilled the saucer and this time when it was finished it curled up by the fire and apparently slept.

I was amused. "Upon my soul, Holmes, if that isn't like a cat. Walk in, treat the place as its own, demand to be fed, and take it all for granted. Typical London stray, it knows when it is onto a good thing"

"Ah, but this is no ordinary cat, Watson." Holmes said quietly. "Nor a normal stray."

I looked at the cat and saw nothing unusual that might lead him to that conclusion. However, I saw that his attention had been caught and rejoiced. If I could only involve him, engage his interest.

"It looks like an ordinary cat to me, Holmes," I said, a little contentiously. "What's so different about a stray that wanders in from the street?"

"Several things. It wears a collar."

"Lost by some old lady then?"

"Consider its condition. The body is sleek, solid. It is in excellent health, and it can be seen that beneath the grimy outer layer, the fur is not harsh as it would be had the animal long gone without food."

"Recently lost by an old lady?"

Holmes produced one of his occasional smiles. "No, no, my friend. There are other points here. The cat is used to being cared for. It came readily to you once you showed yourself friendly. Watch." He spoke gently to the cat, which rose and strolled over to him. His fingers, rubbing under the jaw, produced purring, and eager thumps by the creature's head against his hand.

"You see, Watson, how swiftly it casts off any superficial fear that I may harm it. This is a cat that has always been loved and cared for. The grime on its fur is no more than a few days old." His hands were carefully removing the collar. He turned that and I glimpsed a small copper plaque. "Ah ha!"

"What does it say, Holmes?"

"*Mandalay*, a reward for return to Miss Emily Jackson, 14 South Street."

"As I said," I repeated. "Some old lady." And more cunningly, "It is nothing, Holmes. The case of the stray cat?" I managed a sneer. "You complain of criminals who bring nothing new to your investigations. How far more humdrum is a lost cat? Why, I will bet that the owner is above fifty, a widow or old maid who adores cats, and if we return the animal to that address, she will gush over us, weep over the cat, and expect us to listen for hours to the virtues of her pet."

Holmes rested his chin on one hand and considered the cat. "I think not. Let us take the cat and go there."

"It will be a waste of your time, Holmes. Why, I shall lay down a crown right now that there is nothing exciting or even mildly interesting in all this."

Holmes's eyes gleamed at me. "Very well, Watson. As you know, I do not gamble, but if you insist, here is my crown. Let us leave them here on the table, and you yourself shall say which of us has won the money fairly upon our return."

I allowed him to pick up the cat and followed them as we left the house. Unseen by my friend, I wore a very faint smile. Whatever the outcome of this, I could not lose. If there were a case of any interest, Holmes would be less bored for a while. If not, he would have at least had a day outside our rooms to cheer him, and I would be a crown better off. Holmes hailed a cab, and we were driven off in the direction of the suburb listed on the cat's collar. It was no great distance, and half an hour later we halted outside a pleasant building that looked to be one of those that let out self-contained suites, rather than single rooms with shared amenities.

I paid off the cab while Holmes knocked at the main door, which was opened by a flustered woman of matronly appearance, plump build, and a quantity of frilly apron swathed about her. She gaped at the cat.

"Mandalay, you wicked creature! Oh, how happy I am you're safe. Miss Emily would never have forgiven me." And to us, "Where ever did you find him? Come in, sirs, please come in."

We passed over the threshold, the door was shut behind us, and Holmes released Mandalay. The cat darted along the corridor and cried at a polished door. The woman opened it for him and ushered us into what was clearly the cat's usual accommodation, because he went at once to a padded wicker basket and curled up.

"Please, sirs, sit down."

We sat once she had done so and Holmes took charge. "Your name?"

We found it to be Jane Knox, "No relation to the minister, sirs," and that her husband had been a merchant. This had been his uncle's family home, left to them on the uncle's death twenty years gone. Her husband died soon after, and she had used what money she had to convert the huge rambling old house into five furnished, self-contained apartments, all let to respectable tenants on long-term leases. Miss Knox oversaw the cleaning, the cooking of an evening meal when or if required, and was in general something of a confidant and friend to all in the house.

"It worried me something awful, sirs. Miss Emily is reliable. She has lived here for five years now, and she comes in and goes out each day, and always at the same times. Should she know she is to be late, she always tells me, or leaves a note. And that cat, sirs – she adores Mandalay, she wouldn't ever leave him like this. I didn't know she hadn't come home on the Monday night, not until I found Mandalay was out of food, sirs. I opened the door and he darted past me. Mr. Southby was coming in just then, and the front door being open, too, Mandalay went right outside, and wouldn't come when I called. I tell you true, sirs, I was beside myself with worry. He's been gone four days now, and oh, dear, oh dear, *so has she!*"

We asked questions and it transpired, putting together all we heard, that while Miss Emily had no real need to work, having a small private income sufficient to maintain her and Mandalay in comfort, she also did not believe in being idle. She had therefore taken employment at a typing bureau that catered in particular to writers of scientific works; she, having had an excellent education, was particularly esteemed, and often requested.

"She donates her wages to charity, sirs, good girl that she is. But she enjoys the work. She says it's interesting and she learns so much. And all those old scientific gents think the world of her."

Holmes elicited further details, and after another hour we left the cat content in his home again, and took a second cab to the typing bureau, where we received a similar welcome.

"There must have been some trouble," stated the imposing figure that was the bureau's owner. "I cannot conceive that Emily would have walked out on me or her work without some very strong reason. She is not of that sort."

"Who was her Monday client?" Holmes asked.

"Professor Smithyson. He's in his seventies, a fine old gentleman. He is writing a book on Sumerian Art. Emily finds references for him, and writes at his dictation the text that will accompany the art in his book. It will be his fourth book," she added.

I looked at Holmes, There was no way in which I could see an elderly gentleman obsessed with the ancient city of Sumer as an abductor of young woman or a vile seducer. Yet, it was there she had last been, so far as her employer knew, and it was there we next repaired.

A man we thought must be the gentlemen himself opened the door. "Oh," he eyed us sadly. "You're not Emily."

For once I wasn't far behind Holmes in a deduction. "You hoped it was she? When did you see her last?"

"Monday. She left as usual at five and was to return the next morning at nine. She did not return, and I have not seen her since." Professor Smithyson said succinctly.

Holmes nodded. "She vanished that night. We are asked to look for her."

"You have a client? Whom?"

I caught the glimmer of amusement in my friend's face. "A dear friend of the lady's, one who is deeply concerned for her safe return. He visited my friend and me, and we agreed to help."

"That is wonderful, I had no idea she had anyone. But come in, come in. I am happy to tell you anything I can, to answer any questions you may have. Come in."

We did so and asked our questions. Miss Emily had arrived at nine on the Monday. She had taken dictation for the text of chapter seven, and gone then to check on some aspects of a controversial theory of the professor's. She had returned from the library at one, shared his lunch, and taken further dictation, after which they had discussed the placement of some of the art on the next several pages. She had intended to return to the library before she continued home.

Professor Smithyson smiled ruefully. "I have a theory, I believe that many of the temple friezes were made from templates. That the priests took metal plates, carved patterns into these, and used plant dyes and brushes to produce uniform friezes along temple walls. Look." He waved several sheets of paper at us. "This temple was built over fourteen years, but the basic frieze decoration was considered complete within weeks. How else could that have been accomplished?" He jabbed a finger at the photos.

"Everywhere, along the lower walls, along the door frames, along the places where the upper areas of the walls meet the ceilings. It is unheard of. If I could but prove this was so, it would be a great discovery. We have no clear proof that until this time such a thing had even been thought of, let alone carried out. Miss Emily was almost as excited by the idea as I was. She promised to hurry back with any information she might discover."

We asked more questions, most of which led us to his theory again, and left, certain only that he was likely innocent, and that the mystery continued. I chaffed my friend as we returned home.

"So you have a client? A 'dear friend of the lady's,' you said. 'One deeply concerned for her safe return.' Someone who visited us and we agreed to help." I laughed. "True enough, I suppose."

Holmes looked at me. "True, as you say, my dear Watson. What, would you say the creature was not concerned?" He picked up the two crowns laying on the table. "I think I have fairly won; the lady is question is not over fifty. And there appears to be something of a mystery, does there not?"

I agreed.

His face sobered. "Consider this of the cat also. He lives a mile from Baker Street. Yet the day after she fails to return he not only escapes, he comes to us four days later. With guile and determination, he enters the house, perhaps the only house where he might obtain the assistance he needs to regain his mistress, and that he desperately needs to do. For what is to become of him without her, Watson?"

I saw his point. "Yes, so where do we go next, Holmes?"

"To talk to Lestrade. It is possible he may be able to tell us something."

He could not, although he did his best. "It could be the white slave trade, Mr. Holmes. But the woman, while from the description is pleasant enough looking, is not particularly beautiful, and she is twenty-six. Too old for those who take young women."

He glanced down at a stack of papers that spread across his desk. "As for this professor of yours, he's unlikely to have her captive in his basement."

"There was no basement," Holmes informed him.

"Doubly unlikely then. An expert on Sumerian art? No, not someone I would suspect. Coincidence is a strange thing. Anyhow, I wish you luck, but I can be of no help, so far as I know. I can find her antecedents if you wish." Holmes nodded. "Then that shall be done. Call on me in two days and I may at least tell you somewhat of her."

I was aware that at some stage in this speech, Holmes had tensed slightly. Sumerian art? Could he think a rival had kidnapped Miss Emily to steal a march of the professor's book? Or did he think Professor Smithyson to be the villain after all?"

I waited until we were gone from Lestrade's office and asked. "Holmes, you heard something in what Lestrade told us?"

"A coincidence, Watson. But interesting. Let us go home and in the morning I shall see if Mycroft can tell me anything."

I saw that I was not to hear more on this and resigned myself. The cab let us out on our doorstep and we found, to our surprise, that Jane Knox stood there, a large wicker basket in one hand. Holmes bowed courteously.

"May we be of some assistance, Mrs. Knox? I see that you have brought Mandalay."

"I'm sorry, sirs, I am that, but the creature will not be silent. He howls, and my tenants are complaining. He has cried all day, he stands at the door and tries to run out any time I enter. He has eaten nothing and, well, the long and the short of it is, sirs, I think he wishes to be with you until you find his mistress."

I was bracing. "Really, Mrs. Knox, but cats do not reason in such a way. Take him to his home and let him sleep the night there. I'm sure all will be well in the morning."

Holmes reached out and took the wicker basket. "He may remain with us until we can restore his mistress to him, Mrs. Knox." He suffered her gratitude and promises, her offering of a large bag containing Mandalay's own basket, brush, and bowls, and allowed the woman to go her way while we carried cat and possessions into the house.

I eyed him severely. "If you wished for a cat, Holmes, I could have obtained a kitten."

"Ah, but Mandalay is a client," was all that he said.

I went to change for dinner, cursing my frivolity. I had wished only to engage my friend's attention, I had wanted to find him a case that would fill his days. This whimsy of a cat as client was his own, and, I very much feared, his revenge for the knowledge that I had attempted to manipulate him into the affair. I sighed. Whatever the outcome, he was not bored. That must be set to the credit side of the ledger.

Nor was Mandalay bored, who shared our dinner before vanishing into Mrs. Hudson's realm, where he found and slaughtered two mice, to her delight. "A good creature, he is. And welcome I'm sure if that continues."

We went out the next evening to visit Mycroft at the Diogenes Club. Mycroft is slothful, and disinclined to move, but with a brain so incisive that he out-thinks Holmes on occasion. The club is peculiar – as are its members, Mycroft being a good example. They do not socialize. The club rules forbid this, no member being allowed to address another or even to take notice of him without the desire for that being evident.

On our arrival, Holmes vanished and returned several minutes later with Mycroft, who led us to the club's Stranger's Room, where talk was permitted. Once we had sunk comfortably into opulent chairs, drinks had been provided, and Mycroft had ascertained that our talking would offend no one, he waited politely, looking at Holmes, who began.

"Are there any foreigners currently in London in whom your office takes an interest?"

Mycroft folded his fingers into a steeple and considered. "Several. There is Liebowitcz, who is in the market for guns, Johnson of Miami, who is here because some of his comrades would prefer him terminated, and Lutz of Berlin, who, while here officially to discuss trade, is known to have other interests on behalf of his government."

"What of anyone who might also be of interest to the police?"

"Ah, you may be interested in Vereker of Petersberg. Also, last year we had a refugee from there. A good man who believes in world peace, and his family having been gravely persecuted, he escaped with the aid of friends and came to London, where our Government set him up in a laboratory just outside the city."

"His name?"

"Cmitzhcoh, also of Petersberg." He pronounced the name in a way that sounded like someone coughing during a sneeze, and involuntarily I smiled. Mycroft glared. "I assure you, the situation is not amusing. Vereker always has his own agenda, while ostensibly working at the embassy as an innocent clerk. We believe that he is hunting Cmitzhcoh, and that if he finds him, he plans to steal his discovery and kill the man if possible. He spends much of his time in odd places for a man of his talents, and it is known that twice he has obtained secrets our government would rather his masters not have."

"How?" Holmes inquired.

"He listens, snoops, and pries. Why, it is believed that he obtained the plans for a new type of gun by chatting to a clerk that had the work of copying them. We have grave fears that he is again on the trail of the device Cmitzhcoh is inventing."

"Vereker," Holmes said thoughtfully. "Would the police know of him?"

"He killed a girl in London last year," Mycroft said quietly. "His embassy had much ado persuading the police that he was under diplomatic protection. His masters had him out of the country for a time; now he's back. but they keep him on a short leash."

"I see. Thank you, brother."

We went home to be greeted by Mrs. Hudson. "I've some nice poached fish for supper, and that cat is asleep on the doctor's bed." We enjoyed our supper and later I moved the cat. I prefer my bed unencumbered, although I woke to find that Mandalay had rejoined me. No wonder he wanted his mistress home. She had undoubtedly spoiled him.

Over breakfast, Holmes looked at me. "Watson, if I may ask you, would you take the train out to Chigwell this morning?" I indicated I would be happy to do so. "Excellent. That is where the government has Cmitzhcoh working. There is a Hall there, with surrounding parkland. He is working in the old stables, and living in the gardener's cottage, courtesy of the owner who knows what is afoot."

"What am I to do once I reach Chigwell?"

"I want you to visit hotels, Watson," Holmes said cheerfully. "Call in at bars, discuss the weather, and work around to the odd goings on at the Hall. Ask if they see many strangers there. If so, of what descriptions? Have they noticed suspicious coming and goings, or large vehicles driven by men they do not know? Mysterious loads covered by tightly-drawn tarpaulins on such vehicles. Did any look like artillery?"

"What will you do today?"

"I have a few things to do, Watson, and I regret that I cannot accompany you."

I set off, quite excited by my task. I should not have been. The weather continued wet, and there was no conversation of any value. My one moment of interest came when a young man accosted me. A fresh-faced lad, perhaps in his late twenties, wearing a good suit, and, as I noticed, having soft-looking hands. An office worker of some sort, I presumed.

"You're asking questions about the Hall. About those who live there, them as comes and goes, vehicles that deliver, and what they may carry, and such?" It seemed he had been listening, but what business it was of his, I had no idea.

"Just making conversation," I said speciously.

"In three bars that I've heard."

"If I want to make conversation, what is it to you?" I was becoming annoyed.

"Who are you?"

I frowned. "Young man, that's none of your business. Now, I'm catching the train home, and I'd advise that you return to your friends, should you have any."

I strode away and was furious to find that he followed me all the way to the train station, and stood watching me enter my carriage. He was still looking after me as the train pulled away, and the last I saw of him was that ingenuous countenance. Once returned, I found Holmes leaning back in a chair, a drink in one hand, and the cat at his feet. I unburdened myself.

"A waste of time, I'm sorry to say. I visited half a dozen places. They could tell me of strangers, but none appeared suspicious. No vehicle with any load that resembled artillery, and my only problem was some young fool who affixed himself to me and wanted to know who I was and why I was asking."

"His appearance?"

"Oh, some sort of office worker, I would say."

I described the boy and Holmes nodded. "Vereker."

"What?"

"Yes, Lestrade was here earlier and I had a description from him. I'm told Vereker is the more dangerous, as he looks nothing like the man he's known to be. You thought him ten years younger than his true age. He makes a habit of dressing like a clerk, and while his hands may be soft, he has killed with them. I also called again on Mycroft. He tells me that Vereker has not much time left. It is known to his government that the device being studied at the Hall is on the verge of completion, at which point the plans and a working prototype will be removed, along with their inventor, to an unknown location. Once that is done, his government will recall Vereker, considering him to have failed."

"Will they punish him for that?"

"Not for that," Holmes said thoughtfully. "But no doubt he has other transgressions."

"And was Lestrade able to tell you more about Miss Emily?"

"She is an orphan, her parents having died in an influenza epidemic when she was twenty-one. She inherited family money, she has no close relatives, is of a serious turn of mind, loves cats, and does not believe in idling her days away. She thinks that if the opportunity to do right appears, then this should be acted upon, and she seems to have lived a blameless life. The lease of her apartment is paid yearly, and has almost half a year left to run. The cat is a Brown Burmese, rare in this country, and valuable."

I sighed. "Nothing of any use then."

"That depends on coincidence." Holmes said.

"What coincidence?"

"The one for which we return to Chigwell in the morning." He would say no more, and knowing that, I went to bed early, Mandalay again choosing to join me.

We set off at nine, I bringing my revolver as instructed. To my surprise, we found ourselves joined by Lestrade and two constables, together with a number of men I recognised as the secret service type. I hid my anticipation. It was clear to me that Holmes had made some discovery and that we were in pursuit. We stepped down at Chigwell, and were met with police vans, into which we climbed and sat in silence as the convoy was driven in the direction of the Hall. However, that was not our destination.

At length the vehicles halted, and we exited to stand on the side of a quiet country road. Lestrade gave orders in a low voice. A man appearing to be in authority over our other companions added further commands to that. Holmes, without heeding them, set out. I immediately followed. We circled a large copse and found ourselves looking down into a tiny valley, at the far end of which was a hut. I would have queried events, but one look at Holmes and I remained mute. I had seen that look before. A compound of hunter and one who fears what may be found. We moved down the valley, and once at the shed, I could see the door was not that of the sort normally used in a hut. It was of wood planks, with a strong lock, and a bolt as well.

Holmes looked at that, and I barely heard what he said. "The bolt is shot across. Pray heaven that is for a reason."

And with that he moved to the grimy window with its bars and tapped very gently. There was a pause and then a face appeared, seen dimly through the glass. "Stand back," Holmes ordered. "Help is here. Do you know where your captor may be?"

"He has been gone for days," we heard faintly.

Holmes nodded. "Break the window, Watson."

I used the butt of my revolver, and with the glass gone I could see the woman within more clearly. She looked to be forty, scrawny, and her hair straggled like a witch past her shoulders. Yet spirit gleamed in her eyes, and she was coherent. The bars were stout iron, but I sought out a length of wood, and by levering hard I was able to tear first one, then the remaining pair, from their anchorage. The lady was too weak to climb out alone, so I managed to squeeze past the sill, and once inside I lifted her up so that, with Holmes's assistance, she was able to escape her prison. Once on the ground, she collapsed into a sitting position and surveyed us.

"I am eternally in your debt, gentlemen. But we should leave here at once. My gaoler is a savage. Should he return, he would have no hesitation in attacking you. Oh," she added involuntarily. "I'm so thirsty."

"Has he harmed you?" I asked hastily. "Do not fear to tell us, I am Doctor Watson, and this is my good friend, Mr. Holmes."

She managed a tiny smile. "I am starving, filthy, dying of thirst, and he did strike me a number of times. Other than that, I am unharmed. But, I do wish for water, a bath and food, and my own home again."

I got her to her feet and we found that, brave as she was, she was too weak to walk. While I produced my flask and she drank a few small sips, Holmes produced a police whistle and sounded it, Lestrade came down the hill, a constable at his heels, and we were able to carry the poor lady back up the valley to where a police van waited.

"They'll take her to hospital for a night or two," Lestrade assured us. "Now, we have our man. He has a bullet wound, but he'll live to stand trial for the abduction of Miss Emily Jackson." I stared briefly before I understood that the woman we rescued had been that girl. How a week of captivity had aged her. But then, held in such conditions and in continual fear for her life, it was no wonder.

We gathered the next day at Lestrade's office, while Holmes expounded as I had requested. "It was a coincidence. My brother mentioned Vereker of Petersberg, and also a man, Cmitzhcoh, of the same city."

I demanded an explanation. "Holmes, I see no coincidence."

"No. Yet the name Cmitzhcoh in Russian may be rendered as *Smithson* in English, and that, I thought, would be how Lestrade had heard it."

"I do not . . . oh, Professor Smithyson."

"Mycroft said that Vereker had been known to obtain information by falling into conversation with government clerks. What if, while loitering in a certain research library, he had overheard a woman talking of Smithson – as he thought – and patterns. Might he not take the word as a synonym for plans? Could it be that he believed Miss Emily to work for Cmitzhcoh, and that, with her assistance, willing or unwilling, he hoped to lay hands on the plans for the device of which our admiralty expects great things?"

"He successfully kidnapped her, imprisoned her in that place where we discovered her, and endeavoured to persuade her to talk. What must have been his chagrin to find that he had entirely mistaken things, and what then? If her body was found, his embassy would repudiate him. So he made the decision to take no overt action. He left her, without food, with no more water than remained to her, without bedding against the cold, and hoped that she would die of seemingly natural causes."

"She lives instead," Lestrade cut in. "Thanks to you, Mr. Holmes, and to you doctor, and she is prepared to testify against him."

That she did a month later, and Vereker was given a life sentence. Two days after we freed Miss Emily, she was at our door. I had been talking to Holmes over the breakfast table.

"An interesting case, was it not?"

"Indeed, even if you did persuade me into it."

"You knew?"

Holmes snorted. "Watson, you are many things. Subtle is not one of them. Yet it was a kindly thought, and you did so only for my benefit. I could have no more loyal friend."

I was pleased at the encomium. "Yet," I said, "I regret that while I – so to speak – found you a client, it was not of the paying variety."

"We cannot always have what we want, Watson, But I think that I hear Miss Emily's arrival." Mrs. Hudson was speaking at the door, and as she opened it to usher the girl in, Mandalay came totting past. He halted at Holmes feet, looked up, and carefully placed a large mouse before him, meowed once, then spun to hurl himself into his mistress's arms.

Holmes looked at the dead mouse, and then up at me. "You were wrong, Watson. It seems that the client has been pleased to pay me after all."

Two Plus Two
by Phil Growick

"Watson, how much is two plus two"

The question was so odd and abruptly put that for the moment, I stammered.

Holmes and I had been sitting quite comfortably that morning, the eleventh of June, in our rooms, I, reading the morning *Times*, and Holmes lying on his sofa, in his usual state of morning dishevelment, just staring at the ceiling.

"Pardon me," I was finally able to utter, "could you please repeat that?"

"Certainly. How much is two plus two?"

Knowing Holmes, as much as any person could know Sherlock Holmes, I immediately judged this question to be one of some impenetrable import.

Why would Holmes, with his Olympian intellect, ask such a seemingly foolish question? No, therefore it could not be foolish, and if not foolish, then it must have some profound meaning.

The silence in the room began to weigh heavily, as a hostile humidity in a tropical clime, only abated by Holmes's soft puffs of his pipe.

As my mind spun the possible permutations of a solution to this riddle, Holmes turned his head just so to glance at me, gauge my predicament, and returned it to its former position, transfixed at the ceiling.

If I answered the obvious, "Why, four, of course," I might be the recipient of one of Holmes's more biting barbs, such as, "Oh, really? Are you quite positive, Watson? Have you delved into your Hippocratic method to deduce that answer?"

But if I said nothing, I would appear even more trivial to Holmes. A man of my profession and standing in the community not able to answer a question that a child of six could exclaim most readily? I had to say something, so I did.

"Oh, no, Holmes; you shall not dally with me in such manner."

"Dally? Dally?" He had turned his head full round to my direction, his eyes though soft, still intense in their waiting for my explanation. "In what manner do I dally with you, Watson? Please explain yourself." His head went back to studying the ceiling.

"Holmes, you have given me the simplest of questions which only leads me to suspect a conundrum."

"A conundrum?" He chuckled. "Why, Watson, if I were to make present of a conundrum to you, it would be one of such an intricate nature that I, myself, would find it difficult to puzzle through, for were I to present you with such a conundrum, it would merely be me only listening to myself to hear me through my seminal solution."

Even for Holmes, that last statement was a conundrum in itself. The logic of his utterance was lost to me completely, which left me, once again, being coerced into giving him some sort of an answer.

"All right, Holmes; all right. The answer to your question of how much is two plus two, is, plainly, four." I found that I had raised myself from my chair with my arms pushing unknowingly against the arm-rests and upon the expulsion of my answer, I fell, somewhat heavily, back into my seat. He looked at me once more.

"Four. Are you absolutely positive, Watson? Is there not an iota of apprehension in your posit?"

"No; not one. Two plus two is most certainly four. It has always been four and it shall, until the end of time, be four."

And then I paused for a moment as I heard myself say, "What other possible response could there be?"

Holmes leapt to his feet as suddenly as if he had been stung by a bee in his buttocks, pointed a nicotine-stained index finger at me and shouted, "You see? Watson, you've just opened your mind to the possibility of there being another answer."

"I did no such thing."

He advanced towards me with a self-satisfied grin that recalled a child who had eaten forbidden treats without his parents' suspicion.

"Did you not, just a moment ago, ask if there might be some other possible answer?"

I stammered.

Holmes twirled round in so graceful a manner that would do a ballet dancer proud and reclined himself once again on his sofa, eyes once again studying the celling for perhaps some hidden and eternal truths.

"You stammer, Watson, yet you will not admit that you suspect that somewhere in the cosmos there may be another solution to this very simple question."

"It was merely a figure of speech, Holmes. I did not mean to suggest that there could be any other possible answer. Two plus two must be four."

"Must it?"

"Of course, it must. I'll prove it to you."

With that, I begged him turn his head in my direction as I borrowed some matchsticks from the area in which he kept his pipes and their attendant accessories and proceeded to put two matches down, then another two, counting as I went till I had come to the number four.

"There, Holmes. I have taken two matchsticks and added two more matchsticks and by carefully counting, the sum I have arrived at is four."

"Bravo, Watson. You have just, in your most scientific manner, demonstrated empirical proof that your answer must be correct."

"Precisely."

"However, you are wrong."

"Wrong?"

"Precisely."

I stood erect and stiff as I said, "What do you mean, wrong, Holmes? How can I possibly be wrong?" I believe my voice was rising in such a manner as to make one blush, should one have been in the company of several gentlemen.

"Oh, it is quite possible, Watson, quite possible."

"How can it possibly be possible? Two plus two is four. How can it not be four?"

"When it is not two plus two?"

"What on earth do you mean by that, Holmes? When it is not two plus two? For the last hour or so all you have done is bludgeon me with this ridiculous proposition."

"Watson, I have not bludgeoned you in any manner. Although to you, in so relaxed a disposition, a mental exercise may seem like someone has taken a truncheon to your brain."

"That is unkind, Holmes; even for you."

"I meant no insult, Watson, only that you have been led astray by your own ears and your own powers of total linguistic recall."

"I have not the foggiest notion of what you are talking about."

"Of course, not. Therefore, I will explain. Now, if you would be good enough to reseat yourself and try to return to that relaxed state from which you, yourself, escaped."

Reluctantly, I did as he asked; and when he was quite satisfied that my blood pressure had retreated from the volcanic heights of Vesuvius, he quietly and methodically began his explanation.

"Watson, first, the questioned I posed was a trap."

"Ah, hah!" I exclaimed. "Just as I thought."

"Well, not really; for the trap was such that you could never see it coming. You could only hear it coming."

"Hear it coming? What can that possibly mean?"

"Dare I say, elementary, Watson? Dare I say it?"

I said nothing, which said everything.

"Now, you heard me ask you how much is two plus two? Correct?"

"Correct."

He leapt for exclamation and, it seemed, from the sheer joy of what was next to come, stayed in mid-air for an untenable amount of time.

"Not so. Spell two plus two."

"*T-w-o, p-l-u-s, t-w-o*." As I spelled it out, I took extra care in my reckoning.

"All right and very good."

I smiled broadly.

"But Watson, what if I did not mean *t-w-o, p-l-u-s, t-w-o*?"

"What do you mean, Holmes?"

"Watson, how many words in the English language are there for the word '*two*'?"

I had to think quickly now, and came back with an answer and a question at the same time, "Three?"

"Yes. Perfect. There is the number *two*, the 'also' *too*, *t-o-o*, and the adverb, *t-o*. So yes, there are three twos."

"But how could you ask me to add *t-o* to *t-o*?"

"You see, Watson? *To to to*."

"Yes, well, to to to. But what about *too* to *too*?"

"The same. *Too to too*."

"I believe I'm getting a headache," said I.

"Closer to an earache, Watson. We can go around for days with *two*'s and *to*'s and *too*'s, but that would only lead us to four."

"But that is what I have been saying all along. Two plus two is four."

"Is it really, Watson? Are you forgetting *fore*?"

"The number four?"

"No, how many *four*'s are there?"

"What do you mean how many *four*'s are there?"

"Exactly, just that. How many *four*'s are there in the English language?"

I slapped myself on the forehead and dejectedly came up with the same answer that I'd come up with before.

"Three."

"Precisely. We're back at three from the *two*'s and the *four*'s."

I was shaking my head from side to side in resigned assignation.

"Yes, Holmes: *f-o-u-r*, *f-o-r*, and *f-o-r-e*. Four for fore."

"Astonishing, is it not, Watson? And let us now dismiss *one*."

"One what?"

"How many *one*'s are there in the English language?"

"I would say three but that would be pressing my good fortune. So let me think, and I have it, two."

"So you are saying there are two *one*'s?"

"I think I am. Yes, I am. There is the number one, *o-n-e*, and when you win a battle or game, you won, *w-o-n*."

"Marvelous. We're making wonderful progress, Watson, wonderful progress."

"Progress to what?" My head was truly spinning and as it spun it was draining my energy and threatening to assume to rotation of our Earth.

"Progress to the numbers, and the numbers, whether arithmetic or linguistic, are everything. So, tell me, Watson, how many *eight*'s are there in the English language?"

"Please, Holmes, I beg of you. No more of these semantic gymnastics."

"What a marvelous phrase, Watson. Semantic gymnastics. No wonder you have had such success with your chronicles of our adventures. But I beg you to prolong your stated agony for only two more examples, Watson, only two. Which leads us to the conclusion that no matter what number you choose to study, there are only two or three homonyms."

"And for this, you have wasted a perfectly good morning?"

"Not wasted, at all. I did this to show you that what you hear may not be what is truly meant. And that when you assume what is said by someone to be what that someone says, it may not be what that someone has said, at all. Do you see?"

"See? I do not even seem to hear. Holmes, I am adrift. When this bizarre exercise of yours commenced I, as a physician, was quite positive that I was in the best of health. Now, after these numbers and words and arithmetic and not understanding what perfect strangers are saying to me, I am not sure of what you are saying to me. And you are most certainly not a stranger."

As I sank once more into my seat, Holmes slapped his right knee with his left hand, I suppose for some demonstrative emphasis, and gave a dindle of a laugh.

Oh, please, forgive me here, for there is no such word as *dindle*. In fact, I believe I have just coined it. However, it seems eminently appropriate in this case, as the sound emitting from Holmes was not a full blown laugh, nor a snort, nor snicker, nor chortle, nor most certainly not a guffaw. It was the faintest of sounds of gleeful satisfaction; therefore, it must be considered in the diminutive, and therefore I christen the utterance a *dindle*. You may take the word or discard it, the choice is yours.

"Watson, you still fail to grasp the importance of what we have been doing."

"I suppose so, Holmes; I will give you that."

"What if, Watson, I was paving the way for you and me to solve one of our newest riddles?"

"And which one is that, if I dare ask?"

"I am sure you will most certainly remember the young woman who sat precisely where you now sit, not more than two weeks passed. Miss Emily Kent."

"Of course, of course. She was quite young, very attractive, and she wanted to engage you to find some missing amulet, if I recall."

"Quite right. But the amulet gone missing was not just some amulet. It was the Amulet of Anubis."

"Yes," I was still puzzling over whatever import Holmes seemed to hold so dear, at the moment.

"The Amulet of Anubis was discovered by no one less than Miss Kent's renowned father, the noted Egyptologist, Sir Lionel Kent. And though he perished shortly after that discovery, and many attributed it to an ancient Egyptian curse of some sort, that amulet is the only one found bearing the likeness of Anubis and is considered priceless.

"Miss Kent stated that the amulet lay under lock and key in the home of Mrs. Annabel Brookfield, her grandmother. That only her grandmother, who was quite elderly now, I believe the dark side of ninety, kept that key secreted where only she knew its whereabouts.

"Miss Kent further stated that it was she and her grandmother together who had discovered the amulet missing, and that she had immediately notified the police. After two desultory weeks of police work without success, she came to me to see if I could do what the police could not."

"Yes. But from what I recall, you accepted the challenge without your usual enthusiasm. It would seem to me that finding such a treasure would have given spark to your powers of deduction and elucidation."

"On point, Watson. But it was not any lack of interest. It was that I was in the middle of a coincidence, and as you are well aware, to me, there is no such thing as a coincidence."

"I do not follow."

"Then follow this. Do you ever peruse the *Times* for any retail news of substance?"

"I feel I am falling further behind," I conceded glumly.

"It was approximately two weeks prior to the amulet's theft that Brently & Crafton, perhaps London's supreme fine arts and antiquities auction house, held an auction of the rarest Egyptian treasures and artifacts."

"No, I never bother with such information."

"Well, then, perhaps you should. For the coincidence of the Amulet of Anubis being stolen in so short a span after that auction, is too much of a transparent coincidence."

Once Sherlock Holmes had his mind onto a theory, it is best likened to a snapping turtle's jaws snapping shut.

"You see, Watson, with ancient Egyptian auction fever at high pitch, the Amulet of Anubis would fetch a much loftier price; especially to someone who had not been able to outbid others for specific pieces. And finally, there would be no seller's premium fastened onto the item's sale price."

"Yes, I see that now."

"Good. And now that you are in step, let us take this step by step.

"Do you remember what Miss Kent said specifically about how she and her grandmother found the amulet missing?"

After a moment of sorting through my mental file, I did remember.

"I believe she said that she had asked to borrow the amulet, as she had in the past, to wear at a charity ball. When her grandmother went to retrieve the amulet, she found it missing, and would have fallen to the ground in a dead faint, had not Miss Kent been there to bear her up."

"Indeed. I am most happy to see your memory so facile."

I smiled. "I, as well."

"Now, another question to test that impressive memory. How did Miss Kent get to her grandmother's home?"

"She said she rode to her grandmother's home."

"Watson, please repeat what you just said."

"I said she told us that she rode to her grandmother's home."

"Rode or *rowed*?"

"Pardon me?"

"Words, Watson, words. *R-o-d-e* or *r-o-w-e-d*?"

The import of the question hit me as hard as if Holmes had slapped a brick to the side of my head, and I believe my mouth opened to a width in which a hansom cab could easily have run through.

"There is a rivulet that parallels the vehicular thoroughfare that leads from Miss Kent's home to that of her grandmother. It is a rivulet quite narrow and because of its lack of girth it is not much travelled by boatmen or by the athletic among us who crew.

"Now, do you further remember her answer when I asked her to be precise in the amount of time it took to get from her home to her grandmother's home?"

"Yes. She said it took her one hour."

"Don't you see, Watson? If she had used the thoroughfare and gone by cab, it would have taken her, at most, only half that time. If, however, she needed stealth to sheath a nefarious design, she would have *r-o-w-e-d*, not *r-o-d-e*, and in the darkness would have easily needed that heavy hour. Her statement about the time was a casual remark, but a mistake which led, in part, to her undoing."

"But what led you to the contention of the words?"

"If you remember, it was an unusually hot and humid day for London at this time of year."

"Of course I remember. I had even removed my waistcoat."

"And in such a situation, would not the average person remove any article of clothing adding to the discomfort caused by that heat?"

"Yes, I believe so."

"But did you notice that she did not remove her gloves and that she winced upon me taking her hand in greeting, even in so ginger a manner?"

"I recall that now, but at the time it meant nothing to me."

"In addition, as she was leaving, you touched her lightly on her shoulder as a gentleman would in guiding a woman through a doorway. She gave an almost imperceptible shudder."

"Now that you remark on that, I did notice it but gave it no consequence."

"Ah, but you most certainly should have. Just why would she not remove her gloves? Why was her hand in so delicate a condition that the gentle pressure of my own hand caused her pain which he tried so adroitly to disguise?

"After listening to her description of her travel to her grandmother's home and with all that I have just revealed, I began to wonder about that particular word. From that, I could discern that Miss Kent, while appearing to be a young woman in great distress, was, in fact, the very cause of that seeming distress. Yet how she accomplished that act I, as yet, have not deduced; though I'm in the felicitous process of doing so."

"But the gloves, Holmes, and the shuddering of her back."

"Oh, well, quite easily realized when weighing those words previously mentioned. Because if she *rowed*," and Holmes made the gesture of rowing a boat, "it would be an occupation completely unsuited to her station as a young lady of some stature, and therefore would have not only caused great welts and raw flesh upon her hands from the

105

rowing, but pain in the musculature of the back from such an unaccustomed activity.

"Furthermore, I found her attitude much too easy and flippant. It did not take me long to come to the conclusion that, whatever fee I proposed, unless it was in the vicinity of purchasing the Taj Mahal, would find favour. For she only wanted me as further proof for the insurance company. I am sure you can see that."

"What an astute plan. Holmes. That woman has a criminal mind of the first order."

"Hardly, Watson. Had she a more supple and subtle intelligence, it would have taken me far longer to discern her machinations."

"But would not the insurance be in her grandmother's name? It would seem likely."

"It would under normal circumstances, but as Miss Kent is the sole beneficiary of her grandmother's insurance policy, the monetary restitution falls to her. Then, after a suitable amount of time would pass, I should expect Miss Kent to sell the Amulet of Anubis to any number of discreet purchasers."

"But how did you learn of the particulars of the insurance?"

"It is fairly well known in our upper classes that most great articles of consequential value would be insured by one of only two such companies chartered especially to provide such guarantees. It was easy enough for the police to obtain the appropriate information, once I had suggested they do so."

"Then tell me, how do you propose to reveal to her your knowledge of her theft and plans for the amulet?"

"That you shall see for yourself presently, as I am expecting her to call at any moment."

As if she had been eavesdropping at our keyhole, a gentle rap on our door announced Miss Kent's timely arrival.

She entered and Holmes closed the door behind her.

She was still wearing the gloves and breezed in with such studied insouciance that I saw a very self-satisfied smile on the face of Sherlock Holmes.

"Miss Kent," he said, extending his hand in the usual hand-shaking gesture, yet she simply nodded her assent and sat once more in the chair she had occupied on her previous visit. She used her handbag almost as a buffer between us, so tightly was it clutched and set in her lap. Holmes nodded to me to be sure I had just witnessed the process.

"So, Mr. Holmes, you have called me here, I gather, to give me great news. You have discovered the whereabouts of the Amulet of

Anubis, and you possess the knowledge of who took it and how it was done."

"You are partially correct in that assumption, yes."

"I do not understand," said she; and for the first time, there was the wrinkling of her brow in unforeseen consternation.

"Permit me to explain. I most certainly know the identity of the thief."

At that word, I could gauge an audible, but stifled, gasp from Miss Kent. I must make note here of her remarkable self-control. Though he was no better than a common thief, her presence under fire, so to speak, would have recommended her to be at my side in Afghanistan. I also believed she would have behaved so cool under the attack of Zulus. The woman was cold as an Eskimo's igloo.

"Oh, yes, I have the thief's identity. In point of fact, I have already notified the very officers to whom you reported the crime. They were quite intrigued."

"Intrigued? That is an unusual word to be used such a manner," she said. It was here she began to display only the faintest hint of growing discomfort.

"True, Miss Kent, quite true. But it is not often that the police are presented with the fact that the criminal and the victim are one in the same."

At this she stood, ignoring me fully but fixing her gaze on Holmes, and as she spoke she began to slowly glide towards the door.

"I am not certain what you mean, Mr. Holmes, but I am beginning to feel that you intimate that I am the one in possession of the amulet."

"Bravo, Miss Kent. You have hit the nail on the proverbial head."

Holmes was positively jovial at the exchange, and as he moved to place himself between Miss Kent and the door, he motioned her to sit once more, which she did with some small amount of agitation.

"Mr. Holmes, I am not accustomed to being addressed in such a manner, and I voice my disproval of your insinuation. You forget that I am your benefactress, that I retained you to discover the true criminal, and to return the amulet to my grandmother."

"Of course, you retained me to do so, and as I have just demonstrated, done so. If you would be so kind as to remove your gloves, please."

"I shall do no such thing." She had stood again, in a stance of feminine defiance.

"Come, come, Miss Kent. Enough of the charade."

Holmes then lowered the tone of his voice and all semblance of cheer was gone. "I say once again, please remove your gloves."

"I shall not and you cannot force me to do so. Unless you resort to animal brute force."

"On the contrary, Miss Kent. Watson, would you be so kind as to open the door?

"Of course, Holmes," said I and when I did so, Inspector Michaels and Officer Willets entered the room. At their sight, Miss Kent blushed crimson.

"Gentlemen," said Holmes, "would you please kindly instruct Miss Kent to remove her gloves."

"You heard Mr. Holmes, Miss Kent," said the Inspector, "please do as you are told."

"I must protest this in the strongest terms. I shall speak with your superiors as soon as I am able."

"Well, miss, I can guarantee that you will be speaking with my superiors at the station and then with the magistrates, as well. But this is a serious police investigation, and I must insist that you remove your gloves."

She began muttering to herself, but slowly, very slowly, she placed her handbag between her feet, then removed one glove. It was immediate to all that her hand was still partially bandaged and that part of her hand free was worn and calloused. The same was revealed as she removed the other glove.

Though we all took in the unfortunate sight of her hands, it was Sherlock Holmes who nodded for me, as a medical man, to look more closely at the wounds. This I did, and after concurring nods to me and the police, it was Holmes who spoke.

"Pray tell, Miss Kent, how your hands came to be in so deplorable and painful a state?"

"It is from gardening."

At that, a reflexive laugh let loose from all of us, save Miss Kent.

"From gardening, you say? Miss Kent, for gardening to take such a toll on your hands, I should expect that you were using them in place of trowel and shovel. No, Miss Kent, I propose that your hands suffer from, shall we say, an unaccustomed rowing endeavor."

"I am sure I have no idea what you mean."

"I mean simply that under cover of night you rowed to your grandmother's home so no one could see you on the road, gained access with no great difficulty, since you already possess a key to the premises, and that while your grandmother slept safely and unknowingly in her bed, you took the key from its hidden location, secreted the amulet on your person, replaced the key, locked the front door as you left, and returned home by the same mode of transport."

108

"That is foolish. Only my grandmother knew where the key was hidden."

"That is true to a point. However, being so advanced in age, she would not have heard you surreptitiously watch as she retrieved the key to fetch the amulet for that charity ball for which you requested its use. However, there still is one part of my fee which I have not, as yet, earned." Here, Holmes paused for great impact.

"While I have identified the thief, I have not returned the amulet to its proper owner, your grandmother. I shall do that presently."

With that, Holmes so swiftly grabbed her handbag that the movement could well be compared to the speed and grace of a cheetah. Miss Kent could do nothing to retain hold of the item.

Holmes held the handbag aloft for all to see, then reached in and like a master magician, he pulled out the amulet with a grand, "*Voila!*"

It was Inspector Michaels who now spoke.

"But how did you know that she would have the amulet, Mr. Holmes?"

"Quite simple. With the help of my Baker Street Irregulars, whose noses are always close to the ground, it was child's play to learn that a certain party wishing to purchase the amulet would be meeting Miss Kent this very afternoon in London. Therefore, she must have the amulet with her. She just could not wait to obtain the funds which she would derive from the illegal sale."

"Well, Mr. Holmes, I must hand it to you. And please, sir, you must hand the amulet to me so I can return it to Mrs. Brookfield," said Michaels.

"Now, Miss Kent," he continued, "if you would be so kind as to go with Constable Willets, here. We have a much better mode of transport waiting for you outside. Our own lovely police wagon."

Miss Kent stood, holding herself erect, as Willets took her arm and led her out to the wagon.

"Thank you again, Mr. Holmes, for all of your help. I am not happy to admit that we would never have suspected Miss Kent. We were questioning gardeners, and delivery men, and the help, and, as you have shown me, everyone but the true felon."

With that, he gave a crisp finger to his forehead and was off.

"Good show, Holmes. For it was a show, you know."

"Of course I do, Watson."

With that, he was back to reclining on his sofa, his face once more scanning the ceiling for heaven knows what.

"Now, Watson, might you be more receptive for some more semantic gymnastics? For instance, when someone describes a ghastly sight, are they commenting on a *s-i-g-h-t* or a *s-i-t-e*, as one might find in so many of our historic castle ruins?

"Or let me advance this enticing notion," he proffered, "let us say that we have another female felon, a genuine criminal genius of the first order. And let us suppose that her name was Terry. Would she not then be a true *Miss Terry?*"

"Oh, my word." And with that, I left Sherlock Holmes to ponder the ceiling as I removed myself to a more convivial locale.

The Adventure of the
Coptic Patriarch
by Séamus Duffy

In the early spring of eighteen ninety-eight, a long deep frost had set in over the southern part of the country, freezing the ground and, on one bitter night, our London water pipes. I had gone out in the afternoon with Sherlock Holmes for a stroll in Hyde Park; the paths underfoot were iron-hard and the frozen Serpentine seemed as crowded with skaters as a Saturday afternoon in Piccadilly. We circled the park on our ramble in the still, chilly air, passing the site of the old Tyburn Tree – awakening a reminiscence of our adventures in the grisly affair of the Thirteen Bells. An aimless meander in a comfortable silence; indeed, I was conscious only of the hum of the traffic and the odour of horse manure when, as we approached the Arch, I was stirred out of my reverie and my attention engaged by the newsboy yelling out the headlines of the afternoon editions.

"The usual drivel," began Holmes, "Trivialities concerning the private lives of some famous – "

"Wait, though," I interrupted, for the word "Athanasian" leapt out at me from the lower corner of the front page of the newspaper.

"Holmes, you do recall the business of the Athanasian Scroll?"

"Indeed, Watson."

"Well, here is a story concerning the very same!" I said, fishing in my pocket for some small coinage.

My notes for the previous year recorded Holmes's retention by His Holiness Pope Kyrillos V of the Coptic Patriarchate in Alexandria, over the theft of the ninth-century Athanasian scroll. The affair had necessitated intercession with a cabal of international thieves, and the bargaining for the return of this rare document entailed translation in three separate languages whilst at the same time striving to maintain complete secrecy of the affair.

When we had returned to Baker Street, I was astonished to discover that the newspaper article purported to show that the Scroll, over which Holmes had gone to so much trouble, had been exposed as a forgery.

"A forgery!" cried Holmes.

"So it appears," I replied.

"Well, of all that it is . . . ."

"You see, the real one has turned up."

"The *real* one?" he shook his head in confusion. "Watson, you have resorted to your usual mode of telling a tale by beginning in the middle."

"Very well then, I shall read the entire thing: '*Athanasian Scroll is Forgery, Claims Don,*' it begins. '*The celebrated Professor C.N. Beasley, of the School of Orientalism, has claimed that the ninth century Athanasian Scroll, a sacred relic of the Coptic Church currently exhibited at St Mark's Church, Alexandria, in the Khedivate of Egypt, is a cleverly fabricated forgery. Cedric Norbert Beasley, an authority on the history and linguistics of the Holy Land, claims to have the authentic Scroll in his possession but declines, however, to disclose its source. Beasley's predecessor and mentor, Professor Ignatius Coram, provoked a storm of controversy last year in his three-volume* Athanasius of Alexandria, *which cast doubt on some of the long-standing assumptions of established religion in Britain. The book claimed,* inter alia, *that the Monastic tradition and the techniques of illuminated manuscripts associated with the Early Celtic Church in Britain – particularly those of the Irish Missionaries Columba and Aidan – were developed from Coptic Christians who had visited Glastonbury and Ireland. The Scroll appears to substantiate this, containing as it does, references to the* Book of Kells *and the* Lindisfarne Gospels, *and there is evidence of Alexandrian theology intertwined with that of the Celts, demonstrating an early connection to the Coptic Church, which has a claim to be considered the oldest Christian church in existence. The Scroll recently discovered by Professor Beasley does not differ in content from the original. However a number minor details betray etc., etc. . . . .*' The article goes on to say that the present Patriarch of the Coptic Church in England, the Reverend Father Philxenous, is to meet with Professor Beasley to determine the Scroll's authenticity, and that the latter is resolved to return the document, which is very valuable as well as unique, to its rightful place in St. Mark's in Alexandria."

"Quite remarkable, Watson. You know several thousand *piastres* were paid for that forgery, and I assumed at the time that His Holiness would have recognised the genuine article when he saw it. And now this eccentric academic simply proposes to give it away!"

He shrugged and smiled ruefully, and the conversation strayed back to more secular subjects. Little did we know then that the matter was far from ended; only a few weeks later, on the second day after Easter to be precise, we received an unexpected visit from Inspector Lestrade of Scotland Yard.

Holmes waved our visitor to a chair, rang the bell, and gave an order for coffee. Lestrade's occasional visits had the dual purpose of enabling my friend to discover the latest official developments, and of allowing

112

the Inspector to hear titbits of gossip from the criminal underworld and even, occasionally, to pick my friend's brain without necessarily invoking his intervention. On this occasion, it was clear that the visit was not a social one.

"It's a strange one, Mr. Holmes," said Lestrade, "two definite crimes have been committed, a robbery and a kidnapping, but in the very oddest of circumstances. Have you seen the newspapers?"

"Not yet," Holmes replied.

"I don't suppose either of you gentlemen has ever heard of the Coptics?"

"In that bureau by the window," said Holmes languidly, "you will find a letter of thanks from His Holiness Pope Kyrillos, for whom I undertook a small commission last year."

"And beside it," I added, relishing the spirit of Holmes's rejoinder, "you would also discover my copious notes on the case."

Lestrade laughed. "I might have guessed! What was the affair, then?"

"With the best will in the world," replied Holmes suavely, "I am afraid that I cannot possibly breach a client's confidence – not even to you."

Lestrade looked as though he had been struck.

"All right then, Mr. Holmes," he continued testily, "do you know anything about the . . ." here Lestrade consulted his notebook, "the Athanasian Scroll?"

"Only that it is a ninth century document, dedicated to, rather than written by, St. Athanasias, hence the name; indeed its precise authorship remains unknown, though it is likely to have been collegiate. It was spirited away to Europe for safety during the Arab conquest and returned after the Crusades. It narrowly escaped the fate of burning at the Battle of the Pyramids one hundred years ago, for despite their enmity, both Napoleon and the Mamelukes were united in their scant regard for the Copts. I am aware of the public allegations – allegations which appear to have substantial justification and carry profound academic weight – that the Scroll which is presently in Alexandria is a forgery. The discovery was made by an English academic who was something of a protégé of a certain Russian gentlemen with whom your colleague Hopkins had a professional acquaintance some time ago."

"Ah, Coram, of Yoxley Old Place. That old devil!"

"My understanding is that Professor Beasley recently claimed to have the original in his possession and, once authenticated, it was to be returned to the Coptic Church in Egypt, after he had made a copy for the University faculty."

"You are correct, that was his intention."

"*Was?* What, then, has happened?"

"I have a few notes here from the local man, Inspector Horburgh of the Buckinghamshire Constabulary, concerning a crime that was committed during the night. Yesterday evening, Father Philxenous of the London Patriarchate went to visit the professor at his cottage in Bourne End, in order to examine the aforesaid Scroll. The Patriarch had had a few doubts about whether the Scroll was genuine, but having pored over it for a long time, he agreed that all was in order. The professor then locked the document away in its usual place, following which he and the Patriarch had a conversation, during which, the professor recalled, his visitor became very excited, as was only to be expected. The visitor, who was quite elderly, then said he was tired from the long journey and the excitement – he had come up from Somersetshire, which necessitated three changes of train – and he went off to bed very early without taking any supper, saying he wasn't hungry. He had intended to spend the next few days going over the document with the professor, explaining a few points about the various dialects of the Coptic language. The visitor then went to bed, and that was the last Beasley saw of him. The following morning, the professor awoke to find the house had been entered during the night, and that, not only had the Scroll been stolen, but the Patriarch had disappeared. He had been kidnapped, and a ransom note left demanding ten thousand pounds for the return, alive and safe, of the reverend gentleman."

"Dear me," said Holmes, "a small fortune."

"Of the scroll, however, there was no mention."

"The implication being that the thieves – "

"Singular!" interrupted Lestrade. "One thief, and I think I can also show that the kidnapping was well planned in advance, too, but let me come to those points in a minute."

"Then the thief intends to keep the Scroll and sell it privately."

"Yes, he did a proper job, whoever he was; a clean sweep."

"It is likely, then, that he already has a buyer. A big job, though; there cannot many would handle something of this scale. And yet, taking a hostage surely complicates matters for him considerably. It would have been difficult enough to escape with the booty, but for one man having to subdue and force-march an unwilling party along with him seems madness. Criminals can be greedy, I suppose, and it is never difficult to find instances where greed outweighs common sense."

"Indeed. At about half past seven this morning, the professor had knocked on the visitor's bedroom door to tell him that breakfast would be ready in an hour, as the housekeeper usually comes in about eight o'clock. Receiving no reply, he had opened the door and looked in. He was a bit surprised to find the room empty, and imagined that the old fellow had gone down before him. The professor is a heavy sleeper and possibly wouldn't have heard his visitor stirring; but there was no one downstairs, and it was only when the professor went back upstairs again that he noticed a slip of paper on the dresser beside the bed – the ransom note."

"One moment – had the bed been slept in?" asked Holmes.

"Yes, it had."

"And what of the Patriarch's luggage?"

"It was left behind, and apparently still contained a few articles; a clean shirt and some undergarments."

"And the bedroom window?"

"Closed and locked on the inside."

"Was there a skylight?"

"Let me see . . . Yes, but no lock on the skylight, according to Horburgh."

"Pray continue."

"At first the Professor was incredulous, but there was the empty bed, the abandoned luggage, and no sign of the Patriarch. It was such a shock that he thought to make some strong black coffee to pull himself together. Suddenly he remembered the Scroll and dashed to his study to check, and it was then that he found it missing. It had been in his bureau, which was locked, although the key had been left under a small potted plant nearby. The key to the bureau was missing, so the Professor had to use his spare key to open the bureau. Apart from the note, there was not a single clue as to what had happened, and he had heard nothing during the night. As you can see, there was an unseasonal fall of snow in the city last night, but it had been much heavier out in Buckinghamshire – a few inches. Oh, you haven't heard the best yet, Mr. Holmes, not by a long chalk!

"As Beasley stood gazing out of the study window which looks out to the front of the building, his wits began to return; he noticed with a start that there were no footprints in the snow outside leading away from the front door, as he would have expected, for the snow had stopped before the professor went to bed. He could see in any case that no-one had left the house by the front door for it was locked from the inside. He therefore assumed that the thief must have made his getaway by the rear door, but that was also locked from the inside. A thought struck him, and so he returned to the Patriarch's bedroom, which is at the back of the house, and looked out the window. He could see a clear set of footprints leading from the rear garden fence which backs on to a riverside path, across the garden all the way to the roan pipe adjacent to the window. At that point, the prints were muddled a bit. Furthermore, the snow which had fallen on the window sill had been greatly disturbed too, so that it is pretty obvious how the intruder got in – through the fence, across the garden, up the roan pipe, and in through the window. But nothing to suggest how he got away with the Scroll and the Patriarch. It is a complete mystery!"

"And yet, if the escape was not made above ground . . . well, perhaps it is too early to theorise. I assume you have given strict instructions for nothing to be touched until my arrival."

"Of course. The place is being watched, and Inspector Horburgh, the local man who called me, is in charge."

"I suppose a run out to Bourne End is in order, Watson? Then ask Billy to call us a four-wheeler for Paddington!"

"Unfortunately," I replied, looking at the grey slushy pavements outside, "I detect a slight thaw which may obliterate the footprints."

"Hm, yes. Well, we shall still be able to examine the rest for ourselves."

"Incidentally," said Lestrade, "the ransom note was composed of words cut out from a newspaper, which indicates to me that the kidnapping was aforethought."

"Excellent," replied Holmes, "that seems a bit of a *faux pas* on the thief's part, for there are very few common typefaces which I should be unable to identify, and I should be very surprised if we do not glean something from the note."

The journey down to Bourne End was a pleasant one, especially the final leg from Maidenhead, as we steamed slowly up through Cookham, where, with the sun at our backs, and the Thames glinted and shone in the cold clear air. The top of Winter Hill was still contoured by its light dusting of snow, and although a thaw had set in, there was scarce a breath of wind, the plumes of smoke from the houses and cottages in the sleepy riverside villages rising up in straight lines out of the chimney pots.

Sergeant Canterville of the Bucks. Constabulary had been in conversation with a genial-looking old white-haired railway porter as the train drew in, and he hailed us as we alighted to the platform.

"This is Mr. Merryweather," said the sergeant. "He was on duty yesterday when Father Philxenous arrived."

"Yes, I saw the ole fellow getting off the tray-in," the porter said, in that drawling manner characteristic of the small Thames-side hamlets. "Now I hee-aar as he's been kidnapped. Ha! We haven't had so much excitement since the Marlow Donkey went off the ray-ils one foggy night and nee-aar ended up in the river. Gave me a turn, though, when I heard what had happened to old Nobby!"

"Do you know the Professor?" asked Holmes.

"Went to school together, we did, hee-ar in the village. Nobby were always an odd bod, right enough. While us normal lads would be kickin' a ball arou-and or standin' at a wicket, ten-to-one he'd have his nose in a book. A bit touched, we used to think. But he's travelled all over the Holy Land, and they say he can jabber away to a Bedoow-in or an Ottoman, or a Hebroo like a native. Seems he had these Copticks eatin' out of his hands. Well, the-aar he is now, Principal of whatever-it-is, and hee-aar's me trudgin' arou-and in all weathers, luggin' suitcases and sweepin' draughty waitin' rooms, so who's the mad one now, I say."

"Mr. Merryweather was telling me he remembers a queer lookin' fellow loiterin' about the station yesterday," said the sergeant.

"Yes. He hung about the Waitin' Room most of the day."

"Can you describe him?" asked Lestrade.

"He were a tall, thin, swarthy fellow; he had a broad-brimmed hat pulled dow-en almost over his eyes. Even though there were a coo-al fire burnin' in the Waitin' Room, he had his collar turned up. Lairy lookin' sort of customer, but he weren't breakin' any bye-laws, so I leave him be."

"You could not see his face?"

"That's right. He seemed to be waitin' for someone arrivin' on a tray-in, for he had no luggage of any sort himself. He stood well back from the window, too, except when a tray-in come in."

"Did you examine his ticket?"

"He never come off no tray-in, and didn't buy a ticket hee-aar, to the best of my knowledge, and he never spoke to anyone. From the little I could see, I didn't recognise him as bein' from the village."

"But he was here before Father Philxenous arrived, and remained here afterwards?"

"That's right. He loafed arou-and until after the last tray-in from Maidenhead, then he left."

"One moment," interrupted Holmes. "Were there still trains to arrive from other points after he left?"

"There was the last one off Marlow for the day that terminates hee-aar, and one off High Wycombe that runs rou-and and goes back up empty stock."

"Thank you," said Lestrade, "you have been very helpful."

"This is the address, sir," the young sergeant said briskly to the Inspector, handing him a card.

Professor C. N. Beasley,
1, Lime Kiln Lane,
Bourne End,
Bucks.

"I don't know the place," said Lestrade, "so you'd better take us."

We circled the station and crossed the single track railway by the level crossing, then over a narrow stream, and at the end of the road turned into the Lane, which made a cul-de-sac. A low picket fence separated the houses on one side from the river path which was bustling with people."

"There's a fair goin' at Falconer's," said the sergeant by way of explanation. I had observed, tacked around at various points near the railway station, notices advertising the circus.

"Where exactly?" asked Holmes.

"Just there, that's Falconer's Field under Harvest Ridge," the young man replied, pointing out a steep slope not far off. "In full swing, too, by the sound of it."

"How long has it been here?" asked Lestrade.

"Came on Maundy Thursday – five days now."

Four houses stood in the cul-de-sac, some way back from the street, each with its own front garden: two older cottages at the end, and two newer villas nearest the street crossing. The professor's cottage was at the side of the Lane which backed on to the river.

"The footprints," said Holmes impatiently, "have been lost in the thaw."

"If you please, sir," said the young sergeant, touching his cap to my friend, "the Professor took a photograph of them – we have sent it out to be developed."

"Excellent," remarked Holmes. "The professor seems a model client."

"Ah, here is Inspector Horburgh now," said Lestrade, as an alert-looking man of middle age strode towards us.

"Perhaps it would be better to remain and speak out here," said the local Inspector briskly. "We have not eliminated the professor as a suspect, yet."

"What motive do you think he might possibly have for stealing his own possession?" asked Holmes.

"None, to be truthful. It's a mere formality, but I want to be sure of my ground. The fact that he seems to have been quick-witted enough to take a photograph of the footprints before the thaw set in could cut both ways – take nothing for granted is my motto."

"Excellent!" replied Holmes. "But, assuming the photographs show what the professor described, what would be your theory as to the manner of escape? Can it have been made through some underground passage or other? The cottage hardly looks old enough."

"Eighteenth century," said Horburgh.

"Not impossible but, I should say, unlikely. How long had the professor lived in it?"

"Since a boy."

"Then that appears to take care of the only other conceivable explanation – any place of concealment would be likely to be known to someone who had lived there all his life, so the thief and the Patriarch can hardly have remained concealed in the house, unless the professor is party to the conspiracy."

"I agree," said Horburgh, "but I still intend to search it from top to bottom. We have interviewed a number of people: first I spoke to Mrs. McGill, the housekeeper – she corroborated everything he told me himself. A quiet, simple woman, her husband is chronically unwell, and she lives at the other side of the village. It is extremely doubtful if she has had anything to do with this. The owner of number three – one of the new villas – is a Mr. Selborne, the company accountant. A recent arrival in the village, commutes to the City each day by the eight-twenty, presently on holiday in Switzerland, left last Tuesday. I then interviewed Mr. Joshua Bennett, the former Rector at St. Nicholas, who lives in the other old cottage, number two – he is eighty-two and stone deaf. I think he can be eliminated. In number four, the other of the new houses, lives Captain Tierney. An interesting character, to say the least: formerly of the 7th, Bombay, Mountain Battery, Royal Artillery."

"Retired?" asked Lestrade.

"Dishonourably discharged!" replied his colleague.

"I see."

"Drink and gambling. He had been in India. Youngish chap, bachelor, wild, and a nasty piece when the 'fluence is on him. Motive certainly – gambling debts. Thin as a rake and could easily shin up the roan pipe. He will have had a gun in the house too, I am sure, and could have frightened the old man."

"You mean you haven't searched the place?" asked Holmes.

"Wouldn't let us. Said he knew nothing about it, as he was dead drunk last night – he certainly looked pretty woody this morning. Swears he never left the house yesterday, and what's more, as he put, 'couldn't give a damn about any bloody heathen relics,' and went on about putting 'these devil-worshippers about their business.'"

"Fine fellow!" I replied.

"I had to threaten to run him in after he challenged the young constable to fisticuffs."

"You might get a warrant," said Holmes.

"I have sent to the magistrate for one. I had a word with the circus people too, down at the camp in Falconer's, but couldn't get much out of them. They saw nothing and heard nothing. Don't like policemen around the place, keep themselves to themselves, but they're not a bad lot. If you ask me, they get blamed for a lot of things the settled folk do."

"All the same, I may take a look round there later," said Holmes, to my surprise. "Now, I should like to examine the premises."

My friend first inspected the garden and the outhouses – which amounted to a coal bunker and a tool shed. He stopped for a considerable length of time at a spot by the rear fence which led, through some bushes, on to the river path.

"There is no doubt that there has been someone though here recently," he said, pointing to some broken twigs and twisted branches. "That would certainly corroborate the professor's story."

"Yes, I saw that," said Horburgh.

"It is impossible, of course, to follow these footprints on the path, as there have been so many here. I am confused as to which direction this person passed through."

"Surely it is obvious," said Horburgh, looking at Holmes strangely. "The professor saw the footprints leading from the fence to the house . . . ."

"I thought your motto was to take *nothing* for granted," replied Holmes.

"Well," said the Inspector, somewhat ruffled at my friend's remark, "the photograph should dispel any doubt."

"Yes, possibly," said my friend absently, as he wandered back to the other end of the garden. He then stopped to stare up at the cottage from the ground.

The Inspector followed the line of his gaze, "It's a pity that he didn't take a shot of the window sill, too."

"In point of fact, it wasn't the window sill I should have wanted to examine," replied Holmes enigmatically, to the deepening mystification of the two Inspectors.

"Shall we go inside now?" I asked, breaking the strained silence.

The professor greeted us warmly, and asked the housekeeper for tea. In answer to Holmes's question, Beasley said he had seen no-one unusual loitering in the vicinity of the house about or before the time of the kidnapping. No visitors had called – weeks could go by without one, he said.

"In fact, though," Holmes pointed out, "literally scores of people have been making their way past your garden to the fair at the bottom of the hill. You would scarce have noticed someone keeping a watch. Nothing which was in any way out of the ordinary?"

"The only thing that could be regarded as in any way unusual," continued Beasley, "was that the Patriarch turned up a week earlier than expected."

"Did he give any explanation for this?" Horburgh asked.

"No, and I sought none."

"Do you still have the letter?" inquired Holmes.

"I am afraid not. All it said was that he would come down next Monday and asked for directions."

"Can you describe him?"

"Very dark skinned, as you'd expect; a white beard all over, shaggy eyebrows, and a heavily lined face. He was wearing a dark cassock with a red lining on the inside, a white collarless shirt, and the usual Coptic headgear."

"What age is he?"

"I had thought he was similar to my own, which is sixty-two, but he looked much older."

"Is there anything else you can tell us about him?"

"Not really. I had never met him before, and so know little about him."

"And do you have any theory as to how an escape was effected?"

"Absolutely none – the whole thing amazes me yet. One thing about the Patriarch though: he certainly lacked the courtesy on the average Englishman – he was quite scathing about my grasp of the Coptic language. I must confess, I learnt it as one would learn Latin, as a liturgical language, and therefore I'm conscious that I do not speak it well conversationally. Anyway, he said quite plainly that he preferred to speak in English, which I found disheartening and somewhat rude. He had said, however, that, before he left he would go over some of the finer points of the Bohairic dialect, which is the most common one."

There was such a stark contrast between Beasley, with his accomplishment in ancient languages, as well as his command of English, and the old railway porter with his broad vowels and slurred consonants, that it was difficult to imagine them rubbing shoulders together. There seemed a decade in age difference, yet there could hardly be.

"Dear me, this is an absolutely unique document which I have lost. No sir, which the world has lost! It is literally priceless. As a scholar of Antiquity yourself Mr. Holmes – yes, I read your erudite commentary on

121

the *Sinaitic Palimpsest* and the *Codex Sinaiticus* – you can well understand my loss. Written in an almost extinct language directly descended from that which the Pharaohs spoke – can you conceive that! And the Coptic Church established by Mark the Evangelist is, perhaps the oldest – "

"No doubt that is very interesting," interrupted Holmes, as the professor seemed about to embark upon an elaboration of the subject, "but I forgot to ask if you had informed the Patriarchate in London of the disappearance?"

"Yes, I sent a telegram immediately. The secretary who comes in a few days a week should pick it up."

"Well, we had better move the investigation along. You do not think that there is any part of this house which could be used as a place of concealment?" asked Holmes.

"Absolutely not."

"With your permission," said Horburgh, "we will make a full search of the place – cellar and attic included. We must, you understand, eliminate any possibility of a hiding place."

"Of course, go anywhere, do anything which you need to do," replied Beasley. "The keys are hanging upon the hook in the hall."

Suffice to say that for the next hour or so, between the four of us, we paced and measured every inch of every floor of the house, but in no wise was there any discrepancy which would have allowed for any secret chamber or hiding place. We then unlocked the door to the cellar and started carefully down the steep, narrow, winding stairs. Horburgh lit his bull's eye and shone it round the cellar – what a disappointment! We found nothing there but a few pieces of old junk and four blank walls. No loose flagstone or hidden openings. A mouse could scarcely have been hidden here, and no-one could possibly have escaped this way.

"Before I go down to the fairground," said Holmes when we returned to the upper air, "I should like to inspect the ransom note."

"Here it is."

Holmes turned it over once or twice, his keen eyes raking it for the slightest indication.

"'*Patriarch*' has a capital letter," he said, "and has been made from two smaller words stuck together: '*Patr*' and '*iarch*'. Possibly from '*Patrol*' and '*matriarch*' – a reference, perhaps, to our sovereign. I have closely examined the typeface, but I am disappointed that I am unable to recognise it all as a newspaper type. It is possible that it may be some obscure regional one which I have not seen, though I am familiar with the local 'paper, the *South Bucks Free Press*. Perhaps, though, the other side may be more revealing. Aha, look at some of the words, or rather the parts of words, on the reverse side: '*Batter*' and '*Field*' with capitals, then '*-arriage*'. The complete words which suggest themselves to me very strongly are: *Battery*, *Gun Carriage*, and *Field Marshal*. Where would we be likely to find such a vocabulary?"

"*The Army and Navy Illustrated*!" we three answered almost in unison.

"And we know where we might find a copy of that," said the local man. "The case against Tierney strengthens by the hour."

"Do not be deceived by appearances," said Holmes to our colleagues.

"Looks to me it's as plain as the nose on your face," said Horburgh.

"Nothing so misleading as the obvious," cautioned my friend. "Well, if you two fellows will wait here, Watson and I shall take a turn down to the Field and speak to the show people. I think we may find them less guarded than you did."

We asked about and got to see the Ringmaster easily enough, a plump, white-whiskered fellow in a shiny black suit, puffing away at a pipe in his caravan.

"Not the official Police, are you?" he asked. "Well, come in then. Bartram's the name, Patrick Bartram. I heard from the Inspector what happened, but the Lord knows none of our folk would get up to sich capers. The odd chicken or rabbit here and there, mayhap. I'm not saying as absolutely everybody's above board here, there are a few rogues amongst them I know, but a kidnapping! No sir! Last thing we want is the Police hounding us. You can search any caravan or tent in this camp, mister, but I'd soon know if there was anyone hiding out here. Know how I'd know? The behaviour of the dogs! You must ha' heard them yowling when you come in. Make a lot of noise, but they wouldn't hurt a flea."

"Have you noticed anything unusual, any coming or goings with the fair folk?" Holmes asked.

"Not exackly unusual, no. Only Vittoria the Dancer has ran off with Vigor the Strongman – threw over her other beau, Conrad the Clown. It's been going on for months behind Conrad's back, it was the talk of the camp, and it come to a head on Saturday night after the last house. What else? Well. One of the acrobats, Dino Eusebi, sprained an ankle rehearsing a new move – look, that's him there hobbling by on his stick," said Bartram, as we glimpsed a tall, olive-skinned athletic-looking figure limping past the window and entering a caravan opposite. "His brother, Luigi, has had to get a stand-in. Oh, and two of the performing dogs are ill. That's about it."

"When did the elopement actually take place?"

"Two days ago. Saturday night there's a big row between Vittoria and Conrad; Sunday morning she's gone off with Vigor. I can't see as they would have had anything to do with . . . ."

"Can you show me any photographs of them?"

Bartram went to a shelf and extracted a copy of the *Showmen's Gazette*.

"We're all in here, except the new fellow who come in to work with Luigi," he said, spreading out the sheet on a low table. "I wrote the advertisement meself. This is Vittoria, lovely girl ain't she? If I was young enough, I'd ha' run off with her meself, so I can hardly blame Vigor – that's him there. Left me in the lurch he has, though; very hard to replace a Strongman, you know. They don't come ten-a-penny like dancers or clowns. Well, thank goodness we are having the night off, only the matinee performance today to get through. That's Conrad, the glum looking one, and his mate Tibor; there's the two Eusebis, Kaspar the lion-tamer, and the dancers."

Holmes seemed to take an age in perusing the sheet, as though he were memorising the faces.

"Well?" asked Bartram at last.

"I do not believe the missing man is in this camp," Holmes replied eventually, "nor that you personally have had anything to do with the crime which took place last night, and I will convey that to my acquaintances in the official force."

"Thank you kindly Mr. Holmes, if there's anything I can do . . . ."

"No, thank you. Well, perhaps I might find a copy of that gazette of yours amusing reading for the train journey back to Paddington."

By the time we had returned to the cottage, the photograph which the professor had taken had been delivered to the Inspector.

"The thief came in through the window, that's clear enough – just look at those footprints, clear as a bell," said Lestrade.

"Straight from the fence to the roan pipe, then you can see where he has tried to get a footing, before he shinned up," agreed Horburgh. I could follow their reasoning, but I noticed Holmes was staring very intently at the photograph.

"Something doesn't quite fit here," he said, shaking his head. Lestrade looked at him warily.

"What is it?" asked the local man, rather querulously.

"It's the alignment of the footsteps," replied Holmes. "Look again, more closely. Doctor, you are a man with professional knowledge of the human anatomy, yet I surmise that you cannot see it either."

I shook my head, somewhat annoyed at myself for being so obtuse.

"Start from the fence line and examine the trail of prints, step by step," he said.

It sprang out at me. "You are correct, Holmes," I ejaculated, "there *is* something strange about the pattern of the footsteps, they seem to go off at strange angles and there is an irregular distance between each footfall – it is perfectly clear now."

The two policemen nodded in agreement. I felt that Horburgh's scepticism toward my friend, which had been mounting, was now dispelled.

"He was drunk!" I expostulated. "The irregular footprints show his drunken stagger."

"Excellent, Watson. That is certainly one strong possibility."

"I know a man who was drunk last night," said Horburgh.

"Tierney!" cried Lestrade.

"The very man," said his colleague as Beasley appeared at the door to inquire whether we wanted further refreshments.

"Not for me," said Horburgh.

"We should waste no time in arresting Captain Tierney, warrant or no warrant," said Lestrade, when Beasley had left the room.

"I must thank you sincerely, Mr. Holmes," said the local man, "you have certainly lived up to the reputation which my colleague here intimated to me."

"And yet, my good fellows," replied Holmes, "your case is by no means complete, and I should urge caution. First of all, how did your drunkard ascend the roan pipe in the dark and subdue the old man without making a sound? How did he then escape? Where is the Scroll? Where is the Patriarch?"

"Well, the Scroll might well be in Tierney's house, which is why he wouldn't let my colleague search the place" Lestrade replied.

"As for the Patriarch," said Horburgh, "assuming he is not actually inside Tierney's villa, he could have been spirited away somewhere nearby. We have alerted the local farmers to check all barns and outhouses. You mentioned the *South Bucks Free Press*, Mr. Holmes. They have agreed to carry a front page article in the evening edition."

"It is good to see that at least in some parts of England, there are still pressmen who have respect for the forces of Law and Order," said Lestrade pompously. He was, I presumed, still smarting under a recent lampoon in *Punch*, entitled "Oh Mr. Policeman, What Shall I Do?", which poked fun at Scotland Yard's lack of progress in a capital case.

"There are old derelict warehouses down at the river wharf at Hedsor," Horburgh resumed. "And there are a few empty manor houses too, like Dovecote Hall and Nine Elms House, that haven't had a tenant for years – we have men out searching those at present. We haven't overlooked the old disused Gunpowder Mill, and there are old lime kilns in the district, too. As for Tierney's state last night, it's amazing how much drink some of these sots can swallow and still remain *compos mentis*. He may, in any case, have had an accomplice. If he has had anything to do with this, we'll soon have it out of him."

Holmes looked very thoughtful for a few moments.

"I cannot say yet what involvement, if any, Captain Tierney may have had in this perplexing affair," he said at last. "And I cannot but admire your presence of mind and your verve, Inspector Horburgh. But my earnest advice to you both is to call off the search for the Patriarch – you are wasting your time, for I am afraid your men will never find him."

We three gazed at Holmes in astonishment.

"Then he is dead?" cried Lestrade.

"I am certain as I can be of anything that the Patriarch is alive and well."

"Then, where is he?" asked Horburgh.

"I am unable to say precisely, but I do not think he can be very far away – "

"Is there nothing we can do to rescue him?"

"No; if my theory holds, the mere passage of time will bring about his appearance," Holmes said enigmatically.

"When?"

"Again, I am unable to say, at present."

"What about the Scroll?" asked Lestrade.

"If my deductions are correct, the Scroll has not left the village."

"Come, Mr. Holmes, you are full of riddles and evasions," cried Horburgh at the limit of frustration. "Tell us where it is and we'll get it!"

"Frankly, I am unable to state its exact location, and any premature attempt on your part to obtain it may result in its immediate destruction. However, if you will meet me on the river path just outside this house once darkness has fallen – but say nothing to the professor, you understand. Eight o'clock, then? We will need four constables, two in plain clothes. Oh, and bring two pounds of raw beefsteak."

Lestrade had become inured to my friend's histrionics, but Horburgh looked at Holmes frankly as though he were a lunatic.

"And if you should weary between now and then," my friend said, with a glimmer of amusement in his eye, "I commend you to a few hours' light reading of the *Showmen's Gazette*, Inspector Horburgh. It is amusing and very occasionally illuminating. No? Well, I shall keep it then for the journey back to Paddington tonight, once we have the case tied up." With that, he turned upon his heel and led me off.

We dined exceptionally well at the Old Swan Uppers, and once the plates were cleared, Holmes lit his pipe.

"I must say, Holmes, you have my head spinning. Do you mean to say that you have the case cut and dried already? Or was that a bit of bravado in front of Horburgh?"

"Nothing of the sort, Watson, though I noticed that the Inspector's admiring tone changed somewhat when I disarranged his pet theory."

"I thought you were rather offhand with him, all the same."

"I genuinely admire his energy in getting the case started on a practical footing. But I have presented him with prime clues – including the one on which the case turns - and he refuses to acknowledge it! The problem with the official force is that they have an incorrigible tendency to be seduced by their own arguments. They do not have instilled into them the discipline of searching for an alternative explanation for apparent facts. They are incapable of the mental exercise of falsifying their own theories, which ensures that they never rise above the mediocre. Sometimes, they do not achieve even that."

"As we are meeting outside the professor's house without his knowledge, may I take it that the Scroll and Patriarch are hidden there? Is the professor the guilty one?"

"All in good time, Watson."

The policemen were waiting for us at the riverbank, Horburgh in a sour mood.

"Got your suspect under lock and key?" Holmes asked.

"I'd rather have the Patriarch and the Scroll," he replied curtly.

"If you do exactly as I suggest, I promise that you very soon will have."

"I don't see as I have any alternative."

"Excellent. Your colleague here will attest that I have never yet broken a promise."

Lestrade nodded glumly. Holmes asked if he could speak to the four constables in private, then whispered his instructions to them. Then we made our way in darkness and silence down the river path to the back of Falconer's Field, stopping at a line of trees close to caravans. A low fence at the farther end of the trees separated us from the camp itself, and the occasional voice from one of the fairground people floated across to us. Holmes paused at one point, gave a low whistle once, then turned to Horburgh.

"Have you the beefsteak?" he asked. The Inspector handed him a package, which he opened quietly. He tiptoed towards the fence over which threw the pieces of meat.

"In case the dogs are roaming around," he whispered by way of explanation and then called the constables forward. I could see him pointing out some features of the camp to the constables. Then off they went through the trees. Holmes then motioned to us, and he crept forward, as though leading a salient upon enemy territory, until we were within a few yards of one of the vans, which was lit by a flickering oil lamp. We were still concealed, and I assumed the object of our visit was Bartram's caravan, though in the darkness I could scarcely tell which was which. My attention was suddenly arrested by the two plain-clothesmen who had walked up to the caravan, and began to fiddle with the door handle. Their actions were clumsily in the extreme, and it was no surprise to me when the door flew open with a cry and the inhabitant peered out. I had expected to see Bartram, but I recognised the man as Dino, the acrobat. It occurred to me at that point that Dino was supposed to have sprained an ankle. His recovery since afternoon seemed to have been unusually rapid. A second later, his brother appeared beside him. The startled policemen made off in opposite directions, and the two brothers gave chase with heavy oaths.

"Your men have blown it now!" I remarked to Lestrade.

"Not at all," replied Holmes. "The plan went exactly as I had specified. One moment, and I shall be back." With a few steps, Holmes was inside the caravan, the tails of his long coat flying behind him; in a second he was back at our side.

"I have seen all I need to see," he said, smiling.

"Will you please tell me what on earth is going on?" asked Horburgh, evidently still far from convinced.

"Yes. You have witnessed the arrest of the culprits you have been looking for since this morning. Your men should have the two acrobats under control by now, and all that remains is for us to repair to the professor's, and I shall explain everything to you concerning this interesting little diversion."

But a severe shock awaited us on arrival at the professor's cottage. Sergeant Canterville, who had been left in charge, came rushing out to meet his superior.

"You're not goin' to believe this, sir," he gasped, "but a second person claimin' to be the Patriarch arrived here half an hour ago!"

"What?" cried Horburgh. "What have you done with this impostor?"

""I have him securely handcuffed and under lock and key in the professor's kitchen."

"Good man. Well, Mr. Holmes," said Horburgh with a sarcastic glance at my friend, "how does this fit in to your theory?"

"Confirms it in every respect," Holmes replied with a smile. "Indeed, only a few hours ago I predicted the same – I told you, did I not, that the Patriarch would turn up in the fullness of time?"

"With respect sir," said Canterville, "this is definitely not the same man who arrived last night!"

"Of course it isn't – I never said that it was. It is the real Patriarch, though, and I should lose no time in releasing him if you wish to avoid a charge of wrongful arrest. I suppose I ought to say the same regarding Captain Tierney, though I am inclined to think that a night in the cells will do him no harm whatsoever. Now lead on, Inspector."

It took some time to explain the train of recent events to the newly arrived and astonished Father Philxenous, particularly as to how he received a telegram informing him of his own disappearance; but once the entire party was seated in the professor's drawing room, Holmes began his recapitulation.

"I am afraid, Professor, you were taken badly in – the person who appeared last night, claiming to be the Patriarch, was the thief himself," he said. "It is astonishing how stage make up and a false beard can take one in. It is highly likely that someone had intercepted your mail and knew of the arrangements between yourself and Father Philxenous. That person could not have been from the Coptic community; the reason will be clear in a moment. It was obvious to me from the outset that the escape of a thief, under the conditions described to me, was completely impossible. I had wondered at first whether the thief had got out through the skylight, but the idea that he could also take along an unwilling hostage was, frankly, ludicrous. You will recall the photograph of the footprints – the strange pattern? The thief was not drunk but was – "

"Walking backwards!" I ejaculated, as the realisation dawned upon me.

"Indeed, Watson. I deduced that what happened was that the thief, who was probably Dino Eusebi, once he had stolen the document, opened the window, climbed *down* the roan pipe, and walked *backwards* towards the fence. You will recall my initial difficulty in establishing the direction in which the bushes had been pushed, but it soon became clear that the person had gone *away from*, not towards, the house. Incidentally, as Watson would tell you, the involvement of acrobats in burglaries is by no means uncommon: cases in Hillerød, Denmark in eighty-four, and in Kensington in ninety-two spring to mind. In the latter case, the Eusebi brothers were actually amongst the suspects, but Inspector Gregson lacked the proof to bring the case to court, and, as it happened, I was in Tibet at the time, and therefore unable to assist. On Monday afternoon, Luigi had been lying in wait for the genuine Patriarch at the station, in order to waylay him. You will recall Merryweather's evidence of the man loitering in the Waiting Room. Of course, the real Father Philxenous never turned up, because he had arranged to come on the day after Coptic Easter – *Pascha* – which, as you know Professor, is *next* Monday, not yesterday."

The Patriarch nodded in silence.

"Hence my deduction concerning the person who intercepted the mail. I have no doubt that it was an accomplice of the Eusebis, probably in the sorting office at Mount Pleasant, for the district is full of Italians. So, Inspector, I am afraid that Captain Tierney, despite his behaviour, was something of a red herring. The words which made up the ransom note – which was, of course, entirely spurious and cleverly designed to mislead us – were cut, not from the *Army and Navy Illustrated* as we initially thought, but from the *Showmen's Gazette*, of which I attempted to make you a present. I obtained it from the Ringmaster, a Mr. Bartram who, I should add, is not only entirely innocent in this matter, but has also now lost two acrobats, a strongman, and a dancer, and will probably have to close down. The *Showmen's Gazette*, I observed, contained an advertisement by that gentleman, as well as photographs of the Eusebis, whom I recognised immediately. There was also an article on the plans to develop Battersea Fields as a pleasure garden. Had you read it, you would have discovered such words as '*Patrick*', '*matriarch*', '*carriage drive*', and so on – I need hardly elaborate on their significance. Obviously the Eusebi brothers cut their note out of this.

"I reasoned that the real Patriarch would come here immediately he saw the telegram saying that he had gone missing, and I knew that we should see him soon enough. Thus my advice to you to call off your search. Incidentally, I suppose you will all have deduced that that Dino's sprained ankle was entirely spurious. In fact, this is his walking stick which I took the liberty of rescuing for you, Inspector, as you will no doubt need it as evidence for the trial. It is an unusual specimen, quite an antique in itself. Heavy, too. I should not like to receive a blow from this. Would you like to examine it, professor?"

Beasley took hold of the walking stick and examined it, more, it seemed to me, out of politeness than from genuine interest, for it was clear that one aspect of the case still perturbed him.

"Now, is there any detail which I have missed?" asked my friend finally.

"Where is the Scroll?" Lestrade and Horburgh cried almost in unison.

"The Scroll is in this house," my friend replied with a mischievous gleam in his eye.

"But where?" asked Father Philxenous who had been following the conversation silently.

"It is in the professor's possession," replied my friend.

"My dear Mr. Holmes," began the professor warmly, "whilst I acknowledge that you – "

My friend held up his hand. "Doctor Watson will tell you that I love nothing more than a dramatic denouement to a case. Hand me the stick, please."

With a twist and a click, Holmes produced a roll of parchment from inside the hollow stem of the cane, and placed it upon the table. I recognised the queer Coptic characters immediately. A cry of mingled triumph and relief erupted from Beasley.

"They had to conceal it somewhere," said Holmes, "until they were ready to sell it. An ankle sprain was the ideal bogus injury. It had the ring of truth about it when Luigi actually brought in another acrobat to work with him. It also meant that Dino could go anywhere without letting the precious Scroll out of his sight."

Father Philxenous, stood up and bowed politely to us. "I could not have believed this unless I had seen it with my own eyes," he said slowly and deliberately. "You are blessed with a gift from God, Mr. Holmes."

"Words cannot express my gratitude to you, for bringing this most precious, rare, and sacred relic back to me," said the professor.

"I must add my thanks," said Horburgh frankly, "and to that also my apology for ever having doubted you in the first place."

"We had best be off then," said Holmes, "I believe that there is just time for us to catch the last train."

"But not, surely, before I present you with some reward for your exertions on my behalf," said the Professor, standing up. "My chequebook is in the writing desk. After all, I should have been happy to part with my last penny in order to have the Scroll back."

Holmes held up his hand.

"Not at all, Professor Beasley," he replied. "Success is my reward, as both Doctor Watson and Inspector Lestrade will confirm."

The case of the Two Coptic Patriarchs, as it became known, finally came to court a few months later. It was kept off the front pages, however, by the sensational disappearance of Dr. Ray Ernest in Lewisham during the week that the name of Josiah Amberley gained infamy in the national press.

131

The Royal Arsenal Affair
by Leslie F.E. Coombs

We had just finished our breakfast when Holmes's brother, Mycroft, made one of his rare visits to 221b Baker Street. Despite his massive physical presence and slow, seemingly deliberate movements, I knew that his brain, like that of his brother, hummed with energy, as if it were one of those dynamos that were becoming increasingly more frequent wherever one went. Without further ado, he explained the reason for his unexpected and early visit.

"Sherlock, the Prime Minister has made me responsible for the recovery of a machine that was stolen."

"A machine, you say," responded Holmes.

Mycroft continued. "Yes, a machine or apparatus. Although I am not privy to what its purpose is or how it works. I understand that its loss is of the greatest concern to the government. It must be found, and the villains who have taken it apprehended without delay. Sherlock, you are the only one who is capable of undertaking such a task. I can assure you that if the machine is not found and the villains who took it put it to work, then, as I understand it, the consequences would be disastrous."

"Mycroft, I am sure you are aware that I do not undertake an investigation unless I am given all the facts," was Holmes's response. "I cannot proceed if something is withheld for social, family or political reasons."

"Of course, I understand that."

"Surely, Mycroft, you can tell what sort of machine it is?" Holmes asked. "May I know how big it is?"

"Let me just say, as an estimate, half the size of this room and about a half a ton in weight when its major parts are put together," responded Mycroft reluctantly.

Holmes put down the taper with which he was about to light his after-breakfast pipe. He rarely allowed his features to register surprise, but this time his mouth was open and his eyebrows raised to their fullest extent.

"Half a ton and as big as half this room?" he exclaimed. "An elephant indeed! I shall have to study the place from where it was stolen. Considering what little information you have been able to give me so far, I trust that will not present any obstacle?"

"I can tell you," replied Mycroft, "that it was taken from an annex to the Royal Arsenal at Woolwich only yesterday. There's no time to be lost. I propose that we go there as soon as you are dressed and ready."

Holmes put down his unlit pipe and went to his bedroom, discarding his dressing gown onto the floor.

Mycroft picked up the discarded dressing gown, saying, "My brother has some very untidy habits."

I replied, "That is true. Yet his brain stores information in an extremely ordered manner."

Mycroft then said, "Dr. Watson, despite my brother's frequent failure to acknowledge adequately the invaluable help you have given him on a number of difficult cases, I can assure you he does appreciate it, as I do. Therefore, you'll come with us?"

"If I can be of help, certainly," I replied.

As we went down to the front door, the brothers started to argue over the best and quickest way to get to Woolwich. Mycroft Holmes wanted to use the Inner Circle from Baker Street to Cannon Street Station, but his brother objected because he said he found the sulphureous smoke of the Metropolitan railway's underground lines unbearable. Mycroft and I exchanged meaningful glances that said in effect, "What of the stifling tobacco smoke in the sitting room?"

Once we had gained the pavement, Mycroft lifted an ornate silver cab whistle attached to his watch chain and summoned a growler. Within hardly a minute a four-wheel cab arrived.

During our progress to Cannon Street Station, and then by a slow train to Woolwich Arsenal Station, Holmes said little. I surmised he was going over in his mind the task ahead, and inwardly complaining about the lack of information concerning the missing machine.

When we arrived at the arsenal a number of gentlemen met us. No polite exchange of greetings and introductions. Just a nod or two. I had the impression that they preferred not to say too much about who they were and whom they represented. We were taken immediately to a large shed in the grounds of an annex to the arsenal. Its double doors had been torn off their hinges.

Holmes's first question, after studying the damage to the doors, was, "If the missing machine is of such importance or value, why was it not kept inside the arsenal walls where there would have been some measure of security?"

One of the officials who was with us said, "Mr. Holmes, you are certainly correct in asking such a question. The nature of the machine is such that its purpose could have been betrayed by any one of the hundreds who work in the arsenal. We assumed that this unremarkable shed in this annex, whose sign on the gate indicates that it is nothing more than a clothing store, would attract no particular attention. We have been proved wrong,"

"Perhaps you may be able to tell me of any thoughts you have about who has taken it," said Holmes. "Obviously, because of its size, more than one villain has been involved."

The unnamed official replied, "Mr. Holmes, we are certain that those who removed the machine were those who had built it in the first place. Recently we learned of its whereabouts and took it into our custody. Unfortunately, we were not able to secure those who had invented it. However, we had forestalled their plan to put it into use for a criminal purpose. Our intention, in not destroying it, was to discover certain features that will enable us to be prepared to resist attempts to use similar devices in the future."

"Thank you for that information," said Holmes. "I presume the police are now searching for the thieves?"

"For reasons we cannot disclose, we do not want the police involved," was the reply.

"Oh, and another thing, although not of importance. What do you call the machine?" asked Holmes.

One of the officials replied, "Mr. Holmes, it is just the X Machine. It cannot have a name that might reveal its purpose.

Holmes then started to make a close examination of the interior of the shed. When he had finished and put away his large magnifying glass, he said, "I am right, am I not, in saying that the machine has a number of small wheels, some of which are castors?"

"That is correct," responded one of the officials.

Outside the shed Holmes examined some tracks made by wheels leading to the road. He said, "Gentlemen, the wheel tracks, their disposition, and the size of the wheels indicate, I am certain, that a furniture pantechnicon has been used to take the machine away."

Holmes pointed to a number of footprints, saying, "These prints are those of at least six men; possibly even more. They also tell me that they were having to exert great physical effort; presumably to move the parts of the machine onto the pantechnicon. Furthermore, I conclude that the tracks in the roadway show that it has been taken eastward on this road, and that four Shire horses were needed to move it."

Holmes spent another five minutes examining the wheel tracks and the imprints of the horses' hooves in the dried mud on the road. Fortunately, they were very distinct because it had rained in the night, but later the road had dried out.

"Gentlemen, I suggest that Dr. Watson and I will take a trap and endeavour to follow the tracks made by the pantechnicon and its four Shire horses."

This was agreed to, a horse and trap was hired from a local stable, and we set off. Mycroft Holmes and the others went to the nearest station's telegraph office to await events.

"Holmes," said I, "how did you conclude that the machine had been taken away in a pantechnicon pulled by four Shire horses?"

"The singular nature of the wheel marks in the dried mud suggest the type of small wheels used under furniture vans so as to keep the floor as low as possible. The hooves of heavy draught horses, such as the Shires, are much larger than the average cart horse. However, I am going to have to depend on two clues that presented themselves outside the shed. One was two crushed hops, and the other the cracked shoe of the wheel horse on the nearside. They both provide a strong 'question resolver' whenever we have to decide which of a number of roads at a junction we should take. Furthermore, I have considered that the thieves would not have taken a westerly or southwesterly direction because of the steep hills leading to the high ground around Blackheath. They could, of course, have taken a route through Greenwich, and, despite my reluctance to add gambling to scientific detection, I am going to choose to turn east."

Our progress was slow because at each place where a number of roads branched off, Holmes had to get down and make a close inspection of the surface of the road. This occasionally prompted some coarse comments from bystanders. After two hours, we and the horse needed refreshment, and so we repaired to an inn about four miles to the east of Woolwich, near Plumstead. The White Swan was far from white. It was typical of so many public houses. The interior, even the saloon bar, was in need of some paint. The furnishings were dedicated more to the consumption of ale and spirits, rather than the physical comfort of weary travellers.

I commented, "Did you read that article in one of the newspapers that compared our inns most unfavourably with their equivalent on the Continent?"

"Yes, I did," replied Holmes, "and I agreed with every word. We have stayed in some dreadful places."

As we sat eating bread and cheese and drinking the local ale, we heard the sound of a railway engine's whistle. It came from a level crossing further down the road. This prompted my friend to say, "Watson, I am finding it increasingly difficult to find clear indications of the progress of the pantechnicon. Reluctantly, I shall have to make what I trust is an informed guess."

"I know that that is a step you usually avoid."

"I am going to assume," he said, "that the villains have gone onto the marshes on the other side of the railway. The crossing keeper may be able to provide some useful information."

After we had finished our rather unsatisfactory meal, we drove toward the crossing. As the keeper appeared from his hut, Holmes said, "Good morning. Do many people come this way?"

"Since the brick works over there closed, not many," was the reply. "There ain't not much out on the marsh. Any rate, most uses the road from Abbey Wood station, just down the line."

"Most helpful," said Holmes. "Now we are going to take a walk out on the marsh. There could be some interesting birds to see. We'll leave the horse and trap with you. I hope you do not mind? Here's a florin for your trouble."

"Thank you very much, sir. I'll watch 'em for you."

We set off, trusting that we gave the impression of being ornithologists.

"Did you observe the damage to the gate post of the crossing?" said Holmes. "That could have been struck by the pantechnicon."

"We cannot be certain of that," said I. "It could have been made at any time recently."

"Come, come, my friend. Surely, in the interest of safety, the railway company would have had the gate post mended as soon as possible. That damage was done this morning."

"Holmes," said I, "you know I am not up to too much walking. Slow down a bit please.

"Sorry, old chap. Forgot. Your leg of course."

"Why did we leave the trap?" I asked.

"We could not take the trap, as it would alert the villains of our approach. That is, if we are still on their trail. We may find ourselves standing on the bank of the Thames and having to retrace our steps, and start looking for the trail again."

As so often happened, a day that had started out as a bright summer morning was now overcast with lowering dark clouds scudding across the sky. Neither of us was dressed to resist the heavy driving rain that suddenly assailed us. My protestations at having to proceed in such dreadful weather were answered by Holmes. "This rain will hide our approach, but it is also washing away the tracks of the pantechnicon."

On each side stretched the marshes and numerous drainage ditches. As we progressed, an old fortress and a prison hulk loomed ahead. The latter still retained some features from the time when it had been one of Nelson's ships at Trafalgar. It lay listing to one side on its muddy bed. Its one remaining mast pointed to the sky as if it were an accusing finger for the dreadful life in chains of those who had been confined there, before being sent onward to Australia. The hulk reminded me of the start of Dickens' *Great Expectations*, a battered copy of whose words had provided some relief when I was recovering after being wounded in the Afghan campaign.

My thoughts were interrupted by my friend saying, "That's most interesting. The crossing keeper never mentioned the fort and the hulk. I wonder why?"

"Holmes, do you think we will find the machine in the hulk?"

"No, most unlikely. If it is as big as we have been told, the rotten timbers of the old ship would have collapsed under the weight. If it is here, then it would be in the old fort."

Holmes suddenly said, "Watson, listen, can you hear what I hear? It's the horses and the furniture van. They are going back along another road across the marsh."

"We'll never catch them now," said I. "By the time we get back to the trap they will be long gone."

"Ah, but listen at the speed with which those horses are being driven. That strongly suggests that the van is empty. The machine must have been unloaded inside the fort."

Peering through the driving rain, we studied the remains of the fort. It stood on the only stretch of firm ground at the side of the river. There was only one opening in the wall wide enough to admit a large van. Indicating that I should not speak, Holmes moved into the fort. I followed with my hand on the butt of the pistol in my pocket. I wanted to say, "Holmes, hold on. What are we doing? This is for the police." But then I remembered the injunction at the start of our quest that the fewer privy to the matter, the better.

Holmes grasped my arm and pointed to one side, to indicate I should take the passage on my left. He left me and went to search further into the centre of the fort. I felt my way along in the gloom of what light came from the sky above the roofless fort. The only sounds were the wind and the rain beating against the old stone walls. I could hear no voices until I heard a shout. "Stop or we'll shoot! Drop your stick!" The shout made me jump. I could hear voices coming from the direction which Holmes had taken. I assumed that he had encountered the criminals, but, perhaps, to my dismay, they had seized him.

Once again, Holmes had entered a trap. I thought, "Surely I am not going to have to go through the experience of the *Noble Affair* again?"

For what seemed an eternity, I stood still, listening to the threats being hurled at Holmes. I concluded that there must be at least ten men into whose arms my friend had fallen. My first thought was, "To spring at them with my revolver?" But then the realisation that I might endanger the life of my friend prompted caution. I retraced my steps as quietly as I could. I left the fort. I was intent on reaching the railway and persuading the crossing keeper to let me send a telegram to Mycroft.

My old wounds ached and pained me more than ever as I forced myself to half run back along the road. At any minute, I expected a shot to whistle past my ear, or send me sprawling with a wound or, even worse, to be killed. When I reached the crossing, the keeper helped me to a chair. I was exhausted. My first words were, "I must summon help. Please, you must send a message for me over the telegraphic apparatus."

"Sorry, sir, ain't no telegraph. This ain't a proper signal box. I've only got them indicators that tells me if a train's a-coming."

At that, I struggled to my feet, and with his help, I climbed into the trap and whipped up the horse. I had to get to Plumstead Station telegraph office as soon as possible. I urged the horse onward. Suddenly, part of the harness gave way. I managed to stop the horse and got down to see what was wrong. I soon discovered that one of the buckles had not been fastened properly. I was quickly on my way again.

At Plumstead, I telegraphed, *They've got Holmes. We must rescue him. At least ten villains in old fort on Plumstead Marshes.*

I waited anxiously at the station. An hour later, Mycroft and some of the gentlemen from the Arsenal arrived in two hired cabs. Immediately we set off for the fort. I was relieved to see my companions' revolvers being loaded in anticipation of trouble.

There was no dramatic attack on the fort, no securing of the criminals, and no rescue of Sherlock Holmes. When we entered, we could find neither the machine, nor Holmes. I thought, "Have the birds flown and taken the machine with them?" But then I remembered Holmes deciding that the speed with which the horses had been moving along the other road indicated that the pantechnicon was empty. The machine must have still been in the fort.

With dusk about to make it too difficult to continue searching, we returned to London, leaving a pair of guards in place. As we travelled back, my thoughts became a battle between great concern for the well-being of Holmes and my expectation that, despite all difficulties, as in previous cases, he would survive by some means or other.

The next morning Mrs. Hudson brought up a letter that had been delivered by hand.

"Doctor, this was on the mat when I went down to pick up the papers. Is Mr. Holmes all right? His bed has not been slept in."

"I trust so, Mrs. Hudson."

I tore open the letter. It was in Holmes's handwriting. I had an immediate sense of relief, but then a sense of trepidation as I read the letter. He said that he was in good health but his life was in danger unless £10,000 in gold was handed over to his captors. They would tell me how and where it had to be paid over later in the day.

I was relieved when Superintendent Shershay, of Scotland Yard's Criminal Investigation Department, and Mycroft Holmes arrived soon after. The latter explained that he had been able to persuade the gentlemen we had met at the Arsenal that the wellbeing of the country's foremost scientific detective was of more value, or at least equal, to that of their machine. Therefore, it had been agreed that Scotland Yard had to be told about it. We discussed what had to be done, or rather what might be done, to effect a rescue of my friend and the recovery of the machine. I told them about the letter I had received.

"You say that yesterday's search," said Shershay, "found neither Mr. Holmes nor the machine, and no trace of the thieves. Let me see the letter please, Doctor."

I took it out of my pocket, and as I did so, the envelope that had been with it fell to the floor. As I stooped to pick it up, my eye caught the address that I had ignored when I first received it because I was more concerned with its contents. There, staring me in the face, was a possible clue to Holmes's whereabouts. It read: "*Dr. John Livorno Watson, Private and Confidential, 221b Baker Street*". As with the *Noble Affair*, I had been given a name I did not possess. "*Livorno*. What could that mean?" I thought.

When I pointed out the addition to my name Mycroft said, "Livorno? Surely that's in Italy!"

We debated what had to be done next, and why Holmes had chosen "Livorno" to guide us to where he was being held captive.

"All the same," I replied, "we must make another search of the fort. We will have the advantage of a bright day."

In the sunlight, the old fort looked less forbidding. It was reported that no one had returned during the night. I was determined, as I am sure the Superintendent was, to apply the methods used by Holmes to reveal clues. We examined all the walls, in anticipation that there might be a concealed door or opening. Eventually, we came to a large space, along one side of which were three large hinged iron doors. I thought, "Holmes would advise us to study the floor before anything else."

"Does not look as if anyone has been here," said Shershay. "There are no marks or footprints."

"Superintendent," said I, "the stone floor is covered with earth that appears to have been recently put down. It's too fresh looking. These marks suggest that any footprints were swept away."

I made a furrow in the dirt that covered the floor and said, "I think this shows that there is something in this chamber that the villains want to hide. Let us have a closer look. Don't you agree?"

We managed to push aside some of the earth.

"Look at this," said I. "The floor has been covered to hide these scratches in the stone. They look clean and sharp. Could they have been made by the effort needed to move the parts of the machine?"

"Ah, I see what you mean, Doctor," responded the Superintendent. "You have been most observant. We may find the machine in one of what may have been powder magazines, and, possibly, I hope, Mr. Holmes."

Each door was held shut by a long iron or steel bar set into a socket and secured by a padlock. All parts of the doors, including the padlocks, were covered in red rust and gave no indication that they had been disturbed for many years.

Shershay and Mycroft were examining closely each of the rusty padlocks. The latter began to brush away the rust on one of them.

"Look at this," said Mycroft. "It is a new padlock. They've disguised it with this mixture, I presume, of rust and clay."

"We are going to need a locksmith," said I. "If I had Holmes's set of special tools I might be able to open it. The other day he instructed me in how to use them. An activity, Superintendent, which I suppose I should not admit in front of an officer of the law."

Shershay said, "We'll have to force the lock somehow. We must look for an iron rod or bar. There must be something lying around. Don't suggest that I shoot it off. That idea is only to be found in a Penny Dreadful story. If I used my gun, the bullet could bounce off and injure one of us. Anyway, it will take more than a revolver bullet."

Despite the debris and rubbish that abounded in the fort, it took some time before we came upon a suitable length of iron rod. It took the combined effort of three of us to force the padlock open. Despite the gloomy interior of the magazine, we could clearly see a large black shape having many wheels and levers. But, no sign of my friend.

"That must be what we are looking for," said Mycroft.

I could not bring myself to join in the examination of the strange looking machine. I was too concerned about what might have happened to Holmes. "Livorno, Livorno?" continued to whirl around my brain.

140

Then for some unaccountable reason, it came to me that Livorno, the city in Tuscany, has a breed of hen named after it. And the Livorno Hen in England is called a *Leghorn.*

"Gentlemen," said I, "Holmes may have indicated that he is being held in a place called Leghorn, somewhere in London. Is there such a place?"

"It is more than likely the name of a road," responded Shershay.

"Superintendent, have you got a street directory with you?" I asked.

He produced a well-thumbed copy from his pocket and flicked through the pages. "Ah, here we have a Leghorn Road in Plumstead," he said. "And, of course, there is also a Leghorn Road in Harlesden. I remember a case some years ago of a murder I had to investigate there. But I doubt they have taken Mr. Holmes that far."

"I agree, the villains may not have gone as far as Harlesden," said I. "It is more likely the one in Plumstead."

At Plumstead police station, Shershay, with the authority of Scotland Yard, instructed the local superintendent to provide an inspector and six constables to accompany us to Leghorn Road. They were told nothing more than we were investigating a kidnapping of a prominent person.

When we arrived close to the road, we kept out of sight round the corner. It was decided that I should go along the road by myself, so as not to alert the criminals of an attempt to rescue Holmes. Leghorn Road had about thirty terraced houses: each not more than ten years old, and of the type favoured by shopkeepers and clerks.

"You will attract too much attention." Shershay said to me. "You must disguise yourself." Turning to the Inspector, he said, "let this gentleman borrow your scarf. Now let us make the hat look as if it has seen better days." At that, he took my hat and proceeded to stamp on it. Although it was my best and not very old, I considered it was a small sacrifice if it enabled us to rescue Holmes.

"The gentleman just can't stroll along the road peerin at the ouses. He'll look very suspicious," opined the Inspector.

"What do you suggest?" asked Shershay.

As he spoke, a knife grinder came along, pushing his clumsy machine. The Inspector called him over. "Come er Stringer."

"Come orf it, Inspector. I ain't not done nothing."

"This is Stringer," said the Inspector. "I've many a times had im up for loitering with hintent, and more than once I've nearly nabbed im for nippin into ouses when doors as been left open."

The outcome of this encounter was that Stringer, who had no choice, agreed that I should go along the street with him and pretend to be his mate. It would give me the opportunity to study each house as we went. I had to push the heavy grinding machine, and not appear to be other than what I pretended to be.

We moved slowly along with Stringer, calling out, "Knives, sharpen yer knives!" Without revealing my intent, I examined each house as we passed or stopped. Each of the houses presented a similar appearance: net curtains across the parlour windows, with an aspidistra just visible. For ten minutes or so, when a housewife came out with knives that needed sharpening, I leant against the machine and endeavoured to study the house to see if there were any clues as to what may be happening inside. I crossed off my mental list the house whose knives were being sharpened. I eliminated another three because I could not imagine that the criminals could suffer the appalling noise made by the numerous small children. However, I also thought I might be mistaken, because children could be the perfect distraction. Stringer continued to provide information about the inhabitants of another three: a teacher of music, a town hall clerk and a grocer. He knew all about them and told me that, to the best of his knowledge about criminal activity in that part of London, they were "straight".

As it was a Monday morning, smoke was rising from the chimneys to indicate that the weekly wash was in progress. It was then that I observed that there was no smoke from one set of chimneys.

"Who's in that house, Stringer?" said I, indicating with my head the end house on our side of the road.

"Dunno, guv'nor," was his reply. "Never seen em what's supposed to live there. They ain't never comes art with their knives when I calls."

Despite my impatience to get back to the others and tell them of my suspicions, I had to restrain myself and continue to play the part of the knife grinder's mate for another quarter of an hour.

Back with the others, Stringer was dismissed and threatened with the resurrection of past offences to be taken into account if he told anyone of what had happened.

"Let us hope Holmes is in that house," said I. "Of course, we could be wrong and he is being held somewhere else."

"Now what is our next move to be?" asked Mycroft Holmes.

"We'll have to move most carefully," said Shershay, "or they might kill your brother."

"If he is in there, he is in great danger," said Mycroft. "We cannot just rush the front door."

I considered for some moments about how we could enter the house, seize the villains, and release Holmes. We might create a diversion, such as producing smoke and shouting "Fire!" That had worked on at least two occasions in my accounts of Holmes's career. Or should we force our way in, either from the back or through the front door?

As we stood there debating our next move, a member of the Salvation Army approached carrying copies of the *War Cry*.

With an impulsive decision, I said, "Superintendent, I could wear the uniform jacket and hat of the Salvation Army and get close to the house."

"Doctor, I think you should let me or the Inspector try to do that. It could put you in great danger."

"I realise there is danger in such a plan, but I owe it to my friend to do everything I can to rescue him. I believe I may be able to detect certain clues that Holmes may have left near the house. They could be of a nature that only I could understand their meaning." As I spoke, I was inwardly debating the folly of my decision. Nevertheless I summoned up my limited store of courage to continue.

Shershay spoke to the Salvation Army Captain and asked for his help. At first, he was most reluctant to assist. He did not consider that his duty in the Army equated with helping the police to make an arrest. It took much persuasion to convince the Captain that my intention was to save someone's life. He stood listening to what I intended to do with a frown of disapproval. However, I suggested that I would make a handsome contribution to the Army's funds if I might be allowed to borrow his uniform jacket and hat. Shershay assured him that he would be given full access to any who were arrested, so that he could provide them with both religious and moral support, and try to direct them to a better way of life. He relented.

For the second time that morning, I found myself "play-acting," as my friend would say. I was astonished at the reception I received when the doors of some of the houses opened in response to my knock. Some were polite and made a contribution, and commented on the good work the Army was doing among the desperately poor. Others assailed me with some of the offensive and abusive words I had become accustomed to hearing when I was in the army.

At the door of the house where we assumed Holmes was being held, I knocked but there was no response. I knocked again. I could just hear some voices and then there was a succession of bangs, as if someone was stamping on the floor. Then there was a shout followed by silence. I looked around to see if Holmes had left any clues. All I could find was a flower pot lying in pieces in the small front garden. When I looked closer, I could see that the flowers which it had held were still fresh. I deduced that someone had knocked it flying when mounting the steps up to the door, and that it had occurred recently. I visualised Holmes struggling against his captors as they forced him up the steps into the house. In doing so, I imagined him striking out so as to send the pot down the steps as a clue. I peered through the letter box, and could just make out a cane lying on the floor. I looked again and realised it was Holmes's sword stick with its distinctive silver furnishings. I moved away and rejoined the others.

"He's in there," said I, "no doubt of it."

"There's nothing for it," said Shershay, "we must force our way in. Remember, the villains have guns."

The constables used their heavy boots to kick down the front door. As I followed Shershay and the Inspector into the hall, a shot came from the top of the stairs and I felt a slight burning sensation on my right ear. The bullet smashed into the door frame. An inch to the right and I would not have been able to pen this account. Another shot was fired at us but missed, and a voice shouted, "Comes any closer and this bleedin interfering detective bloke gets it. Get art of the ous."

"That's not done much good," said the Inspector. "They've got Mr. Holmes, alright."

"How many of them do you think there are, Doctor?" asked the Superintendent.

I replied, "In the old fort, I am sure there were about ten of them. Whether they are all in the house, I cannot say. Of course, there may be only two or three, because they have not been moving the heavy machine about."

"There's nothing for it. We've got to charge up the stairs," said Shershay.

Although as a doctor I had not been expected to be in the van of a charge against the enemy in Afghanistan, I had had to follow as close as I could to tend to any wounded. Now, I was expected to lead. What followed was a confused scene of shouting and the sound of my gun being fired up the stairs. I did not aim it, but fired off all six shots one after the other to confuse whoever was guarding the landing. To my astonishment, one of my shots hit someone. There was a cry of pain and one of the villains tumbled down the stairs.

"Good shot, Doctor!" exclaimed the Superintendent.

I will not dwell on the method used by the Inspector to convince the villain who lay on the hall floor to reveal how many of his companions were above.

"Damn yer bleeding eyes. Find out yerselves. Ouch, ouch." After a pause, the Inspector put the question again to his prisoner, and this time the answer was, "There's only one, it's me mate. Ouch, es in the front bedroom."

We rushed up the stairs. At any moment I expected to be shot. Once on the landing, we approached the front bedroom door. Keeping to one side, Shershay pushed the door open to reveal Holmes, tied to a chair and gagged, with a pistol pointed at his head by one of the villains.

"Don't come any closer or he gets it," came the response. "Only one of yous got a gun, and I counted six shots."

Had this been a play, it might have seemed to have been well rehearsed; which of course it was not. What followed took only a few seconds, but at the time it seemed as if time stood still. I could not take my eyes off the villain's trigger finger. I could see the muscles tightening. Simultaneously Holmes bowed his head and Shershay's life-preserver hit the gun. The gun fired, and before the villain could draw back the hammer again, we were on him.

Holmes was released. Apart from the back of his head suffering a burn from the gun being fired less than an inch from his skin, he had not been harmed much, although he admitted his ears were ringing.

Back in Baker Street, Mycroft said that he was free to tell us what the affair had been about. However, we were enjoined never to reveal what he was about to tell us.

"Apparently the machine is capable of printing five pound notes, and at the rate of five hundred an hour. The paper and the quality of the printing are such that it is hard to distinguish one of the counterfeit notes from the real thing. Had the villains succeeded in the first place, they could have flooded the country with counterfeit five pound notes, and also distributed them in other countries and throughout the Empire to an extent that would have undermined the value of Sterling."

I am pleased to record that, once again, the nation was in debt to my friend, the great scientific detective. However, the monetary reward he received from the Treasury included a proviso that, for the foreseeable future, neither he nor I must reveal the existence of such a lethal, in financial terms, machine. That is why this account has had to remain locked away for many years.

As with all my friend's cases, there were a number of questions for which I sought an answer. One was, "What was the significance of the two hops you picked up?"

"Oh, those. Well, you see, they provided me with a possible indication of the direction taken by the furniture van. One, or all of the villains, may have come from the northern part of Kent where hops abound. I deduced that there was a slight, I emphasise slight, possibility that they might have been intent on going in that direction rather than in any other. However, I did observe one lying on the road that led down to the crossing and the marshes.

"Watson, you said you were delayed during the dash to Plumstead station because the harness came apart."

"Yes, I found one of the buckles had come undone. Did the crossing keeper attempt to delay me?"

"Too much drama, my old friend. Neither he nor the gang of thieves would have anticipated our presence at the crossing. It was nothing more than a buckle that had not been fastened properly."

The Adventure of the Sunken Parsley
by Mark Alberstat

The summer heat of 1898 had somewhat abated as Mr. Sherlock Holmes and I enjoyed a rare morning of inactivity in early September. We had left the city on several occasions throughout the all-too-short British summer, but each of those trips had been in response to a summons for Holmes to help untangle the rat's nest of clues and scents of some mystery laid before us. This morning, however, was a leisurely one. We sat in front of a cold fireplace, tobacco at hand, and a variety of the daily papers scattered about our intimate sitting room.

The year so far had been a busy one. My notes, however, indicate that there was only one case which I could lay before the public, and that was the affair at Wisteria Lodge. The other undertakings of my friend Sherlock Holmes were to that point either inconclusive, repetitive tropes from previous exploits, or too delicate for those involved to even consider exploring in the public press.

"Is it your eyesight or your reflexes, Watson?" asked Holmes.

"My eyesight or my reflexes? What are you getting at, Holmes?" I replied

"Is it your eyesight or your reflexes that are not quite what they used to be to allow you to be hit so hard on the knee with a cricket ball that you are not playing today?"

"Once again, I feel you are partially a warlock. How on Earth did you know I was hit yesterday? You did not see me come in after the match, and I was seated here when you came down to breakfast. And, I would like to add, it is neither my eyesight nor my reflexes. I was distracted by someone in the crowd which led to my injury," I replied.

"Yes, someone in the crowd. I am sure that was it. As to how I know you were hit is simplicity itself. There in an account in this paper of the Players versus Gentlemen match in which you were participated yesterday at Lords. That was the second day of a three-day match. Although today's activities do not start for another two hours, you are clearly not preparing to be there. That raises the question as to why. You are sitting in the chair a bit more stiffly then is your usual relaxed mode, and your left leg is crossed over your right, an atypical pose for you. I have to conclude an injury to your leg is keeping you home today, and being hit in the leg by a pitched ball seems the most likely injury event to a non-sportsman like myself."

"As is often the case, Holmes, you are correct in your observations and conclusions. Although I hate to let my side down, I just can't make it to the pitch at Lord's today, despite it being a stone's throw from our door. If I were there, the pull to put on my whites and have a go would be too strong and, I feel, detrimental to the Gentlemen who were kind enough to invite me to play with them," I said.

"Your injury could not have come at a better time. I am in need of a sounding board, and you would do well with some country air and a ramble to reinvigorate your leg,"

"Sounds capital, Holmes. Where are we off to?"

"Hertford. County town for Hertfordshire. If you would be so kind as to reach for the timetable, we can plan our trip."

My military background did me proud, as within ninety minutes Holmes and I found ourselves settling into a first-class carriage that was pulling out of London's Liverpool Station. Holmes said it was to be a day trip, so nothing more was needed other than a Bradshaw.

The countryside often put Holmes in a philosophic mood, and today was no different. Although attached to the great metropolis by a thousand filaments, he longed for the clean air and solitude of the realms beyond. He often talked about buying a cottage somewhere, and as he gazed out the window, I was sure he was thinking about it again.

"How many pounds of honey per annum, Holmes?" I asked.

"Honey? Pounds per annum? My dear Watson, you are attempting to break into my thoughts as I have often done to you on occasion. Well done, well done indeed," replied Holmes.

"However, I will disappoint you and inform you that I was not thinking of my retirement cottage, but the mystery at hand."

"We have slightly over an hour in this carriage for me to give you an outline of the errand we are on. An hour to pass through the metropolis and into the pastoral setting of Hertfordshire's farms. Sadly, Watson, we are heading into dark matters, a far cry from Austen's *Pride and Prejudice*, set in this bucolic locale," said Holmes, gazing out the window.

"And what is it that whisks us out of the city and into rural England, Holmes?"

"A summons, Watson. A summons from Inspector Neal."

"I am not aware of that name."

"Possibly not. Neal is still young and putting in his time away from the city. He does have promise and shows enough intelligence to call me in when he is out of his depth. This is one such incident," said Holmes.

"Neal has a murder on his hands, Watson. A murder with no physical trauma, and the local doctor has said that his initial tests for poison have been inconclusive. This is why you are with me. You may see something medically that the local doctor has missed, and with your ever-growing knowledge of murders, thanks to my practice and our partnership, you may be considered an expert in your own right."

These were indeed high words of praise from Holmes. However, finding fault in another professional man's work and opinion is something I did not look forward to.

"The Thorntons have been a prominent family in the town since Elizabethan times, and their estate, Hartham House, at one time was the largest in the county. You may remember, Watson, that Queen Elizabeth spent time in Hertford when the Plague was on in London. It was the Thorntons who hosted her until Hertford Castle was ready for the Queen and her retinue. Today's family, of course, does not host royalty, but they still have cache and sway in the town, if not the county."

"And the murder, Holmes? Who has been murdered?"

"Always the man of action. Sir Evan Thornton is dead, Watson. He is the latest patriarch of the family and was found deceased in his bed this morning. He and his wife, Lady Elizabeth, have separate bedrooms, and it was Sir Evan's valet who found him. From the pained expression on his face, the state of his nightclothes, and the bed itself, it was instantly believed that Sir Evan did not die peacefully," said Holmes.

"And there are no suspects? No smoking gun?"

"No, there are no smoking guns, as you put it, Watson. After the body was found, the local doctor was immediately sent for. Neal tells me in a telegram that what this local practitioner found was so far out of the ordinary that he immediately thought of us. You for your medical background, and myself to see and find things which he cannot."

With that brief *précis*, we arrived at Hertford Station. We were immediately met by Inspector Neal when we alighted the train.

"So good of you to come on such short notice, Mr. Holmes," said Neal.

"Murder rarely finds a convenient time, Inspector."

"Quite so, quite so. Hartham House is just at the other end of town," said the inspector, issuing us into a carriage which was clearly marked as property of the local constabulary.

"As you instructed, Mr. Holmes, the body has not been moved. The rest of the house has also been left as it was when I arrived earlier this morning and began the investigation," said Neal.

"Tell us about the household. Who lives there, size of staff and the property itself," commanded Holmes.

"The primary concerns in the house are Mr. and Mrs. Thornton, of course, but also Mrs. Thornton's brother, who arrived a couple of months ago. He is here studying horticulture, and splits his time between the estate and a rental property in London. The household staff includes Sir Evan's valet, Michaels, who is the only staff who lives on the estate. He is much more than a valet and butler to Sir Evan. He assists in running the estate. There are a few other domestic staff who do not live in the house, as well as a full-time gardener. Lady Thornton is expecting us."

"What can you tell us about Sir Evan and his wife?" asked Holmes.

"Well, sir, they are generally well-liked in the town. They are the benefactors for various charities and events through the year, which brings them in contact with most of the town. They received their honorary titles just last year for the work they have done with the local poor. Lady Thornton has established three charities in the town, and her husband donated land and resources for people to grow their own produce. Despite their prominence, Sir Evan has never sought public office, and seems to spend most of his time managing the various businesses the family owns, puttering in his extensive gardens which are open to the public once a year, and attending various private functions through the summer months. Sir Evan was born in this house some forty years ago. His father was a bit of a queer duck, and had the boy schooled locally and not sent away as most of their class do," reported Neal.

"And Lady Elizabeth?"

"Almost the polar opposite, Mr. Holmes. Although also well-liked in town, she is not from here, and when I say 'here,' I mean to say England. Sir Evan took a two-year world-tour after his father died, and he arrived back on these shores a married man. Lady Elizabeth is actually an Elizabetta who grew up rich and privileged in Italy. She is a charming, warm woman who has captivated the local social scene and has turned more than a few heads. But here we are, and you can meet her momentarily for yourself."

We alighted from the carriage and were standing in front of a large three-storey block of a manor house. The door we were about to enter was set into the right front façade of the home. Its curved header was mimicked in all of the long windows on this, the ground floor of the home. I glanced about as we entered the portico and saw that the house stood on a large plot of land that was probably once a much larger estate.

We were greeted at the door by Michaels, the Thornton's valet and butler, who informed us we could wait in the library for Mrs. Thornton to come down and speak to us.

"Before we do that," said Holmes, "I would like to examine the body."

"Right this way, Mr. Holmes," replied Neal, leading us up the central stairs and into a well-appointed bedroom.

Sir Evan Thornton's body was on the bed, covered by a single sheet. Neal closed the door behind us and Holmes removed the temporary shroud.

Sir Evan's face was contorted in a paroxysm of agony. His knees were drawn up to his chest and his hands were clenched.

"Note the rigidity and the facial expression. This was not a natural death. What do you make of it, Watson?" asked Holmes.

I leaned over and looked into the corpse's eyes and mouth. The eyes were that of any dead man, and the mouth and odour from it were also no different. Many poisons leave traces or tell-tale signs in both locations, but in this case there was nothing. From a small mark on the arm it was clear that the local doctor had drawn blood to have it tested.

Holmes watched me as I made my examination of the body. As I rose and stepped away, he asked for my opinion.

"I would have to agree with the local doctor. At this point I would say poison or poisons unknown is the cause," I replied.

After this morbid examination, the three of us left the death room and walked downstairs and into the library.

The library was a typical one for a country estate. The room, which featured doors leading into the garden, was lined with book cases. A long table dominated one end of the room, while a large, heavy desk commanded respect at the other. As we waited, the ever-curious Holmes wandered the room, looking at the collection of rare and not-so-rare books.

"Mark my words, Neal. You can learn a lot about a man by the books he keeps, and even more by the books he reads," said Holmes, looking over the shelves near the desk.

Shortly afterwards, Michaels opened the door and Lady Thornton, dressed in full mourning, glided into the room, aided by a man who could only be her brother.

"Gentlemen, I am Lady Elizabetta Thornton, and this is my brother, Mario Conti," said our host as we introduced ourselves.

Lady Elizabetta was a raven-haired Italian beauty.

"I will do whatever I can to help you in your investigation. My husband's murderer must be found. Stop at nothing, the cost is immaterial," she said.

"Madam, I am here to find the truth, not a pay day," replied Holmes. "Can we begin with last night?"

"Certainly, Mr. Holmes," said Lady Elizabetta, sitting on the settee, while her brother stood resolutely behind her.

"My husband returned home late from the city. He often returns on the six p.m. train, but that night it was the 8:15. He was picked up at the station by Michaels. I saw my husband briefly and then retired for the evening. I know nothing more of his movements until the next morning when Michaels found him."

"Do you know who he saw while in the city?" asked Holmes.

"No sir, I do not. My husband kept the various business aspects of the estate very close to himself. He once told me the firm of lawyers he uses, or I should say used, but I have no idea what took him to London yesterday," answered Lady Elizabetta.

"Very succinct, Lady Thornton, thank you. Mr. Conti, did you see Sir Evan yesterday evening?"

"I did, indeed. In fact, I dined with him, which, no doubt, Michaels will confirm, since he served the meal. I was also in the city that day, doing some research at your British Museum. I arrived here about 7:45 and discovered that my brother-in-law had not yet returned but was expected soon, so I waited for him. We had some matters to discuss and I saw no reason to delay. I may as well tell you now, the conversation over dinner was a heated one, as I am sure the spying staff will report."

"And what was it that you were discussing?" asked Holmes.

"None of your concern, I can assure you."

"That is for me to decide. What matters did you discuss, heatedly, with the late Sir Evan?" repeated Holmes.

Conti glanced down at his seated sister; she looked up at him and nodded slightly, giving her permission to discuss what must have been a private subject its public airing.

"We were discussing a member of staff, and also my sister's return to Italy. The marriage has been less than she dreamt of, and she was looking for a split. We are staunch Catholics and revere the word from Rome. We know there will be no divorce, but a separation of thousands of miles will help the situation. Sir Evan would have nothing to do with the scheme and threatened to cut her off financially should she ever even attempt to leave England," said Conti.

"Surely your family fortune would be enough," said Holmes.

"The fortune is not what it once was, and our father, who is a strong nationalist, was very hurt when his only daughter left Italy to be with an English knight," replied Conti.

"You corroborate this, Lady Thornton?" asked Holmes.

"Yes, it is true, and it now looks bad for us, but it is true. I loved Evan when we met, and when we travelled together around Italy and the rest of the continent. He seemed to this young girl so worldly, so knowledgeable, I was swept off my feet. When we came to this house, he became a different person. He was so involved in the estate and the local community, he forgot about me and the life we had planned to share. He was more concerned with his house, the grounds, and the gardens, than he was with his new bride," said Lady Thornton.

"I told myself this would change. He would, as you say, come around. He didn't, and after five years of this marriage, I decided to leave him. By this time, my brother was here studying and I confided in him. We went to my husband as a united front, but were rebuffed and denied as if we were merely asking to redecorate a room," continued Lady Thornton.

Holmes looked over at Inspector Neal and said, "I would like to talk to the valet now."

"You have nothing more to ask us, Mr. Holmes?" asked Lady Thornton.

"Not at the moment. Your statements are clear and concise, and I do not want to keep you any longer than necessary. I am sure you have arrangements to make, and further questions can be asked later."

Lady Thornton and her brother left the room and Michaels was invited in. He soon confirmed the tone and content of the dinner conversation which Conti had disclosed.

"How long have you been with the family?" asked Holmes.

"Man and boy, Mr. Holmes. I started here in the stables when I was just a lad and my father was the game keeper. I went to school with Sir Evan, and also went with him as his valet when he was on his Grand Tour. The estate and Sir Evan has changed a lot over the years," reminisced Michaels. "The estate has gotten smaller, with outer parts being sold off or given away to the poor. Sir Evan expanded the garden and now wants to eat as much as he can from his own property. Did you know, Mr. Holmes, we grow four different types of carrots? And that's just a start of the variety of vegetables gown right here."

"Did Sir Evan actually do the gardening, or was that left up to staff?" asked Holmes.

"Oh no, sir. Sir Evan was in the garden most days during the season, and planning and reading about gardening through the winter. Those bookcases there," said Michaels, pointing to three glass-fronted cases near the large desk, "are full of books on the subject and his own journals and plan books. Mr. Conti was the same. Although they didn't agree on all topics, as you have heard, they certainly did when it came to matters of the soil and garden. I have been of assistance to both of them, although, of course, much more assistance to Sir Evan, having served him for so many years. I take some pride in being able to say there is not a bed, a tree or a plant on the grounds that I do not know, or have not had a hand in planting, pruning or shaping. "

"Thank you, Michaels. That will be all for now," said Holmes. It was just as Michaels was leaving the room that a local constable came in and handed Neal a sealed envelope.

"This will be the coroner's report, Mr. Holmes. I asked the office to send it to me, wherever I was."

"Excellent. It may prove to be interesting reading," said Holmes.

Neal sat at the desk, with Holmes and me standing over his shoulders. The report was one page and outlined Sir Evan's general health, age and other vitals. The final paragraph was the critical part for us. However, after each of us reading, the conclusions we were no further ahead.

"Well, Mr. Holmes. Death by poison unknown. Nothing much new here, I'm afraid," said Neal.

"On the contrary. It confirms our earlier suspicions, rules out other possibilities, and sets us on our track. Let us walk in the garden and think," replied Holmes.

Our forty-minute walk through the famed gardens was a quiet one. Holmes had brought along his briar-root pipe, a favourite of his for country walks. The two detectives walked together while I trailed behind them. The beds ranged from showy flowers, which I have not the faintest idea of what they are, to a large vegetable and herb patch, which featured items I was more familiar with. Several times Holmes stopped at a bed, examined a plant or two, and continued.

"Like the library, Neal, a man's hobbies can tell much about the person. In this case, I believe we can learn as much about his death as we can his life," said Holmes.

"Mr. Holmes, I know of your queer ways and obtuse remarks, but I am completely at sea if you think I can learn about who killed Sir Evan by a stroll around the garden," replied Neal.

"Like my friend Watson here, you see but you do not observe," said Holmes.

By this time, we had reached the front of the house again. Michaels was standing near the police brougham, and Conti was on the top step, examining a large ornamental planter.

"I am here at the behest of my sister, Mr. Holmes. Is there anything further you need from any of us?"

"Not at the moment, thank you," said Holmes as we approached the four-wheeler.

"I believe I have forgotten my walking stick in the garden," added Holmes. "I will just nip round and retrieve it, I will only be a moment," Holmes said as he hurried away.

Holmes returned a few minutes later without his stick.

"Age is a cruel master, Mr. Conti. I don't believe I had my stick with me at all today. Tricks of the mind," said Holmes, stepping into the brougham.

"Please let your sister know I will be in touch in a day or two. We will get to the bottom of this, be assured."

"What now, Mr. Holmes? I don't see that we are any further ahead in this murder investigation," asked Neal.

"On the contrary. We are near the end, I believe. It is back to the police station for you, and back to London for Watson and me. Can you meet us in at Baker Street in London for dinner tomorrow evening? I think by then, the fog shall lift and I will provide you with a solution to this very pretty little murder," said Holmes.

"Yes, of course. But what shall I do until then?" asked Neal.

"Whatever policemen in the country do. Except, I would advise you not to dine at Hartham House."

With that we drove back to the station and were in our Baker Street rooms before sunset.

"Before dinner, Watson, I would like to conduct a chemical experiment. You are welcome to assist me if you care to."

"Today's exertions and the meandering garden walk has not helped by injured knee at all. Also, your experiments often put up such foul smells I may not be down for dinner at all. However, for now I will retire to my room and rest," I replied, leaving our sitting room to Holmes's machinations.

When I awoke two hours later, I was pleasantly surprised with the clearness of the air. When I made my way down to our sitting room, Holmes sat amidst a scattering of papers, a satisfied look upon his face.

"Well, Holmes, you don't have to be a detective to see that you are pleased with something. However, from the air and lack of an acrid smell, I would suggest that you did not, after all, conduct any experiments."

"Quite the opposite," said Holmes. "I did, and they were a success. One cup of butter will never be the same, but this time the experiment was self-contained and proved my theory regarding the Thornton murder."

"Clearly he was murdered with poison, Holmes. However, how you could sit here and positively discover how or with what is beyond me," I replied.

155

"Not the biggest stretch for us, but a pretty little case in a pretty little corner of our country," said Holmes. "I do hope that Neal has fathomed his way through it better than you, Watson."

"So, you will not tell me who killed Sir Evan?"

"Not at the moment. You know my love for the dramatic. All will be revealed at dinner tomorrow when the good inspector joins us. Until then, Mrs. Hudson has prepared a full cold dinner for us, which we shouldn't put off much longer."

The next day was a long one for me. Not only was I anxiously awaiting Inspector Neal to arrive so we could get on with the explanation of the murder, but my knee had swollen due to the previous day's outings, and I read in the paper that The Gentlemen had lost the match, an outcome my superior batting prowess may have been able to avoid.

Time did pass, as it always does, and we soon heard a knock on our door. Inspector Neal was led into our room by our landlady. As Mrs. Hudson was about to leave, Holmes said, "We will now take that dinner you and I had discussed, Mrs. Hudson."

She closed the door, and the three of us stood around the cold fireplace.

"Well, Mr. Holmes. Here we are. I am no further ahead in the murder investigation, but I certainly hope you are."

"Murder, and especially poisonings, are nothing to discuss on an empty stomach. Once our dinner is laid out, and we are sitting enjoying Mrs. Hudson's repast, all shall be revealed," said Holmes.

While we were waiting for our landlady to set the table for the three of us and bring out a cornucopia of cold dishes for our dinner, we discussed the latest news from Scotland Yard. The trials and tribulations of the growing force was of interest to me, while Holmes seemed, of course, most keen on the C.I.D., or Criminal Investigations Division. After mulling its existence and structure, we were ready to sit down.

"Now, Inspector. Our landlady is not renowned for her cooking, but she is certainly more than adequate. Before we partake in the cold joint, I would like to bring your attention to the long serving dish with two squares of butter on it. Squares identical to these aided me in unravelling our Hertfordshire mystery."

"Really, Mr. Holmes? You have me at a complete loss," replied the inspector.

"Perhaps so. Allow me to recreate a small experiment I conducted here yesterday evening."

With that, Holmes gestured toward the long, glass-covered dish containing the two squares of butter. He then revealed two smaller glass dishes. Each of these, seemingly, had parsley in them, and I commented as much.

"You are correct, Watson. They do seem alike, and they do seem like parsley. Both of these samples I liberated from the garden at Hartham House yesterday when I returned for my mislaid walking stick."

"The sample on the right is the type of parsley found all too often on the side of plates in restaurants throughout the city and the country. The parsley on the left is something very different indeed," said Holmes.

Holmes then took a pair of pincers from his laboratory table and put a few springs of each in its corresponding square of butter.

"Now, gentlemen, I request from you nothing more than some patience," said Holmes.

With five minutes, the results of the experiment were clear. The parsley on the right pad of butter was just as Holmes had placed it. The one on the left, however, had sunk three-quarters of the way through the butter and would soon be resting on the bottom of the dish. The butter around that piece of parsley was melted and oozing into a puddle.

"Gentlemen, let me introduce to you the very rare, *petroselinum virdi mortem*, or Green-Leafed Death, as it is known in parts of northern Italy. It is particularly insidious, in that it initially tastes and acts like any other type of parsley. Once it mixes with food and other acids in the victim's stomach, however, death surely follows."

"But what is it, Holmes?" I asked.

"It is a distant relative of the common parsley plant, but one that has a long and checkered past. This is what Sir Evan died from, and this is why the coroner could not find it in any toxicology books. The plant is virtually unknown outside of a small area around Lake Como, and even there it is rare and hardly ever grown in a garden. As soon as the leaves are picked, the plant excretes a very toxic, acid-like sap. The few sprigs I brought back with me almost ate through the envelope in which I placed them," said Holmes.

"But how did you find this, Mr. Holmes?" stammered Neal.

"I found it because I was looking for it. When the coroner's report spoke of unknown poisons, and we were at an estate known for its gardens, my mind immediately linked the two. At that point, of course, I only had a suspicion, but that would soon be proven to be true."

"As we walked around the garden," continued Holmes, "I noticed that many of the beds thrived with a type of planting called 'companion gardening'. There were actually a few books on the subject in the library; the library I told you to pay attention to, Neal."

"During the walk, I noticed that a rose bed was fringed with parsley plants. The dark green of the parsley set off the delicate roses nicely, and the companion planting helps both thrive. In the vegetable beds, I found more parsley. However, there was one bed that had a slightly neglected look about it, despite it showing some signs of care. On closer inspection, I noticed that one parsley plant had a dead patch all around it. This is the plant I returned to and took a snippet of for my experiment."

"But who gave Sir Evan the poisonous parsley?" asked Neal.

"That we shall soon discover. If I am not mistaken, that is Mr. Conti I hear in our entrance way, coming to join us for dinner. Quickly now, Watson. Cover up the two butters and follow my lead."

Just then, Mr. Conti entered our sitting room. The three of us rose to greet our new guest.

"I came as requested, Mr. Holmes, although I do regret leaving my sister at such a time."

"And I thank you for your indulgence, sir. We were just about to sit down for dinner, if you would care to join us. Michaels was kind enough to send us a fresh-produce package," said Holmes, striding back to the table.

"Here we have some fresh carrots and beets from the estate's garden, which will go lovely with this parsley butter," said Holmes lifting the covers off the two squares of butter.

"Won't you join us?" asked Holmes, taking a bread roll from a heap of them on the table and slathering some of the tainted butter on it.

Conti stared at the two butters and stammered, "These items came from the Chequers Estate?"

"Indeed. In addition to the telegram I sent to you to come here this evening, I sent one to Michaels to let him know how we were progressing, and he was kind enough to send this fine selection back."

Conti rushed over to Holmes, snatched the dinner roll out of his hand and placed the covers back on the exposed dishes.

"You mustn't eat any of this," he declared.

"Come, come, I am sure it is all fine, is it not?" replied Holmes.

"No, Mr. Holmes, I assure you it is not!" replied Conti. "This is poison and was meant for you," he said, pointing to the parsley that had melted through the butter.

"Time to tell your tale, Mr. Conti. Be warned, however, Neal here will take down a complete recording of that tale, and his notes may be used in court."

"That is quite alright. It began about eighteen months ago when I received a letter from my sister. It was clear she was no longer happy with her husband, her situation, and her future. He never raised a hand to her, Mr. Holmes, but he abused and belittled her in a hundred different ways. She wanted out and away from him."

158

"I had been planning on a visit before, but that letter sealed my plans. I was in Hertfordshire within two weeks. I used my interest in horticulture and the chance to study at the British Museum and Sir Evan's own library as a guise for the trip and extended stay. "

"My sister and I decided we would make a united front and approach her husband about a separation. We did, one Saturday morning a month ago. He did not take it lightly. He flew into a rage and railed at us. For a man who is often reserved, he yelled and went on, loud enough and long enough for there to be no doubt among any of the staff as to what we were discussing. It was clear that my wife's husband was not going to let her leave. He said they could lead independent lives under the same roof, but that was as far as he would allow."

"We left Sir Evan in the library. As we did, Michaels went in. He seemed to always be lurking somewhere obvious in the house."

"After that initial discussion, if you can call it one, Sir Evan wouldn't speak to me except on the subject of horticulture. On that point we talked often and freely. If I were to bring the subject of my sister into the conversation, he would either put an end to the conversation, or rage at me for bringing up a closed subject."

"While I was in the garden one day, I noticed this plant," continued Conti. "Where I come from it is a known poison, but it is far from common. Anyone with an interest in plants, however, will have come across it and know its evil legacy. I knew that neither I nor Sir Evan planted it. Sir Evan had been far too busy with other aspects of the estate, and I would never grow something so deadly in an open garden. It is not an easy plant to remove, Mr. Holmes, or I would have pulled it from the ground then and there. The leaves, as you know, are very dangerous and must be handled correctly. I made a mental note to return with proper gloves and a spade to remove it from the garden and burn it."

"Later that day," continued Conti "I returned to the bed, but before I got there, I saw Michaels tending it. It was he who had planted the Green Death; I knew then that I was dealing with a very serious-minded man and refrained from approaching him. A man who grows poisons in the open is not to be lightly dealt with. I approached Sir Evan about the matter that evening, and he was dead by morning. Mr. Holmes, Michaels murdered his employer and has tried to do the same to you!"

"Calm yourself, Mr. Conti. I know. In addition to the telegram that I sent to yourself to join us, I took the liberty of sending another to Inspector Neal's office with instructions to arrest Michaels. By now, he should be making himself at home in a holding cell in the Hertford police station."

With that, Holmes removed the tainted parsley from the table and invited our guests to dine with us.

"But how did you know it was Michaels?" asked Neal.

"My first suspicions naturally fell on yourself, Mr. Conti. However, when I saw the dead patch around the suspected poison, I realized it couldn't be you. You would be aware of what plants can co-exist with the Green Death and would have been able to hide it better."

"I also surmised that when you and Sir Evan were discussing a member of such a small staff, it may have been Michaels. I also noticed that Michaels kept very close at hand when we were questioning Lady Elizabeth. It seemed more than usual staff curiosity. When Michaels entered and Lady Elizabeth left, the look in his eyes was unmistakable. He is in love with your sister, Mr. Conti. He was angered that Sir Evan would not allow her her freedom. I believe he had seeds for this plant from when he visited Italy with Sir Evan years ago. Why he kept it all this time is difficult to say. A look at the history of this plant does show that more than one staff member has murdered their employer with it. Maybe he found the history of it before and kept it in the back of his mind. It is not always an easy thing to plumb the depths of the mind of a murderer."

"Another murderer brought to heel," I said to Holmes later that evening, after our guests had departed. "Not often you bring down a villain by watching parsley sink in butter."

"Very true, Watson. This may be a fine study for your chronicles. The parsley not only brought down a murderer, but I was also able to garnish a fine fee from Lady Elizabeth," added Holmes with a chuckle.

The Strange Case of the Violin Savant

by GC Rosenquist

The language of music can solve crime, if one only listens.

As I sat in my chair by the fire enjoying my evening cheroot, I watched Holmes with an intense fascination, studying his every move as he quietly set up the cherrywood music stand in front of the parlour window in our flat in Baker Street.

The window behind stood black and featureless, while outside in the cool November night, spackles of rain tapped out time on the glass like a metronome.

Holmes, with the rapt single-mindedness he so often demonstrated in the past during his most difficult cases, grabbed up a stack of sheet music from a nearby table and placed it on the stand. Then he moved an oil lamp from one area of the table to another, so that it shined on the pages without giving shadow. Satisfied, he reached down and lifted his Stradivarius out of its case with such care it might have been a living thing. He took the bow up in his other hand then gently placed the violin under his chin.

He stood there a moment frozen in time, his eyes closed, his mouth clenched so tightly it was nothing more than a small slit, his right arm out front and high but bent at the elbow, the violin bow motionless in his hand, suspended above the strings like a storm cloud ready to burst. I waited expectantly for that first delicate but commanding touch of horsehair upon catgut.

Then Holmes took in a deep breath, lowered the bow, and she sang. Her voice cut through the silence of the room like a bolt of lightning. Rising up through the octaves, she trilled with laughter and joy, electrifying the molecules in the air with bright white light. Then her mood suddenly changed, her voice dropped like a falling star, spinning down into the murky depths, wailing mournfully. The room suddenly grew dim, the air thick and heavy with foreboding. After a tear here and a sob there, she finally recovered, coming up out of the darkness, howling like a banshee, defiant and victorious.

I'd never heard Holmes play with such passion before. He seemed possessed by the music, at one with the profound tragedy of its story, and it brought to my recollection the recent case of young master Eric

161

Leighton, whose way of playing the violin was so powerful, so unearthly, it provoked murder . . . .

It was a mild late summer evening in London as I was making my way back to Baker Street after completing a house call when a cab rolled up to me and stopped. The side door opened and out leaned Holmes's head. "Get in, Watson," he said. "We're needed."

Without a moment's hesitation, I did as he ordered and sat down next to him. "Where are we going?" I asked.

He handed me a note from Inspector Lestrade of Scotland Yard. I read it in silence.

Good Evening, Mr. Holmes,

Scotland Yard once again has urgent need of your skills. Please meet me at the Leighton Estate in Watford immediately. Young Master Eric has disappeared.

Regards,
Lestrade

"It's happened again!" I ejaculated, folded the missive, and handed it back to Holmes.

"I'm afraid so, Watson," Holmes said. "First, a month ago, both of his parents go missing, now the boy. Something is amiss in Watford, but I promise you that we shall get to the bottom of it this time."

As the cab hurried through the streets of London, heading north for the country, I tried to remember everything I could about the Leighton family, especially the boy, Eric. He was a pure savant, genius in everything concerning the violin. He could read or hear a piece of music once and play it back with perfect recall. His own compositions were so sophisticated they were nearly impossible for other violinists to play. He'd played his first private recital at four years of age, completed a command performance for the Queen at Earl's Court at five, and had since locked in a lucrative contract for five performances a week at the Garrick Theatre on Guilford Street. The boy, nine years old now, was a curiosity and was celebrated across Britain, becoming one of its wealthiest citizens. Indeed, Holmes and I had attended one of the boy's performances back in the spring and he was magnificent. I found myself moved to tears half a dozen times.

But as is so often the case with savants, their genius came at a terrible cost. He was mortally shy and completely incapable of speaking

162

even a single word. It seemed only Conrad Dyson, his violin instructor, knew how to communicate with him on the most rudimentary level – through music. And then the boy's parents mysteriously disappeared back in August, leaving a note for authorities, claiming they couldn't handle the difficulties of raising such a special child so they were going abroad, away from all the excitement and demands the boy's genius manufactured. The note went on to say they thought it best to leave the boy in the hands of a person who knew how to deal with a savant – Conrad Dyson.

Suspicious? Yes, but the note was proven to be written in the mother's hand and since authorities couldn't locate the parents, either in America or the Continent, to confirm the contents of the letter, nothing legally could be done about it.

This infuriated Holmes, who knew foul play had occurred but couldn't prove it. It had taken the heavy hand of Commissioner Carruthers of Scotland Yard to force Holmes to stand down from any further investigation. The case went cold quickly, but with this disturbing new event, I knew my compatriot would warm it up again, this time with the blessing of Scotland Yard.

When we arrived at Leighton Manor, it was well after dark had fallen. The grounds, as well as the exterior of the monolithic seventeenth century stone dwelling, were lit by a neat, continuous line of gas lamps that surrounded the perimeter of the mansion like an army guarding a King. This was what all that new money the boy had earned had bought him. He would have done better to purchase a real army.

As Holmes and I got out of the cab, we were met on the drive by a well-dressed butler, a man over six feet tall, with a face seemingly carved out of living granite. All the lines in his face were sharp and angular, his eyes were deeply set in two cavernous pits that were constantly hidden in shadow, his mouth and chin were stern and unmoving. I had the feeling that if I'd seen the man stub his toe, no evidence of the incident would appear anywhere on his face. He held a blazing lamp high in his left hand.

Holmes handed the man Lestrade's note. After a short perusal the big man nodded.

"My name is Killkenny, sir," the butler said. An unfortunate name, I thought. "Everyone is in young master Eric's rehearsal parlour waiting for you. Please follow me."

As we followed Killkenny up the steps and into the mansion, I listened as Holmes, unbeknownst to the butler, subtly began his first interview.

163

"Killkenny, I hadn't seen you here a month ago when we first investigated the disappearance of the Leightons. A man named Wyckoff was in your position. Where did he go?"

"I don't rightly know, sir," Killkenny replied, his voice monotone and calm. I didn't like it at all. He continued. "Mr. Dyson hired me on two weeks ago. I'm not aware of anyone named Wyckoff."

"Two weeks, you say? So, you know the boy?"

"Yes, sir."

"Are you close with him?"

"Not particularly, sir. My duties center mostly on running the household. It's Mr. Dyson who mainly interacts with young master Eric."

"I see. So you hadn't met Mr. and Mrs. Leighton before their disappearance?"

"No, sir."

"Were you aware of the suspicious circumstances surrounding their disappearance?"

"I was told that they had left young master Eric in Mr. Dyson's care and went abroad. All this about a suspicious disappearance is news to me. I fully expect Mr. and Mrs. Leighton to return to the manor in proper health."

"Did the boy share your optimism, Killkenny?"

"I wouldn't know what young master Eric thinks, sir. He is an enigma to me. I don't understand his genius at all."

"Oh, yes, I'd forgotten, Killkenny. You said earlier that you aren't particularly close to the boy, is that right?"

We came to a pair of huge, closed, elaborately gilded doors. I could hear angry men's muffled voices rising and falling in the chamber beyond them. The big man stopped, turned and faced Holmes. Without the least bit of emotion, he said, "I have already answered that question, sir."

Holmes smiled then nodded. "And so you did, Killkenny. Shall we go in?"

As Holmes and I stepped into the dimly lit room, we saw three men standing in front of a massive fireplace arguing. Their faces were red and pinched, and so completely involved in their grievances they didn't notice our presence. Lestrade was between them, trying to keep them separated with outstretched arms.

Two of the men we'd already become acquainted with from interviews taken when Mr. and Mrs. Leighton first disappeared. The first of the two men was Alger Archer, owner of the Garrick Theatre, where young master Eric fulfilled his contract. He was a short, pudgy man, and wore a dark green suit that desperately needed to be let out in certain places. He was entirely bald except for a pair of slate-colored sideburns that fanned out from his face like extended pigeon wings. The features of his face were delicate and rounded and seemed too small in relation to the large size of his head. It looked as if his head had continued to grow after puberty but his face failed to follow suit.

The other man Holmes and I knew was Conrad Dyson, the boy's violin instructor, and now guardian. He was as tall as Killkenny but had a body reminiscent of a whooping crane – long legs with knobby knees, thin lanky arms, hands with unnaturally long fingers. His face was compact, lacking a chin, but his beak of a nose more than made up for that. Even when he moved, it was distinctly birdlike.

The third man, unfamiliar to Holmes and me, was of medium build. He wore a gray suit jacket that went all the way down to his shoes, and a neatly folded white handkerchief stuck up out of the breast pocket, pressed and as perfectly smooth as his suit coat. A thick beard of blazing red hair lined the man's aged face, slivers of silver woven through the hairs flashing in the lamp light whenever he moved his chin. His eyebrows were the same fiery red, framing a pair of clear green eyes that nearly popped out as he shouted down the other two men. He wore a tall black top hat which lent him an aura of dignity.

Holmes and I watched the spectacle. The room was large, spacious, and highly decorated with gold leaf wallpaper, wood floors covered with expensive Middle eastern rugs, and a crystal chandelier hung from the ceiling that, when fully lit, would look as if the sun was exploding inside the room. A pair of French doors against the back wall were closed, the keys still dangling out from the keyhole. An oak music stand stood in front of the doors, stacked with penciled-in music sheets, and at its feet was an open, empty violin case. A fireplace as tall as a person stood against the north wall. On the mantel were seven empty wine glasses, lined up side-by-side. A strange place to store your wine glasses, I thought.

Lestrade finally saw us and made our presence known to the other men. They silenced their debate immediately.

"Thank heavens you've arrived, Mr. Holmes," Lestrade said through a relieved sigh. "A few moments more and I would've arrested the lot of them."

"I appreciate your patience in the matter, Detective Inspector," Holmes said as he approached the men. He greeted Dyson and Archer with a few shallow-pumped handshakes, then took the red haired man's hand. "I'm Sherlock Holmes – "

165

"I know who you are, Mr. Holmes," the man abruptly interrupted as he took his hat off and bowed slightly. "My name is Bartholomew Oxtoby."

"And what is your association with these two men?" Holmes motioned at Dyson and Archer as he said this.

"An unhealthy one at the moment, Mr. Holmes," Oxtoby replied. "I own the New Britain Performing Arts Theatre."

"On Charterhouse Street?"

"The very one."

"That's a few blocks from the Garrick. May I assume there is a bit of competitive blood being spilt here?"

"More than that, Mr. Holmes," Oxtoby said. "They accuse me of kidnapping the boy! I came over here to have it out with them before I involve the courts. My good name is at stake!"

"Good name? Bah!" Archer spat. "You've been trying to steal young master Eric away from me for years. Well, you finally did it – by kidnapping him!"

Oxtoby's green eyes popped out again and his face flashed red. "My representative will peel your skin like an onion in court, Archer! Your lies won't stand up against a barrister's questioning!"

"Is this true, Mr. Oxtoby?" Holmes interrupted. "Have you been trying to steal the boy away from the Garrick Theatre?"

"Of course I have!" Oxtoby replied, his temper still white hot. His red hair was no lie. "The boy is overworked and treated like a stable mule. More than once his parents came to me, pleading for me to buy out his contract from Archer, but Archer refused to sell, even at one-hundred percent profit."

"There's nothing that says I have to sell his contract to you or anyone else, Oxtoby," Archer interjected. "He's my legal property for five more years."

"You talk of the boy like he's a piece of furniture!" Oxtoby bellowed. "It's outrageous! He's a human being!"

I noticed that Conrad Dyson stood in the background, his mouth locked shut like a bear trap. Holmes noticed it too.

"Mr. Dyson," Holmes began. "Were you aware of this plotting between Mr. and Mrs. Leighton and Mr. Oxtoby?"

Dyson's eyelids fluttered like moth wings as he answered. "Yes, I was, Mr. Holmes. They asked my opinion in the matter a few weeks before they went abroad."

"And what did you tell them?"

"That I thought it best to fulfill the remaining years of the contract out. Then, if they still felt the same about it, make the change – sign with Oxtoby."

"Did you fear they might change you as well?"

Dyson's bird face went pale. "Now wait a minute, Mr. Holmes, I'm the only person in Britain young master Eric trusts. I've been with him since the beginning. Mr. and Mrs. Leighton would never – "

"Mr. Oxtoby," Holmes interrupted. "In your negotiations with the Leightons, did they include anything about Mr. Dyson's services being carried on while under contract with you?"

"Never, Mr. Holmes," Oxtoby snarled. "It was understood that I would tutor the boy, give him my undivided attention."

"Yes, all the while filling your seats and swimming in the windfall of treasure that was sure to come your way!" Archer shouted.

"Hmm," Holmes mused as he rubbed his chin, his eyes closed in thought. "So you see, gentlemen," he said. "The three of you have perfect motives for kidnaping the boy – all of them rooted in greed."

"I love the boy!" Dyson exclaimed.

"When was the last time you saw him?"

"Last night. I put him to bed myself. When I awoke this morning, he was gone."

"Where's your room in relation to the boy's?"

"Across the hall."

"And you heard nothing during the night?"

"Nothing, Mr. Holmes. Nothing!" Tears began flowing out of Dyson's eyes. Whether they were real or not I couldn't judge. He was either very clever or genuinely upset.

"What happened to Wyckoff, the butler?"

Dyson composed himself enough to answer. "A few days after Mr. and Mrs. Leighton went abroad, he informed me he was leaving the estate's employment."

"Did he give a reason why?"

"None, Mr. Holmes. But after all the rigorous questioning and chaos generated by you and Scotland Yard during your initial investigation, I assumed he'd found other – quieter – employment elsewhere."

"And you, Mr. Archer?" Holmes asked. "When did you see the boy last?"

"At his last performance in the Garrick, two nights ago."

"Mr. Oxtoby?"

"Not since his parents disappeared."

Holmes, as he listened to their responses, made his way across the room to the music stand. He paged through the sheet music, then knelt

167

down next to the empty violin case. He stared at it a moment and stood up again. Lestrade and I exchanged quick glances, knowing Holmes was onto something. Holmes turned and faced the three men, his hands clasped behind his back.

"Gentlemen," he began. "You may be guilty of greed, but not of kidnapping the boy."

"Are you mad, Holmes?" Archer muttered. "Of course Oxtoby here kidnapped the boy, and he had good reason. He stood to make hundreds of thousands of pounds!"

"Would that be the same amount you're currently making off the boy, Mr. Archer?"

That shut the tiny fat man up.

Holmes shook his head. "No. It's clear to me after seeing the evidence that young master Eric ran away. The real questions are why and where to?"

"Ran away?" Dyson asked, his hands up. "That's impossible! Young master Eric would never do such a thing. He's not capable of it."

"You underestimate the boy, Dyson," Holmes said. "He's smarter and more aware of things going on around him than you realize."

"How can you possibly know that, Mr. Holmes? You've never personally met him."

"Look for yourself," Holmes said as he pointed at the French doors. "No evidence of break in here or anywhere else on the grounds." He pointed at the empty violin case. "And the boy's violin, a rare, priceless 16th century Amati, is missing."

"Perhaps the boy's kidnapper, realizing how much it was worth, took it with him. Perhaps he plans to sell it on the black market," Archer reasoned.

"Ridiculous, Mr. Archer," Holmes said, almost laughing. "Something like an original Amati violin suddenly appears in the black market, flags go up, police are brought in. Black marketers don't like that. The violin would be useless to them. The boy took it with him. For proof of what I say, gentlemen, come have a look for yourself."

The three men ambled over and looked into the violin case.

"You see it?"

Only Dyson answered. "Yes, Mr. Holmes."

"Please tell the others what you see, or should I say, don't see."

Dyson sighed so loudly it almost became a whistle, then he looked up at Archer and Oxtoby. "The bow . . . it's missing," he said.

"Exactly," Holmes said. "What interest would a kidnapper have for a bow? Absolutely none, but it's of vital importance to someone who plays the violin. That's why it's missing. The boy took that with him also."

"So, young master Eric ran away, taking his violin and bow with him," Dyson repeated, sounding almost relieved. "But that's wonderful. He's not in danger."

"Oh, he's very much in danger, Dyson," Holmes said. "I suspect the special way his brain works is strictly centered on music. Am I correct, Dyson?"

"Yes, Mr. Holmes. In fact, the only way he communicates with me is by music, either written or played. The way he plays a note, for example, lets me know what he wants or doesn't want, or if he's hungry, thirsty or sleepy."

"Like these compositions?" Holmes asked as he swept the sheet music off the stand and held them out. "Are they written by young master Eric?"

Dyson went over, took the pages from Holmes and fanned through them. "Yes, Mr. Holmes, that's his handwriting. And these compositions are new."

"So, realizing that his mind only relates to things concerning music, he wouldn't have thought to bring food and water with him wherever he went?"

This idea struck Dyson like an earthquake. His eyes grew large, his face went pale again. "Oh, dear, Mr. Holmes! You're right. He's like an infant that way."

"We'll have to find him before he starves to death or dies of thirst," Holmes suggested.

"Call out the bloodhounds!" Dyson panicked. "Get every constable in Scotland Yard on the job, search every field, wood, river, cave, home – before it's too late!"

"We could do that," Holmes said taking the sheets from Dyson. "Or I could decipher this sheet music the boy left behind."

"What does that sheet music have to do with the boy running away?" Archer asked.

"Everything, Mr. Archer," Holmes replied.

"But, Mr. Holmes," Dyson said. "Those compositions are unlike anything I've ever seen young master Eric write before. Much more sophisticated. They made no sense to me at all."

"Because they're maps, Mr. Dyson. Musical maps!"

Back in the privacy of our Baker Street flat, Holmes and I worked diligently on deciphering the music maps hidden in young master Eric's compositions. Lestrade gave us until morning to decipher the sheets, and then we'd have to return them to Scotland Yard where, even now, they were organizing search parties to find the boy.

Presently, we'd gone through two pots of tea and I was boiling another when Holmes called me over where the sheet music was spread out across the table. He had a pipe in his mouth and a magnifying glass in his hand.

"See here, Watson," he said, leaning over the glass like a hunchbacked monk reading a scroll. "There are two separate compositions here."

"How can you tell?" I asked, inspecting the pages myself but without the benefit of the glass.

Holmes pointed at one of the pages. "This first composition is only one page in length. See the Coda mark at the bottom of the last measure?"

"I do, Holmes," I said, remembering some of what I learned from piano lessons during my childhood. "But there's only one note throughout the entire thing – a high 'A' on a ledger line above the staff."

"Correct, Watson, all of them joined by a slur signature, which means we are to play them in one breath, forming a single musical phrase. And the *Fortississimo* above the notes mean we are to play it as loud as we can."

"What does that '*D.C.*' in front of the Coda mean?"

"*Da capo*, or to *repeat from the beginning*."

"Very curious," I said. "What are all those '*N*'s' above the bars?"

"I believe it means '*North*'," Holmes said. "They're on the second composition as well, along with '*E*'s' and '*W*'s', meaning '*East*' and '*West*.'"

"Direction prompts," I said.

"Quite right, Watson. I'm impressed."

I counted out the pages of the second composition, ending at thirty-three. But most of the pages were riddled with single '*G*' notes played *Pizzicato*, or by plucking the violin strings along the measure in four-four time. Then, on the last three pages, the staffs broke into two lines, each in treble clef, which meant two violinists were playing at the same time. Or was one playing and the other responding, like a conversation? Strange. I'd never seen anything like it before.

It was all too much for my meager detecting skills, so after I took the tea pot off the burner and filled Holmes's cup, I retired to bed, knowing my compatriot would burn the lamp oil all night trying to decipher young master Eric's map.

It was near dawn when I was awoken by the unmistakable violent poundings of an altercation going on in the parlour. I threw my robe on, ripped the door open, and ran out just in time to see Holmes lying on the floor rubbing his head and the swift shadow of a man running out through the open door of our flat. Heavy feet thundered down the stairs as the intruder made a break for it.

"Holmes! Are you all right?" I asked as I knelt next to him.

"Yes – yes, I think so. He took the compositions, Watson."

Realizing that sheet music was our only hope for finding young master Eric Leighton, I jumped to my feet to give chase but Holmes grabbed my arm.

"No! Stay put, Watson. It's fine," he said as I helped him to his feet.

"But, Holmes!" I protested. "He's run off with – "

"I suspected something like this would happen, Watson, so I took the precaution of copying the compositions down to the last detail. I was just finishing up when the assailant burst into the room, knocked me over, and stole the originals."

I should have known Holmes was a step ahead of everyone else.

"But who was he? Did you get a good look?"

"Unfortunately no, Watson," he replied as he sat down at the table. "He was wearing a black mask. But I have a suspicion. We'll wait a few hours until we hear from Scotland Yard."

"Concerning what, Holmes?"

"What else, my dear Watson? Murder."

And hear from Scotland Yard we did.

At nine, Lestrade sent a cab for us, and we were taken to an alley a few blocks from our flat. It was a warm but drizzling morning with puddles already filling in everywhere we stepped. Constables had the entrance to the alleyway cordoned off. Lestrade met us there and let us through.

"We received word of this about a half hour ago, Mr. Holmes," he said as he led us down the alleyway. "When I saw who it was I knew you'd want to see him for yourself. He's been dead approximately three to four hours."

"Which puts time of death just before dawn," Holmes added.

"The same time as our assailant," I said.

"Assailant?" Lestrade asked, his eyebrows went up like two birds taking flight.

"Yes, Inspector," Holmes said. "We had a break-in at Baker Street. The thief stole young master Eric Leighton's original compositions right off my table. Tell me, was anything found on the corpse?"

"Nothing, Mr. Holmes. Not even a wallet."

"How was he killed?"

"Stabbed once in the lower back and once in the abdomen. No sign of the weapon anywhere."

We came to where the corpse lay, dressed all in black, its arms and legs still grotesquely deformed from the effects of rigor. The black mask Holmes had spoken about earlier had been pulled off and lay next to the body.

"Yes," Holmes said, staring down into the face of the dead man. "Just as I had suspected."

I leaned over and had a look for myself. "Why, that's Wyckoff," I said, nearly breathless. "The original butler, missing from Leighton Manor!"

Finding nothing of consequence on Wyckoff's body, and deriving no clues from the bleak alley surroundings, Holmes told Lestrade to once again assemble Archer, Dyson and Bartholomew in young master Eric Leighton's rehearsal parlour that evening. Everything would be cleared up for Scotland Yard in the matter of both Mr. and Mrs. Leighton's and young master Eric's disappearance once and for all.

I waited the rest of the day at Baker Street, ruminating over that confounding sheet music, while Holmes went off to the Public Records Office to do some research. When he returned, just before dusk, he had a sparkle in his eyes and a confident grin on his face.

"Come, Watson," he said, as he grabbed his violin case. "Take up those compositions I copied and bring them with you, or would you miss my first public performance?"

Flabbergasted at the prospect of such a thing, I nearly knocked the table over in my exuberance.

"At once, Holmes!" I said. "At once!"

The last one to arrive in young master Eric's rehearsal parlour was Bartholomew Oxtoby. Killkenny escorted him in, and he took his place next to Dyson and Archer in front of the giant fireplace with the seven wine glasses on the mantel, which was unlit due to the very warm late summer weather.

"Honestly, Holmes," Oxtoby started, removing his hat and running his hand through his fiery red hair. "I don't know why I have to be involved in all of this nonsense. The only thing I'm guilty of is thinking of young master Eric's best interests."

Holmes, standing in front of the music stand, nodded. "This will be over very soon, Mr. Oxtoby," he said. "I appreciate your cooperation. Killkenny, please lock the door."

Detective Inspector Lestrade, two young constables, and I were standing near the French doors, watching with great interest the drama Holmes was staging. The copied pages of young master Eric's compositions were sitting upright on the music stand for everyone to see. Holmes's violin case sat open on a nearby table, his Stradivarius shined under the bright, constant sunlight provided by the chandelier above.

Once Killkenny took his place near the others, Holmes began.

"Gentlemen. Early this morning I suffered an insulting attack in the sitting room of my flat in Baker Street. The assailant burst through my door, knocked me down, and stole young master Eric's original compositions, the ones I took upon myself to decipher."

Dyson, Archer and Oxtoby traded surprised glances. Then Dyson pointed at the music stand. "What are those?"

"Transcripts. What the assailant didn't know was that I had spent most of the night copying the compositions down, perfectly, to the last musical signature, in case something of that nature happened."

"Brilliant thinking, Holmes," Archer said, his big gray sideburns waved slightly when he talked.

"A few hours later, I was contacted by Detective Inspector Lestrade and shown the corpse of the assailant, lying in a rain-drenched alley a few blocks from my flat. He was stabbed in the lower back and abdomen."

"Ghastly, Holmes!" Oxtoby exclaimed. "Who was he?"

"Wyckoff, the previous butler employed here, before Killkenny."

The only one who didn't betray any emotion was Killkenny. I thought this very suspicious.

"But, why – " Dyson started, but Holmes cut him off.

"We'll return to Wyckoff later," Holmes said. "For now, let's concentrate on young master Eric's musical maps."

"You've deciphered them, then?" Archer asked.

"I believe so. The trick was to think like a nine year-old violin savant desperate to communicate with someone, anyone, in the only way he knew how."

The men stood there listening to Holmes, in the process they'd forgotten how to breathe.

Holmes reached down and picked up the Stradivarius and the bow. With the bow he pointed at the sheet music on the stand. "There are two compositions. The first is one page in length and contains a single sustained note to be played very loudly. The second composition is

173

thirty-three pages in length and contains, for the most part, a confusing mish-mash of string pluckings, ending with three pages of double grand staffs where it looks as if two violinists are trading responses."

"I've never heard of such a thing," Dyson said, and the three of them moved closer to the music stand to see for themselves what Holmes spoke of.

"Nevertheless, it's all there," Holmes countered. "The boy was trying to tell us something. Or rather, he was trying to show us something. You see, above every measure is a single letter. The first composition has only one, an 'N', meaning north. Killkenny! Has this music stand been moved since the boy ran off?"

"Not an inch, sir."

"Good, because the boy meant for the location of this music stand to be the starting point – the place where the two maps begin. From this very spot, Eric's compositions should lead us to two separate, important locations."

"But to where exactly? And why?" Archer asked.

"Let's find out," Holmes said and brought the Stradivarius up to his chin. "If you gentlemen will stand back and give me some room, I'll demonstrate how clever young master Eric is."

The men stepped back. My heart was jackhammering with the excitement.

"Now, the first composition tells me I should be facing north from this location when I play the sustained note. A high 'A.'" Holmes turned, faced north, and he was staring straight at the giant fireplace with the seven wine glasses on the mantel. Holmes brought the bow down upon the violin string, took a slight breath then gave a long, slow upward stroke. The note filled the air of the room completely, it was like a long, slow blade cutting across a piece of glass. Holmes brought his arm forward, skillfully completing the downward stroke without interrupting the note, then forward again, the note singing, crying with deafening passion.

But there was something audible just underneath the crying, a distinct ringing an octave higher, and the harder, the louder Holmes played the 'A' note, the higher and louder the ringing became. All of us in the room heard it and our attention was brought to the fireplace, the place where the ringing seemed to be coming from.

Holmes played the last measure as hard as he could then stopped, lifted the bow from the string – yet the music played on! To our amazement, we listened as the seven wine glasses on top of the fireplace mantel rang in tandem. Stepping closer to the mantel, I could see how the edges of the wine glasses were blurred with vibration as they cried. After a few seconds, the ringing faded and a stunned silence fell over the room.

"Remarkable!" Exclaimed Holmes.

"Dyson!" Holmes called as he placed his Stradivarius back into the case. "Who put those wine glasses up there on the mantel?"

Dyson, still staring at the wine glasses in awe, replied. "Young master Eric did, Mr. Holmes. The night he disappeared. I didn't think anything of it. I just thought it was something he fancied for the moment. His mind works that way sometimes . . . I didn't think – "

"Lucky for us, no one did," Holmes interrupted. "Or those glasses would have been taken down. The boy knew that a high '*A*' played a certain way would create sound waves that would affect the audible frequency of those particular wine glasses, causing them to vibrate and sing. Using sound to create sound – just remarkable!"

"But what does it mean?" Oxtoby asked.

"I should think that would be obvious," Holmes said, walking over to the fireplace. "The boy led us here for some reason." He put his hands on the mantel and slid them across, feeling for something. Then he leaned forward and inspected the bricks that made up the sides of the fireplace. "Ah! Here we are!" He pulled at a corner brick, it opened out like a door on a hinge, there was a thick cable attached to it.

The floor rumbled, and something thumped in the wall behind the fireplace. Then the interior wall of the fireplace went up, revealing a dark, stone-walled hallway large enough for a person to walk through.

"A secret passage!" Oxtoby exclaimed.

"Gads, Holmes!" Lestrade ejaculated. "You never cease to amaze me!"

"Thank you, Inspector."

"But where does it lead?" Dyson asked.

"The answers to all your questions are in there," Holmes said. Then he grabbed an oil lamp from a nearby table and motioned towards the passageway. "Shall we?"

Lestrade and I took up lamps of our own and brought up the rear of the party, with the two constables following closely behind. After thirty feet, the passage turned ninety degrees to the west, continued on for another twenty feet then opened up into a large cavernous chamber, cobwebs dangling like dusty tree branches from the ceiling.

Mixed in with the scent of dirt and old, stale wood smoke was the unmistakable hint of death. I feared what our lamps would uncover in there.

"Oh, Lord!" Dyson suddenly screamed out and turned his face away, his long hands covering his bird face.

On the floor, lying next to each other, were two bodies, one male, the other female. Their skeletal forms, still covered with patches of desiccated flesh and hair in some places, were dressed in high class eveningwear. The female was missing one of her shoes. They were lying face up with their hands tied behind their backs, their horrible, skeleton mouths were open, as if screaming. The clothing over their lower abdomens was sliced open and stained with blood. Obvious knife wounds.

"Do you recognize them, Dyson?" Holmes asked, holding the lamp over the two corpses.

"Yes . . . Mr. and Mrs. Leighton! As I live and breathe! Oh, Lord!" Dyson cried.

"Get hold of yourself, man!" Holmes ordered. "I presume you knew nothing of this secret passageway?"

Dyson swallowed hard, never looking at the Leightons, then answered. "Of course not, Mr. Holmes. I'm as surprised about this as the rest of you are."

"At least one of us here isn't surprised," Holmes said. "And look, they're stabbed to death, just like Wyckoff, in the lower abdomen, telling me it was a short man that committed these murders."

Everyone's gaze fell upon Alger Archer. Dyson and Oxtoby stepped away from him.

Archer's eyes glowed wide in the lamp light, like a demon hound. "You're blaming me for these murders because I'm short, Mr. Holmes?" he stated. "Rubbish! You'll need more than that to convict me!"

"And I have it, Archer," Holmes countered. "Who else but you knew about this secret chamber? Who else but you would gain by Mr. and Mrs. Leighton's deaths?"

"You can't prove any of what you say! This is completely ridiculous, and I swear, sir, that I shall sue you dry before this month is out!"

"Save your threats for your cellmate, Archer! You knew the Leightons were secretly going behind your back to Oxtoby, trying to figure out a legal way to break your contract with the boy and sign with him."

"How the blazes would I know that?"

"Because you had a spy here at Leighton Manor – Wyckoff, the butler!"

"Wyckoff? Why, I hardly knew the man!"

176

"You lie, sir!" Holmes reached into his inside breast pocket and handed an envelope with folded papers inside to Lestrade.

"What are those?" Archer asked, his face went from angry and demonic to pure white with fear.

"A transcript of the contract you signed with the Leightons five years ago. I went to the Public Records Office yesterday in London to procure it. Everything Scotland Yard needs to convict you is inside those papers."

"They'll prove nothing!" Archer spat, but I could tell it was all bluster.

"They'll prove the fact that it was you who was contracted to find the Leightons a palatable place to live, this old seventeenth century estate, of which you were very familiar because you grew up here – the old Archer Estate. They'll prove the fact that it was you who was contracted to find them a butler. You chose a man who used to work for you as a prop man at the Garrick, a man you found trustworthy, and would tell you everything that was said in this house – Wyckoff. But after you murdered the Leightons, Wyckoff's feet grew cold. Fearing he would be blamed for their deaths, he quit and hid himself someplace he was familiar with, the Garrick Theatre. But you found him and sweet-talked him into serving you one last time, by stealing the boy's compositions from me. You see, young master Eric was there in the parlour just beyond the fireplace when you murdered his parents. He saw you drag them into this passage that terrible night a month ago, and he heard their screams when you committed your dastardly deed. You counted on the boy not being able to speak or function like a normal human being, in order to get away with your crime. But he ruined your plans by hiding the location of his murdered parents in a musical composition. That's why the boy ran – he knows how valuable he is, and he knew the investigation of his disappearance was the only way to bring intense scrutiny to those compositions."

"Clever boy," Lestrade said.

"Quite, Inspector," Homes agreed, then continued, focusing his attention upon Archer, whom was trembling now. "So, taking a calculated risk, I purposely let it be known last night that the boy's compositions were actually maps. You panicked, took the bait, and ran, Archer. And when that task was done and the original compositions were in your possession, you tied up that one final loose end in your plot by killing Wyckoff in the alley, the same way you killed the Leightons – a knife in the belly. But to make sure he was dead, you stabbed him again in the back."

"What about the note the boy's mother allegedly wrote, the one giving Dyson guardianship over the boy?" Oxtoby asked.

"Archer forced her to write it just before he murdered her. He knew the authorities would confirm it as her handwriting and that there would never be a way in which to confirm its story, so it would be treated as a temporary writ of guardianship. Perfectly legal and binding. It stopped any investigation of foul play in its tracks."

"You're the devil himself!" Dyson shouted and rushed at Archer, but one of the constables grabbed him. "The poor boy!" Dyson cried, struggling to get free. "The poor boy!"

Lestrade glanced at the other constable. "Secure Archer and take down him to the Yard. I'll be along shortly. And get a wagon up here to collect the bodies."

As the constable put the chains on Archer's wrists, Archer's face was red, his sideburns flattened with perspiration. "I'll be set free, Holmes," he muttered, staring up at my compatriot with a hatred I've never witnessed before. "You'll see."

"Yes, we'll see, Archer," Holmes said, grinning. "When your neck is stretching on the gallows."

Back in front of the music stand a few minutes later, Holmes picked up his Stradivarius again. "Now, time to find the boy," he said.

Lestrade, Dyson, Oxtoby, Killkenny, and I watched Holmes read over the scribbles on the sheet music.

"Have you figured out what all those *Pizzicatos* are about, Watson?" Holmes asked without remove his gaze from the pages.

"I'm afraid not, Holmes," I said meekly.

"They represent footsteps. Apparently we are to go on a night time walk through the fields. Has everyone brought their walking shoes?"

We laughed, but knew the underlying seriousness in which Holmes took to the task.

"I'll need someone with an oil lamp to hold the pages as we go."

Dyson, properly in control of himself now, went over with an oil lamp in one hand and took the pages up in his other hand, making sure Holmes could see them. Holmes then faced west, the first direction prompt the composition required.

"Watson?" Holmes said. "Be a trooper and open the French doors, will you?"

I hurried and did as he asked. The night air smelled of flowery fragrance and grass, a cool breeze wafted into the room.

Pluck! Went the first *Pizzicato* note. *Pluck! Pluck! Pluck!*

We followed Holmes out into the darkness of the Leighton Estate. When the composition said to go north, he turned north; when east, he went east. We went through well-landscaped vales of grass, up over a series of small hills, came to a thin wood, followed a path that wound through it, and came out on the other side at the gates of a cemetery. Holmes didn't seem to notice. He plucked and stepped, plucked and stepped along the white gravel path until we came to a crossroads. There, the *Pizzicatos* in the composition stopped and the violin conversation was to begin. We were surrounded by ancient, weathered gravestones and high, glossy, marble statues. A large mausoleum stood about twenty yards away, its iron doors rusty. The name *Diebold* was carved over the entrance.

"Everyone must remain absolutely quiet now," Holmes instructed, his voice nearly a whisper. Then he stared a moment at the sheet music Dyson held up in the lamp light, and with a slight flourish, played the first four bars of the composition. When he finished, we listened.

Nothing.

We waited for a solid minute, holding our collective breath, before Lestrade finally told Holmes to play it again. Holmes did, it sounded exactly the same as the first go round. This time, after he stopped, the answer came out of the night wind like a woman singing a lullaby from a very far off distance. Her voice rose up and was carried on the breeze, gently, caringly, towards us. When her singing stopped, Holmes played the next four bars. She replied a moment later, her voice louder, closer. Dyson, staring in the direction the other violin's song emanated from, was shaking with relief, his face glistening with tears.

Back and forth the violins sang, one high, the other low, one laughed, the other cried, but as their conversation wore on, their voices grew louder and louder until they crescendoed at the very high end of the scale, becoming a single voice. Then the singing stopped and we waited.

The silence lasted for an interminable amount of time before we finally heard the creak of a rusty door split the air. Out from the depths of that huge mausoleum stepped the boy, his thick, curly black hair a tangled mess, his face pale, violin and bow in his hands.

I took the lamp and the sheet music from Dyson and told him to go to the boy. As Dyson and the boy embraced in the darkness between gravestones, I heard Holmes breathing heavily in the shadows next to me, exhausted, drained and spent of all his energy.

As it turned out, the mausoleum in which the boy hid himself, the one named *Diebold*, was one that he had visited often with his mother. It was her side of the family laid at rest there, so he knew it well and felt safe there. And Dyson, as the boy's permanent guardian, swiftly signed on with Oxtoby at the New Britain Performing Arts Theatre. No doubt the boy would be well taken care of now.

Sitting in my chair by the fire, finishing the last of my evening cheroot, I watched as Holmes completed his amazing display of musicianship with the dramatic cut of a down bow, then Coda. He placed the Stradivarius and bow in its case then glanced at me sideways.

"Tolerable?" he asked, grinning.

"Tolerable?" I repeated in disbelief. "Why, Holmes, I've never heard you play better."

"You think young master Eric will agree?"

Knocks rattled from the door behind me. It was young master Eric, with Conrad Dyson, arriving for the boy's monthly private violin session with Holmes.

"Why don't we let him in and find out," I suggested.

The Story Behind the Story

I was supremely honored one day in early April 2015, when I received a message through Facebook from David Marcum, editor of this fantastic anthology, asking if I would be interested in being a part of it. Flattered, I told him I would, and promised to send him a story by June of 2015.

I'd been kicking around a story in my head since I finished the final edits of The Pearl of Death *the summer before. It had to do with a young violin savant who could communicate only through writing and playing music. I've always been fascinated with Holmes's use of the violin and I wanted to write a story where it played a more integral part in the plot, but the story I was thinking up was getting so complicated I hesitated at even starting it. Mr. Marcum's missive changed that. It forced me to rethink the story, simplify it, and soon I had great motivation to complete it.*

Whenever I write a Sherlock Holmes story I try to add something new, push the envelope a little bit, while staying within the strict guidelines of the original Canon of stories. It's a technique that forces me not to repeat myself. "The Strange Case of the Violin Savant" was no exception. Testing Holmes's genius against a completely different form of genius excited me and I believe made for an interesting story. I hope you agree. More importantly, I hope you received some modest amount of entertainment from it.

The Hopkins Brothers Affair
by Iain McLaughlin and Claire Bartlett

I have known my good friend, Sherlock Holmes, some many years now. In that time he has never failed to amaze me, both with the breadth of his knowledge on some matters and the depth of his ignorance on others. I am certain that he would take no offence at my use of the word "ignorance," because it is a state he both recognises in himself and dismisses as unimportant. His interests lie only in facts which may be of some use in his deductive work. However, the breadth of his knowledge can be quite startling, even to myself after these years of his friendship. I will admit, I am also, on occasion, quite set upon the back foot by his actions. Sometimes, he makes a small decision which I find reveals a new aspect of his personality.

We were seated in Baker Street on a dull, grey morning when summer was turning to autumn, and occasionally the clash of warm and cold weather brought a thick, cold fog upon the city. We were enduring just such a day. For myself, I was content to sit by the fire reading the paper, but Holmes was noticeably in need of stimulation, lest he fall back upon the relief he found at the point of a sharp needle. He rarely made any attempt to hide his frustration when overtaken by ennui. For that reason, I was delighted to hear a firm knock at the front door which, at that time of day, could only mean the possibility a client. I say "possibility," for Holmes has often been in the depths of despair and yet rejected a case as being beneath him. More than once I know he has deduced the answer to a client's malady before the individual has taken their seat. I found myself hoping that Holmes would find this case worthy of his time.

A minute later. Mrs. Hudson's familiar knock brought her into our rooms. "A gentleman to see you," said she, ushering a tall fellow into the sitting room. I gauged he was north of his fortieth year, but only just. His face was tanned from an outdoor life in a climate far better than that which we endured that morning. His clothing was of reasonably high quality, and he bore himself with the confidence of a man used to being in control of his situation. It afforded little surprise when the fellow introduced himself as Captain Hopkins.

"Matthew or Jonathan?" Holmes asked, drawing deeply upon his pipe. He waved a hand to suppress the obvious incredulity from our guest. "You are clearly a seafaring man," Holmes said briskly. "You introduced yourself as a captain and carry yourself with the manner of a gentleman. By my reckoning, the only gentlemen captaining ships out of London by the name of Hopkins are the owners of the Hopkins Brothers Sailing Fleet. I deduced nothing. I merely recognised a name." He turned those pale eyes to me. "People see my methods when there are none in use, Watson, and the cause of it is those penny dreadfuls you churn out."

I ignored the barb from my friend and invited Captain Hopkins to sit.

"I am Jonathan Hopkins," said he. "The younger of the brothers. Matthew is my senior by almost two years."

Holmes nodded, locking the information into that great mind of his. "Please tell us why you are here, Captain Hopkins," said Holmes. His tone was flat and far from interested. I found myself hoping that this visitor would have a tale of interest for Holmes, and then a pang of guilt stabbed me, for if the story did interest my friend, there would undoubtedly be some degree of suffering involved for this fellow sitting with us. I offered Hopkins a cigarette or a fill of tobacco, but he declined politely.

"Thank you but no, Doctor Watson. I have fallen from the habit of smoking these past few years. The smoke irritated my brother's chest and so I desisted."

"You gave up the habit for your brother?" Holmes enquired. "You have a close relationship with him?"

"Oh, indeed," Hopkins agreed readily. "Should not brothers have such a friendship? That is why I find myself at your door this morning."

Holmes sucked again on his pipe and cast his gaze upon the fire. "Go on."

Hopkins did as he was bid. "Mister Holmes, I believe something has happened to my brother, and I am sorely in need of assistance in discovering what has occurred."

"Do you suspect foul play?" I asked.

Holmes waved a hand to silence me. "It must be in his own words," said Holmes with some irritation. "You know well enough we must not interfere or place our interpretations on the facts until we know what the facts really are." Having duly chastened me, he glanced at Hopkins. "Continue."

The captain picked up his narrative as requested. "As you are apparently aware, Mister Holmes, my family's fortune relies upon our sailing ships trafficking cargo to and from London. We sail to every corner of the world. However, as the new century closes upon us, our customers demand greater and greater speed from the carriers of their goods. Those of us who still rely upon canvas and the Good Lord to provide the wind to fill those sails are in danger of losing our livelihoods."

"Why do you not change to steam driven ships?" Holmes asked. There was neither judgement nor condemnation in his tone. He sought information, nothing more.

"I would happily make that change, Mister Holmes," said Hopkins. "However, with finances as they are, we need to keep all our ships at sea. While they sail, we continue to make a profit, albeit one that diminishes each year. Buying a steam ship is not financially an option we may entertain at this time, and were one of our current ships to be taken out of service long enough to be adapted to steam, it would surely send us into bankruptcy." He sighed heavily. "Unfortunately, I fear we are sailing towards losing money and ultimate bankruptcy anyway. Our dwindling profits will, in a year or two, surely become losses."

"What shall you do then?" I asked, hoping the fellow had a plan in mind to rescue his fortunes. I was to be disappointed.

"That I do not know," he answered in a forlorn tone. "My brother . . . ." his voice faltered and he steadied himself. "My brother took the blame for our situation upon himself."

"Why so?" Holmes's voice was calm but insistent.

Hopkins leaned forward in his chair, gripping his hat tightly. "Some years ago, Matthew and I discussed the future of the business. We were doing well. Steam was not yet the force it has become and we were profiting well from our fleet. However, I could see the advantages of this new technology. I am firmly of the belief that once a new idea has secured its footing it will quickly take strides forward. I felt this was the case with steam. In their Civil War in the Americas, they had steam battleships. We ourselves have them now also. Steamers had already taken to the ocean, and I was of the opinion that they should come to dominate within a decade or less. I believed that we should invest in this new technology. I argued for it very strongly."

"And your brother refused the idea?" said Holmes, tapping the bit of his pipe against his lower lip.

"Sadly he did," our guest confirmed. "I have regretted that decision ever since, though he is still loudly in favour of sail over steam as a means of propulsion for ship. In truth, I fear steam will one day be as obsolete as sail soon will be, but by then we shall be scuppered."

Holmes sat forward and fixed his gaze upon Captain Hopkins. "While I undoubtedly concur with your opinions on maritime matters, I fail to see why you find yourself upon our doorstep."

Hopkins cleared his throat. "I was coming towards that matter."

"Please do so," said Holmes, settling back into his chair. I offered Hopkins an encouraging smile.

"I am only recently returned to this country," Hopkins said. "I have been on a voyage."

"Africa," Holmes said carelessly. He peered at us, aware that his audience awaited his reasoning. He gave it quickly. "Your skin is tanned but the weather in Europe has been uncommonly poor these past few months. As a newly married man, you are unlikely to have sailed far afield from your bride." He paused before admitting with a smile, "I also remember reading of your recent marriage in *The Times*, which means you could have sailed no further than Africa to have returned so quickly."

"You are perfectly correct, sir," affirmed Hopkins. "And I was sorely reluctant to be away from home even for that time. I am late to marriage, and I would enjoy as much of it as I can, but business requires my hand also."

"Your brother?" prompted Holmes.

"When I returned, my wife handed me a letter from Matthew. She said that he had delivered it by hand, and that it was solely for my eyes upon my return."

"You have the letter with you?" Holmes asked.

"Indeed."

"Read it," instructed Holmes.

Hopkins produced an envelope and drew folded sheets of paper from within. What he read aloud followed thus:

My dear Jonathan,

I trust you are well and in good fettle following your trek to Africa. A also trust that your voyage was a swift and profitable one. I choose the words "swift" and "profitable" with good reason. As you are aware, those of us who sail under canvas are frequently subject to slights and comments from those using more modern but less reliable means of propulsion. Last week, Henry Meek of the Charters and Meek Company chose to round upon me with such taunts as I could no longer resist the urge to prove the fellow wrong. He issued a challenge of a race between one of his ships and one of ours. Sail against steam. He even sweetened the pot with a wager of a hundred guineas. I could not resist and so there shall be a race between our fastest ship, the Charlotte Hill, *and his steam ship, the* Spirit of Dorset. *The first to reach Lisbon shall be the winner. I am confident enough of victory that I shall captain the* Charlotte Hill *myself. I look forward to seeing the defeat etched upon the face of Meek's captain as they arrive to find me waiting for them.*

I shall see you upon my return and we shall dine well on Meek's hundred guineas.

I am, always, your devoted, loving and proud brother.

Matthew

Reading the letter had affected Hopkins rather deeply, and he needed a moment to compose himself. I made a slight motion to halt Holmes when he began to appear impatient.

"Take your time," I said to Hopkins, though my eyes were firmly set on Holmes at the time.

"Thank you, Doctor," said Hopkins, putting the letter back into the envelope.

"Did your brother win?" I asked, eager to draw the fellow towards facts which would interest Holmes.

"The *Charlotte Hill* never made Lisbon," Hopkins said sadly. "She set sail as planned, but she was never seen again. She is assumed lost with all hands."

"Oh, I am so sorry," I said with some feeling. I had not imagined that his brother might be lost at sea.

Holmes, too, offered a few words of comfort. "My condolences, captain. However, with utmost sympathy, may I ask why you gave come to me when a more maritime authority would surely be of greater assistance to you?"

"Normally I would agree with you, sir," said Hopkins firmly. "However, my brother was a man who never once in his life took on a wager when it was offered. He did not believe in gambling. Our father . . . our father was prone to it, you see, and prone to losing when he did so. Neither my brother nor I followed his stead in that manner."

"Men do occasionally act in a manner outwith their normal character," Holmes said slowly, but I could see that he had slowly become intrigued by the story being unfolded in front of him. "Pray continue, captain."

Hopkins resumed as requested. "I was surprised to find the crew of the *Charlotte Hill* still ashore. The bosun came to me and had some harsh words for me on the manner in which Matthew had told them that they were all stood down from this voyage. He replaced them with a much

185

smaller crew. He claimed these were sailors who specialised in speed rather than in handling cargo, and that was what he needed for this voyage. It did not sit well with the bosun or the men, Mister Holmes. Every sailor prides himself on doing his job the best he can. To be replaced in such a manner was a huge insult, and that was not Matthew's way either." He raised the envelope containing the letter he had received. "But I should say that the most uncommon aspect of this was that my brother finished his letter in such an emotional manner. He signed himself 'devoted, loving and proud' . . . my brother was not a man given to emotion, gentleman. The affection we bore for each other was never expressed in words. That was the first time he had ever inferred love in our relationship."

"Intriguing." Holmes was tapping his pipe against his bottom teeth, making an annoying hollow sound. "Yes, indeed, intriguing. Tell me, Captain, what do you know of the men he signed aboard for this voyage?"

"Nothing," Hopkins admitted. "And the records my brother made of his crew were somewhat perplexing. They gave only names rather than addresses and details of their sailing experience, which was his normal way."

"Do you know how quickly he sought and obtained the services of this crew?" Holmes asked. I could tell from the way he spoke that his mind was already sifting the facts.

"Quickly, I believe," Hopkins replied. "Although I cannot be sure of that."

"No matter," Holmes said briskly. "I shall have the Irregulars visit my informants at the docks to find what they know."

The relief upon Hopkins' face was palpable. "You will?" he cried. "Mister Holmes, I do not know how to thank you."

Holmes raised a hand to silence the fellow. "It is possible we will learn nothing from my informants. You tell me your brother has been acting in a manner quite unlike his normal self."

"I do, sir."

"Then I will require to make some assessment of the man for myself," said Holmes rising swiftly to his feet. "Would you be willing to show me his home?"

"I would," replied Hopkins firmly.

"Will his wife object?" I asked.

Hopkins shook his head. "As I said, Doctor, my brother was not a man for allowing emotions to seep into his day. He has never married."

"Come, gentlemen," said Holmes. He had already removed his dressing gown and tossed it casually onto a chair. "Let us not waste time."

Within half an hour, a carriage had delivered us to Matthew Hopkins' townhouse, a fine looking three storey building near Hyde Park. The housekeeper, a small and fussy woman by the name of Mrs. Priddy, let us in with some considerable lack of grace, which was only slightly eased by the presence of her master's brother.

"Kindly do not venture far," said Holmes. "I may have questions for you."

The woman's protests were harshly quieted by Hopkins, who clearly bore no affection towards the woman. "She is a shrew," said he when the woman had left us. "But she ran the house to Matthew's satisfaction."

The interior of the house was comfortable enough, but lacking in warmth or individuality. It was how I imagine it had looked when Matthew Hopkins had moved in. Even the paintings of ships which adorned a few walls were too generic to actually be ships from the Hopkins Brothers' line. It felt like a house still waiting for someone to give it life and turn it into a home. I found it a deeply sad place.

Holmes's eyes were scanning the room, taking each piece of information and storing it. He moved around the ground floor, inspecting each of the rooms in turn, asking if there had been any changes that Captain Hopkins could recognise. After some coaxing, Hopkins agreed that within the study the desk had been shifted so that the light now came over the shoulder of anyone seated at the desk, rather than falling onto the desktop at an angle from the side. The alteration afforded the person sitting at the desk a direct view of the doorway.

I could tell Holmes has far from satisfied, and Hopkins also sensed my friend's restiveness. He suggested continuing the exploration upstairs, which duly outraged Mrs. Priddy. None of us cared a whit for the woman's protests and soon we found ourselves on the first floor. Here, Hopkins showed us to his brother's bed chamber, a large, well-appointed room with a splendidly sized bed. The room was unnaturally tidy. With permission from Captain Hopkins, Holmes opened cupboards and wardrobes, inspecting clothes and whatever else he found. The bedside cabinet was locked, and Hopkins said that he would call for Mrs. Priddy. Holmes smiled wryly, stating that would not be necessary. A few moments later, the cabinet was open. Holmes has learned a number of skills from his experiences with the criminal classes, which can occasionally prove to be of use in his cases.

The contents of the drawer took Captain Hopkins by surprise. "These are family letters," said he in a hushed voice. "Letters between our parents while our father was at sea, and letters from Matthew and me to our parents when we were at school."

There were also photographs and family documents. "An odd place to store them, surely?" said Holmes.

"Indeed," concurred Hopkins.

As Holmes pulled the drawer, we heard the round of something hard rolling within. Reaching to the lack, Holmes found a small glass bottle containing a reddish brown liquid. He removed the stopper and sniffed. He and I both knew the identity of the contents before he spoke them aloud for Hopkins' benefit. "Laudanum."

"No," protested Hopkins vehemently. "My brother would never use a drug such as this. You must be mistaken."

"I am not mistaken," Holmes said with a wry, humourless smile. "I have some expertise in these matters."

"I cannot believe my brother would use such a drug," said Hopkins. "He did not drink or smoke, and oft times castigated me for doing so. Why should he use it now?" He paused as thoughts raced through his mind. "Would the use of this terrible drug explain why he would change character and make such a terrible decision as to take on a race with an unknown crew?"

Holmes handed the laudanum bottle to me, as if handing away a temptation. "I have seen all I need to see here." He headed for the door. "Captain Hopkins, please come to Baker Street tonight at seven o'clock. I shall have your answers for you then."

With that, Holmes strode from the room. I bade Hopkins a good day and assured him Holmes would be as good as his word before following my friend from the room.

For the rest of the afternoon, Holmes did not speak at all on the matter of Matthew Hopkins. I myself had developed a theory which ran thus: Matthew Hopkins had become aware that his intractable devotion to sail was destroying his family business. Overtaken by guilt, he had begun to use opiates such as laudanum as a relief, and under the influence of these drugs, he had begun to behave in an aberrant and unwise manner, such as wagering with a rival and taking aboard an unknown crew in the desperate hope he could be proven right. That behaviour had led ultimately to the ship being lost and the deaths of all those aboard. However, when I presented my theory to Holmes, he merely requested that I ask Mrs. Hudson to bring tea.

188

Early in the evening, Holmes was visited by a pair of his Irregulars, who quickly delivered their information and were equally swiftly rewarded with a coin.

"Dare I ask?" I enquired.

Holmes looked to the clock. "Captain Hopkins will be here shortly," said he. "I have no mood to tell the story twice."

As anticipated, Captain Hopkins arrived precisely upon the hour of seven. He was soon seated comfortably with a cup of tea in his hand and an impatient expression upon his face. "Well, Mister Holmes?" he asked. "Do you know what has happened to my brother?"

"Not everything," Holmes admitted. "But the material facts of the matter are quite clear."

Quite by chance, I had placed the laudanum upon the mantelpiece. I cursed my foolishness and promised myself that I should remove it from the house at the earliest instance. For that moment, it had Hopkins' attention. "Had my brother taken to using laudanum?" he asked.

"He had," Holmes confirmed. "Though I think it was only in the last few months he had taken to its use."

Hopkins' shoulders slumped. I imagined that he had come to a similar theory as I had reached. I knew only too well the despair which came with the thought of someone dear to us being taken by an opiate. "I can scarcely believe he would become a slave to the poppy," sighed Hopkins. "I thought him stronger than that."

I fancied I saw Holmes flinch just for an instant at any hint that use of an opiate was a weakness. His calm mask was in place within a moment. "Then I will tell you that he was not in thrall to laudanum," Holmes replied. "Do not ask me to explain that yet. I shall give all the details I have at my disposal, but I shall relay them in my own manner."

Lighting a taper on the fire, Holmes lit his pipe. "I sent the Irregulars to find information on the crew taken aboard the *Charlotte Hill* by your brother. What I discovered was that each man had made no plans to return. Several had given up their homes. The families of some were noted as having more money than would have been expected. When people live in poverty, even those trying to hide a little more money than usual are quite obvious." He took a long draw on his pipe. "But we shall set that aside for the moment. In your brother's home, I was most intrigued not by the laudanum or the family effects, but your brother's clothes. It was clear that your brother had lost weight recently."

Hopkins nodded. "Mrs. Priddy said that he was hardly eating. I thought little of it. When I have a concern, I, too, go off my food, and we have both been deeply concerned by business matters."

Holmes looked at Hopkins, and those pale eyes were not unkind. "I fear your brother was not merely concerned, Captain Hopkins. I believe he knew he was dying."

"What?"

"You mentioned that your smoke had irritated his chest. I think rather it will have been his throat. I noticed that his newest clothes were several sizes smaller but the collars of his shirts had been altered to offer less pressure on the throat. Your opinion, Doctor?"

I was aware of Hopkins' eyes alighting upon me. "Difficult to be sure without seeing the patient," I said. "But a throat cancer would be my guess."

"Deduction, not guess," Holmes corrected me. "And it is also the conclusion I drew. I believe that Matthew Hopkins was aware that he was dying, and also aware that his business was dying. To save the business and the brother he cared for but, as is often the way with brothers, was unable to show his affection in life, he chose to show his affection in death." He turned to Hopkins. "If your ship is lost at sea, will your insurance company compensate you?"

"Fully," Hopkins confirmed. He paused, staring at Holmes. "What are you saying, Mr. Holmes?"

"I am saying that your brother knew he was not long for this life. He wished to give you the best chance possible to help your company survive. With the insurance from his life and for the lost ship, you will be able to take your company forward. He crewed the ship with other men who did not have long left to live, and he took them on a voyage from which none of them expected to return."

"Are you saying he scuppered the ship?" Hopkins sounded aghast.

"I do not know," admitted Holmes. "He may have taken it to a remote cove and scuppered it, or he may have sailed it to a foreign port to sell in order to raise money to look after the crew and himself in their final days. It is largely irrelevant. He surrendered the comforts he could have gained by dying at home so that you could prosper. The family documents in his drawer were a clear indication of the value he placed on family."

"So he may be alive?"

Holmes held his hands wide. "Even I cannot tell that, but even with the most extensive of searches, by the time we track his whereabouts, he will certainly be dead."

I cannot express the mixture of emotions I saw upon Jonathan Hopkins' face. He did not know if his brother was alive or dead, but he did know his brother was gone, having executed a plan for the love of his only remaining family.

"Be assured," Holmes said quietly. "I have no intention of discussing this matter with the insurance companies. I have no real evidence to prove my theory, though I know I am correct. Nor do I have the wish to thwart the dying wish of a brave man."

"But the law?"

"The law did not engage me, Captain. You did. That is an end of the matter."

"Thank you, Mister Holmes."

I sensed that Hopkins would want to say something more but that would make Holmes uncomfortable. "Let me show you out, Captain," I said.

"Thank you, Doctor."

I ushered Hopkins towards the door but was halted by Holmes's voice. "Watson."

"What is it?"

He had picked up his violin and was pointing the bow at the bottle resting on the mantelpiece. "Show that out as well."

"Yes, Holmes."

The Disembodied Assassin
by Andrew Lane

In my forty-eight years on this Earth I have buried both of my parents, my brother, and my dear wife, as well as numerous comrades in the British Army, and countless patients whom I was unable to save from their injuries. I have also mourned the death of my dearest friend, Sherlock Holmes, and his later reappearance alive and well did not in any way console me for the three years in which I considered him lost. I am no stranger to grief, and yet the death of Queen Victoria on the 22nd of January 1901 came as a considerable shock to me. Victoria had been on the throne since before I was born, and despite the fact that I knew intellectually she was elderly and infirm, there was something in me that assumed she would go on forever. She embodied everything that was great about the British Empire, and I believe there was a large element of the British public which thought that, without her clearheaded guidance, that Empire would begin to crumble. Certainly her successor, her eldest son Edward, was not the immediate focus of the same love, affection and trust that his mother had enjoyed, for reasons that readers of some of my earlier reports of my friend Sherlock Holmes's investigations will be well aware.

The only person who seemed untouched by Queen Victoria's death was Sherlock Holmes. He had been granted audiences with Her Majesty on several occasions, thanks to the work he had done directly or indirectly for the Crown, and she had presented him with an assortment of medals which he had immediately and carelessly thrown into a desk drawer on his return from Buckingham Palace, On picking up the black-bordered edition of the *Times* which reported her death, he turned immediately to the *Small Ads* page.

I stared blankly across the room at that same front page, as he held the newspaper up, wondering what would become of the country in this new century, with a new ruler. Somewhere downstairs, I could hear Mrs. Hudson weeping as she cooked our breakfast. I already knew that outside our rooms, in the street, men and women were wearing black armbands, and hansom cabs were draped in black ribbons, as if they had all lost a close relative.

When Mrs. Hudson finally delivered our breakfast – red-eyed and unable to talk coherently – there was a telegram on a plate next to the kippers. Holmes immediately snatched it up, sliced it open, and scanned its contents.

"Brother Mycroft requests my immediate presence," he announced. "Would you like to come with me, Watson?"

"I would," I replied. "Do you believe this request has anything to do with the death of the Queen?"

He frowned at me, as if he wasn't sure what I was talking about. "I doubt it," he said eventually. "Unless, of course, Her Majesty was murdered, but I consider the probability of that to be relatively small. After all, why murder a rheumatic woman with failing eyesight in her eighties? Surely one could trust natural processes to carry her off in fairly short order."

"Does the death of Her Majesty mean nothing to you?" I snapped, angry at his casual attitude.

He shrugged. "Depending on which historians one believes, Victoria was perhaps the sixty-third monarch this island has seen. I have not mourned the loss of the previous ones, and see no reason to mourn this one. She was an interesting lady, but in the end the monarchy has little practical function in society, despite the beliefs of my brother. Which leads us back to the question – will you come with me, or not?"

Despite my irritation, I agreed to travel with Holmes. Some of Holmes's most interesting cases had come from his brother, and I was intrigued to see what Mycroft wanted this time.

We secured a hansom cab quickly, but our progress was slow due to the number of people who had spontaneously come out onto the streets of London to show their respects. Oxford Street was almost impassable, and our driver had to go up and around Trafalgar Square, which was so full of mourners that there was scarcely room for a single newcomer.

"A good field for the pickpockets," was all that Holmes would observe as we drove past the crowds.

Mycroft Holmes was, as usual, comfortably ensconced in the Diogenes Club. This time, however, he was not waiting for us in the Strangers Room. Instead, we were led through the hushed enclave to a different location – this one being a meeting room placed directly in the centre of a much larger hall. As such, it had no windows, and only one obvious door.

I glanced at Holmes as we approached, and saw that he was smiling. He noticed my interest, and put his finger to his lips, lest I inadvertently break the Club's rule of silence by asking him what had amused him so. When we were safely inside the room – which was empty apart from the two of us – and the door shut behind us, he turned to me.

"I have only been in this room once before," he said, "and that was thirty-three years ago. I found Mycroft standing in the doorway with a knife in his hand. There was blood on the knife, and a dead body on the floor. Nobody outside had seen anyone else enter or leave apart from Mycroft and the other man. I had to prove that my brother was innocent of the murder in order to save him from the scaffold."

"You were fourteen!" I exclaimed.

"It was not the first murder I had solved," he said. Looking around, he added: "I see they have not redecorated since then."

"But the murder?" I asked when it became clear that he was not going to elaborate on the matter. "If it wasn't Mycroft who stabbed the man, then who was it? And how was it done?"

He shrugged. "Perhaps another time," he said. "The matter had some points of interest, but not many." He paused. "We both ended up in Moscow as a result," he observed, tantalising me even further.

Before I could demand more details of this period of my friend's life – a period he had refused to speak of until this throw-away remark – the door to the room opened and Mycroft Holmes entered.

He was, if anything, even larger than the last time I had seen him. His girth filled the door from side to side. I was aware, from my own observations and from comments made by his brother, that Mycroft Holmes lived almost exclusively in his office in Whitehall, in his club in Whitehall and in his lodgings – which were also in Whitehall. It would be fair to say that he rarely, if ever, walked for more than a few hundred yards.

"Ah, Sherlock," he boomed. "I am grateful for your attendance." He walked over to a large chair that I suspect had been brought into the room especially for him and settled himself in it. He waved to two other chairs on the other side of the table. "Please – be seated. Refreshments will be served shortly."

We sat, and Holmes gazed critically at his brother. "You are looking well," he said. "I perceive a change of maid or of your gentleman's gentleman."

"Lord Humberstone has been murdered," Mycroft Holmes announced baldly.

Sherlock nodded. "It was clear from the latest edition of *The Times* that something had occurred which they were unable to report," he said. "The story on the front page had been rewritten to fit a space which had obviously been set for something else, and then changed at the last minute."

"We issued them with a notice of Prior Restraint," Mycroft said. "Given the currently unsettled political and social situation, we felt it best that the report of the murder of a prominent dignitary be withheld from the public for a few days."

"Until you have established whether it is a crime of passion, an unfortunate result of a burglary gone wrong, or an assassination," Sherlock Holmes said.

"Until," Mycroft corrected, "*you* establish whether it is a crime of passion, an unfortunate result of a burglary gone wrong, or an assassination."

Holmes shrugged. "You have police for that kind of thing," he pointed out. "I have my disagreements with them, but they have become significantly more professional in their approach to evidence-gathering and analytical thought since I first started as a consulting detective. Is there some reason why they cannot be bought in?"

Mycroft Holmes made a "*Harumph!*" noise, and looked away. If there had been a window in the room then he would have gazed out of it, but as it was he merely ended up looking at a gas lamp.

"Let me give you the bare bones of the matter," he said eventually. "Lord Humberstone is a member of the Privy Council, and a special advisor on Royal Protocol. He has been writing a document which sets out the terms under which power will transfer from Queen Victoria, following her sad but not unexpected demise, to her son."

I remembered Holmes's comment about there having been perhaps sixty-three monarchs before Victoria. "But surely this has happened many times before," I said. "There must be precedents."

Mycroft fixed me with a gimlet eye, as if he had only just noticed my presence. It was a pose, of course – he noticed everything.

"It has not happened during any of our lifetimes," he pointed out, "and besides, there is a significant movement advocating that our country abandon a monarchy altogether and becomes a democratic republic under the leadership of an elected President, along the lines of the United States of America. Such talk leads us down a path that ends up in Socialism, if not out-and-out Anarchy, and must be stopped in its tracks.

"America has not ended up succumbing to Socialism or Anarchy," I pointed out.

"Give them time," he growled. Turning back to Sherlock Holmes, he continued: "Lord Humberstone was addressing these points, attempting to ensure a clean and clear transfer of power in a way that would bring the population behind its new King. His murder is at best inconvenient, and at worst tantamount to a declaration of rebellion."

"Give me the details," my friend snapped.

"Lord Humberstone was in his study, working. The door was locked and the curtains drawn. He had a personal bodyguard of three men, one of whom was in the room with him, one outside the door, and the third outside the window. Hearing a cry from inside the room, the man outside the door knocked and entered. He found the man who had been stationed *inside* the room bending over Lord Humberstone, who was slumped over his desk. Humberstone had a knife in his back that had penetrated through to his heart. The man who had been outside the door and the man outside the window quickly searched the room, but could see nobody else but the man who had been with Lord Humberstone all that time. He was quickly arrested for murder, and is currently in police custody."

"But you do not believe that he is guilty."

"The man has been one of my top agents for many years now. I trust him implicitly – as much as I trust anyone, that is. I cannot believe that he is responsible for the murder of Lord Humberstone."

"You mean that you cannot believe your judgement is wrong," Sherlock Holmes said.

Mycroft sighed. "He has no reason to have committed such a deed, and he maintains his innocence. Apart from his presence in the room, there is no reason to connect him to the crime, and if he *did* want to murder Lord Humberstone, then poison in his brandy decanter would have been a much more subtle means – and I should point out that my agent is no fool." He paused, as if considering whether he should speak the words that were forming in his mind. "He has killed before, professionally, on behalf of the Crown. His assassinations have been subtle and have never been traced back to him. He would not choose a method this clumsy."

"He may have been suborned by some Socialist or Anarchist group," Sherlock pointed out.

"There is no evidence indicating such," Mycroft countered, "and besides – they, or he, would quickly have claimed responsibility and tried to obtain as much publicity as possible for their cause." He sighed deeply. "Sherlock, I would deem it a personal favour if you would look into this case for me."

Sherlock Holmes stared at his brother for a long moment. "There is no need to invoke personal favours," he said eventually. "Of course I shall investigate. Besides, the crime as you have described it has features of interest – the locked room, the presence of two people, one of whom dies and the other one of whom is not apparently the murderer." He looked around the room in which we sat. "Strange how things in life appear to repeat themselves."

"What did your agent say happened?" I asked Mycroft Holmes.

Holmes made a small, dismissive gesture with his hand. "Irrelevant," he said. "Personal recollections are fraught with uncertainties and ambiguities. I prefer not to taint my mind with them until I have real evidence."

"He told his colleagues," Mycroft answered regardless, "that he was looking out of the window – which was closed and locked, by the way – when he heard Lord Humberstone cry out, and fall forwards onto his desk. When he went across to check, he found a knife in Lord Humberstone's back."

"At what time did this occur?" Holmes asked.

"There is some uncertainty as to that," Mycroft said. "My man claims that the clock in the study was winding itself up to strike, but the men outside say that it was five minutes before the hour of one o'clock this morning when he called out to them." He paused, and his lips pursed into a thin line. "That discrepancy is, I have to admit, another strike against him."

"Speaking of 'strikes'," Sherlock said, "did he actually *hear* the clock strike one o'clock?"

"He did not. He says that he was so distracted by the strange events that had occurred."

"Hmm," Holmes mused, then: "We must go, before the evidence is unrecoverably contaminated. May I presume that you have transport waiting?"

Mycroft nodded. "There is a brougham awaiting outside," he said. "Lord Humberstone's house is in Richmond. I have ordered that his body be left undisturbed."

"Did you mention that refreshments were on their way?" I asked Mycroft Holmes.

"Yes – for me," he replied, raising an eyebrow. "Please keep me informed as to your progress."

We made our goodbyes and left Mycroft Holmes sitting in that windowless room, staring at the wall and awaiting his refreshments.

The journey to Richmond Park took less than an hour, during which time Holmes and I barely exchanged three words. I spent most of my time looking out of the window at the passing panoply of London life.

There were police guards on the gates of Lord Humberstone's manor house, which was set in its own walled-off grounds within Richmond Park. Deer grazed peacefully on the grass both outside and inside the walls.

As the brougham clattered up the gravel drive towards the house, I saw, from my window, what appeared to me a group of military personnel in uniform standing behind a row of cannons which were directed at a copse of trees. It took me a few moments to realise that they were not moving. They appeared to be models, of the same kind that one might see in Madame Tussaud's exhibition, just a few hundred yards down Baker Street from where Sherlock Holmes and I had made our lodgings. Their skin was flesh-coloured, but slightly too shiny to be real, and their uniforms were faded by constant exposure to rain and sunlight.

I looked to where the cannons were pointed, and saw that there were other stationary figures in the trees. These figures were wearing what looked to me like French uniforms. I indicated them to Holmes. He merely gazed out of the window for a moment, and then shrugged.

"As well as being an able diplomat, Lord Humberstone was a noted collector of mechanical models," he said. "I understand that he has, in his collection, a perfect replica of Vaucanson's duck, which allegedly can eat corn and pass the remains from its system, although I would dispute the accuracy of any digestive process which takes place inside a mechanical creature. Rather than statues in his house, he has various realistic automata that move their eyes, speak, write, and even play the flute. I believe that he also has a mechanical man designed and built by Leonardo da Vinci. This creation is dressed in armour and is able to sit down and stand up."

"I remember," I said, "seeing a mechanical Turk playing chess, when I was a child."

"The mechanical Turk was a fake," Holmes pointed out. "There was a dwarf inside who could play chess extremely well, and manipulated the Turk's hands from beneath."

"Oh," I said, deflated.

The brougham came to a stop outside the main door of the manor house. As I climbed out, I found myself looking again at the motionless soldiers. "They do not appear to be automata," I said. "They are not moving."

"Look at the ground between the cannons and the trees." Holmes came around the side of the brougham to join me. "Do you see there are holes in the ground near the trees – some circular and some like long, straight gashes?"

"I do."

"I would think that perhaps once a day these mechanical soldiers come to life and perform some kind of show. The holes in the ground are the result of cannonballs projected from the muzzles of the cannons – probably by springs, rather than by gunpowder, for the sake of safety and consistency. With a spring of a certain size, compacted by a certain amount, the cannonballs will always follow the same path and end up in the same holes. Servants probably collect them up afterwards, unless there is some form of automatic recovery mechanism beneath the ground."

"And the regular gashes?" I asked.

"They mark the paths which the French figures in the trees will follow when they advance towards the cannons, which will fire. Repelled, the French will retreat back into the trees. It is probably a recreation of a moment from the Battle of Waterloo. There must be some machinery – again, beneath the ground – which allows the French soldiers to move as if they are actually walking. I would imagine that it is powered by hydraulic action. I doubt, by the way, that true repeatability could be achieved if the automata were actually walking on their own legs – they will be held up, somehow, from beneath."

We started up the short run of marble steps leading up to the front door of the manor house. Another automaton was standing just to one side of the door – an elderly man with a wig of long, white hair, dressed in a dusty black suit. It stood motionless, gazing in the direction of the military automata. I wondered who it was meant to be.

The door opened as we approached, revealing a butler. He nodded to us. "Gentlemen, you are expected," he said in a dry voice. "Please – come in." As we passed him he looked over to the automaton in the dusty black suit. "Mister Drescombe – will you be here for dinner?"

"I will not," the man who I had taken for a mechanical contrivance said, turning his head and gazing at the butler, ignoring us completely. "I will be watching the performance in . . ." he checked a gold Hunter watch hanging from a chain on his waistcoat, "fifteen minutes, and then I shall be heading for the workshop to make some adjustments to the duelling swordfighters. Their timing is slightly out. Perhaps you could have a cold collation sent over on a tray."

"Of course," the butler said, and closed the door behind us.

"Mister Drescombe was employed by Lord Humberstone as what?" Holmes asked as we were led across a white and black-tiled hall. "A mechanic?"

"More of a curator," the butler replied smoothly. "Although he *is* responsible for repairs and maintenance of Lord Humberstone's collection."

He took us down a corridor that led off to the right. The hall and the corridor were both lined with realistic human figures on podia, or realistic busts on pedestals. Some were stationary, awaiting whatever vital force was required to activate them, while others moved their heads from side to side, or nodded at us as we passed. Some of the busts were moving their lips and jaws as if speaking. One even seemed to track us with its eyes as we walked by – a small gesture, compared to the others, but I found it disturbing. I noticed that one particular whole automaton held a flute, as Holmes had mentioned. As I watched it raised the instrument to its lips and, apparently, blew. I heard the notes of *Greensleeves*, perfectly formed and phrased.

I found the whole scene very macabre. In my experience, life is life and death is death, and the two should never be confused. These automata looked like corpses, with their waxy skin and lack of normal expression, but they mimicked the appearance of life. I shivered as I walked, and felt the hairs rise up on the back of my neck as I wondered what they were doing behind me.

"Is it possible," I whispered to Holmes as we walked down the corridor, "that Lord Humberstone was killed not by a human being but by an *automaton*?"

"Unlikely," he said in his normal tone of voice. "Consider – Mycroft's trusted agent saw no other figure in the room."

"But – " I continued.

He interrupted me. "You are about to suggest that an automaton could be constructed of glass, with glass gears, glass rods and glass springs. Please, Watson, save your imagination for the written version of this case which, no doubt, you are already formulating in your mind. Such a creation might serve for the works of Mr. Wells or Monsieur Verne, but not for reality." Before I could reply, he continued: "And please put from your mind the idea of an invisible man, in the same vein as Mr. Wells wrote about a few years ago. There is no logic that could explain such a thing. It is a romance, nothing more. This death was caused by something visible and tangible, I assure you."

I remembered that when I first met Holmes, some twenty years before, I had constructed a list of things that he knew about, and things of which he was ignorant. As the first item on the list I had written: "Knowledge of Literature – nil." I am unsure whether I got that wrong then, whether he had developed an interest in literature since, or whether my own interest had rubbed off on him.

The butler took us to the door on the right hand side at the far end of the corridor. It was guarded by a policeman, who saluted us as we approached. Mycroft Holmes must have sent word ahead that we were to be afforded every courtesy.

I was five paces into the room, and gazing at the body of Lord Humberstone as it lay sprawled face-down on the desk, when I realised that my friend was not by my side. I turned to find him examining the door lock, and then the hinges. Once he had finished, he moved, not in the direction of the body, but towards the single window that looked out over the grounds of the house. Based on our path to the room, I assumed that it faced the front of the house, and the military simulacra that stood eternal guard outside. Rather than look through the glass, Holmes examined the frame carefully, taking his magnifying glass from his pocket to get a clearer view.

I stepped towards the desk, gazing at the knife projecting from the back, and the dark stain of dried blood that surrounded it. I could not see the face of the corpse: it was hidden by the unfashionably long hair that had fallen forwards to touch the green leather blotter. The hands were stretched out to either side. I gently touched the wrist, and the neck. They were cold but flexible. I raised the right hand and tried to bend the arm, but *rigor mortis* had completely set in. The arm was stiff and straight, and the hand clawed.

"Are you confident that Lord Humberstone has not been replaced by a life-like simulacrum?" Holmes asked, leaving the window and moving across to where I stood at the desk. He had a slight smile on his lips.

"The thought had never occurred to me," I replied. I did not say, but the thought that *had* occurred to me was that now I had seen Lord Humberstone's actual body, I had stopped thinking of the man as "him", and had started thinking of the body as "it" – not unlike the way I had been thinking of the automata outside.

As Holmes bent over the body, examining the knife carefully, I looked at the wall behind him. It was lined with shelves, and the shelves contained hundreds of books. Looking across the titles, I saw that they were mainly histories, some military and some not, with a smattering of philosophy amongst them. I could also see, but in my mind's eye, Lord Humberstone sitting upright at his desk, writing away with the same antique fountain pen that even now lay a few inches from his outstretched hand, turning around every now and then to consult a book from the shelves behind him on some obscure point.

"Interesting," Holmes murmured, still looking at the knife. "Interesting and instructive."

He turned around and looked at the shelves of books, examining the wood carefully.

"Are you looking for some sign of a secret door or panel?" I inquired.

"It is an obvious possibility," he answered, face still pressed close to the wood and the leather, "but I believe I can rule it out. These shelves are solid, and there is no evidence of gaps or hinges that might indicate an opening. However . . . ."

"What is it?" I asked.

He shook his head impatiently. "Perhaps nothing."

I was about to press him further when I heard the sound of explosions. I was momentarily startled, but then I remembered the recreation of a scene from the Battle of Waterloo outside. It must have been time for the performance to start, and the death of its owner had not impeded the running of whatever mechanism set it off. I crossed to the window and gazed out. Had I not seen the automata close up earlier, I would have believed that the figures outside were real men in uniform. The British soldiers were moving as if they were loading the cannons with cannonballs, ramming them down the muzzles with ramrods and then setting them off with lit tapers, while the French soldiers advanced in a most realistic manner from the trees. The cannonballs fired with flashes of flame and bursts of smoke, and followed a shallow trajectory until they hit the ground exactly where they had hit the last time, and the time before that. The French soldiers threw their hands up in recreations of panic, and began to retreat.

I could imagine Lord Humberstone getting up from his desk, leaving his work behind, and crossing to where I stood now so that he could see the performance. How it must have cheered him to see it – but no more. Now the performance went on bereft of an audience, apart from me.

"And who are you?" a querulous voice asked from the doorway.

I turned, and saw a middle-aged woman in fine clothes standing there, staring at us. Her face was pale and drawn.

"Lady Humberstone?" I asked, moving towards her from my position in front of the window. "I am Doctor John Watson, and this is my colleague, Sherlock Holmes. We are here on behalf of Mycroft Holmes."

Her gaze moved from me to Holmes and back again. "I believe that I saw a telegram to the effect that you would be here," she said.

I could see that she was trying to prevent her gaze fixing on the body of her late husband. Instead, it kept flitting around the room – settling for a moment on the curtains, the books, the window, and each of us before starting off again.

I moved tactfully so that I was standing between her and the desk. "Please accept our sincere condolences on your tragic loss, your Ladyship," I said, bowing slightly.

She nodded her thanks. "Are you able to tell me when you might be finished?" she asked. "There are arrangements to be made. I have a funeral director standing by, ready to take my husband's body."

"I am sure we will be as quick as possible," I responded.

"I see your husband was anticipating a new post," Holmes suddenly interrupted. He was by now leaning over the body like some predatory spider, making close observations.

"How do you know that?" Lady Humberstone sounded surprised. "No announcement has been made, or will be made until after the coronation of the King!"

"He had written a letter to His Majesty, thanking him for the honour and accepting it," Holmes said. "The letter has obviously been sent already, but he blotted it on the blotting paper here before sealing it in the envelope. There are enough traces of the ink to make out the sense of it, and I am more than able to read reversed writing." He bent closer to the desk. "If I am not mistaken, he would have been taking up the post of Governor-General in Canada."

Lady Humberstone sniffed. "Indeed," she said.

"You were not in favour of your husband accepting the position?" Holmes asked.

"It is a great honour," she replied carefully.

"You can be honest with us," my friend pressed. "Somebody else will be chosen now."

She briefly met his level gaze. "It is a long way away," she admitted grudgingly, "and the weather is not pleasant. There is much snow, and much ice, and the social life is not as we are used to here."

"But you would have accompanied Lord Humberside?"

"Of course!" she said, affronted. "It would have been my duty, and we never shirk our duty!"

A sudden flurry of cannon fire attracted her attention to the window. Her face creased into an expression of distaste. "Of course, there would have been some advantages," she added quietly.

"You were not in favour of your husband's hobby?"

She shuddered. "I find these automata to be an affront to God, Mr. Holmes. If we had uprooted our lives and moved to Canada, then my husband had promised to sell each and every piece in his collection."

"He had agreed to that?"

She nodded. "He said that rather than let these mechanical abominations rust or rot, as I would have preferred, he would make them available to the collectors who would be lined up, begging him to sell."

"I see." Holmes nodded. "Thank you."

Lady Humberstone raised an aristocratic eyebrow at his abrupt dismissal. She paused, just long enough to make it clear that her leaving was her idea rather than his, and then turned towards the door. Turning back, she said: "Please try to finish as quickly as you can. Leaving my husband here is . . . undignified."

As she swept out, I turned to Holmes. "If Lady Humberstone did not wish to go to Canada with her husband," I said quietly, "then surely that would give her a motive to kill him. Perhaps this murder was not a result of some political act, but a simple crime arising from a marital disagreement, a crime of passion of the kind one might find at any level of society."

"You have been reading too much sensationalist fiction, Watson," he said, straightening up. "Motives are like flies: they multiply uncontrollably, and they inevitably cluster around a death. Motives will not lead us to a murderer – only the evidence will do that."

"And have you found any evidence?"

"Some," he said noncommittally. He turned and took something from the shelves behind him, then moved from behind the desk and headed towards the door. "I would draw your attention in particular to the timepiece on the mantelpiece."

I glanced across to the fireplace. Above it, on the marble ledge, an Ormolu clock sat.

"What about it?" I asked, speaking to his back as he moved past me.

"What time is it?" Holmes asked. I saw that he was holding a large tome, bound in blue leather, in his hands.

"Five past three in the afternoon," I answered.

"And did you hear the clock strike, or even wind up to strike, in the twenty minutes or so during which we have been in this room?"

"I did not," I replied, considering. The point was well made – if it hadn't been the clock that Mycroft Holmes's agent had heard winding up to strike, then what had it been?

By the time I followed Holmes out into the corridor, Holmes had found the butler. "Where are the two men who were outside the study when Lord Humberstone was killed?" he snapped. "The guards that were provided for him?"

"In the Orangery," the butler replied. "If you gentlemen would care to follow me?"

We walked back along the corridor that had led us there, with the various automata lining it watching us go, or otherwise performing for our benefit.

The Orangery was a glassed-in conservatory abutting the rear of the building. Large ceramic pots containing small citrus bushes were placed in regular array on the tiled floor. The afternoon sun shone through the glass, creating a humid atmosphere. Two men in dark suits were sitting uncomfortably on bamboo chairs amongst the foliage. In the distance the sound of cannons could still be dimly heard.

"My name is Sherlock Holmes," my friend announced as we walked in. He was still carrying the blue book. "My brother, Mycroft Holmes, with whom I believe you are acquainted, has asked me to investigate the murder of Lord Humberstone. I have two questions." He glanced from one man to the other. They had both straightened up in their chairs at the mention of Mycroft Holmes. "Firstly, what is your opinion of your colleague – the one who has been arrested for murder? Be honest – I need to know whether he has ever expressed any political opinions, and to what extent you would trust him to do his job properly."

The men shared a glance. One of them – the older one – stood up. "Mr. Holmes," he said in a well-educated voice, "we have, as you can understand, been speaking of little else while we have been sitting here waiting. The answers from both of us are this: we have both been working with the man for several years now. We have trusted him with our lives on many previous occasions, and would do so in future, despite the accusations made about him. As to his political opinions – he has never expressed any to our certain knowledge."

"Excellent. And as to the second question – what time was it when he called out to you, informing you that Lord Humberstone was dead?"

The second man stood. "I was outside the door, Mr. Holmes. My colleague here was outside the window. I looked at the clock on the mantelpiece when I entered the room. It was just shy of one o'clock this morning when he shouted that there was something wrong."

"You are sure?" Holmes pressed. "Perhaps it was just *past* one o'clock?"

"No sir – it was four minutes to one. I checked it on my own watch."

Holmes stepped across to where the man stood. "Show me your watch."

My friend pulled his own watch from his pocket and compared it with the one that the man held out. "Very good," he said. "The time is accurate." Holmes turned to leave, then turned back. "A third question, if I may. Was the fire burning in the fireplace?"

"Strongly, sir," the first man answered. "The flames were high."

Holmes glanced at me. "I needed to rule out the slim possibility that someone had entered through the chimney," he said.

Holmes made as if to leave the Orangery, but the first man coughed. "Sir – if I may? Was it our fault? Did someone somehow manage to get past us and kill Lord Humberstone?"

"You did your jobs perfectly well," Holmes answered. "Whatever happened in that room was beyond your control, and I shall report as such to my brother. Oh, and rest assured – your colleague is innocent, and his name will shortly be cleared."

He strode away, and I followed him. "To the workshop!" he called over his shoulder – the blue leather-bound book still clutched in his hands.

We left the main house and crossed the lawn towards a rough wooden building that had been constructed in the grounds of the house. The automated replay of the Waterloo skirmish had finished by now: the various automata were stationary, caught in their various poses, and I thought I could feel some vibration beneath my feet as the cannon balls that had been fired were transferred mechanically back underground through hidden tunnels to recreate the piles that would be used the next day as ammunition, and the day after that, and the day after that. The senseless, mechanical repetition of warfare without the blood and the shattered limbs offended me, and I found myself wondering if whatever was providing the power for the mechanism – be it clockwork or perhaps the movement of water in pressurised pipes – would keep it going, time after time, long after we were all dead ourselves, or whether it needed humans to keep winding it up.

"Those who have never experienced war have no conception of how random and uncontrolled it is," Holmes said over his shoulder. He seemed to be fiddling with the book that he was carrying.

"How did you know what I was thinking?" I called back, amazed as always at how he could penetrate to the heart of my deepest thoughts.

"Your hand moved to your shoulder, to the point where that Jezail bullet impacted," he said. "It was clear that your thoughts had turned to comparing this clockwork conflict to the real thing."

We approached the workshop, with me marvelling at Holmes's uncanny ability to cut to the heart of an emotion merely by observation.

Holmes pushed the door to the workshop open and entered without knocking. "Mr. Drescombe!" he called, "are you in here?"

The interior of the building was immaculate, without any trace of dust or any other contaminant. One wall was completely taken up with metal shelving, on which were set labelled cardboard boxes. I could see *"Gears – Large"*, *"Gears – Medium"*, and *"Gears – Small"*, as well as *"Rods"*, *"Springs"*, *"Axles"*, and many, many other types of mechanical component. The rest of the room was filled with wooden benches on which were numerous simulacra in various states of disrepair. It struck me as very much like the kind of room in which I and my student colleagues had trained as surgeons on various dead bodies that had been donated to our medical school, but without the smell of rotting flesh and chemical preservatives.

Opposite the shelving, near the door, I saw a set of levers, like those in a railway switching box. They were perhaps three feet high, and were set into slots in the wooden floor. I wondered, as I passed them, what their purpose was.

"Who is asking?" a voice called from the far end of the room.

"My name is Sherlock Holmes," my friend announced, striding along the aisle between the benches. "I am here to bring to justice the murderer of Lord Humberside."

"And good luck to you," the voice responded. As we got closer, I saw that the last bench was taken up with the figure of a swordsman dressed in padded white clothes. The automaton's face – if it had a face – was hidden by a protective mesh mask, and its sword had been removed from the extended hand and placed beside it. The cloth covering its limbs had been pushed back, and I could see that the joints were articulated in polished metal, and instead of muscles there was an elaborate construct of cogs and gears and metal struts. The elderly man who I had mistaken for an automaton earlier on was sitting on a stool and bending over it with a pair of pliers in his hand. "With the death of Lord Humberstone, my employment has come to an abrupt end," he said without looking up.

"I understand that it would have come to an end regardless," Holmes countered. "His move to Canada would have resulted in his entire collection being sold."

Drescombe glanced up at my friend, and his expression was twisted in anger. "Her Ladyship is not fond of these exquisite creations," he snapped. "She has no appreciation of the true beauty that comes with recreating life."

"I presume," I said, "that her Ladyship is of the mind that only God can create life."

Drescombe gestured at the half-dismantled fencer on the bench before him. "When this automaton is fixed and back on its plinth, I guarantee that you would not be able to tell its movements from those of a real swordsman."

"Ah," Holmes said, moving to stand in front of the bench, "but could it *engage* with a real swordsman? Could it see the man's lunges and parries? Could it anticipate attacks and take advantage of momentary vulnerabilities? I think not. When all is said and done, this object is no more than a very sophisticated clock mechanism dressed up to look human." He placed the blue-bound tome that he had removed from the library in a clear place on the bench. He positioned it so that its leather spine was directly facing Drescombe.

The mechanic and curator, for his part, stared at the book with a frown on his face. "That is one of Lord Humberstone's books," he said.

"You should return it to the library immediately, or face the consequences of an accusation that you are a thief."

"These automata have no consideration or thought of their own," Holmes continued, as if Drescombe had said nothing. "They merely follow their creator's instructions."

In the silence that followed, I thought I could hear a whirring sound, as if a clock spring was unwinding in preparation for the clock itself to strike, I glanced around, wondering from where the sound originated. There were no clocks in the workshop, and none of the automata that were scattered around appeared to be moving.

Drescombe's gaze was fixed on the book. He put his pliers down carefully on the bench and placed his hands flat on the wooden surface. He appeared to be tensing himself, ready for some precipitate action, but I couldn't understand why.

I moved closer, and I realised that the sound I could hear was actually coming from the book itself!

The whirring noise came to an end with a sudden *click!*

Drescombe threw himself to one side, falling to the floor, as the spine of the book sprang open on hidden hinges down one edge. From my position I couldn't see inside, but I knew now that it wasn't a book at all but a simulacrum of a book filled with springs, gears and cogs.

A sudden loud *choing!* assaulted our ears, and the book jerked as a spring inside was suddenly released. I half-expected something to be projected out of the cavity inside, but there was nothing.

Holmes gestured to me to come closer. "Please, help Mr. Drescombe up," he said. "I fear he has had a shock. He suspected that I had not only found his little automated murder weapon, but that I had also refitted the knife inside. I had not, of course, but he could not take the chance, and by his reaction he has given away his guilt."

I moved around the bench and took Drescombe by the shoulder, pulling him to his feet. As I did so I noticed that the spine of the book was slowly being pulled closed, hiding the interior mechanism and making the device look just like an ordinary book again. "How did you know?" I asked Holmes.

"It was commonplace." Holmes shrugged. "Firstly, it was clear to me that there was not enough space between Lord Humberstone's chair and the bookshelves for an assailant, invisible or not, to stand, let alone to bring his arm back in order to thrust the knife into Humberstone's back. The knife had scratch marks from a metal spring on the pommel. In addition there were marks in the dust on the bookshelves showing where Humberstone had pulled books out to consult them, but the marks were straight, running directly from the books to the edge of the shelves. Only in the case of *this* book were the marks curved, as if the entire spine of the book had been pulled to one side. Or been *pushed* to one side, as I realised."

Drescombe snarled. "The fool would have broken up the collection and sold it! I begged him not to, but he wouldn't listen to me!"

"And so you cold-bloodedly murdered him," Holmes said dispassionately. "And you would have let another man accept the punishment that was due to you. For that you will be called to account."

Drescombe suddenly pulled away from my grasp, lunging for the bench. "I think not," he shouted, grabbing the sword that had belonged to the simulacrum of the fencer and whipped around to face us. The blade slashed towards my face as I moved towards him, and it was only Holmes's hand pulling me back that saved me from a nasty injury.

Drescombe ran for the workshop's door. I raced after him, but he grabbed the shelving as he passed and pulled it over. I jumped to one side as boxes and mechanical components spilled everywhere. Drescombe vanished through the door. I had to clamber over the shelving to follow him. The shelving had fallen against the levers that I had noticed by the door, and as I tried to get past it, the weight of the metal pushed three of the levers across into a different position.

I virtually fell out of the door, and saw Drescombe sprinting across the lawn and towards the Waterloo recreation. He moved fast for a man his age, but I was confident that I could catch up to him before he got to the trees. I began to run, but from behind me I heard Holmes shout: "No! Watson – stop!"

I turned to look back. Holmes was standing in the doorway of the workshop, gesticulating to me. When he saw that he had my attention, he pointed to where Drescombe was running through the British soldiers and their cannons.

I felt, rather than heard, a vibration beneath my feet. The uniformed automata started to move, almost as if Drescombe's presence had disturbed them. I realised with a flash of terrible understanding that the levers inside the workshop – the ones that had been knocked by the falling shelves – controlled the entire display. Drescombe had set it off by accident, and he was running right through the middle of it. If Holmes hadn't stopped me, then I would have been in amongst it myself.

It was the French simulacra emerging from the trees that alerted Drescombe to what was happening. He turned to see what was going on. His face was caught somewhere between desperation and sudden fear.

"Stay where you are!" I yelled. "Stay down!"

The British troops went through the motions of loading the cannons with cannonballs, and ramming them down. Regardless of the man in the middle of the field of battle, they operated as they always had: automatically and without thought.

If Drescombe had stayed where he was he might have been safe – the cannonballs would follow the same paths they always had, and he knew the mechanism so intimately that he could have anticipated them, but he panicked. He tried to run sideways, to safety, but his foot caught on a tuft of grass and he fell. His head blocked the patch of darkness marking one of the holes where the cannonballs ended their flight, and from where they would be conveyed by some underground apparatus back to their starting points. I saw him turn his head and gaze in horror at me, just as the cannons fired.

I turned away. I have seen far too much of the horror of war in my life, and had no great desire to see any more.

Holmes had dived back inside the workshop and tried to pull the levers back again, in order to shut the recreation off, but either the shelves were pushing too hard against them or the apparatus, once initiated, had to keep going until the end. Cannon after cannon fired, and I could imagine only too well Drescombe's body jerking and twitching as the cannonballs hit.

I walked slowly back to the workshop.

"Poetic justice?" Holmes mused as I got to the doorway.

"Perhaps." I sighed. "At least you have proved the innocence of Mycroft's agent. Do you want to convey the news to him in person?"

Holmes shook his head. "I shall send him a telegram informing him of the outcome of my investigations."

I glanced inside the workshop, at the various disassembled simulacra. From behind me I could hear the sounds of the fake, recreated battle. I found myself comparing the automata and simulacra that I had seen with my friend and his brother – two men who never showed emotion and regarded logic as being the most important of characteristics, and who believed that the world ran along predictable, rational lines. And I found myself wondering if there was really a difference between them.

Holmes reached out to take my shoulder. "Come on," he said quietly, "let's head back. I'll treat you to dinner at Simpsons in the Strand. They have some particularly fine bottles of Beune at the moment."

"And will you tell me more about your childhood, and this case when you saved your brother from a charge of murder?" I asked.

He pursed his lips. "Almost certainly not," he said.

210

The Adventure of the Dark Tower

by Peter K. Andersson

Inchwood Cottage sat on the edge of a large field, just where it sloped down towards a small brook and gave way to scattered shrubs that were the beginnings of a dour copse. It had a thatched roof, looking slightly too big for the building underneath it, and the two stories of the house were so low-ceilinged that, when one examined the rows of windows from the outside, it seemed that there was barely enough room for a grown man to stand upright in both floors together. I came upon it on one of my walks during a brief holiday in the farther reaches of Herefordshire, where I had gone to finish a few long-overdue articles for a medicinal journal, while my wife was holidaying elsewhere visiting friends.

The sight of the cottage startled me somewhat, for I had been walking for a good twenty minutes, through woodlands and across fields, without seeing any signs of civilisation, and so I was led to believe that this part of the area was totally uninhabited. I conjectured that it was the dwelling of some gamekeeper or poacher, but as I came nearer, the sight of a man in the garden, busy pruning the rose bushes on the gravel path, forced me to alter my assumption. He was in his mid-thirties, dressed neatly in tweeds similar to my own, and with a head of pomaded hair and cropped side-whiskers that suggested a respectable townsman rather than a man of the wilderness. His appearance contrasted starkly with the rugged moss-grown look of some of the more colourful characters I had encountered in the village. The neglected state of the lane made my approach quite audible from some distance, and the man had had time to react to my advent and walk leisurely down to the gate of his garden before I had arrived at it. His look was not entirely pleasant – there was something akin to anxiety in his eyes – but the faint smile he met me with was more than I had come to expect from these suspicious country dwellers.

"Have you lost your way, perhaps?" he said, absentmindedly hooking a thumb in the pocket of his waistcoat.

"Not particularly. I have been wandering aimlessly for a few hours, and am not really going anywhere."

"Well, this lane leads nowhere. It continues down to the brook and a few yards into the woods, and then it just stops."

"Can one not walk on through the rough country?"

"Hardly. The woods are thick and virtually impenetrable. My best advice to you would be to turn back and take the first turning at the fork in the road, about half a mile up the hill."

"I would, only this road seemed to me to be a shortcut back to the village. It cannot be far beyond the trees."

"Many people think so, but the lay of the land is deceiving. One hardly notices that the lane bends to the north here, leading in the wrong direction. In fact it is the other road that leads to the village."

By this time, I had sensed that this man had a reason for deterring me from going further, a reason that did not have anything to do with the fact that the road ended, but as he was so adamant, I did not wish to infuriate him by insisting, and replied that I would return and go the other way. This news relieved him noticeably, and he became more friendly, asking me whether he could help me in any other way. I told him I thought the cottage was most attractive and that it was partly the sight of it that had encouraged me to continue this way. He seemed delighted, and told me it was over two hundred years old.

"In the old times, the people who dwelled here earned their living on sheep farming, but now the house is owned by a local squire who lets it to people in need of a secluded getaway. Nobody seems to know where the name Inchwood comes from, however, and most likely it descends from a place name associated with the area since medieval times."

"I see. So you lease the cottage? For the season?"

"You might say that."

My question appeared to have made him watchful once more, and I realised that I had overstepped the boundary.

"Well, I can certainly understand why one would want to retreat from the world to a place as peaceful as this," I said, in order to return to the discourse of small-talk. "I have done the same thing, if only for a few weeks."

Seeing an opportunity to steer the conversation away from himself, he enthusiastically inquired about the reason for my holiday, and when he eventually understood who I was, he proclaimed with delight that he was familiar with my name and was an admirer of my accounts of the work of Sherlock Holmes. This naturally led to a series of slightly awkward but heartfelt exchanges of courtesies, and I was both surprised and glad to come across a reader of my work in such a remote place. My identity seemed to sweep away the last remnants of reserve in the man, and the conversation resulted in an invitation into the house, a suggestion that me and my weary limbs were only too glad to accept.

He introduced himself as Elmsley Purkiss, and continued questioning me about my holiday and the walks I had made in the last few days, seemingly most interested in where I had been and just how much of the area I had actually seen. It was not until we were both comfortably seated in two easychairs by a back window overlooking the bordering field that I was given the opportunity to pose similar questions to my host.

"How long have you been living here?"

He sipped his tea, looking into the air with a distant stare.

"A bit too long, perhaps."

"Are you here on holiday?"

"It began as some sort of holiday, I suppose. It then evolved into an obsession. Eventually it turned into a curse."

"You interest me, Mr. Purkiss. If my human experience is anything to go by, I would say that you are a man with a heavy heart."

"Either a heavy heart or a heavy head." He put down his teacup with something akin to resolution. "I feel I want to tell you about my predicament, Dr. Watson, since I trust you and know you to be a man of knowledge and wisdom. One could hardly have hoped for a better receiver of my confession than a man whose writings have convinced me of his honesty and decency. Very well then, I shall tell you my story, but only on the condition that it travels no further than this room, unless of course you should someday wish to share it with your detective friend.

"I am a scholar by profession, a historian as a matter of fact, and I am attached since several years to the University of Cambridge. I came here at the instigation of the squire I mentioned earlier, who is the owner of this cottage and the surrounding land. His name is Marchmont, and I met him at a function in Cambridge about six months ago. We struck up a conversation for no apparent reason, and he seemed genuinely interested in my work, researching the late-medieval tax registers of northern Shropshire. As the hour grew late, our discussion turned to more personal matters, and eventually he put his brandy down on the table and looked at me with a more grave look than before.

"'I wish to tell you something, Dr. Purkiss, a certain personal quandary that a man of your learning might make heads or tails of.'

"I was intrigued, still enthused by our conversation, which had until now remained quite lighthearted, and I encouraged him to continue.

"'There is on my land,' he said, 'not three miles from where my garden gives way to wild unfarmed countryside, a small cottage overlooking a small stream and the edge of a copse. It is a charming and picturesque place, and I have several times let it to holidaymakers with much success, but it is also connected with a piece of local folklore that has a tendency to ward off prospective tenants. It is said that the ford across the stream where the path enters the woods is haunted, and that several people who have walked down that path and crossed the ford have never returned. The story goes that sometime in the sixteenth century, when Marchmont Manor was in the possession of one of my ancestors and his two sons, a local maiden was abducted by a woman who was rumoured to be a witch and taken to an old medieval turret in the midst of the woods. One of the Marchmont sons, Sir Roderick, swore to the locals that he would bring back the girl, and entered the woods on his horse by crossing the stream that bordered it.'

"'From that time, nothing was heard or seen of him for over a year, until suddenly one day he staggered out of the woods at exactly the place where he had entered it, weak and stripped of his armour, walking up to the little cottage where the shepherd and his wife had stepped out on the front steps, curious of the strange, ostensibly tramp-like, wanderer. Sir Roderick collapsed before their feet and they took him in, nursing him for several days. It was clear, however, that he was too enfeebled to regain his strength, and he died there, although not without first providing undeniable proof that he was who he claimed to be by producing the sword branded by the family crest that he had once carried with him into the woods. The shepherd and his wife took the sword to his father and brother at the manor and told them what he had told them, that he had spent a year searching for the maiden but being perpetually misled by the witch, whose magic transformed the woods into a bewildering maze, constantly changing appearance and form.'

"'Sir Roderick's brother, upon hearing the sad news, swore that he would avenge the witch by putting her on the stake, and rode off himself into the woods, only to disappear completely. His father declared that no one was to enter these woods again, and the matter was laid to rest. Since that time, however, there have been continuous reports of strange events in connection with the woods, especially concerning the ghost of a pale-faced maiden who has been seen standing on the other side of the ford, beckoning to passers-by. It is said that this is the girl whom Sir Roderick originally set out to rescue, only now she is seen as a decoy, luring innocent men and women into the woods to become victims of the evil witch.'

"'This would all have been nothing but a colourful piece of folklore, if it had not been for the events of the recent past. Last year, I let the cottage to a newlywed couple who were looking for a romantic hideaway from the bustle of their metropolitan lives. They decided to go home after only a week. The husband came to me and claimed that they had been harassed at all hours of the day by strange screams, and whenever they approached the woods on their walks, the sight of a spectral young girl following them on the other side of the brook, in among the trees, made every attempt at peace of mind futile. Inclined to ascribe the incident to the personalities of the tenants rather than something in the physical reality of the place, I shortly thereafter let the cottage to a young ornithologist who had a special interest in the owls of that region of Herefordshire. But pacing the terrain at night in search of nocturnally active birds only served to make the experience more tangible, and he only lasted a couple of days.'

"Marchmont paused in his narrative and removed his spectacles to wipe the sweat from his eyelids. I was intrigued by his tale rather than unnerved, and the details appealed to my historical interests. I asked him about the continuing fate of the dead knight's family, and he answered as I had suspected.

"'Sir Roderick was my ancestor, and I am now the resident at Marchmont Manor, where my family has lived since the sixteenth century. Somehow I feel a sense of responsibility now that the old family curse has reared its head again, and I feel I should do something, but at the same time I am afraid. You are a scholar and a historian, Dr. Purkiss. What do you suggest I should do?'

"My brain had already begun to make plans for a new research project, and I saw a potential for making exciting new discoveries in the Marchmont family archives that would make me the envy of my peers.

"'I suggest, Mr. Marchmont,' said I, 'that you invite me down to Marchmont Manor this spring. I will come and have a look in your family papers, and maybe even spend a night or two in the cottage. I am certain that some light will be shed on this mystery.'

"Marchmont was hesitant. 'This is a very bad business, indeed, Dr. Purkiss. I would not want to lead you into anything you might regret.'

"'Come now, Mr. Marchmont. Your previous tenants were obviously impressionable and weak-minded people. I hardly expect that a man like myself would react to such events in the same way. My impulse is towards reason and investigation. You forget that you are talking to a Cambridge man!'

"In the course of the following minutes, I managed to persuade him, and arrangements were made for me to come to Herefordshire after the end of term. I looked forward to a peaceful and not too demanding break from my daily routines, but the moment I arrived in this area, it seemed that a cloud of misapprehension appeared above my head.

"You know how it is, Doctor, when you travel and the sensation of actually being in the strange place you have been looking forward to visiting makes you feel much more quaint and bewildered than you could ever have anticipated. This feeling tends to wear off in the first few days, but with this place the process was the opposite. The longer I stayed at Marchmont Manor – a grim Elizabethan mansion in a dreadful state of disrepair – the clearer I felt this unease, and so when it was suggested I go out and stay at Inchwood Cottage for a couple of days, I welcomed the change of scenery. To this point, I had been searching the Marchmont archive for anything that either pertained to the legend of Sir Roderick, or that simply attracted my interest, but to my great disappointment, all I could find were bills, deeds, and dreary farming accounts. I fancied that if I came out to the cottage, I could study the landscape instead, and perhaps even indulge in a bit of amateur archaeology. But whatever self-confidence I may have felt before relocating to the cottage was swept away quickly after the first night here.

"It was not exactly the cottage itself that filled me with dread. You can see for yourself that it is a pleasant and well-kept house, and Mr. Marchmont has made sure it is fitted with the most modern conveniences. The curious feelings were from the beginning connected to the woods. Whenever I glanced out of the window at it, or walked down to the brook, I felt a cold creeping sensation running through me. I decided at first that it was all nonsense, and set out one morning, determined to find my way through the woods and learn whether any remains of a witch's tower could be seen on the other side. I must say, Dr. Watson, that it was probably the most horrendous experience of my life. The screams that I had intermittently heard the previous night were as nothing compared to the terrors of the woods. The first thing that met me after I had crossed the ford and walked up the slope on which the copse was located were the scarecrows. Not ordinary scarecrows, made of straw and old clothes, but scarecrows made of the bones and skulls of animals, tied together and placed on poles that had been driven into the ground at various places.

"These macabre creations seemed to have been erected for the purpose of warding off intruders, and the sight of them made me change direction several times, causing me to lose my way. I believed I had finally come upon a path that would lead me in the right direction, when I look up the hill and saw a human figure standing twenty yards ahead of me. It was like no human I had ever seen before. To all aspects, it was a young girl, but she was emaciated and gaunt, her cheeks sunken as if from starvation, and her eyes contorted into a haunting dark stare. Dressed in nothing but her undergarments, which were tattered and torn,

216

she stretched her long thin arms out towards me, with hands that seemed to have been bound up so that she could not separate her fingers, and she whispered in a voice that imitated the restless wind in the treetops a word that sounded strangely like 'bedrock.' She repeated it a few times, and the last time the uttering of the word transformed into a piercing scream, so full of terror that my nerves failed me, and I ran away from there as fast as I could. I am not proud of my capitulation to supernatural speculations, Dr. Watson, and I trust that your friend Mr. Holmes would be even less proud of me, but that evening, I started to wonder whether Marchmont's story was not true after all, and concluded that what I had encountered in the woods could be nothing other than a ghost, as clear and as horrifying as one might appear.

"My realisation led the way to harrowing contemplations that forced me to question the very foundations of my beliefs. I suppose there was some particle in me that refused to give in to the acknowledgment of the supernatural, and so I decided to stay on in the cottage, to see if anything further could be concluded from the matter. I could not bring myself to enter the woods again, however, and was condemned to wander along its borders like a dog around a cat in a tree. On several occasions, I saw the spectral maiden peering out at me from among the trees, stretching out her arms and calling to me with a strange high-pitched screech reminiscent of some birdcall, and every time I saw her, I ran all the way back to the cottage, my nervous state forcing me to lie down for the rest of the day. Now I have been here all summer, and I have come no closer to an answer in this matter, having little doubt that this obsession will eventually steal away what little reason I have left in me."

The man looked out of the window with a dreamy gaze long after he had finished his story, giving me time to sort out the many impressions and questions that it had left in my mind. When he finally turned his eyes to me, my first question was evident:

"Do you believe the maiden in the woods to be the ghost of the one that Sir Roderick rode out to rescue?"

Dr. Purkiss pursed his lips.

"Yes, I cannot deny it. She is undoubtedly a ghost, and who else would it be? There are no records of any other crime in this part of the world, and the only instance of civilisation here is this cottage. I know it sounds incredible, and you are right to be critical, but if you had seen her like I have, you would feel the same conviction."

"Is she dressed in Elizabethan clothes?"

He smiled.

"She is dressed in undergarments which are torn to pieces, making it quite impossible to judge what period they come from."

217

"I see. Have you made any attempts to walk around the perimeter of the copse, to see if the tower can be seen from the other side?"

"I have had plenty of time this summer to get acquainted with the area enough to be able to draw up a detailed map of it. On the other side of the woods there is a lake which has a reputation for being exceedingly deep. When you observe the woods from the other side of the lake, you can see that the land rises and that the woods are growing on a large hill upon which it is perfectly possible that there has once been a manmade structure, but no documentation in the Marchmont archives, or indeed the village archives, make mention of such a structure. The legend may very well have exaggerated this particular ingredient, as it has been passed down through the generations. I do not expect it to reflect reality completely."

"What do you intend to do?"

"I suppose I will have to leave sooner or later. I have made arrangements with my college to allow me to remain here for a longer period than I had intended, but I cannot prolong my stay indefinitely, and come October, my time here must be terminated."

I found the company of Dr. Purkiss stimulating, and I stayed for another hour while we chatted about other matters – a pastime he seemed to be in desperate need of – but when it started to grow dark, I decided I would not stay to see what would emerge from the woods, and started on my way back to the hotel in the village. That evening, I had dinner on my own in my room and found time to ponder the strange story I had been told. There was something unfulfilled about it, as if Dr. Purkiss had not exactly told me the whole truth, or his supernatural experiences had discouraged him from investigating the matter in full. But above all, it was the fearful images his narrative had evoked that stayed in my mind, and as I went to bed, I found that my brain was at work trying to shed some light on it, making it quite impossible for me to fall asleep.

Instead, I rose from my bed and sat down at the writing-desk by the window, trying with the help of ink and paper to disentangle the jumble of impressions in my head. I started making a list of the various factors of the problem, and as I did so, I realised what would put my mind at rest. I promptly crumpled up my list and produced a fresh sheet of writing paper, immediately starting on a letter to Sherlock Holmes that related Dr. Purkiss' story in detail. I knew deep down that whenever a mystery like this came my way, old habits had taught me that laying the matter before Holmes was the only certain path to peace of mind. I remembered that Dr. Purkiss had, in passing, given me permission to communicate the story to Holmes, and although this remark might have been an unreflected impulse of courtesy, my insomniac self seized upon this vague consent to be able to obey its natural instincts. I consequently gave a full description of the story I had come in contact with that afternoon, using a few months of silence between me and my friend as an excuse to write to him.

The next morning I posted the letter in the village, before embarking on a new walk that would circle the boundaries of the haunted copse. As I trudged the wild terrain, my mind wandered, and the legend of Sir Roderick made me think of that strange and mysterious poem by Browning, *Childe Roland to the Dark Tower Came*, about a young knight on an aimless quest, approaching a dark tower at the edge of an inhospitable wasteland. The parallels were not obvious, but I suppose it was the way Dr. Purkiss had called the witch's dwelling a "dark tower" that made me recall the poem from long ago, and especially the passage that went –

> *What with my whole world-wide wandering,*
> *What with my search drawn out through years, my hope*
> *Dwindled into a ghost not fit to cope*
> *With that obstreperous joy success would bring,*
> *I hardly tried now to rebuke the spring*
> *My heart made, finding failure in its scope.*

– which to me conjured up the same sense of hopelessness that distinguished both Sir Roderick's undertaking and Dr. Purkiss' research. My walk did not produce any knowledge beyond what Dr. Purkiss had already told me, except that I was allowed to see for myself the lake on the other side of the woods, and the difficulty one would meet by trying to penetrate it from that side. I forced myself to devote the afternoon to my article and continued with my writing the next day, which eventually made me think less about my visit to Inchwood Cottage. Two days after my meeting with Dr. Purkiss, the girl at the hotel reception stopped me on my way from breakfast to tell me I had received a letter. It was from Holmes of course, and I rushed up to my room to see what he had written. The letter read as follows:

My dear Watson,

Glad to hear you are well and everything, but more importantly, I must thank you for bringing the Inchwood case to my attention. Your report was most detailed, and I have gone over the basic facts several times since I received your letter. On the whole, however, I must conclude that you could have posed much more probing questions to Purkiss than you did. Firstly, when it comes to his willingness to accept a supernatural explanation, we must ensure that there is nothing in his background that facilitates this, such as the loss of a loved one, or a history of supernatural belief in his family.

What exactly is his experience of women? His reaction to seeing a frightened and helpless girl in the woods seems most ungentlemanlike. Secondly, what can we really know about what is going on in the woods beyond what the legend would have us think? It is very easy to view a problem from one side without being able to imagine the completely different appearance it would have were it viewed from another angle. This lack of imagination is usually what divides us from our fellow man. I therefore encourage you to go back to your feebleminded historian and ask him to describe more fully what he has actually seen. Then write to me again as soon as possible.

Holmes's sparse but sober words reassured me that there were still avenues of inquiry that needed to be explored before a supernatural explanation should be seriously considered. At the same time, I think that Holmes's physical distance from the scene hindered him from appreciating the non-verbal nuances of the case – Dr. Purkiss' way of telling the story, the grim and unwelcoming atmosphere of the copse – thus being less inclined to see it the way I did. Always taking my friend's advice, however, I followed his instructions and paid another visit to Inchwood Cottage.

I found Dr. Purkiss as I had the previous time, hard at work on the rose bushes, a hobby that seemed to take his mind away from the sad reasons for his continued tenancy. There is no need for me to put down the words that passed between us on this occasion. It was a pleasant visit, and Dr. Purkiss was delighted to see me again. Much of our conversation was devoted to other matters, but I did press him on the details of his narrative, and he was most insistent in defending his interpretation of the events. I left him none the wiser than when I came, and feared that my next letter to Holmes would be dissatisfying to him. However, when I returned to the hotel, I learned that a new letter had arrived. It was from Holmes, written only the day after the previous one:

My dear Watson,

I had just sent Billy to the post office with your letter when I sat myself down with the task of pasting the week's newspaper clippings into my scrapbook, and came upon a most tantalising but brief report from the Gazette of the 15th inst. The connection to your story was not clear, but the outline of this followed too closely the outline of yours to keep me from investigating further. I ran off to the library to consult the regional newspapers of that particular part of the country.

My findings confirmed my suspicions and stirred vague thoughts about this case at the back of my mind that I had been unable or too lazy to verbalise in my letter to you. For instance: what invisible border allows a woman to appear inside a forest but keeps her from appearing outside it? The way she – or they – appeared at the edge of the woods seemingly beckoning to passers-by made me increasingly suspicious. The state of her hands will, I am sure, provide the key to this. And then there was that word she had used when encountering Purkiss: "Bedrock." This constitutes nothing short of evidence, Watson!

My following course of action was to purchase as comprehensive Ordnance Survey maps of the area as I could find, and I have now spent a few stimulating hours in their company, exploring the region in much the same fashion as I have no doubt you have been doing for the past few days. The expedition reveals something quite extraordinary. In an old 18th-century book on the Marchmont family that I found at Cecil Court, there was a reproduction of an old map of the estate. It was done by a visiting surveyor, which explains why it would not have been in the family archives, and it shows the copse much as it looks on modern maps, apart from one thing. There is a building in the middle of the woods that has disappeared in the later maps. Now, why is this? Has it been demolished? Is someone trying to hide its existence?

I think the real answer is more prosaic. No one has bothered to look at this map when drawing up the new ones, and the resurrected legend might explain why no 19th-century surveyor has felt the urge to penetrate the woods, while a Georgian man of the Enlightenment found little reason for apprehension. After all, if one disregards the legend, it is just a boring grove of trees.

So where does this lead us, Watson? It leads us to a very exciting development. There is something in the woods, but not what Dr. Purkiss thinks. And the circumstantial evidence of the newspaper reports tells us to act, with speed and determination. It is a matter of life and death, and I fear you would not forgive yourself – if I know you correctly – should you be too late to avert a tragedy, or at least to prevent a tragedy from progressing further. By Heavens, I wish I was there to assist you! Pressing engagements and a lack of time prevents me, but I wish you luck, my friend, and good hunting.

The letter explained nothing further, but enclosed with it were two newspaper clippings, which Holmes would have thought would be sufficient data for me to put two and two together. In the upper corner of each of them, I recognised his handwriting giving the date and name of the publication from which it was cut. The first one was two weeks old and came from *The Times*:

MYSTERIOUS DISAPPEARANCES IN HEREFORDSHIRE. The Echo reports that another local girl has vanished in the area of the town of Great Rumsey in northern Herefordshire. Readers may recall the mysterious disappearance last summer of Jenny Mayle, 19, who worked as a milkmaid at Crossways Farm. She lived in a stable building adjoining the main house and vanished overnight, the farmer and his family having heard no suspicious sounds. According to a witness statement from a farmhand, it was as if she had been dragged away from her bed and out into the night. Although the police initially suspected the farmer and his family, no evidence could be found against them, and it seemed increasingly likely that the crime had been perpetrated by an outsider.

This case was elicited by the locals in late May of this year, when a similar incident took place. The victim was a Miss Millicent Ellis, 23, the daughter of a local butcher, who walked home one evening from the village of Bramhurst to her family home two miles away, but never arrived. As no traces have been found in over three weeks of searching, the police are beginning to abandon the possibility that Miss Ellis has been the victim of a crime, instead believing that she has met with some sort of accident, possibly drowning in one of the treacherous meres hidden in the surrounding forests. The similarity of the two cases is striking, and the newspapers are starting to speculate on whether they might be related, but the local police insist that there are still too few indications of a shared culprit.

After reading this account, I was beginning to see what Holmes was driving at in his letter, but when I read the second clipping, things started to fall into place. It was from a local paper, dated the previous spring:

ESCAPE FROM GLOUCESTER. A dramatic escape took place yesterday at Gloucester County Gaol of the notorious criminal Julius Bedrock, who was caught three years ago on suspicion of assaulting several young women in the area of Ledbury, Herefordshire, including his own former wife, Mrs. Elizabeth Bedrock, who subsequently died of her injuries. Only a lack of evidence saved Mr. Bedrock from a death penalty, but now that he is once again at large, the police fear that he will continue his rampage, and possibly commit even more heinous crimes than before. The escape was carried out by means of a rope that had been secured to the prison wall, but it could only be successfully executed through the willful neglect of one or several members of the staff, which is why the director has ordered a full investigation and interrogation of the guards on duty at the time of the escape.

There was only one thing that related this item to the story of Dr. Purkiss, but it was enough to make me see it in an entirely new light. It was, of course, the name of Bedrock, which was not unique, but uncommon enough to consider the possible parallels. The evidence that Holmes had provided me with indicated several things: that this man Bedrock was in some way connected to whatever was going on in the woods, that there was possibly a building in the woods, and that the spectral maiden or maidens that Purkiss had seen were, if not ghosts, then the ghostlike manifestations of young girls abducted from the surrounding area.

Whether they were alive or not, I was still too committed to Purkiss' perspective to say, but there were no doubts that I should contact the local police immediately. I chose to do this without contacting Purkiss or Mr. Marchmont, and I feared that the men at the sleepy little provincial station would dismiss me as a highly-strung city dweller overreacting on my encounter with something rural and uncivilised, but to my delight they listened to my story and sensed my earnestness. The Superintendent looked at the newspaper clippings that I had brought with me, and ordered that all his men be rounded up to assist us in investigating the matter.

Daylight was beginning to fade as we arrived at Inchwood Cottage and the ford that constituted the main entrance into the copse. I saw no light in the windows of the cottage and concluded that Dr. Purkiss had gone to bed, deciding that it would be unnecessary to worry him with what was going on until we had been able to acquire some answers. The Superintendent led the way into the woods, and although I was prepared for it, I was a startled as the policemen to see the grotesque scarecrows of animal bones that lined the path up the hill. Some of the men suggested we do it in the morning, but the Superintendent urged them not to mind about attempts at deterrence, and we continued on our way.

Eventually we came upon something resembling a bundle of clothes lying by the foot of a birch tree. As we came closer, it turned out to be the lifeless body of a young girl, wearing nothing but her petticoat. One of the men kneeled beside her and declared that she was still breathing. I examined her quickly and concluded that she had been starved and assaulted, but thanks to her youth she was not dying. What struck me most of all, however, was her hands, which had been bound up so that her fingers could not be separated, just as Dr. Purkiss had described. I also noticed that there was a strong rope tied around her waist which led away from her body, snaking up the hill through the trees. I called the policemen's attention to this, and we followed the rope up the hill.

It led us twenty yards onwards, to a small clearing in which was standing some sort of structure. In the fading sunlight, it appeared to me like a wide and crooked tower, about three stories high, but ruined, suggesting that it had once been higher. At this moment, a curious and not particularly pleasant sensation was roused in my stomach. It was the presentiment of darkness, not physical night-time darkness, but human darkness, the bottomless pit of the diseased human soul. And I was once more reminded of Browning and his pathetic knight, who was beginning to prefer the prospect of failure to the potentially overpowering chance of consummation.

Was this consummation, the confrontation with the fact of the matter, too horrendous to imagine? Was it perhaps better to revert to unworldly fantasising, interpreting the grim consequences of human actions as signs of the wondrous and supernatural, instead of having to acknowledge what they really were? I let the professional policemen walk ahead of me into the building, which, I suppose, was nothing more than an old cowshed or hay barn, preserved in this remote corner since a time when this copse was a field, but turning in my defensive fantasy into something more romantic and more manageable.

Julius Bedrock was brought out of that building screaming and kicking, and it took three strong policemen to be able to hold him down and convey him to the prison wagon. Inside were also found the remains of Jenny Mayle, the lost milkmaid, who had been abducted by Bedrock the previous summer and kept in his secret hideaway for as long as her powers allowed her. The other girl was identified as Millicent Ellis, the butcher's daughter, and in spite of her delicate state, she eventually managed to regain her strength and her health was restored, although the mental scars that her experiences at Bedrock's lair would take much more time to heal.

The police initially considered the possibility that Bedrock had been able to hide in the forest barn thanks to the assistance of Mr. Marchmont, or someone in his household, but upon further investigation, these suspicions were abandoned, and it seemed that when Marchmont presented his trepidation concerning Inchwood Cottage and the adjoining woods, he truly believed the matter to be a supernatural one. Since Bedrock's escape the year before, he had hidden from the world in the woods, but being unable to curb his unnatural urges, he kidnapped the two girls, keeping them from running away by tying them to a rope that was fastened to a tree by the barn, and then tying up their hands so that they would not be able to loosen the ropes when Bedrock looked away.

Just as Holmes had implied, the state of the girls' hands provided the key. The ropes allowed them to wander freely around the copse, but they were just short enough to prevent them from venturing outside its borders. In some moments, however, they were visible to passers-by from outside. Fortunately for Bedrock, there was an old legend tied to the place that made people interpret what they had seen in ways that prevented a full investigation. I cannot deny that I myself was also taken in by this collective misapprehension, and not until it was brought to the attention of Sherlock Holmes could it be brought to a satisfying conclusion.

I naturally conveyed the news about the raid to Dr. Purkiss, who received it with considerable delight and relief. It was as if a stone had been lifted from his chest, and he said to me that the shackles that had tied him to this place in the shape of a mental obsession had been loosened, thanks to me. Our meeting through this case became the beginning of a continuing friendship, and I still regard him as one of my more insightful and humble acquaintances, his modesty perhaps improved by the experiences he had in connection to this mystery.

Holmes's attitude to his handling of the matter remains more reserved, as the resort to supernatural considerations that Purkiss was guilty of is his constant enemy. To me, it is only a too-endearing proof that he is human, something that I realised the depths of when I came to the Dark Tower of Inchwood Copse. Nevertheless, I have taken to heart the words that Holmes wrote to me in a telegram shortly after the events, upon learning the gratifying conclusion of the case:

> *I have always been suspicious of scholars, Watson. They are so certain of themselves that when their worldviews are undermined, they turn into the only other workgroup that is as presumptuous – priests.*

The Adventure of the
Reluctant Corpse
by Matthew J. Elliott

It would not be entirely fair to say that with my second marriage, my partnership with Sherlock Holmes came to a conclusion. I trust, however, that I am not telling tales out of school when I say that my wife's feelings regarding my old friend certainly made the continuation of our working relationship rather more difficult. I was never entirely certain of the reasons for her enmity towards the man with whom I had stood shoulder-to-shoulder throughout numerous adventures, but a married man's obligations must, first and foremost, be to his bride. That is why the evening of the 24th of December 1902 did not find me at Baker Street, sharing a pipe with an old friend, but at the Kensington home of Sir Boris Wyngarde, that well-known figure in fashionable society. I must confess, we owed our presence there at least in part to Holmes; as a result of my published accounts of his investigations, I was at that time enjoying a certain celebrity, which resulted in our invitation to that festive occasion.

Sir Boris, whose reputation was enhanced by a suggestion of improprieties in his distant past, was at our side within moments of our arrival. I had earlier informed Kate of our host's peculiar disability, and she did not so much as blink when the heavy, elderly gentleman took her hand, voicing his regret that we had been unable to join him at his home in the country for the pheasant shooting a week earlier.

"We hoped very much to attend, Sir Boris," I replied, "But I'm afraid medical duties required my presence in London."

"*And* Mr. Sherlock Holmes," Kate added, pointedly. Clearly, my absence when serving as a witness to the confession of the Fitzrovia Strangler still rankled with her.

"Ah, the illustrious Mr. Holmes! I understand he couldn't be persuaded to join us this evening."

I explained that my colleague was not of a particularly social disposition, a fact anyone who had actually read my narratives would have realised.

"I hear talk that he is to be immortalized in wax," said Sir Boris.

I tried to avoid my wife's glance as I replied that, yes, Holmes had indeed been approached by Madame Tussaud's, but that that he had declined the honour. And perhaps unsurprisingly, the possibility of a wax

227

effigy of myself without Holmes was deemed quite out of the question. This was a matter of small concern to me, but once she had me to herself again, I could tell that she was quite incandescent with displeasure.

"Why didn't you tell me any of this?" she demanded. "My own husband, in Madame Tussaud's?"

"There was never any real chance of that," I explained. "And I didn't want you to get your hopes up, dear."

Thankfully, Sir Boris came to my rescue at that moment, returning in the company of another guest. It did not take a Sherlock Holmes to deduce that this fellow was a military man like myself; his uniform and smartly-trimmed dundrearies told me that. He was introduced to me as Captain Enoch Courtney of Her Majesty's Cavalry, but I could not for the life of me shake the sensation that I had encountered him elsewhere, and that when I had, he had not been going by that name.

"I thought the two of you might have a good deal in common," our host explained, "both of you being former soldiers."

"You'll forgive me, Captain," said Kate, "but you seem a little young to be retired."

Courtney lowered his head and smirked in what I thought a most ungentlemanly fashion. "Sadly, Mrs. Watson, an old bullet wound means I am no longer able to sit astride a horse. Are you a cavalry veteran, also, Doctor?"

"A humble army surgeon," I replied. "Fifth Northumberland Fusiliers. I have the strangest feeling, Captain, that we may already have met, Captain?

"I don't believe so," he replied. "Of course, I saw a number of doctors after I was shot."

"No, that's not it. But I'm quite certain I've seen you before."

"Certainly not in your other capacity, dear," Kate suggested.

The casual observer might have failed to notice any change in the Captain's countenance, but thanks to my years spent at Holmes's side, I flatter myself that I am no casual observer. A sudden flurry of blinking told me that something had unnerved the fellow.

"Are you by any chance the same Dr. Watson who assists the famous Mr. Sherlock Holmes?" he asked.

Kate began to explain that, in her opinion, I was more than a mere assistant, and could surely have solved many, if not all, of the cases I had chronicled unaided. Thankfully, before my embarrassment could become too acute, the chime of the doorbell and Sir Boris' consequent excitation captured everyone's attention. Prevented by his missing thumbs from opening the door himself, I stepped forward to perform the task while Kate took the lull in conversation as an opportunity to refresh her glass.

Our host's glee at discovering a group of carollers waiting on his doorstep was a joy in itself to behold, and he clapped his thumbless hands together with a delight I had previously only observed in children or the simple-minded.

"Splendid, my friends, splendid!" he cried.

It may be that I am at fault in recalling that the singers had chosen *In the Bleak Midwinter* with which to regale us; very likely, I am confusing this moment with the incident, far later in the evening, when Holmes and I found ourselves desecrating a grave, like a modern-day Burke and Hare. But I am getting ahead of myself.

All those present registered their approval with enthusiastic applause; so enthusiastic, in fact, that it was a full minute before I noticed Captain Courtney's distress. He clutched his throat with one hand while waving the other frantically to attract attention. The guests ceased their gestures of approval and began to panic; the carollers, however, continued their melodious celebration, entirely unaware of the drama that was occurring inside the house.

Stepping forward, I was in time to catch Courtney as he collapsed, but the weight of his form was almost too great, and I struggled to rest him gently on the floor. By now, a circle of guests had formed around us, shocked and fascinated by this incident. Sir Boris urged them to allow me enough room to examine the fellow, before kneeling at my side, as eager as his friends to sample this fresh sensation.

"What's the matter with him, Watson? Too much wine, do you think?"

It was the matter of a moment to confirm that the Captain's condition was far more serious – I could detect no pulse; he was most certainly dead.

Sir Boris tugged at his remaining strands of hair with distress. "This is infamous! Nothing like this has ever happened before!"

"The authorities will have to be sent for," I informed him.

"Yes, of course, of course. I say, I suppose I can rely on your for a death certificate, old man?"

I assured him that I would take care of all the formalities, requesting that the servants carry the body into the kitchen, where I might conduct a full examination in private. I confess that I was not being entirely forthcoming with my host; I hoped that the removal of the corpse might give me enough time to speak to Kate without being overheard. She was not entirely overjoyed by my request that she take a cab to Baker Street at once.

"I need you to fetch Mr. Holmes," I explained. "You are the only one here I can trust. There is something very strange going on, something

I am unable to account for."

"And you imagine that Mr. Holmes can?" she asked.

"I sincerely hope so. Tell him that Scotland Yard must be notified also."

It would certainly have been of use to my friend had I scribbled even the briefest of notes of explanation, but at that moment, when I could scarcely accept the evidence of my own eyes, I feared it might do more harm than good. At the moment of his death, I had at last remembered where I had last seen Captain Courtney. And on that occasion, as now, he was quite dead. How could I expect anyone, even Sherlock Holmes, to believe my claim without the opportunity to see the man for himself. Surely, then, there could be no doubt in his mind.

I was somewhat irritated when Sir Boris insisted on following me into the kitchen where the dead man presently lay on a table, looking for all the world like a reveller who has imbibed too freely and found the first place to lay his head. But as I began to loosen Courtney's clothing, prior to beginning my examination, my host blanched, before excusing himself, explaining that he had rather a lot of guests who required calming down, and only a limited amount of champagne with which to accomplish that task. It was a relief to be able to carry on my work without interruption, I thought, though this was certainly the strangest Christmas Eve I had ever experienced!

"And now, 'Captain' . . ." I said as much to myself as to the corpse, "let's see if I can ascertain precisely *how* you died." I began to roll up his shirt sleeves when something caught my attention. I peered at the man's left hand. Had I not been thus distracted, I might have heard someone creeping up on me, but the first I was aware of another presence in the kitchen was when I felt the cold sting of metal brush against my cheek. I did not need to see it to know that it was the barrel of a revolver.

"There's nothing here that need concern you, Doctor," said the man behind me. I recognized his accent as Canadian, or perhaps American.

"Who the devil are you, and how long have you been hiding here?" I demanded.

"You worry too much," replied the stranger, calmly. "It's not healthy. If you continue to fret like this, you could end up with a bullet in your chest. And, yes, that is my way of telling you that if you even think of calling for help, I'll shoot you."

I was in no position to do anything other than comply with the stranger's wishes. "Just what do you want of me?" I asked.

"Simply some heavy lifting – a task far below your station in life, I'm afraid. I'd like you to drag your patient outside, where I have a vehicle waiting."

It seemed to me strange that he should refer to the Captain as my "patient," since, it seemed to me he was very far from recovery.

"You might want to grip him under the arms – I should hate for you to get a bad back."

Despite the tendency of my knee to give way beneath me in the cold weather, I was nonetheless able to drag the body out of the house via the servants' entrance and into a nearby cab. I felt quite winded by the time I was done, but that was by far the least of my concerns, since it seemed entirely likely that this foreigner, whose face I had still not seen, would kill me as soon as I had completed my task.

"Are you happy now?" I asked, leaning against the vehicle, exhausted.

"Don't I look happy?" he asked, stepping closer. In truth, I was unable to answer his question, for though he was at that moment standing beneath a street-lamp, a scarf concealed the lower portion of his features. As odd as it may sound, I took heart in this, for I knew – or perhaps I should say, I hoped – that as long as he continued to conceal his identity, he had no reason to do away with me. That was not to say, however, that he would not hurt me considerably, if he so chose, and as he swung the revolver at my head, I recalled thinking that he had evidently come to a decision.

"'Physician, heal thyself . . . .'"

"Shakespeare," I murmured, "*Macbeth*, I think." My eyelids seemed absurdly heavy. Opening them would require all my strength.

"Luke, Chapter Four, actually. My knowledge of the *New Testament* is more reliable than that of the *Old*."

Finally, my weary old body obeyed its master's instructions, and with a struggle, I found myself staring up into the face of Mr. Sherlock Holmes. It was evident even to my addled senses that he had discovered my prostrate form in the snow, and brought me back into the house.

"This is really most inconvenient, you know, old fellow. Mrs. Hudson promised me a goose."

"And you have my profound apologies, Holmes," I replied, slowly raising myself up and realising that I had lain upon the kitchen table that had earlier served as a temporary resting place for the body I had been forced at gunpoint to remove.

"I deduce from the marks in the frost," said Holmes, "that *you* were the one who transported the deceased to a waiting vehicle. Under duress, one hopes."

"At gunpoint, in fact," I explained. "Where's Kate, Holmes?"

"Attempting to calm your excitable host. She was most concerned for your well-being. I explained to her that her presence at your side was entirely unnecessary, and that you have sustained far worse injuries in my company – for some reason, that seemed only to annoy her."

Glad to be on my feet after occupying the bed of a dead man, I was prepared to ignore the throbbing pain at my temple, the result of being struck with a revolver earlier in the evening. In any event, Holmes's arrival meant that I could at last divest myself of the suspicion I had held since first encountering the so-called Captain Enoch Courtney.

"Holmes, I know you'll find this hard to believe, but I'll swear the dead man was Erasmus Crow – the man behind the British Railway Owner's Society fraud, among other criminal coups."

Sherlock Holmes did not so much as blink, even though he knew as well as did I that Crow had been dead for some three months. "Why should I find that hard to believe, Watson? This may be the time of year for miracles, but I suspect there is, in this instance, a logical explanation. Please don't imagine for a moment that I don't believe you, old friend. If you are confident that you saw Erasmus Crow alive, then I am quite satisfied that is what you saw."

I must own, I was relieved and gladdened to hear that Holmes was prepared to take me at my word, when any other man might call me deranged; not only that, I realised, but he had followed my instructions to the letter, and summoned the police, which now seemed an eminently sensible course of action, given that the corpse of Erasmus Crow, or whoever it happened to be, had been forcibly removed from the premises. The rodent-like face of Inspector Lestrade peeked in through the kitchen door.

"Did I hear someone mention Erasmus Crow, the one that got away?" he asked. I bade the policeman a good evening. "Of course, the only reason he got away was because he dropped dead before we could charge him."

"Nothing less than the grave would deter an officer as tenacious as yourself, Lestrade."

We all three recalled the incident of Crow's demise, but I had particular cause to do so – he had complained of chest pains for several weeks prior to his eventual demise, and his personal physician had no hesitation in identifying a heart attack as the cause of death. There was surely no question that the doctor was a willing participant in any deception, however; Marcus Foxborough and I both belonged to the Hippocratic Club, and I was actually present when he arrived with a guest, that very same Erasmus Crow who collapsed and died before my eyes – but seemingly not for the final time. I confirmed Foxborough's state myself, and I was satisfied that the man was most sincerely dead. And yet, how could I account for his appearance at Sir Boris' festivities?

"Crow *is* definitely dead this time, I suppose?" asked Lestrade, with some amusement.

"He had no pulse, Inspector – that is a very common indication, one of the first they teach in medical school, in point of fact."

"One wonders whether this might signal the end of a permanent state of decease," Holmes mused. "What might that mean in return for my craft? I could, for instance, be called upon to solve multiple murders of a single victim. Or, the police may no longer view it as a particularly serious offence, and I'll be forced to seek an alternative profession. I understand the Liverpool Symphony has a vacancy for a lead violinist." My friend has the oddest ideas of what constitutes humour. It can be rather trying at times.

With a shrug, Lestrade queried whether there might even be a crime to investigate, and though it pained me to admit it, I could understand his position: with Crow having been pronounced dead so many months ago, why should Scotland Yard take any interest in his second death?

"Perhaps because," Holmes suggested, "during his period of resurrection, he impersonated a military officer. Unlike the good doctor, I am no betting man, but I should be prepared to wager a hefty sum that His Majesty's Cavalry have no record of a Captain Courtney. It's unfortunate, Doctor, that you were unable to conduct an examination before you were waylaid."

I so rarely have the opportunity to surprise one of so great an intellect that I took appreciable satisfaction in informing him about the small bruise I observed on the back of Crow's left hand.

"So he may have been injected with some poison?" Lestrade suggested, demonstrating the instinctive grasp for the obvious that had made him the envy of the Yard. "It must have happened just after those carollers arrived – everyone's attention was distracted, the perfect moment. Which means that everyone present is under suspicion. Except for yourself, Doctor. And this Sir Boris Wyngarde, I suppose. You don't invite someone 'round to celebrate Christmas and then murder them. Do you?"

"I imagine it would be rather difficult to use a syringe without thumbs," Holmes noted, adding to my considerable surprise, "although from what you've told me, I have no doubt that he would be quite capable of murder. Didn't you ever read pirate stories when you were a lad, Watson? You remember the standard punishment for piracy?"

With mounting unease, I realised that I did indeed know: the penalty was to be strung up by the thumbs. Though he had always hinted at a colourful past, I saw at that moment that it may have been more colourful than any one of us could have imagined. "Holmes . . . do you suspect he and Crow may have been involved in something nefarious?"

"In the absence of evidence, suspicions are entirely worthless, my dear Watson."

I have often been duped by Sherlock Holmes when he has assumed a role, in particular on a night shortly after my first marriage when he managed to convince me that he was alarmingly close to death. I am rarely so easily duped by anyone else, however, and had I been required to swear on the Bible that Sir Boris was genuinely surprised to be told of Captain Courtney's true identity, I would have done so willingly.

"Then . . . then . . . What about the expedition?" he blathered.

"Not, by any chance, to the treasure-laden tomb of some previously unknown Egyptian Pharaoh? I'm afraid to say that the late Mr. Crow has tricked several wealthy men out of their fortunes with the same scheme."

His chins wobbled in protest. "No, no! I've seen the map!"

"I imagine I could show you its twin," Lestrade informed him. "We still have it in evidence. What a fellow this Crow was, eh? No better than a pirate, one might say. Please don't tell me you gave him any money. Funds for the expedition, that sort of thing? You did? Oh dear! I suppose if you were to give me an address for Captain Courtney, there's just a chance I might be able to recover some of it."

Sir Boris raised eight fingers to the sky in a gesture of despair. "I really don't know. I always just saw him at the club. I was under no illusions that the address he provided when he applied for membership was certainly false."

"Well, that leaves us with nothing," said the policeman, regretfully. "No clues, and no body."

Holmes was not one to be disheartened. "A funeral must have been carried out on the occasion of Crow's first death, Lestrade. Perhaps an examination of his coffin would be enlightening."

I am certain that the Inspector would have joined me in considering grave-robbing an unsuitable past-time during the festive season, but Holmes was a man of progressive notions, and I doubted that anything I might say would deter him from this course of action. Thankfully, Kate's interruption at that moment at least meant a temporary respite from such an unpleasant and – without the proper permissions – illegal activity.

"John, dear," she said, "I've been observing the constables interviewing the guests . . . and it seems to me that someone is missing."

"I'm afraid you're mistaken, Mrs. Watson," Sir Boris assured her. "Everyone I invited is still present."

Kate, Lord bless her persistence, would not be put off. "I'm certain I saw a woman . . . rather short, and dumpy . . . grey-haired . . . and wearing a faded red dress." The more details my wife added to her description, the more I was able to picture the very woman. I, too, had seen her, conspicuous at the time by her lack of ostentation, but who was now noticeably absent from Sir Boris' home.

My own admission seemed to spark something in our host's memory also. "Ah, yes!" he cried. "That would be Mrs. Warrender – but she wasn't a guest; she just popped by to wish me the compliments of the season."

Lestrade enquired who this Mrs. Warrender, whom Sir Boris apparently didn't like well enough to invite to his annual festivities, might be.

"Please don't misunderstand me, Inspector – she's is a fine lady . . . just not exactly of the 'first rank,' if you understand what I'm getting at." I sensed from the tightening of Kate's grip upon my arm that she, for one, did not understand. "As you may know, I am exceptionally fond of the unconventional, but there *are* limits – I mean, a working woman, I ask you!"

"And precisely what *is* that work?" I felt compelled to ask.

"Oh, the importation of exotic animals. I believe she inherited the firm from her late husband. Her son, Ridley, provided me with a Burmese Jungle Fowl for my country estate, and I'm presently negotiating for a Bengal Tiger." He placed a finger to his chin in a gesture of thoughtfulness. "I wonder if there's time to cancel the order and get my money back?" It seemed that his forgetfulness regarding Mrs. Warrender extended to being able to say with any certainty just when she left the celebration. It was, he suspected, some time before the arrival of the carollers. Then again, it may very well have been afterwards. With regard to the lady's address, he was only slightly more helpful, suggesting that she might be found in Lewisham, possibly somewhere near the brick-works. It did not seem like too great a task for our police force to locate an importer of strange beasts in Lewisham, but my hopes that the home of Mrs. Warrender might be our first port of call were soon dashed; Holmes was almost indecently keen to discover who might be buried in Erasmus Crow's grave, since the man himself had been alive and well until just a few hours ago.

It pains me to acknowledge that this was not the only impromptu exhumation in which I participated during my association with Sherlock Holmes; readers may recall the ghastly events that plagued the Canadian village of La Mort Rouge. On that occasion, we were without assistance from a member of the police force, but our position was now no less precarious, Lestrade having allowed himself to become infected by Holmes's insatiable curiosity and thus, after identifying the cemetery in which Crow had supposedly been buried, rapidly procured a couple of shovels, but none of the appropriate legal documents.

And so we set about our work, a cloud masking the moon, and the lateness of the hour preventing us from being seen. If anyone had observed our actions, Holmes at least would have been deemed entirely innocent, for he was reluctant to assist with the digging, preferring instead to examine the nearby grass through his lens.

"Holmes, if you wished, you could give us a hand," I suggested, with, I hope, a certain chilliness in my tone. "The ground's not all that hard, you know."

"And don't you find that interesting, Watson?"

Indeed I did not, since at that particular moment, I was wondering how I'd strayed so far from my notion of the ideal Christmas as to find myself several feet down in the earth in the process of uprooting a corpse.

"You have no doubt failed to notice that the grass around this grave is scorched."

"That's hardly surprising, Mr. Holmes," Lestrade complained. "How could I have noticed that when I can hardly see my shovel in front of my face?"

Holmes might have explained himself right away, but he was at that moment enjoying our discomfort and bewilderment rather too much. "Do you by any chance recall the words of *In the Bleak Midwinter*, Watson? 'Earth stood hard as iron' . . . ."

I saw at last just what he was driving at. In December, the ground should certainly have been as hard as iron, but our digging had gone fairly easily – easier still for Holmes, who had not participated in any way.

"It has, in point of fact, been softened with the aid of a small, controlled fire," he explained to a still-befuddled Lestrade. "Someone has been here before us, gentlemen."

The Inspector was most displeased by this revelation, and threw down his shovel in anger. The noise of its impact – that of metal striking wood – informed us that we had at last discovered the coffin for which we had been digging. Holmes at least offered the use of his muscles in raising it from the pit and resting it upon the ground; from its weight, it was clear that someone or something lay inside.

Lestrade's foresight had not stretched to the acquisition of a crowbar, and a shovel proved too unwieldy, so in the end, it took the sheer brute force of three men to wrest the lid from the casket. There was, as I suspected, something exceptionally heavy inside. But the fact that I had seen Erasmus Crow earlier that night could not prepare me for the presence of his body in the coffin. He was, for the third time, quite dead. But the cause of his demise on this occasion was not an injection of some unknown potion; the blood surrounding the hole in his chest served as proof that he had been alive at the moment he was shot.

The three of us would have some questions to answer concerning the circumstances under which we discovered the body, but Crow's obviously violent demise meant that we had no difficulty in securing the use of the mortuary for his long-delayed autopsy.

I had already dismissed the idea of identical twins – or even triplets – as the sort of far-fetched nonsense one might find in a yellow-backed novel, but I knew that Holmes would not discount it entirely until it had been proven impossible rather than simply improbable. Thankfully, I was able to provide this assurance almost immediately, for the dead man bore the same mark on his hand that I had observed at Sir Boris' home.

"Surely there can be no further doubt that this is, in fact, Erasmus Crow," I remarked.

"But how is it that the body's quite fresh, when your friend Foxborough pronounced him dead three months ago? And you pronounced him dead earlier this evening, yes? By poisoning? And yet now he's dead *again*, lying on a mortuary slab – and judging from the blood, his heart was still beating when he was shot."

I was forced to admit that it was a very troubling development.

"If this is the third death for Mr. Crow, we can at least take comfort in the knowledge that there is unlikely to be a fourth," Holmes observed.

"I wish I shared your confidence, Mr. Holmes."

I could at least say with certainty that the coffin did not contain a body when it was first buried – unless, of course, the chemistry volumes were placed beneath him in order to give him something to read in the afterlife, in the manner of the pharaohs of Crow's imagination.

"Who do you imagine shot Crow and buried him in that grave – *his* own grave?" I asked. "Sir Boris Wyngarde, perhaps?"

"If he had attempted to use a shovel, Watson, I venture to suggest he would still be digging."

"He *might* be able to fire a gun," Lestrade suggested, "on a man who somehow keeps coming back from the dead. Any idea how he does that, Mr. Holmes?"

Holmes, however, seemed distracted by a tinge of yellowish powder on the dead man's lapels. Distractedly, he said: "Perhaps more than at any time of year, married gentlemen should be at home with their families. I have a few telegrams to send, gentlemen, and then I suggest we meet up again tomorrow, when we shall pay a visit to Mrs. Warrender."

To extricate oneself from home, hearth and spouse on Christmas morning proved every bit as difficult as might be imagined, but despite Kate's protestations, I was determined to see this case through to its conclusion, whatever that might be. Hailing a cab was not without its challenges, but I soon joined Holmes at Baker Street, where Lestrade was already impatiently awaiting my arrival.

Our journey to Lewisham was conducted for the most part in silence; none of us, it seemed, feeling the desire to wish one another a Merry Christmas, so powerful was the desire on my part and that of the Inspector to unravel this puzzle. Sherlock Holmes, who, I suspected, had already reasoned it out, held his peace solely because he was waiting for just the right dramatic moment.

The Warrender residence served also as the family's place of business, which perhaps explained why there were no indications of the festive season anywhere; wicker baskets containing squeaking, snorting and howling animals of various sizes and odours were stacked along the walls, and we were forced to walk single file in order to avoid the shredding of our coats by the claws that reached out at us as we made our way to the office of the head of the firm of Warrender and Son, Animal Importers.

Mrs. Minnie Warrender did not make much of an impression on me when I had observed her at Sir Boris' home the night before, but bathed in the greenish glow cast by sunlight shining through a row of tanks containing exotic schools of fish, her squat form and grim expression appeared positively malevolent. She sat behind a badly-splintered desk, her hands folded in front of her. I was reminded of the matron at my old school, a ghastly toad-like individual named Makins.

"I must say, Mr. Holmes, it's rare to have such distinguished guests in my offices," she said, after the formal introductions were concluded.

"And you must forgive me if say I find that hard to believe, Mrs. Warrender. You claim Sir Boris Wyngarde as one of your clients, for instance." He spoke distractedly, as he studied the fish darting about before him.

Lestrade's features wrinkled in an expression of disgust. "Ugly looking brutes, the lot of them."

"You should know better than to judge by appearances, Lestrade.

The blue-ringed octopus, for instance – I've always found it a fascinating creature. A most rewarding purchase for the discerning customer."

Mrs. Warrender's gave no outward indication of unease, but I detected a degree of caution in her voice as she asked: "You are . . . familiar with the blue-ringed octopus, then?"

"And also the porcupine-fish – both native to the Caribbean, and both possessing remarkable qualities. Perhaps you'd care to enlighten the Inspector?"

Her smile was very far from ingratiating. "I'm afraid I have no notion of what you're talking about, Mr. Holmes."

"Really? Then permit me to enlighten you, dear lady. Both produce a remarkable toxin which, when injected into the human system, result in a state which even the most tenacious and well-trained medical mind might mistake for death."

I knew then that Holmes had been expecting to find such creatures on the premises, and that their excretions might well explain how a man such as Erasmus Crow might be declared dead when he was, in point of fact, still alive, and how he might die again, under the name Enoch Courtney.

Mr. Warrender continued to feign ignorance. "This is all astonishing news, Mr. Holmes."

"I think not, madam. I rather suspect that when you inherited your late husband's enterprise, you realized that you might acquire the animals necessary to start a more profitable, and entirely secret, business – selling a foolproof escape route to anyone anxious to evade the clutches of the police. How on Earth can anyone arrest a dead man? The toxin, in its pure form, is not without its side-effects, of course – it frequently results in damage to the brain, and is sometimes mistaken for a form of living death. You are perhaps familiar with the legend of the zombie? But a gifted chemist such as yourself must have found a way of altering the toxin to create a new and harmless formula, perhaps by combining it with an extract derived from the Black Fish of the Bering Sea, which I see in *this* tank. They are frozen every winter and revived during the spring thaw, are they not?"

Before she had a chance to respond, a young man appeared in the doorway. He wore a leather apron and thick gloves, and spoke with a vaguely cockney accent, but there was something familiar about the tone. The height and build were right, too. And though he had covered his features as best he could the evening before, I recognised the eyes. Yes, this was the fellow, all right.

"Is there a good reason why you're intruding on these premises on Christmas morning?" He demanded. "We've a good deal to do before we close up for the festive season."

Holmes turned to greet him. "And this must be your son, Ridley Warrender."

"Your manner is very familiar considering we haven't yet been introduced. What on earth is going on here?"

I gave young Warrender a hard stare. "Be warned, I am armed, sir – and I owe you for that blow on the back of the head." He attempted to laugh it off, but no-one else in that cramped room seemed to find it particularly amusing, in particular his mother.

"My son and I are still uncertain what crime it is you are actually investigating, gentlemen," she said.

"The breaking of good faith, Mrs. Warrender. In order for your scheme to work smoothly, the individual whose death you stage must, logically, agree to disappear completely, perhaps to another country. But Erasmus Crow disobeyed your instructions, and came dangerously close to undermining your entire operation. He had to be dealt with swiftly. When you came to Sir Boris Wyngarde's party, injected Crow with the formula once again, which resulted in a second simulated death. Your son Ridley here removed the body on your instructions, and waited until the formula had worn off before shooting Crow and burying him in his own grave."

Thrusting his chin out in defiance, the Warrender boy asked: "Who is this 'Erasmus Crow' I'm supposed to have killed?"

"He is a man with yellowish dust on his lapels, Mr. Warrender – dust which came from the gloves you're now wearing, dust which matches exactly the colour of the London stock brick. And Lewisham brick-works is just next door, is it not? Should further doubt remain, the chemistry textbooks buried in the coffin contain numerous notations in a female hand. I have no doubt, Mrs. Warrender, that were we to obtain a specimen of your handwriting, it would be an exact match."

Lestrade reached into his pocket for a set of handcuffs. "You probably should have just dropped the body in the Thames. Hands out, Mr. Warrender."

Unexpectedly, the lady rose from her chair. She was not much taller standing than she had been sitting down. "You are correct on all points, save for one, Mr. Holmes. My boy did not shoot Crow – *I* did. No, not a word, Ridley! I am quite content to go to my fate, but if there's a chance my son might escape the noose, I wish him to take it."

It was far from the perfect outcome, but the young fellow obeyed his parent and would not say another word, nor, despite Lestrade's coaxing, would he provide us with a list of former clients. Holmes always suspected that both Warrenders were aware of the formula for simulated death, and that the son would eventually be released from prison for his lesser crimes, to a waiting clientèle of influential individuals in the criminal world, anxious to be avail themselves of his services. It might have been Mrs. Warrender's idea of the perfect Christmas gift, but it seemed to me a gift laden with malice.

The Inspector of Graves
by Jim French

This script has never been published in text form, and was initially performed as a radio drama on July 16, 2006. The broadcast was Episode No. 71 of The Further Adventures of Sherlock Holmes, *one of the recurring series featured on the nationally syndicated* Imagination Theatre. *Founded by Jim French, the company has currently produced over 1,000 multi-series episodes, including 117 (as of this writing) original Sherlock Holmes pastiches.*

In addition, Imagination Theatre is in the process of recording the entire Holmes Canon, featured as The Classic Adventures of Sherlock Holmes, *and when completed, this will be the only version with all episodes to have been written by the same writer, Matthew J. Elliott, and with the same two actors, John Patrick Lowrie and Lawrence Albert, portraying Holmes and Watson, respectively.*

THE CAST

SHERLOCK HOLMES – John Patrick Lowrie

DR. WATSON – Lawrence Albert

B.W. HOLCAMP – Cynthia Lauren Tewes: *Barbara Woolsey Holcamp, unmarried, mid-20's, middle class accent, bright, spunky, well-educated, former teacher, well-off but not wealthy*

MRS. LUCY PACKER – Pam Nolte: *Brusque, coarse sister of the mother of Frank Ellis, the man Barbara Holcamp loved. She's about 60*

MRS. ELLIS – Ellen McLain: *The late Frank Ellis's mother. Lived several years in Australia, and could have picked up that accent, but she's a middle-class British widow, slightly younger than her sister*

CABBIE – Dennis Bateman: *An old Cockney*

WATSON: I am Doctor John H. Watson. Having now lived one year beyond the half-century mark, and having been assistant and biographer to Sherlock Holmes for nearly half of that time, it was not surprising that we would, on occasion, find ourselves thinking along the same lines. Although I no longer lived in our Baker Street rooms, our years of investigating cases together had created a bond much like that often found between brothers. So on the first day of March, 1903, although we hadn't spoken since January, I strongly felt that he would be contacting me that day, and sure enough, just before noon my telephone rang, and it was Holmes.

MUSIC – OUT

HOLMES: (FILTER) Have you read this morning's *Daily Chronicle*?

WATSON: (PAUSE) Holmes? I was just thinking about you! How are you?

HOLMES: It's a small article, third page. "Grave Robbing in Lambeth. Mystery corpse found in the wrong coffin in Loburn Abbey Cemetery, Kennington."

WATSON: I don't think I read that.

HOLMES: Aren't many of your comrades from the war buried there?

WATSON: So *that's* the connection! All morning long, my thought have been on you, while you apparently were thinking of me! How remarkable!

HOLMES: Not at all; someday it will be discovered that there is a substance in the atmosphere that connects the minds of congenial human beings in the same way that piano strings vibrate when the same notes are bowed on a violin. Sympathetic resonance, I believe it's called.

WATSON: But . . . .

HOLMES: I've received a telegram from someone who needs our help and is in a position to pay handsomely for it. I'll need your medical knowledge, Watson.

WATSON: But –

HOLMES: And if you turn to the agony columns on the back page, you'll see a bit more information on the same matter.

WATSON: But how –

HOLMES: I'll tell you all I know of it on the way to Kennington. How soon can you be ready, with your surgeon's bag and apron?

WATSON: Er – my wife will want to know if I'll be home for dinner.

HOLMES: Ay, yes, my best to your bride. I'll be round in twenty minutes. Dress warmly, it feels like snow.

SOUND EFFECT – CLICK OVER WIRE

WATSON: On the back page, among the personals, was this: "Anyone having information concerning the removal of the remains of the late Dr. Frank Ellis from his grave in Loburn Abbey will kindly contact B.W. Holcamp, 19 Bethune Road, Kennington, Lambeth. A reward is offered for accurate information. All confidences kept." Not long after I read the notice, Holmes appeared at our door with a hansom waiting.

SOUND EFFECT – FADE IN HANSOM CLATTERING DOWN STREET

HOLMES: You're looking fit, Watson. Put on a pound or two, I see. Your new bride must be a good cook.

WATSON: She is. I'm a lucky man.

HOLMES: Yes; and let's hope wife number three will be luckier than your first two. Now; to the task at hand. The missing body is that of Frank Ellis, a physician. Due to his service with our forces during the Boer War, he was buried in the veterans' section of Loburn Abbey Cemetery.

WATSON: Why was his coffin dug up?

HOLMES: Mr. Holcamp gave only a few details in his telegram, but the nature of the case intrigues me and calls for the professional services of my oldest and dearest friend.

WATSON: That's most generous of you, Holmes, but it doesn't answer my question.

HOLMES: Speculation is no substitute for investigation, Watson, you know that. Now, if I remember London's geography correctly, we should be across the river and in Lambeth within half an hour.

SOUND EFFECT – HANSOM DOWN SLIGHTLY, HORSE STOPS AT *

WATSON: From Holmes's remarks and the personal ad in the paper, I somehow expected Mr. Holcamp would be living in a finer neighbourhood, but when we arrived * in Bethune Road we saw only a line of gray, run-down row houses, of the sort ordinary wage-earners live in.

SOUND EFFECT – IN DISTANCE, YOUNG CHILDREN PLAYING

HOLMES: [EXTERIOR] (EXERTION AS HE STEPS DOWN) I don't imagine cabbies drive out here very much. Would a guinea keep you waiting to take us back to Baker Street?

CABBIE: [EXTERIOR] (OFF) Two guineas would, sir.

HOLMES: Done. Here you are.

CABBIE: (OFF) Thanks, guv'nor. I'll be right 'ere.

SOUND EFFECT – TWO MEN WALKING ON PAVEMENT

WATSON: [EXTERIOR] Well? Is this what you expected?

HOLMES: Reserve your judgement until all the facts are in.

SOUND EFFECT – STEPS STOP

HOLCAMP: [EXTERIOR] Yes?

HOLMES: We're looking for the residence of Mr. B.W. Holcamp.

HOLCAMP: I am B.W. Holcamp. And you'd be Sherlock Holmes!

HOLMES: Correct.

HOLCAMP: And Doctor Watson?

WATSON: I am.

HOLCAMP: Come right in, please!

SOUND EFFECT – THEY WALK INSIDE, DOOR CLOSES
    (CHILDREN OUT)

HOLCAMP: You expected me to be a man, no doubt.

HOLMES: Indeed.

HOLCAMP: I didn't intend to deceive you; the B.W. in my name stands
    for Barbara Woolsey. Barbara Woolsey Holcamp.

WATSON: Don't think a thing of it, Miss Holcamp; or is it Mrs.
    Holcamp?

HOLCAMP: It's Miss.

HOLMES: So perhaps you'll begin at the beginning and leave out no
    detail of your problem, however minor.

HOLCAMP: Of course. But first, may I offer you tea? The kettle's just
    off the hob.

HOLMES: Not for me, thank you.

WATSON: Yes, I could use a cup.

HOLCAMP: Very good. Mind you, it'll be very hot.

<u>SOUND EFFECT – TEA BEING POURED AND SERVED UNDER:</u>

HOLCAMP: Here you are, Doctor. Lemon or sugar?

WATSON: Neither, thanks.

HOLCAMP: (AS SHE SITS) Now, to begin at the beginning. I lost both
of my parents in a disaster at sea just before the turn of the century.
Eighteen ninety-nine, December to be exact. I had no other family,
and for a time, I didn't know whom to turn to. I held a teaching
position in Dagney, third form, and if it had not been for the kindness
of those dear children, I think I would have chosen to end it all, out of
loneliness and grief.

WATSON: (MURMURS) My dear lady!

HOLCAMP: But as Providence would have it, there came upon the
scene a remarkable man, a doctor like yourself, Doctor Watson, and I
became his regular patient. His name was Frank Ellis. Doctor Ellis
was unlike any man I had ever known. He recognized that I needed
someone to guide me, someone to trust and rely on, and he became
that person in my life. I was only twenty at the time of my parents'
death, and Doctor Ellis became like a counsellor, a father, and a good
friend to me. He was like a father, as I say, but in many respects you
might say he was like a mother to me; tender and gentle,
understanding of a girl's emotional needs.

HOLMES: (DRILY) Quite remarkable. Do go on.

HOLCAMP: I'm afraid that from this point on, my story is darker and
more tragic. As our relationships grew, it became more personal. You
see, I had fallen in love with him, and I believed that Frank – Doctor
Ellis – felt the same for me. The first time I sought to speak to him
about it, he changed the subject. I realized he was struggling to . . .
maintain a professional relationship with me, when part of him longed
to be much closer.

HOLMES: And was there intimate physical contact between you?

247

HOLCAMP: No. Not so much as a kiss. And yet, there were moments when our hands might touch, accidentally, and his cheeks would colour and he seemed about to say something . . . and then think better of it. And so I finally determined to let him know that I understood the change in our relationship, and would welcome his feelings for me . . . the he need have no fear in declaring his love for me, for I felt the same for him.

WATSON: That must have taken courage.

HOLCAMP: Oh, Doctor, you have no idea! On the next evening when he called on me with some cough syrup he prescribed, I took his hands in mine, sat down beside him – here on this divan – and told him of my love for him.

WATSON: And what was his reply?

HOLCAMP: He looked stricken! He rose, trembling, and stammered like a schoolboy, telling me I'd misunderstood his concern for me as affection. He explained that he took care of his widowed mother in her home, and that she was his first responsibility for as long as she lived. He said he wanted to be my friend and physician, but anything beyond that was impossible. That was the last time I saw him. And so, barely a year after I lost both of my parents, once more I was utterly alone and without hope!

HOLMES: And what happened to Doctor Ellis?

HOLCAMP: Within a few weeks, Doctor Ellis became seriously ill, and the next thing I knew, he passed away!

WATSON: Miss Holcamp, speaking as a physician myself, let me suggest that at the time you confessed your love to him, the symptoms of a fatal illness might well have already appeared, which would certainly explain why he told you that marriage would be impossible.

HOLMES: At any rate, we regret your loss. And now, to the matter at hand: you say that the body of Doctor Ellis is not in its grave?

HOLCAMP: That's right.

HOLMES: How do you come to know that?

HOLCAMP: I paid to have the grave opened and his body exhumed.

HOLMES: Why would you want to do that?

HOLCAMP: Is it absolutely necessary for you to know?

HOLMES: Is there a reason why we should not know?

HOLCAMP: Very well. After that night, I was wracked with misery; first there was humiliation, then anger, then infinite sadness. I knew that I would never see him again, but I wanted him to have something of mine, something that was precious to me, that would always be a connection between us.

WATSON: A keepsake.

HOLCAMP: Exactly. I had a ring, a silver ring mounted with four large diamonds. It had been my mother's. When her estate was settled, the stones alone were valued at more than a thousand pounds! I had it engraved, "Dear love, Barbara". And I sent it to him with a note that said, "Wear it or return it, but never give it away. If you will wear it, send me a blossom from a plum tree."

WATSON: And – did he?

HOLCAMP: See what is in this glass case on my mantel, Doctor.

WATSON: It looks like a bough from a tree.

HOLCAMP: Dead and dried out now, but when it was delivered to me, it held a fresh plum blossom! No note, just the blossom on its bough. But that told me that he loved me too, even though he could never say it. I had it mounted as a keepsake. It is precious to me . . . because it came from him.

HOLMES: A most poignant story, Miss Holcamp, but you haven't yet explained why you wanted his body exhumed.

HOLCAMP: (PAUSE) To prove that the ring had been stolen and he had been murdered!

HOLMES: And why, Miss Holcamp, do you think Doctor Ellis was murdered?

HOLCAMP: Several months earlier, he called on me and asked if I had been "bothered" as he put it by a man he called Toby. "Bothered in what way?" I asked him, and he said that the man was a crook who specialized in fraud and blackmail. When I asked him how he came to know such a person, Doctor Ellis said he had treated him as a patient some time ago. He said this "Toby" person was spreading lies about him. I asked him if he had reported "Toby" to the police, and he said the police knew him well. He'd been in prison many times.

HOLMES: And you think "Toby" murdered Doctor Ellis and stole the ring?

HOLCAMP: I did think that, yes; but the police ruled out murder. He died at home, with his mother by his side. She told them he'd been sick for a long time; she said he died from some disease he contracted in Australia, the same disease that killed his father.

HOLMES: You learned that from the police or from Mrs. Ellis?

HOLCAMP: The police. I've never spoken with Mrs. Ellis.

HOLMES: Not even at the funeral? I assume you both were there.

HOLCAMP: There were only five or six mourners. I wasn't certain which one was Mrs. Ellis, so I remained very much in the background and spoke to no one.

WATSON: Didn't Mrs. Ellis have to give her permission for her son's body to be exhumed?

HOLCAMP: She was too ill, and with no other living relatives, I was able to secure that authority from the Inspector himself.

HOLMES: Which Inspector, Miss Holcamp?

HOLCAMP: The Inspector of Graves.

HOLMES: I see. Watson, while we still have the sun, I think we would do well to visit the cemetery ourselves. Miss Holcamp, would you act as our guide?

HOLCAMP: Gladly, Mr. Holmes. I'll get my cloak. (MOVING OFF) I'll only be a moment . . . .

WATSON: (SOTTO) In all my years of practice I never heard of an "Inspector of Graves." Is there such a thing?

HOLMES: (SOTTO) If there is, it would be in the Revised Laws of 1888. I have them all in one of my files; we shall investigate when we get home.

MUSIC – UNDERSCORE

WATSON: The cabbie drove us to the cemetery located on the grounds of Loburn Abbey, a crumbling old landmark abandoned by the church some time ago. The best-maintained part of the burial grounds was the War Veteran's Memorial Cemetery, and that was where Miss Holcamp led us. On a rise of ground, amid row upon row of crosses and headstones, we came to a raw plot of newly turned earth. We were quite alone.

MUSIC – OUT

SOUND EFFECT – GENTLE WIND IN BACKGROUND

HOLCAMP: [EXTERIOR] This is where he was buried, in the Veterans' section. Frank served in the medical corps during the Boer War.

HOLMES: [EXTERIOR] Who besides you witnessed the exhumation?

HOLCAMP: The two workmen who opened the grave, and a constable who took one glance inside the coffin and walked away. Then came the moment I most dreaded. *I* had to look into the coffin.

HOLMES: Yes?

HOLCAMP: It was *not* Frank Ellis! The body was in a burial shroud, but nothing could conceal what was immediately apparent. It was not a man's body! It was the body of a woman! Quite unmistakably a woman!

HOLMES: Hmm! Most interesting! And was the ring missing?

HOLCAMP: The shroud had come apart, revealing the hands clasped across the breast. There was no ring. Whoever stole the body stole the ring as well.

WATSON: And no doubt pawned it immediately.

HOLMES: To whom did you report this?

HOLCAMP: I tried to report it to the local constable who came out to watch them dig. I sent one of the gravediggers to fetch him, but he came back alone and said the constable told him he had other duties.

WATSON: And Mrs. Ellis? Was she informed?

HOLCAMP: I sent word, but never received a reply.

WATSON: [INTERIOR] Holmes turned away and stood briefly at the side of the grave with his head bowed; not in prayer, but in deep thought. A minute passed, and then he turned back.

HOLMES: It is of paramount importance that I speak with Mrs. Ellis. Where does she live?

HOLCAMP: I've never been to her home, but I know her address. Number Five, Cambridge Lane, Empire Park. Do you want me to come with you?

HOLMES: That would be unwise until we know the circumstances.

MUSIC – URGENT MOTION MOTIF

WATSON: [INTERIOR] We took Miss Holcamp back to her home in Bethune Road, and then set off for the cluster of fine old residences that made up the neighbourhood of Empire Park. Number Five, Cambridge Lane was a house of Greco-Roman style, not overly large, but architecturally impressive. It took some time before an elderly woman came to the door.

SOUND EFFECT – FRONT DOOR OPENS

MRS. PACKER: [EXTERIOR] What do you want?

HOLMES: [EXTERIOR] I am Sherlock Holmes, and this is Doctor Watson.

MRS. PACKER: *What do you* want?

HOLMES: We are investigating the death of Doctor Frank Ellis, and we came to speak with his mother.

MRS. PACKER: Mrs. Ellis is ill. I am her sister, and I can tell you anything she could tell you.

WATSON: Er, could we step inside, Miss . . . ?

MRS. PACKER: *Mrs.* Packer. I'm the only one taking care of my sister and I'm busy morning to night, but yes, you may come in.

WATSON: We very much appreciate it, Mrs. Packer.

SOUND EFFECT – THEY WALK IN, DOOR CLOSES

MRS. ELLIS: (FAR OFF MICROPHONE) Who is it, Lucy?

MRS. PACKER: There! Your doorbell must have woken her. (YELLS) It's two men asking for you!

HOLMES: (PROMPTING HER) Sherlock Holmes and Doctor –

MRS. PACKER: (YELLS) One of 'em's name is Sherlock Holmes, he says.

MRS. ELLIS: (A BIT CLOSER) I'll be right out. Have them sit down, please, Lucy. (PAUSE, MOVING ON MICROPHONE) I am Mrs. Ellis.

WATSON: Forgive our intrusion, Madam; we –

MRS. ELLIS: Lucy, go and freshen my bedclothes, will you dear? And the flower are dying. Some yellow ones this time, I think. Daffodils, perhaps? Yes, Daffodils. Forgive me for wearing a robe, gentlemen. I've been rather ill.

(MRS. PACKER WALKS AWAY, MUMBLING AD LIB)

MRS. ELLIS: I know who you are, Mr. Holmes. And I presume you are Doctor Watson.

WATSON: Just so, madam.

HOLMES: We are most obliged, Mrs. Ellis, and we'll be as brief as possible.

MRS. ELLIS: Won't you sit down?

HOLMES: I trust we'll be here not more than five minutes.

MRS. ELLIS: I began reading of your exploits when I was living in Australia, so I know a thing or two about you. Now, you want to know about . . . my son?

HOLMES: There is a report that he died of natural causes. Kindly tell us about that.

MRS. ELLIS: When we lived in Australia, my husband and I fell upon hard times. We had just the one child, but we had great difficulty in making ends meet. Then, one day, a medical college in Sydney ran a competition for young men just finishing high school. The winner would receive four years of medical training, free of charge.

WATSON: Ah, and Frank won the scholarship?

MRS. ELLIS: Not only the scholarship, but he graduated at the top of his class. He joined the Royal Medical Corps and was commissioned as a leftenant. But while serving in Africa, he contracted a strange disease that became known as "Breakbone Fever" because it causes horrible pain.

WATSON: "Breakbone Fever"! Yes; its true name is dengue [*den*-gee] fever. It thrives in hot climates! I saw a few cases in India when I was stationed there in the Medical Corps.

MRS. ELLIS: My husband died of it. I was able to scrape together enough money to return to England with Frank. He sailed through the British medical exams and went into private practice. He was very successful; so much so that he bought me this house. I think that brings you up to date.

HOLMES: Are you acquainted with one of his patients, a woman named Barbara Holcamp?

MRS. ELLIS: Oh yes, I heard her name frequently.

HOLMES: And were you aware that she had your son's grave opened?

MRS. ELLIS: *What?* (CALLS WEAKLY) Lucy! (SHE FAINTS)

HOLMES: Grab her, Watson!

WATSON: My dear lady!

MRS. PACKER: (OFF) What is it? What happened? (ON) Oh dear Lord!

WATSON: Ease her down onto this divan!

MRS. PACKER: What have you done to her?

HOLMES: Nothing! She fainted.

WATSON: Mrs. Packer, do you have any smelling salts?

MRS. PACKER: I don't know. If you're a doctor, where's your bag?

WATSON: I didn't bring it. Now, please be quiet for a minute while I take her pulse. (PAUSE) Her pulse is weak and irregular. She should be hospitalized. Is there a telephone?

MRS. PACKER: Had it taken out, now that she doesn't need it any longer!

255

MRS. ELLIS: (STIRS)

WATSON: She's stirring. I'll rub her wrists to start some circulation. Mrs. Packer, where is her medicine?

MRS. PACKER: In her room. I'll go get it.

MRS. ELLIS: (WEAKLY) No . . . I'm all right. I'm all right.

WATSON: Please! Don't try to rise up just yet, Mrs. Ellis!

MRS. PACKER: Do you want me to get a pillow, dear?

MRS. ELLIS: I don't know. I'm so light-headed. Mr. Holmes: I thought I heard you say that Holcamp woman had the grave opened.

HOLMES: We can discuss such things another time.

MRS. ELLIS: No, I have to know!

HOLMES: We were told that you were too ill to be consulted, and so permission was granted to Miss Holcamp. Now it appears you knew nothing about it.

MRS. ELLIS: Nothing! I never would have permitted it! What was her purpose? Why did that woman want the grave opened? Was – was the body touched?

WATSON: The body was perfectly intact.

HOLMES: Or so we were told. Watson, do you think it would be safe to leave Mrs. Ellis now? We have some pressing matters to take care of . . . .

WATSON: Who is your physician, Mrs. Ellis?

MRS. PACKER: I know him; he's not far away. I'll fetch him.

WATSON: Yes, I think that would be wise. And here is my card. I no longer practice but I would be only too glad to be of service.

HOLMES: Please don't bother seeing us out. Good day to you both.

<u>SOUND EFFECT – TWO MEN WALK TO DOOR, OPEN IT, STEP OUTSIDE</u>

<u>SOUND EFFECT – DOOR CLOSES</u>

WATSON: [EXTERIOR] I feel like a fool, Holmes! Barbara Holcamp lied to us!

HOLMES: [EXTERIOR] And she's not the only one; unless I'm greatly mistaken, this entire matter is founded on lies. Come along, Watson; we have work to do!

<u>MUSIC – SHORT STING</u>

WATSON: And in a minute, I'll tell you the conclusion of this strange case.

<u>MUSIC – OUT</u>

<u>MUSIC – UNDERCURRENT</u>

<u>SOUND EFFECT – HANSOM IN LONDON STREET, HORSE TROTTING</u>

HOLMES: [EXTERIOR] It was a capital blunder on my part to have taken the Holcamp woman at her word!

WATSON: [EXTERIOR] But it's possible that she did send a letter about the exhumation, but Mrs. Ellis might not remember receiving it; or she might not have seen it at all, due to her illness.

HOLMES: And when she told us that Mrs. Ellis had no living relative! Now, I question whether she had anyone's permission to dig up the coffin! Who was the "Inspector of Graves"? Who were the men with the picks and shovels? And why is the gravesite still raw dirt and not being resodded? Pull up here, driver; I want to send some telegrams. Watson, drive on back to Baker Street, consult the file for 1888, and look for any official title called "Inspector of Graves"!

<u>MUSIC - UNDERCURRENT</u>

WATSON: I did as Holmes asked, and after a careful search of not only the Revised Laws of 1888, but the previous laws and regulations concerning burials and exhumations, the title of "Inspector of Graves" did not appear.

<u>SOUND EFFECT – ADD: HORSE TRAFFIC AND TICKING CLOCK</u>

WATSON: It had grown dark and the street lamps were burning before Holmes returned.

<u>SOUND EFFECT – DOOR OPENS, HOLMES ENTERS, DOOR CLOSES</u>

<u>MUSIC – OUT</u>

HOLMES: Have you had anything to eat?

WATSON: No, I thought I'd wait for you. Have you eaten?

HOLMES: No, I'm famished! Get Mrs. Hudson to bring us a hearty supper, and I'll tell you where I've been and what I've found. And while we're waiting for our meal, we shall change into workingmen's clothes and fortify ourselves against a cold night in a graveyard. Break out your electric torch, a bottle of brandy, and . . . oh yes; your revolver!

WATSON: Good grief! You're not proposing that we dig up that coffin!

HOLMES: Of course not. I've hired two strong men to do it for us.

WATSON: And why the revolver?

HOLMES: As a precaution, should we be interrupted.

WATSON: I don't know, Holmes. How will exhuming the body once more be helpful?

HOLMES: Go tell Mrs. Hudson that we want a substantial supper as soon as she can bring it, and as we eat, I'll explain.

<u>MUSIC – SHORT BRIDGE</u>

258

HOLMES: You will recall Barbara Holcamp mentioning a criminal called "Toby"

WATSON: Yes?

HOLMES: This afternoon, the Metropolitan Police were in a cooperative mood, and allowed me a look at the record of "Toby." Toby Luster makes his living practicing fraud and blackmail, explaining the non-existent title "Inspector of Graves". No doubt it was he who gave our client the idea of opening the grave. Operating on the premise that everyone has a secret or two to hide, Toby selected Doctor Frank Ellis as a target for blackmail. (Reach me the salt, will you, Watson?)

WATSON: Yes, here.

HOLMES: Thank you. It seems that Toby had discovered something damning about the good doctor, and he proceeded to demand payment to keep quiet, or he would inform all of Ellis's patients *and* the medical board of the secret Ellis was hiding. This would have meant strict disciplinary sanctions, loss of patients, and perhaps most distressing for the doctor, it would probably result in the suicide of his loving patient, Barbara Holcamp.

WATSON: I'd like the salt now.

HOLMES: Take it.

WATSON: Thank you. Go on!

HOLMES: After we parted this afternoon, I returned to the Ellis home to have a talk with Mrs. Ellis's sister, Lucy Packer, and with a bit of coaxing, she provided a fountain of information. First, she said she might have opened the letter to Mrs. Ellis from Miss Holcamp, requesting permission to open the grave, but she threw it away. Then Mrs. Packer told me Doctor Ellis had been living and keeping his office there in his mother's house, so as to be nearby to minister to her. One night, Toby Luster came to see the doctor, complaining of illness. But once inside the surgery, there arose a clamour of shouting

259

and cursing, and Mrs. Packer, a formidable figure as you'll recall, armed herself with a kitchen knife and dashed into the room. She saw that the doctor had picked up a scalpel to defend himself. Before any blood was shed, Luster ran away.

WATSON: My word! What did he want?

HOLMES: Money, Watson. He came to blackmail Doctor Ellis. But the incident was not reported to the police.

WATSON: Why on earth not?

HOLMES: The answer, friend Watson, lies buried in Loburn Abbey Cemetery! Now, if you're finished, let's be on our way!

MUSIC – GRIM UNDERCURRENT

WATSON: Of all the hazards Holmes and I had faced, the illegal opening of a grave was one of the most risky. The two men he had paid to dig up the coffin worked silently and fast in the cold dark night, while I kept watch for one last member of the party to arrive. The coffin was just hoisted out of the ground when that fifth person appeared. Barbara Holcamp!

MUSIC – SEGUE TO NIGHT SOUNDS

HOLMES: [EXTERIOR] Ah, good evening, Miss Holcamp. So glad you could join us.

HOLCAMP: [EXTERIOR] What are those men doing?

HOLMES: Just what you had them doing a few days ago.

HOLCAMP: But why?

HOLMES: As a means of proving that we have done our work and solved the mystery of the missing man. Go ahead and open the coffin, gentlemen. Now Watson, I'll need the light from your torch. Just shine it into the coffin as the lid comes up . . . .

SOUND EFFECT – A SQUEAK WOULD BE NICE HERE

HOLMES: . . . Very good. Now, Miss Holcamp?

HOLCAMP: You want me to . . . ?

HOLMES: Yes. Please have a look inside the coffin.

HOLCAMP: (HESITANTLY) Very well . . . .

HOLMES: (PAUSE) That should be sufficient. What did you see?

HOLCAMP: I saw exactly what I saw when I looked the first time! I don't understand. Why have you put me through this revolting experience, gazing upon the decaying body of some woman? I thought you said you'd found Frank Ellis's body!

HOLMES: I have. Or more accurately, I found that Frank Ellis doesn't exist and never has! The body in this coffin is that of the woman who pretended to be Frank Ellis!

HOLCAMP: You must be insane! That isn't true!

HOLMES: The record proves otherwise, Miss Holcamp. This afternoon I got the complete story from Mrs. Ellis's sister. Her niece, *Francine* Ellis, could never have entered and won the Australian Medical College Scholarship as a woman. And so she became known as *Frank* Ellis. As Frank Ellis she was able to get a commission in the Army. As Frank Ellis she was able to pass the examination allowing her to practice medicine here in England. And as Frank Ellis, she became your doctor, and . . . .

HOLCAMP: Stop! I don't want to hear another word!

MUSIC – POIGNANT UNDERCURRENT

WATSON: [INTERIOR] Some time later, back at his rooms on Baker Street, Holmes leaned back in his chair and looked with great satisfaction on the shining object he held in his hand.

HOLMES: What do you think she'll do with this when she gets it?

WATSON: She'll probably wonder how you came to have it.

HOLMES: I was thinking of enclosing a note, telling her that Doctor Ellis must have told his mother to conceal the ring in the casket, but not on his finger, knowing the danger of grave robbers. But then that might convey the unsavoury image of Sherlock Holmes, the great detective, rummaging amongst the remains, when in fact I paid one of the gravediggers to look for it.

WATSON: (PAUSE) Just send her the ring, Holmes.

MUSIC – *DANSE MACABRE*

NARRATOR: You have heard "The Inspector of Graves", written and directed by Jim French. *The Further Adventures of Sherlock Holmes* features John Patrick Lowrie as Holmes and Lawrence Albert as Doctor Watson.

WATSON: And this is Doctor John H. Watson. I had many more adventures with Sherlock Holmes, and I'll tell you another one . . . when next we meet!

The Adventure of the
Parson's Son
by Bob Byrne

I followed Sherlock Holmes along the edge of the field, clambering with no great grace over a wooden fence. "Hsst, Watson." He had enjoined me to silence more than once during our midnight sojourn, in which we had crossed a railroad line, wandered through fields, and climbed more than one fence, all in moonless dark, with aid of neither lantern nor torch. I had fallen thrice and stumbled several more times across the uneven ground. My clothes were splattered and I had even momentarily lost a boot in a mud hole.

Holmes, of course, had strode silently, barely making a whisper, whereas I moved through brush as if a herd of moose had come to graze, and he often had to wait for me to catch up. This latest admonishment finished, we continued on. I estimated that our journey had taken approximately fifteen minutes when Holmes stopped and put a hand to my chest.

His mouth close to my ear, he whispered, barely audibly, "This is the field we seek. Not a sound."

I nodded my head silently and moved over the fence as quietly as I could. Not earning a remonstrance from Holmes, it seems I did well enough this time.

I could just make out the silhouette of a horse in the field and the outlines of the buildings to the east. By prearrangement, I stayed where I was, knowing Holmes would indicate if I need join him. As he approached the horse, it nickered gently, shuffling its hooves uncertainly. I judged by Holmes's movements that he was removing my gorget from his pocket while soothing the horse, though I could not hear his whisperings.

The near total silence of the night was shattered by the blast of a police whistle and the field was suddenly bathed in lantern light as several officers rushed in from all directions. "Halt, in the name of the law!"

The horse bolted while Holmes and I raised our arms in surrender, he dropping the gorget to the ground at his feet. One of the constabulary men stooped and picked it up, eyeing it critically. He sneered at Holmes and said, "Looks like we got another horse mutilator, boys."

"I've had my eye on this George Edalji for many a year, Mister Holmes."

We stood facing the local Chief Constable, the honorable G.A. Anson, the second son of the Earl of Lichester. He reminded me far too much of some of my army officers in Afghanistan: A lot of bluster that attempted to compensate for a lack of practical experience. We had been escorted roughly into his office after our capture. To his credit, upon recognizing Holmes, he immediately realized how improbable it was that we had intended to cut open that horse and did not place us under arrest.

Holmes explained that we had been retracing the route that George Edalji had allegedly taken a few nights before to mutilate a horse in that very field at the Great Wyerly Colliery. He also told the chief constable why we had come from London.

"I'm afraid you've come on a wild goose chase, sir. Naturally, the reverend wants you to prove his son innocent." The way Anson said "reverend" indicated that he did not like the elder Edalji.

He almost leered at Holmes. "Why, after he had been arrested, Edalji said, 'I am not surprised at this. I have been expecting it for some time.' Those were his very words, I can tell you."

The man actually snorted. "Now, I ask you, what better confession of guilt could we have asked for?"

"Or perhaps it was the natural response of a man who knows he has been a suspect, be it for valid reasons or not," Holmes replied levelly.

A flush rose on Anson's cheeks.

"I happen to know that Edalji was not innocent of strange goings on at the vicarage some ten years ago." He said this last with a knowing look, as if he had let us in on some great secret.

Holmes was unruffled, as always. "I'm sure your men are gathering all sorts of evidence to establish Edalji's guilt." I thought I detected a faint inflection on the word "establish."

Anson seemed a bit uncertain what to make of this statement. "I'm sure with so many crimes in London, Scotland Yard is in need of your assistance. But here in Wyerly, we've got things under our thumbs."

"Yes, I'm certain there's no doubt in your mind that you've secured the guilty party. We shall not trouble you any further at the moment." Holmes sighed softly and moved a few steps to the door but stopped short. Turning, he said, "If it wouldn't be too much trouble, could I see the plaster of Edalji's boot marks?"

Anson was startled at the sudden change of subject, just when he thought Holmes was leaving. "Why, we had no need to make one."

My friend stared at him in obvious disbelief. "No cast made? Surely there are photographs, then?"

Anson was more than a bit uncomfortable at Holmes's tone. "Not necessary. One of my men took Edalji's boot and made an impression in the mud next to the boot marks. It was clearly a match."

"And he will testify to that effect in court, with no evidence to buttress his claim?"

The chief constable seemed to come to the conclusion that Holmes was not necessarily on his side. A bit late, in my opinion. "We'll do just fine on our own. We don't need the help of a publicity-seeking private detective from London. Perhaps you and the doctor would do well to leave!"

Holmes smiled thinly and I moved towards the door. "I think we'll enjoy some of your fine country air. It's always so refreshing to get away from London's thick climate. Come, Watson, let us retire to our rooms."

With a curt nod to Anson, I followed Holmes out. A sharp glance from my friend told me to hold any questions to myself until we were in more secluded surroundings.

It had been a long night; or rather, morning. After but a few meager hours of sleep, we had gathered in the secured environs of Holmes's room, settled in with warm but tepid tea, courtesy of the innkeeper. "This is weak stuff, Holmes," I commented as I swallowed unenthusiastically.

He grunted noncommittally, ignoring the cup at his elbow. "Well, old fellow, you have now traversed the same route that George Edalji allegedly did, in almost total darkness, to mutilate a horse. Could he have done it?"

I reflected on our nocturnal journey. Granted, I had struggled over the unfamiliar ground. Edalji, a native, would have an advantage. But there was his vision to take into account.

"Holmes, if the degree of myopia is as severe as his father attests, I find it all but inconceivable that young Edalji could have followed that path, undetected, attacked the horse, retraced his route and commenced home without anyone the wiser, no matter the time."

He laughed. "As do I. You have the benefit of excellent sight and you struggled throughout." I ignored this careless slight, the receipt of which was my burden as Sherlock Holmes's assistant. "Edalji could not possibly have succeeded in such a mission. And for him to evade an alert police force; it beggars reason.

"Though 'reason' and Captain Anson may be only nodding acquaintances," he muttered.

He took a drink of the lukewarm tea, made a face, and put it back down. "Parson Edalji said that the police have offered not one, but two possible scenarios. That his son attacked the horse in the evening before coming home from an errand in the village: or that he snuck out of the parsonage, which was under observation, in the middle of the night, completed his task, and snuck in, undetected."

I reflected on this. "It seems rather incongruous."

"Preposterous would be a better word, Watson. The man wears no corrective lenses. And it is implied that he was involved in the previous maimings, though the police have been careful to avoid direct mention of that."

"I must say, matters seem to favor the young solicitor, though I fear many facts will need to be marshaled in his defense to blunt the police's seeming animus. I believe that we shall next look into the matter of the horse hair found on Edalji's coat. I am sure that it will be a cornerstone of any prosecution case."

"Yes, gentlemen, I removed twenty-nine hairs from the jacket. There can be no doubt that they were from a horse."

We were conversing with the police surgeon, a Doctor Butler. He was rather nondescript, except for the somewhat disconcerting habit of looking at a spot approximately four or five inches to the right of the person to whom he was speaking.

"Well, you certainly couldn't be mistaken in that, Doctor," Holmes replied, pausing. "And I understand that a portion of hide was cut from the mutilated horse and brought to you?"

"Yes, a piece was removed from the belly." Again, he looked at a point next to Holmes's head.

"Indeed." Holmes turned thoughtful eyes to me and then casually looked to the ceiling, as if the following question was a mere trifle. "And did you find any similarity between the hairs on George Edalji's coat and that portion of horse flesh?" His piercing gaze then centered on the doctor.

"Why yes, I did. Nearly all of the hairs on the jacket were similar in color, length and structure."

I felt that Holmes was baiting a trap for the unwary police surgeon. I had seen this many times before.

"I take it that the coat was sealed at the parsonage and brought directly to you that morning?"

The man blinked owlishly. "No, not directly to me, Mister Holmes."

266

Holmes's expression affected surprise. "Not directly? I would think that such a vital piece of evidence would be put into your care post haste. Surely no more than an hour or so elapsed?"

Dr. Butler seemed somewhat discomfited. "Err . . . no, it was a bit longer than that."

Holmes stared placidly at the man. The silence hung in the air like a blanket, both of us waiting for the doctor to add more. Holmes raised an eyebrow. "I believe that the police went to the parsonage at about eight o'clock in the morning. Surely you recall when the coat was brought to you here."

Butler rubbed his hands together as if he were washing them. "I believe that I examined the coat at nine o'clock in the evening."

"Surely not!" Holmes's voice was like the crack of a whip. "That is some thirteen hours after it was secured at the parsonage. Where was this coat during that period of time?"

"I . . . I do not know, sir. I had no knowledge of the coat until it was brought to me."

"According to young Edalji's father, there were no hairs on the coat when it was examined at the parsonage. Even Inspector Campbell could claim he found only two hairs. Yet you found twenty-nine? How do you explain that, sir?"

The man was clearly shaken. "It is not my task to explain it, gentlemen."

I felt sympathy for the poor doctor. I did not believe he had done anything untoward regarding the questionable provenance of George Edalji's coat and the horse hairs. "Come now, Holmes. Surely Doctor Butler is not responsible for what happened to the coat before it came into his possession."

His face softened. He looked apologetically at Butler. "Of course, I intended no offense, Doctor. You have been of great assistance and I thank you."

He offered his hand, which Butler shook with some relief. "Yes, yes, of course. No offense taken. Please let me know if I can answer any other questions." He seemed relieved that we were departing.

I wished him well and followed Holmes out of the room. He chuckled as we walked along. "You played that well, Watson. I have found that sometimes having a 'good' inquisitor and a 'bad' inquisitor provides an effective balance when questioning someone."

Surprised, I replied, "Glad to help, Holmes. I must say, I'm rather dubious regarding the disappearance of the coat."

"Ha! I believe we have discredited the coat entirely. Though I wish I could get Thorndyke to examine it. Would that we were back in London."

I was a bit startled by this pronouncement. "Entirely? Really, Holmes?"

His eyes gleamed. "Upon its initial examination, there is a dispute to whether any hairs at all adhere to the coat. The local police say only two are visible. The coat is taken into police custody and reappears over a dozen hours later, covered with twenty-nine identifiable horse hairs. And those hairs are consistent with the hairs on a piece of skin cut from the mutilated horse.

"It does not take a great deal of imagination to consider that the hairs on the coat came from the sample cut from the dead horse."

I was shocked! "Holmes, surely you don't mean to imply that the constabulary intentionally placed the hairs from the sample onto the coat?"

He gave me a flat smile. "I suppose it is conceivable that the two objects came into contact with each other, or someone unintentionally transferred the hairs from one to the other. But I find that the less likely of our possibilities. The circumstance of the hairs on the coat does not buttress the case against Edalji."

I ruminated on this as we continued our walk. While I had seen my share of less-than-efficient police work in my years with Holmes, I found it hard to imagine the official force manufacturing guilt against someone!

I looked around to the realization that we were near our inn. "I say, Holmes, where are we going now?"

He stopped. "I suggest that you enjoy the local fare. I am going to delve into the case of young Edalji's boot marks and will not require your assistance at present."

I took a short walk after enjoying some adequate shepherd's pie and assorted trimmings. I was back in my room, dozing in the almost comfortable chair, when Holmes knocked and entered unbidden. I shrugged off my torpor and greeted him. "What did you discover, Holmes?"

He carelessly tossed his deerstalker onto the small table. "Either the local force is more incompetent than I believe possible or is intent on convicting Edalji." He shook his head. "I cannot imagine even Lestrade would have arrested the man on such specious evidence."

He moved over to the window and looked out upon the whitewashed walls of the shop next door to my room. "The good Inspector Campbell took a pair of Edalji's boots at the same time as the coat supposedly covered in horse hairs." He snorted in derision. "Then, some eight hours later, after hundreds of miners had tramped all over the area like a herd of buffalo, he located boot prints that matched those made by Edalji's boots."

"Definitively?" I queried.

"Of course not! It would appear that he spotted some likely marks, made an imprint in the ground next to them with Edalji's boot and then declared them a match!"

He shook his head. "It is clear that the man has not read my little monograph on the subject of footprints. As Captain Anson verified, he did not make a print, take a photograph or even sketch the muddied marks. There is no evidence of any kind that can be examined." He paused, then added, "Or refuted."

I knew my friend to be angered by such shoddy police work. Something occurred to me then. "If there was rain off and on all night, and if Edalji committed the crime before returning home at 9:30, wouldn't any prints almost surely be gone by the following afternoon?"

His laugh was as sharp as a pistol shot. "Very good, Watson. I could wish that you were on the local force. To find a print over half a day later, with the ongoing rain and the scene unsecured; the unsubstantiated claim of finding a match is almost absurd."

He stared contemplatively at his hat on the table. "Surely if Anson has not already had the same thought, someone will. Which would further induce the police to favor the scenario in which Edalji snuck out of the house in the middle of the night, rather than committing the crime on his way home from the village.

"I should laugh at the whole affair if the consequences for young Edalji were not so serious, my friend."

I pondered Holmes's words. Edalji was a successful young barrister, having written a well-received manual on railway law. A conviction would surely strike him from the rolls, in addition to sending him to prison for a time. It certainly was no laughing matter.

Holmes stared levelly at me. "The coat, the boot marks, the rusty razor that clearly could not be the mutilating weapon, his poor eyesight: it is surely a poor case they have to bring against him."

I had already dismissed the razor from my thoughts. Inspector Campbell had taken a razor, supposedly wet and with blood stains, from the parsonage, along with the coat and boots. It was almost immediately determined that the stains were rust, and it was wet because young Edalji had used it that morning to . . . shave! Regardless, the razor was not consistent with the type of weapon that could make the fatal wound.

"Watson, I fear there is something dark under the surface here in Wyerly. Some menace for George Edalji."

"Foul, vile stuff." I put down one of the letters sent to the Edalji family. Parson Edalji patted his wife's hand, the two sitting across from Holmes and me.

"Yes, Mister Holmes, we were subjected to a variety of accusations, vandalism and pranks malicious and harmless, beginning in 1892 and lasting for three years. Goods arrived for orders we did not place. People were summoned to our home for meetings that did not exist. Things I cannot repeat were said about ourselves and others."

We sat in the modest parsonage inhabited by the Edaljis. It was a humble room with no signs of ostentation. We had been served a much better tea than that from the inn, and were asking the senior Edalji about the family's past problems.

"And the local authorities believe that your son was behind these letters. Even the ones that maligned himself and his own family?"

Pastor Edalji was from Bombay, raised in a Parsi family. He had been given the see in Wyerly by a relative of his wife. As the area was a rough, rural parish with a tough, mining mentality, I could guess that the locals had not been overjoyed to have a foreigner brought in to oversee their spiritual needs.

"Yes. For example, a key was stolen from the Walsall School, several miles away. It was found on our doorstep. Chief Constable Anson was convinced that George had taken it. To what end? And he did not even attend Walsall. It made no sense!"

His wife, clearly suffering from a long history of unpleasantness surrounding her family, remained silent.

"It certainly seems unfair," I interjected.

He smiled weakly at me and continued. "The letters simply stopped in 1895, the culprit never identified. Then, this past February, a horse was mutilated in the night. More attacks followed, and malicious letters began appearing. The police again believed that George wrote them."

Holmes had listened with rapt attention. "Of course, it is far more likely that someone else wrote the letters. And that the person left the area in 1985, when the letters ceased. They then returned, renewing their attacks on your family."

Mrs. Edalji gave a genuine, if broken, smile to Holmes. I sensed that she had received little support related to the persecution of her family.

Parson Edalji nodded his head. "That would certainly . . . ." The sentence went unfinished.

Holmes asked some additional questions regarding who might feel such hostility towards the man and his son. We learned of the expected

I shall now tell of the discussion that preceded that interruption. We had examined the letters given us by Parson Edalji. They were a malevolent collection of threats, inanities, and slanders. While not all directed at the family, clearly someone hated George Edalji.

Holmes left me to my own devices and pursued his own investigations for a time. I knew of no man who could elicit information from someone as well as he. Several hours later, he returned to our rooms and related to me the fruit of his inquiries.

"Watson, it is surely of note that the letters stopped suddenly for a time, then resumed. I also wondered about the key to Walsall School appearing at the parsonage. You agree?"

I had not given the matter any thought. "Why, yes, surely."

He gave me a knowing grin as he loaded his pipe with some tobacco he had brought from Baker Street. Once he had a small stream of blue smoke emanating from the briar, he resumed.

"You may, of course, open the window if it becomes a bit thick in here."

I nodded but made no move to do so.

"Very well." He puffed contentedly. "I think it quite possible that the person or persons, for I believe there is more than one, who could write those letters could also be involved in the mutilations. We are not dealing with the greed and cunning of a Milverton, or the shrewd planning for profit of John Clay. I believe in this case, we deal with a simpler, base meanness of spirit. Someone who is lacking in the mores of right and wrong. The type who, as a youth, tortured small animals just for the fun of doing so."

I listened in silent agreement.

"So, I asked shopkeepers, tradesmen and the like about such a lad from several years ago. Some were recalcitrant, while some obviously took advantage to disparage folk they have disliked for years. With each name, I also inquired if the person had left the area for some time and recently returned."

He looked at me with a grin.

"Come now, Holmes," I blurted out. "You can't refrain from telling me what you discovered. It's obvious you have a suspect in mind."

He chuckled. "Good old Watson. You know me well."

He adjusted himself in his chair and fiddled with his pipe. "There is a young man named Royster Sharp who was quite unpopular in this town. He was a troublesome youth, consistently performing vandalous acts, bullying the weak, and just behaving like a rotten egg."

He eyed me with amusement. "Would you care to guess what school he attended?"

273

I thought for a moment. "Walsall!"

He nodded. "Yes. The same school from which the mysterious key was stolen. He was suspended more than once before being expelled. His younger brother, Rodney, is rather simpleminded and followed his brother's lead, often joining him in his trouble making."

I was excited, seeing a much more likely suspect than George Edalji, though whether for the letters, the mutilations or both, I could not yet say.

"Sharp signed on to a boat as a butcher's apprentice. He was at sea for some eight years, returning not long before the letters and mutilations began."

"Why, Holmes! A butcher's training. Surely he would know how to cut these animals and would have an instrument for doing so. Or know how to easily obtain one!"

He removed the pipe from his mouth and eyed it critically. "Most assuredly, Watson."

I continued on, excitedly. "And if his character is as poor as you indicate, he's just the type of man who would write those letters and be involved in the mutilations. His easily led brother could be a confederate!"

"While it's by no means a sure thing, I have no doubt that Captain Anson would have done better to look into the Sharps, rather than pursue George Edalji." He paused, grimaced. "At least, if his aim were justice."

I was one who always gave the official force as much benefit of the doubt as I could. But in this instance, I feared their intentions towards Edalji were less than honorable.

"What now, Holmes?"

"We eat, my good man. I have worked up an appetite this day." So saying, he arose and opened the window, dissipating some of the blue cloud that had formed at the ceiling.

It was shortly after that we encountered the Sharp brothers, to their unfortunate experience.

Sadly, I do not set forth before you, dear reader, a story of one of Holmes's great successes. The defense counsel, whom I shall not name here to avoid the direct casting of an aspersion, ignored all advice on the path to follow. He believed the evidence was so weak that a thorough defense was unnecessary.

Ignoring the insistent pleas of the Reverend Edalji and Holmes and myself, he did not call a single expert to testify to young Edalji's extensive myopia. Nor did he point out the speciousness of the footprint identification. He was so convinced that the jury would see the local prejudices against the Edaljis and the lack of fair investigation by the local constabulary that there was no need for "unnecessary expense and potential confusion by clouding the matter."

While recognizing the local antipathy towards the Edalji's, said counsel clearly underestimated the degree of it. Also, by failing to establish a vigorous defense, he did not account for the fact that the police investigation did not bring evidence against any other possible culprit.

The jury, hearing from a confident police force and a handwriting expert, and knowing the local feeling against the Edaljis, brought in a verdict of guilty. Young George was sentenced to seven years, hard labor.

Holmes, disgusted by counsel's obstinate refusal to properly defend his client, had returned to Baker Street in my company. I read him the verdict as it was reported in the *Times*. He sighed and stared into space.

"Ah, Watson. There is no greater bastion of legal justice than the English courts, but I do believe it is lacking some type of court of appeal. I fear that our American cousins have excelled us in that particular area."

I silently read the article, my heart sinking into despair as I thought of this earnest young lawyer confined to a prison cell. Holmes puffed away on his pipe, a cloud of blue smoke ever expanding in our rooms.

"Watson, you recall that journalist, Sims, raised quite a hue and cry at the wrongful conviction of Adolph Beck."

I paused, letting the paper settle in my lap. "Yes. Gordon . . . no, George R. Sims, I believe his name is. Say, Holmes, didn't Gurrin testify in that case as well?"

"Yes, Watson. I believe history will show that Thomas Gurrin, handwriting charlatan, played a significant role in sending two innocent men to the gaol."

"Sims made Beck's conviction a bit of a *cause célèbre*." He shook his head. "Though I don't know that it played any part in his parole for good behavior."

He eyed me with the faintest trace of a smile. "The Home Office is as stiff-necked as an oxen in harness, but perhaps your agent could lead a memorial on Edalji's behalf . . . ." His voice trailed off.

I jumped to my feet, the paper falling to the floor. "By Jove, Holmes, this is just the sort of thing that would get Conan Doyle's blood boiling. Now that you mention it, Arthur had mentioned to me that he believed Adolf Beck was innocent."

I moved over to my writing desk and began a letter to my literary agent, setting down those findings of Holmes's that were contrary to the verdict. *"My dear Doyle, as a man of integrity and with interests in the world of crime, I am sure that you have closely followed the trial of*

275

George Edalji. Holmes and I were involved in the investigation, and I would like to share with you the terrible injustice . . . ."

I have several notebooks with events and partially written accounts of affairs involving Sherlock Holmes. For a variety of reasons, they remain fragments. There are also a few that are complete and could be published at any time, but won't be for reasons I choose not reveal. It is possible that in time, the injustice involving the parson's son, George Edalji, will find print. Through absolutely no fault of his own, Holmes's work could be declared unsuccessful. So, I write this record of the matter, knowing that it will likely be placed in my tin dispatch box for some time.

The Adventure of the Botanist's Glove
by James Lovegrove

The autumn of 1903 found my friend Sherlock Holmes in a ruminative and occasionally melancholy frame of mind. Again and again in our conversations he would raise the subject of retirement, not only his own but mine. "Watson, do you ever feel you have done enough?" he might say. "Seen enough patients, cured enough ailments, fulfilled your vocation as a general practitioner? Do you begin to wonder if it is not time to step back and take the respite that more than two decades of hard work has earned you?"

I might respond by telling Holmes that I was in fine fettle and believed I had another four or five good, productive years in me. If he took the hint – for I was, of course, encouraging *him* not to sheathe his sword just yet – he did not show it. Poring over the property sections of various Sussex-based periodicals had become one of his favourite pastimes. He had estate agents in the South Downs area scouting for a suitable smallholding for him to purchase. Increasingly his thoughts were turning to a rural retreat and a life of quiet contemplation and research.

As if to confirm his general state of ennui, the cases he had been accepting of late displayed a marked penchant for the macabre and the outré. It seemed that nothing else was sufficiently spicy for his jaded palate. There was the affair of the blanched soldier, and the bizarre episode that I have chronicled as "The Creeping Man", not to mention those adventures of that period which I have yet to set down on paper such as the sighting of fairies in Epping Forest, the hair-raising affair of the Dorking Demon, and the Gerrards Cross meteorite which had such a singular effect on any who touched it.

Thus it came as somewhat of a surprise that Holmes agreed to investigate the death of Sir Peregrine Carruthers, given that on the face of it the eminent botanist's demise appeared to be nothing more than a tragic accident. There were no eerie overtones, little of the Gothic about it – yet it piqued his curiosity nonetheless.

It was as I was paying one of my increasingly infrequent calls at 221b Baker Street one September evening that an unannounced guest arrived. Billy, the page, had gone home for the night, so it was left to Mrs. Hudson to escort the visitor up.

"A Miss Mary Smith," she said, ushering in an anxious-looking woman of perhaps only twenty, comely in a rather unremarkable way, with features that spoke of honesty and a familiarity with hardship. "No card," Mrs. Hudson added, with all that that implied.

Indeed, Mary Smith was a person of no great means, as was evident the moment she opened her mouth.

"I am sorry for coming at such an inconvenient 'our, Mr. 'Olmes," she said in broad Cockney tones. "Especially when you already 'ave a guest."

"Dr. Watson is no mere guest, my dear girl. He is a colleague, a coeval, a comrade, and you may speak as freely in front of him as you would me."

"Thank you, sir. Really, I am at my wits' end, and I pray that you can 'elp."

"I shall endeavour to assist if at all I can," Holmes replied. He was never less than gracious in his dealings with the fairer sex. "Please be seated. I see that you have travelled up to London by train and that this has depleted your financial resources, such that you walked here from the station rather than took a cab. I see, too, that you are in service to a wealthy household and that your late mistress was a larger-proportioned woman. Is it on the matter of her death that you have come to consult me?"

Miss Smith's look of astonishment was one I had beheld many times before, on many a face. Holmes's facility for inferring facts about a person through logical analysis of their appearance and comportment was old to me but never failed to elicit startlement from those on whom it was practised for the first time.

"'Ow did you . . . ? Why, it's incredible! It's true, Lady Jane was not small and is, as you say, no longer with us. Are you one of them psychic mediums, sir, what 'as the power to read minds?"

"Hardly. There is nothing supernatural about anything I do. I merely observe. In this instance, it was immediately clear to me that your dress – a very expensive silk creation – is a hand-me-down. It has been substantially altered to fit your figure, which is by inference much trimmer than that of its erstwhile owner, since so many extra seams have been required to take in the material, especially at the waist and bust. The needlework is good, but not of professional quality, leading me to the conclusion that you yourself carried out the alteration."

"That is so. But 'ow could you tell Lady Jane is dead?"

"It is unlikely a woman would part with so elegant and fashionable a garment otherwise. You must have, as it were, 'inherited' it. Either she bequeathed it to you, or her widower insisted you have it rather than let it be thrown out. As for your being in service to a wealthy household, the dress – in tandem with your, if I may say so, un-aristocratic accent – allows room for no other interpretation. I can tell you came up by train because the ticket stub is tucked into your sleeve, making an unmistakable impression against the material, but the fresh mud on your boots suggests you had to walk across town thereafter. It has been raining lately and the streets are not at their cleanliest. You would not have gone on foot if you had the funds left over to hire a cab." He shrugged his shoulders. "These deductions are mere child's play."

"You are incorrect only on one point."

Holmes arched an eyebrow.

"It is not Lady Jane's death what brings me 'ere. 'Er ladyship succumbed to dropsy two years ago. Dreadful it was. The doctors kept draining the fluid but there was nothing else they could do, and in the end 'er poor 'eart gave out from the strain. No, the problem is what's become of my master, Sir Peregrine."

"Sir Peregrine Carruthers?"

"None other. You know 'im?"

"Know of him. I have read several of his books. His survey of orchids of the Amazonian basin is second to none, and his *On the Reproductive Habits of British Wildflowers*, while flawed, has much to commend it, as does his textbook on graftage. A great man."

At this encomium, tears welled up in Mary Smith's eyes, and all at once she was wracked with sobs. So overwhelmed by emotion was she that she became almost hysterical, and I summoned Mrs. Hudson from downstairs to comfort her. Holmes's redoubtable landlady succeeded in calming the girl, using the empathy and gentle blandishments that are the peculiar gift of womenfolk. Once Miss Smith had recovered, she was able to provide an account of her recent travails, the nature of which made her fragile inner state both explicable and forgivable.

"Sir Peregrine and Lady Jane were the best of employers. When 'er ladyship passed away, Sir Peregrine was almost inconsolable with grief. 'E came through it right enough in the end, however, and was back to 'is old self more or less, although a man can never be the same after losing 'is wife, can 'e? And after nearly thirty years of marriage and all. Now, 'e didn't really need me anymore, being as I'm a lady's maid, but 'e kept me on nonetheless out of kindness. Said 'e knew 'ow fond Lady Jane 'ad been of me, which is true, and she wouldn't 'ave wanted me turfed out if it could be avoided. I'm a 'ard worker and ever so reliable, and 'e appointed me as 'ousemaid instead."

"Are you Sir Peregrine's only domestic employee?"

"At Bridlinghall Place? No, there's a 'ousekeeper as well, Mrs. Frensham, and a couple of gardeners what come in every day from the village nearby. Anyway, I was glad to stay on. I'm a foundling, you see. 'Ence the name Mary Smith, because no one at the orphanage 'ad the imagination to christen me anything fancier. Don't know 'oo my mum or dad is. I was taken on by the Carrutherses when I was fourteen, and 'aving no children of their own they soon became like parents to me. And now . . . ."

With an effort, Miss Smith composed herself once more.

"All was fine – as fine as can be expected, given the shadow cast by Lady Jane's death – until about six months ago. That's when Mrs. Frensham just turned on me for no good reason. Before, we'd got on well enough, 'er and me, even if we wasn't what you'd call bosom friends. Then, all at once, she starts being 'ateful, treating me like I'm something stuck to the bottom of 'er shoe."

"You hadn't done anything to offend her?"

"Not as I can recall. It was like an electric light switching off, that quick. She was frosty. She started bossing me about, whereas before she'd been polite in her requests. Once or twice she even 'issed at me, calling me vile names, using words one woman should never say to another."

"How frightful," I declared, with feeling.

"I bore it," said Miss Smith. "I wanted to snap back at 'er but I couldn't bring myself to. There was enough upset in the 'ouse without me making it any worse, and I was loath to do anything as might jeopardise my position."

"Could you not have complained to Sir Peregrine?" I asked.

"Even if I'd wanted to, there was never any proof. Mrs. Frensham was sweetness and light towards me whenever 'e was present. She was only ever mean behind 'is back, so it would have been my word against 'ers. She was cunning in 'er cruelty."

"*La donna è mobile*," said Holmes with a tinge of impatience.

Seeing Miss Smith frown in incomprehension, I said, "What my friend is implying, in his rather abrupt and abstruse way, is that he feels Mrs. Frensham's treatment of you is not necessarily the germane issue here. Please tell us more about Sir Peregrine."

"What's to tell, sir? Sir Peregrine is dead too, now. Just this morning it 'appened, and I'm the one what's going to get it in the neck for it!"

Holmes leaned forward in his armchair. He was intrigued again, and fully attentive to what the girl had to say.

"Sir Peregrine is a great botanist, as you know," she continued. "Foremost in 'is field, I've 'eard said. 'Ighly respected. What 'e don't know about plants, particularly flowers, en't worth knowing. There's just one problem. It's not something that's ever been made public. 'E wouldn't 'ave wanted the world to know. Thing is, 'e's fatally allergic to bee stings."

"Bee stings?" I ejaculated. It was ironic: the flower expert, endangered by the very species that propagates his subject of study.

"He discovered it the 'ard way when he was off on one of 'is field trips abroad a few years back. Africa, I think it was. A bee stung 'im, and 'e nearly perished on the spot."

"Anaphylaxis," I said. "The violent reaction of the body as it attempts to rid itself of a particular substance. The immune system overcompensates, with the consequence that the throat can swell up so much that a person cannot breathe. There can be failure of the internal organs as well. Jenner first noted the phenomenon when experimenting with his smallpox inoculations at the turn of the century, and bee stings are one of its commonest causes, along with certain foodstuffs."

"That was Sir Peregrine's condition, yes. Anaphylaxis. 'E barely survived that first time. A local tribesman, one of 'is guides, somehow knew what to do. Shoved a sharp 'ollow twig into 'is neck for 'im to breathe through until the swelling went down. After that, Sir Peregrine 'ad a mortal terror of bees."

"Understandably," said Holmes.

"'E made sure there were no 'ives within five miles of Bridlinghall Place. 'E'd run for cover if 'e ever 'eard so much as a buzz. That was until 'e got 'old of this stuff, a new medicine called epiniff – I can't quite remember the name."

"Epinephrine," I said. "I read about it in *The Lancet* just last month. It's a natural hormone, more commonly known as adrenaline. It has been isolated and synthesised by two American chemists, Abel and Takemine, and is now available in a form that can be injected."

"That's it. Sir Peregrine 'ad some of it in a 'ypodermic syringe what 'e carried with 'im at all times in case of emergency."

"One shot would constrict the blood vessels, relax the bronchial muscles and inhibit the release of antihistamines. A life saver, for someone like him."

"Only not this time," said Miss Smith. "There's a conservatory at Bridlinghall Place where Sir Peregrine would do 'is research. It's full of flowers, potted plants and so forth, and always kept warm because some of the plants are tropical and sensitive to the cold. One thing everyone in the 'ousehold knew not to do, and that was leave any of the conservatory windows open. Not only would it let the 'eat out, it might allow a bee to come in."

"Attracted by the scent from all those blooms," said Holmes.

"Exactly. But that, alas, is what occurred this morning. A bee got in. It stung Sir Peregrine. And now . . . now . . . ."

"He was unable to inject himself with the epinephrine?"

"We found 'im on the floor of the conservatory, shuddering 'is last. Oh, it was 'orrible. 'Orrible! We 'eard 'im cry out. Then 'is nephew broke down the door what connects the conservatory to the rest of the 'ouse and tried to revive 'im. Sir Peregrine 'adn't managed to dose 'imself, so Cecil – that's the nephew, Cecil 'Arrison – got the syringe out of 'is pocket and stuck it in 'im. But it was no good. Too late. 'E died right in front of us. And there, on the floor beside 'im, was the bee what caused 'is death. It was a goner also, of course, because that's what 'appens when a bee stings, en't it?"

"Yes," said Holmes. "The barbed end of the stinger becomes stuck in the victim's skin and is ripped loose from the bee's abdomen. It is a somewhat defective defence mechanism, if you ask me, in so far as its use is tantamount to suicide. I presume, then, that there was a window open after all?"

"One of the little awning windows near the roof. It was only a tiny bit ajar, but that was all that was needed."

"And you have been accused of leaving it that way?"

"I 'ave, only I never. I never did. I wouldn't 'ave put Sir Peregrine's life at risk like that. Not in a million years. It was my job to wash them windows inside and out. Mrs. Frensham made me do it just last week. I know I didn't open any of them, not even a crack. I'll swear to it on the 'Oly Bible. But that's what she's saying. That's exactly what she told the police when they came. She all but accused me, right in front of them, of killing Sir Peregrine. As if I would. Like I said, the man was like a father to me."

Holmes leaned back, steepling his fingers. His expression combined sympathy and a faint, detached amusement. I knew then and there that he believed Miss Mary Smith's innocence, as did I, but also that he was determined to prove it and exonerate her.

"Now listen, my girl," he said. "If you are adamant that you did not leave the awning window open, someone else must have. I shall find out who, and dispel the cloud of suspicion that is hovering over you."

"Can you, Mr. 'Olmes? Will you?"

"Indubitably. You have been wronged, and that must be set right."

"I cannot pay you much, if at all."

Holmes waved a hand. "It would be churlish of me to accept your money. I have been remunerated more than generously over the years by various deep-pocketed clients, meaning I am in a position to work *pro bono* if I so choose, for deserving causes. You most assuredly belong in that category."

"Oh, thank you, sir."

"Bridlinghall Place. That is near Haywards Heath, is it not? Watson, be so good as to fetch down *Bradshaw's*, would you? If memory serves, there is a train departing from Victoria at half past the hour. We can be at our destination by eight o'clock if we hurry. The sooner we arrive, the better, I think."

The daylight was dwindling as the three of us journeyed south by train to Haywards Heath, and thence by trap to Bridlinghall Place. It was a Georgian manor set in grounds extending for several acres, with an impressive portico and the somewhat fantastical air of a gigantic doll's house, the plaything of some Titan child. As the sun sank towards the horizon, its rays gilded the stucco façade and lent the windows a diamond-like dazzle.

We were met at the front door by a tall, gaunt, hatchet-faced woman in her late middle years who could only have been Mrs. Frensham. A black cloth band encircled her left arm. She barely acknowledged Holmes and myself, instead launching into a vituperative tirade against Miss Smith.

"Where have you been, child? Sloping off like that without a by your leave. The nerve! On a day like this, of all days. The police are wondering about your whereabouts. They are still very keen to interview you. No surprises there, of course. Now you have made yourself look not just neglectful but downright guilty."

"I 'ave brought friends," Miss Smith said, indicating us. I was pleased to see her standing up for herself against the housekeeper's scolding. It was not something that came naturally to her, but she clearly felt emboldened by our presence. "I did in fact tell you I was going up to London, Mrs. Frensham. Perhaps in all the commotion you forgot."

"Why, you – !" Mrs. Frensham checked herself. Had Holmes and I not been there, she might well have given free rein to the enmity she felt towards her subordinate. In the event, she simply gritted her teeth and said, "We shall discuss this further later. As it is, I neither know who these gentlemen are, nor care. This is a household in mourning. We are not in a fit state to receive guests."

"I am not a guest, madam," said Holmes. "I am here at Miss Smith's request, with my associate, in order to make enquiries into Sir Peregine's terrible mishap. You are entirely within your rights to turn us away. However, we shall only come back tomorrow, and the day after, and the day after that. We are nothing if not persistent, and shan't rest until we have got to the bottom of the matter. So it would be simpler just to invite us in now, and save yourself a great deal of trouble."

Mrs. Frensham weighed up his words, and relented, reluctantly. In we went, but no sooner were we across the threshold and congregated in the hallway than a male voice said, "Who are these people?"

The speaker was a young, tousle-haired man who appeared at the top of the staircase, rubbing his face as though he had just woken up from sleep. He shambled down to join us, yawning and fixing us with a bleary eye.

"Master Cecil," said Miss Smith, "may I introduce Mr. Sherlock 'Olmes and his colleague, Dr. Watson. Mr. 'Olmes, Dr. Watson – Cecil 'Arrison."

"Ah yes," said Harrison in a *louche* drawl. "The detective fellow. I've read about you. And you're the chap who writes the stories about him. Well, welcome to our humble abode. I've no idea why you feel the need to be here. Poor old Uncle Perry. It's dreadful, but it was an accident, that's all. I know you're into murders and sinister doings and suchlike, but I can assure you you won't find any of that at Bridlinghall Place. I say that as the man of the house."

"You are Sir Peregrine's nephew, I take it," said Holmes.

Cecil Harrison nodded. "His closest living kin. He and Aunt Jane had no offspring of their own. I've always regarded myself as a surrogate son – more of a son to them than I am to my own parents, who have rather disowned me."

"Master Cecil was the 'ero of the 'our," said Mary Smith. "The way 'e put 'is shoulder to the conservatory door and 'ammered it open. Proper 'Ercules, 'e was."

Harrison cast down his gaze, as though embarrassed by the flattery. "Legacy of rugby at school. But if only I had been a fraction quicker off the mark, got there a fraction sooner. I came running as soon as I heard Uncle Perry cry out. He was calling for help. He knew, once he'd been stung, he had only moments. I imagine he was trying to fumble his syringe out of his pocket but couldn't because he was already going into shock and his hands weren't working properly."

"Are you a resident here?" Holmes asked.

"On and off, when I'm not up in town gallivanting. My uncle employs me from time to time as an assistant. A kind of glorified secretary, really. I take notes for him and type them up. Don't know tuppence about plants, but I've been learning. Don't think I'll ever make a scientist, but I'm grateful for the work. *Was* grateful. Oh God . . . ."

Sorrow trembled through his body. I found myself unable to warm to this youth, who struck me as something of an over-privileged ne'er-do-well. All the same, one would have to have a heart of stone not to feel compassion for him.

"May we take a look at the conservatory?" Holmes asked Miss Smith.

"Of course. It's this way."

We followed her to the rear of the manor. Mrs. Frensham, while not invited to accompany us, did so anyway, with a fussy, peremptory air, as though she could not allow any activity under this roof to go unmonitored by herself.

Before we entered the conservatory, Holmes bent to examine the door, which was large and wooden and sported a broken lock. The jamb, where the lock engaged, was splintered.

"Was Sir Peregrine apt to lock himself inside the conservatory?"

"'E was," said Miss Smith. "Sometimes 'e didn't want to be disturbed. It ruined 'is concentration, 'e said, knowing there was the possibility of someone walking in at any moment."

"Not that any of us would," Mrs. Frensham interjected. "We knew his ways too well for that. But locking it from the inside gave him that sense of security he needed."

"And both of you watched Cecil Harrison break the door down?"

The women nodded.

"I was first 'ere," said Mary Smith. "Then Mrs. Frensham. Then Master Cecil. The two of us was in a right state before 'e came. We could 'ear Sir Peregrine all gasping and choking, and not a thing either of us could do about it. Cecil rode in like the cavalry."

"Most useful thing the boy ever did in his life," Mrs. Frensham muttered. "Not that it benefited the master in the end."

The interior of the conservatory was muggy and humid. Underfloor hot water pipes radiated warmth up through grilles. The atmosphere was ripe with the smells of verdure and soil. Every inch of available space was occupied by plants, from ferns and shrubs to bromeliads, brightly coloured orchids, and other even more exotic flora. Sir Peregrine's body had been removed, but not so the hypodermic syringe, which lay on the floor beside its steel carrying case. Also on the floor was the tiny agent of the botanist's doom, a humble little honeybee. Holmes picked it up in a gingerly fashion, holding it by the wings between thumb and forefinger, and brought it close to his eye for scrutiny.

"Yes, you can see by the wound at the base of the abdomen," he said. "This bee has stung, and has pulled itself half inside out in the process. Amazing creatures, bees. I have always found them appealing – their industriousness, their organisation, their adherence to a rigid hierarchy. Mostly their lives are about productivity. They are difficult to provoke to ire, in spite of all the folklore about angry swarms. A bee stings only if it is frightened or protecting its queen. It would rather flee than fight."

"Sir Peregrine must have alarmed it," I said. "Perhaps, when it flew in, he panicked. He tried to swat it, and missed."

"That would seem a feasible scenario," Holmes allowed. "One would think he knew better, however. Given that bees posed a fatal danger to him, he might surely have done his level best not to antagonise this one."

He turned his attention to the syringe. Having examined it minutely, he proceeded to perform a highly unwise action. There was a small amount of clear liquid left in its glass cylinder, and he tipped it upside down so that the droplets collected at the needle's base; then he pricked the point of the needle into the tip of his thumb and depressed the plunger.

"Holmes!" I cried. "What are you doing? Are you mad?"

"Merely a test, Watson," replied he, eyeing his thumb. A bead of blood had formed, and gradually the skin around it paled, until soon the entire top segment of his thumb from the knuckle upward had gone stark white.

"Tingles," he said. "A numb sensation. The syringe undoubtedly contains epinephrine."

I continued to upbraid him. It had been an act of the utmost foolhardiness to inject an unidentified substance into himself. Holmes just gave a dismissive shake of the head, as though I were a bothersome nagging wife whom he had learned to ignore.

"Hullo, what's this?" he said, sucking the thumb to restore the blood flow. His gaze had alighted on one of the many workbenches, where sat a pair of secateurs and next to them a few leaf clippings and a solitary leather gardening glove. "Miss Smith, was Sir Peregrine in the habit of wearing gloves while he worked?"

"As far as I'm aware, yes."

"Yes, he did," Mrs. Frensham asserted firmly. She seemed keen to demonstrate that she had greater familiarity with their employer's practices than did Mary Smith. "Especially when he was using secateurs to prune or take a cutting, in order to safeguard his fingers."

"Clumsy, was he?"

286

"Just sensible and cautious."

"Hmmm. Was he right- or left-handed?"

"Right."

"This is a left-handed glove. That is suggestive."

"Of what?" I enquired, but Holmes had already put down the glove and moved on. Now he was applying himself to the little awning window which stood open, held by a bar fastener on its inmost peg. Standing on tiptoe he was able to swing the window in and out, assessing the ease with which the hinges operated. He went out into the twilit garden and surveyed its exterior by the beam of his pocket-lantern. On hands and knees he inspected the ground immediately around the conservatory, which was laid to lawn. He pronounced himself satisfied.

"The only footprints I can discern match yours, Miss Smith," he said. "But that is only to be expected, since you were the one who washed the windows last week."

Mrs. Frensham snorted. It was all the confirmation she needed that Mary Smith had, through carelessness, signed Sir Peregrine Carruthers's death warrant.

"Do not be discouraged, my girl," Holmes went on. "All is not lost. Watson and I will engage rooms for the night at a hotel in Haywards Heath. There are anomalies here that merit further enquiry. Tomorrow we shall return, and by then I hope to have all the data I need to deliver a definitive verdict on the incident."

As we were leaving the house, Mrs. Frensham waylaid us on the front steps.

"There is something I must tell you," she said. "If I interpret aright your remark about 'anomalies,' you are of the opinion that there may be more to Sir Peregrin's death than meets the eye."

"Some of the evidence at the scene does not add up."

"In that case, I imagine that you are considering one of us three as the guilty party, since we were the only persons on the property at the time."

"Do you have a confession to make, madam?"

"Oh no, sir! Perish the thought. It occurs to me, however, that the finger of blame might point, if not in Miss Smith's direction, then in Master Cecil's. If this was murder, who would seem to gain the most from it? Master Cecil, of course. As the obvious heir to Sir Peregrine's estate, he stands to become a very rich young man. Now, he is a feckless boy, to be sure, and has yet to make something of his life. He hardly knows the meaning of responsibility. If Sir Peregrine had not been giving him work, it is doubtful he would be able to obtain gainful employment elsewhere. That said, I believe him not to be of an acquisitive nature, certainly not to the degree that he would kill someone for whom he bore a great familial fondness. That is not my reading of his character."

"Well, you know him better than I do, Mrs. Frensham."

"Miss Smith, on the other hand, is just the kind of girl who would stop at naught to get what she wants."

"You dislike her."

"I resent her. And would you care to know why?"

"Very much so."

Mrs. Frensham leaned close to us and said in viperish tones, "She is in Sir Peregrine's will. To be precise, she is his heir, not Master Cecil."

Holmes's eyelids narrowed. "How fascinating. You know this for a fact?"

The housekeeper looked very smug. "I do. Sir Peregrine had the will redrafted not long after he lost Lady Jane. Naturally, with his wife gone and the pair of them childless, someone had to be the inheritor. He chose Miss Smith over Master Cecil, for reasons one may only speculate at. I saw the new will on his desk earlier this year. Mr. Cramb, his solicitor, had brought it over personally. Sir Peregrine had been verifying the wording of it and had left it out on the blotter. By chance, while he was absent from his study, I went in to empty the waste paper basket, and there it was. I couldn't help but notice the name of Mary Smith listed as sole beneficiary."

"Why her? Why not Harrison?"

"That was for Sir Peregrine to know, and he now cannot tell us."

"Are you insinuating that there was impropriety between the two of them?"

"A widower. A young woman of no breeding but a certain coarse attractiveness. It is not unheard of."

"Does Harrison know about this?" I asked. "That he is not to see a penny?"

"I can't aver to that with any authority, but how likely is it that he was *not* aware? My point is this: of the three of us, there is only one who would profit at all from Sir Peregrine's death. She, the wicked little minx, must have worked her wiles on the poor man during the period when he was grief-stricken and at his most vulnerable. Do not be fooled by her guileless demeanour. She has not brought you here to clear her name, but to mock us, to rub our noses in her immunity from prosecution. No one can prove that she left the window open on purpose, but we who know her know she did."

We drove to Haywards Heath with Mrs. Frensham's words ringing in our ears. Holmes was absorbed in deliberation, and remained that way – aloof and reticent – all through supper and at breakfast the next morning.

Eventually, as we left the hotel, he broke his silence. "Watson, we have two ports of call today before we return to Bridlinghall Place. The first will be innocuous, the second less so."

The first was the offices of Geraint Cramb, Sir Peregrine's solicitor. Holmes prevailed on him to show us his copy of the will. Cramb was reluctant, but it transpired that he was an admirer of Holmes's and something of a devotee of my writings, and his personal enthusiasm overcame his professional discretion.

The will, formally notarised and fully official, was as Mrs. Frensham had said. Once probate was complete, Mary Smith would own outright the manor and Sir Peregrine's substantial capital assets, aside from a few trifling charitable disbursements.

"It is a somewhat unconventional bequest," said Cramb, "and I counselled against it, but Sir Peregrine was resolute. He felt this Miss Smith was the most deserving person of any of his acquaintance, more so even than a blood relative."

"Was there any indication of a romantic relationship between the two?"

"Not that I could tell, Mr. Holmes, although I was not privy to the workings of Sir Peregrine's heart. In my judgement, his decision, although out of the ordinary, was made in a spirit of sincerity and with a sound mind. He liked the Harrison lad well enough, even felt a sort of paternal duty of care towards him, but I remember him telling me once that a man ought to make his own way in the world and that to confer a large sum of money on somebody with little gumption or ambition would unquestionably be the ruin of that person."

"Did Mary Smith know she was in line for a sizeable legacy?"

"If so, she would have learned it only from Sir Peregrine, not from me."

After bidding Cramb adieu, we travelled to the local hospital, where Holmes inveigled us a visit to the morgue in which the body of Sir Peregrine Carruthers was being held in advance of the coroner's post mortem examination later that same day. The procedure entailed, I am afraid to say, bribery. An orderly whom Holmes identified as burdened with gambling debts took half a crown off us and led us furtively to the little mausoleum-like building that was set apart from the main bulk of the hospital, an old-fashioned "dead house." Sir Peregrine was laid out on a shelf there, under a sheet. I kept watch at the entrance while Holmes pored over the cadaver. Within a few minutes he had found what he was looking for.

On the journey back to the manor, I enquired about the fresh evidence he had discovered.

"A puncture mark on the inside of the forearm."

"Is that it? But we know already that Harrison injected Sir Peregrine with epinephrine."

"Ah, but there are puncture marks and there are puncture marks, Watson. I also learned where he was stung."

"Where?"

"On the tip of the index finger of his left hand."

"That would make sense. Presumably he was trying to swat the bee with that hand. The bee would have none of it and stung him."

"But why was he not wearing his gardening glove at the time? If he had a glove on his right hand, why not the left as well? And let's not forget that the fellow was right-handed. He would have instinctively used his dominant hand to try to kill the bee, would he not?"

"He took the glove off to swat the bee with it. Yes, that's better still. In an effort to obviate the risk of getting stung, he stripped off the left-hand glove and turned it into a weapon, which he wielded with his right hand."

"An inefficient weapon, I would say. It would have been safer, surely, to keep the glove on and utilise some other implement. Or, for that matter, simply to vacate the conservatory and avoid a confrontation with the bee altogether, knowing that it would be potentially deadly for him."

"He was not thinking straight. Fear got the better of him."

"Watson, your insights, while well-meant, lack rigour. They succeed in showing only how little you have learned about the art of scientific deduction during the time we have been together, and thus how little respect you accord it."

"Well, dash it all, Holmes," I said hotly, "why don't you simply tell me what you know happened, and put me out of my misery? All these years you have derived an almost sadistic pleasure from watching me flounder as I try to arrive at solutions you have already fathomed. For once could you not come out with the answer and not make me feel imbecilic and muddle-headed? Is that too much to ask?"

"And deprive you of the dramatic dénouement you require for your narratives?" Holmes chuckled. "No, old friend. I must leave you twisting in the wind a little longer. All will be revealed once we arrive back at Bridlinghall Place."

And so, in due course, all *was* revealed. Holmes gathered the three disparate members of the household in the drawing room, and addressed them as follows.

"Any coroner worth his salt would assess the circumstances of Sir Peregrine Carruthers's demise and deem it death by misadventure. Even if the awning window had been left open deliberately by someone who knew of Sir Peregrine's fatal allergy to bee stings and was counting on a bee finding its way into the conservatory, there would be no way of proving malfeasance beyond a reasonable doubt. As murders go, it would be a cunning method. It would also, by the same token, be a highly unreliable one. Who could guarantee that a bee would even enter? Who could ensure the creature would actually sting the intended victim? The odds against achieving the desired result by happenstance alone are astronomical."

"So he wasn't murdered," said Cecil Harrison. "That's what you're telling us."

"Oh no. He was. Just not by that exact means."

Mary Smith gasped, as did Mrs. Frensham.

"No," Holmes continued, "the way Sir Peregrine was despatched was altogether more calculated. A bee did not end up in the conservatory by chance. It was put there. It was, moreover, secreted in a place where there was an almost one-hundred-percent certainty it would sting him."

"Where would that be?" said Miss Smith.

"As if you didn't know," Mrs. Frensham muttered under her breath. I was standing close to her, so that only I overheard.

"Why, inside his gardening glove, of course. It would be a simple matter to insert a worker bee into the finger of one of the gloves – the index of the left, to be precise – and leave it there, trapped by the weight of the material, unable to free itself. If the deed was performed sufficiently in advance, during the small hours of the morning, then the bee would have stopped buzzing in frustration and would have quietened down by the time Sir Peregrine made his daily foray into the conservatory. He would have had no inkling that the insect was sequestered in the glove until he came to slip the glove on."

"'Ow 'orrid," said Miss Smith.

"Quite. A tiny living bullet waiting in the barrel of the gun, set to fire when the person pulling the trigger was not around. As simple as it is sinister. But of course, Sir Peregrine had his hypodermic full of epinephrine on him, ready to save him. Once he had been stung, the first thing he would have done was inject himself. But what if the injection failed to work? What if our murderer had taken the precaution of replacing it beforehand with another syringe containing a liquid of no medicinal value, such as water?"

Holmes cast an imperious gaze round the room.

"Then, when Sir Peregrine thought he had counteracted the effects of anaphylaxis, it turned out he had not. He rapidly realised this, and that was when he began screaming and calling for help. Help came. It came, however, too late, and more to the point, it was not help at all."

"But Master Cecil administered an injection after he broke in," said Mrs. Frensham. "He used Sir Peregrine's own syringe."

"Did he? Or did he only purport to?"

Cecil Harrison shot to his feet. "This is absurd. Preposterous. Am I to take it that I stand accused of my own uncle's murder?"

"Please sit down, Mr. Harrison. Posturing and chest-beating will get you nowhere. You know as well as I do what you did. You barged your way into the conservatory with the original syringe hidden in your hand. You took advantage of being first into the room, ahead of the two ladies here. You shielded Sir Peregrine from their view with your body and brandished that syringe as though it was the one from his carrying case, at the same time slipping the other syringe, the ineffectual counterfeit, into your pocket. You then injected Sir Peregrine in precisely the same spot where he had injected himself moments earlier, so that there would be only a single puncture mark."

"I defy you to back up that assertion with proof," said the young man vehemently. He was puffed up with indignation, like a cornered cat with its fur bristling.

"There'll be proof enough," said Holmes. "What alerted me to the possibility that Sir Peregrine did not die by accident was the fact that he had removed his left glove. Why, if he was using secateurs with his right hand, would his left hand be bare? It would be rash to deploy a sharp instrument like that and leave the fingers of your other hand uncovered when you had the option of protecting them. This led me to the inference that Sir Peregrine snatched the glove off almost as soon as he put it on. This, in turn, gave me a location for the bee to have been lodged. The open awning window was merely misdirection. You left it ajar, Mr. Harrison, at the same time as you introduced the bee into the glove. You had been taking a nap yesterday when we turned up in the evening. Our arrival woke you. Doubtless you were catching up on the sleep you had lost through your nocturnal activities. That misstep aside, you are shrewder than people give you credit for. The terrible thing, as far as you are concerned, is that it has all been for nothing."

"What do you mean by that?"

"I mean that killing your uncle, a man who did what he could to support you and keep you solvent, is going to reap you no reward save the gallows."

"Reward? Are you referring to the inheritance? But I get nothing, Mr. Holmes. Didn't you know that? Uncle Perry changed his will. He left everything to *her*, lock, stock and barrel." Harrison gestured intemperately at Miss Smith. "She gets the lot. The Lord alone knows why. Is she kin? She is not. But that was his decision, and he informed me of it, and there is a major plank of your case against me taken away."

"Maybe," said Holmes, "but it sets another plank, just as firm, in its stead. If money was not the motive, what is a no less powerful and compelling a reason to kill? Revenge."

Harrison's eyes flickered. I saw it, and in that moment realised that Holmes had hit the nail on the head. Cecil Harrison had planned and executed a cold-blooded murder simply to get his own back on the uncle who had cut him out of a lucrative legacy. His reason was not greed but a pettier one: peevishness.

"And with your revenge," Holmes added, "you sought to make it look as though Miss Mary Smith had been the agent of Sir Peregrine's death. You wished it to be ascribed to her inattention, so that at least the responsibility would be attached to her thereafter, if not the technical culpability. She would live for the rest of her life dishonoured, with shame and opprobrium heaped upon her. She would be known forever as the careless housemaid who caused the world to lose a great scientist."

Harrison continued to remonstrate and deny, but by that stage the local constabulary were at the door. Holmes had summoned them earlier, with instructions about the timing of their arrival. He bade them search Harrison's room, and sure enough, there they found, hidden in a drawer, a second syringe which was identical to the other and which proved to have contained only water.

As for Mary Smith, her face had turned ashen upon learning the news about the will, and as the police officers led a fulminating Cecil Harrison away from the premises, she sank into a swoon. I tended to her until she came round.

"I can scarcely credit it, Doctor," she said in a wan voice. "Such benevolence. Such generosity. Oh, Sir Peregrine . . . ."

A severe glare from Mrs. Frensham was aimed her way, after which the housekeeper, without another word, exited the room. Her baseless suspicions about Mary Smith's relationship with their employer would never be allayed, and indeed, not an hour later, she was seen departing Bridlinghall Place in high dudgeon, with a packed valise, clearly having no intention to return. I try not to editorialise in these chronicles of mine, but in Mrs. Frensham's case I can only say good riddance.

"It is a terrible pity," said Holmes on the train back to London, "that someone should prefer a young woman who is not family over a young man who is. Yet Sir Peregrine clearly felt the virtuous, industrious Miss Smith a worthier recipient of his largesse than the shiftless, unenterprising Mr. Harrison, and it was to prove his undoing."

"Might I ask, purely in order to tidy up a final detail, how you knew he had been injected twice in the same spot?"

"Oh, that." My companion waved a hand airily. "The puncture mark was a fraction too large for the bore of needle on the syringe. Harrison was accurate, but nonetheless could not avoid widening the original hole, however slightly. It was easy to discern because I myself have been guilty of the same thing."

"You?"

"When, in the not too distant past, I habitually partook of cocaine, I would sometimes reuse a puncture. For that I have you to blame."

"Me?"

"You constant disapproval over my use of the drug worsened whenever the puncture marks on my arm multiplied. In order to forestall that, I would inject in the same spot twice to keep their number down while maintaining the same frequency of doses. Hence, it would appear that I was moderating my intake, when I was not. I am not proud of that, but at least it was of benefit in this instance."

I did not know whether to laugh or chastise him. In the end I chose the former. It seemed better to make light of that dark episode in his life, and thus lay it to rest, instead of reviving it.

Holmes's mind, at any rate, seemed to be focused more on the future than the past. He turned his head to gaze out of the window at the Sussex countryside speeding by, into whose rustic embrace he would consign himself a few months thence. In its golden autumn finery, the landscape had rarely looked better.

"The bee," he said, half to himself. "Admirable, captivating little insect. It would not be a waste of one's declining years to devote oneself to the study of it. Yes, bees . . . ."

A Most Diabolical Plot
by Tim Symonds

From the Notebooks of Dr. John H. Watson MD, late of the Indian Army

Not 'til the day the bugle blows for me shall I forget the most diabolical attempt ever made on my friend Sherlock Holmes's life. My wife was away, and I was seated in the airy living-room of the lodgings I had shared with Holmes on the first floor of 221, Baker Street. Our landlady, Mrs. Hudson, came in with my breakfast, together with the morning edition of the *Westminster Gazette*. The newspaper contained a summary of the year's significant events so far – on February 3rd a British expedition captured the mud-walled city of Kano, in Northern Nigeria. Under Pelham Warner's captaincy, the first cricket tour of Australia was in its final planning stages. I was about to turn my attention to the plate of kidneys, kedgeree, and ham, when my eye was caught by a short article on an inside page titled "Mystery Disappearance of Society Murderer."

> *Nothing has been seen of Colonel Sebastian Moran, formerly 1st Bangalore Pioneers and well-known at London's card-playing clubs, since his unpublicised release from Newgate last year when the gaol was closed for demolition. The Colonel served only half of a twenty-year sentence for the willful murder of his gambling partner, the Honourable Ronald Adair, second son of the Earl of Maynooth. Moran fell into a trap laid by Inspector Lestrade of Scotland Yard less than a decade ago when the former attempted to assassinate the famous Consulting Detective Sherlock Holmes, employing an ingenious air-gun designed to shoot bullets instead of small lead pellets. To gain early release, Colonel Moran vowed to turn his considerable talents to good causes.*

I lowered the newspaper and stared unseeing at the wall. We were in the autumn of 1903. More than forty determined attempts had been made upon Holmes's life in the twenty-plus years since we had taken up lodgings together, yet I recalled in exact detail Moran's failure in 1894, which led to his arrest and imprisonment. It was preceded by a murder taking place in unusual and inexplicable circumstances. At the time, Holmes remarked, "That had all the hallmarks of Colonel Moran." He

295

reached up to a bookshelf for his Index of biographies, adding, "My collection of M's is a fine one. Morgan the poisoner, and Merridew of abominable memory, and Mathews, who knocked out my left canine in the waiting-room at Charing Cross. And, finally, here is our friend."

He passed the Index to me.

MORAN, SEBASTIAN, COLONEL. Born London, 1840. Son of Sir Augustus Moran, C. B., once British Minister to Persia. Educated Eton and Oxford. Served in Jowaki Campaign, Afghan Campaign, Charasiab (despatches), Sherpur, and Cabul. Address: Conduit Street. Clubs: The Anglo-Indian, the Tankerville, the Bagatelle Card Club. Recruited by the "Napoleon of Crime," Professor Moriarty, serving as his Chief of Staff, but used solely for assassinations that require rare skill with the rifle.

Scratched in the margins in Holmes's precise hand were the words, *"The second most dangerous man in London."*

"As you have a fountain pen in your hand, Watson, please update the entry," Holmes had requested. "Now the Napoleon of Crime Moriarty is dead, could you strike out 'second' as in 'The *second* most dangerous man in London.' Moran has inherited the rank as our principal foe."

Once Moran had been safely tucked away in Newgate Prison, I gave him less thought throughout the years than to the industrious navigators repairing the canals of Mars. It came as a nasty shock to learn of his release. I assumed the murderer would stay locked up for many years to come. I folded the *Gazette* and cast a glance across the back garden to a wall giving access into Siddons Lane. More than once, in fear of attack from Baker Street itself, Holmes and I achieved a quick exit by that back route. I made a mental note to inform my comrade that Moran was on the loose, and turned to my writing-desk to put the final touches to our most recent case for submission to the *Strand Magazine*.

Within the hour the manuscript was finished. I threw down the pen and looked out of the window. A warm, lazy summer lay behind us, the third since Edward VII assumed the throne of England. I could spend a leisurely hour in nearby Regents Park watching the herons' antics on their tiny island before strolling on to the *Strand's* offices on Southampton Street. The Art Editor would commission a few simple line drawings from the well-known artist Mr. Sidney Paget to illustrate the story. With luck, it would be picked up across the Atlantic by the editor of *Collier's* magazine.

The grandfather clock struck the hour. Holmes came up the stairs at his customary three-at-a-time. On most days, as he had that day, he left the flat before daybreak for London's East End, forever observing the rapacious ivory-traders and dragsmen in the welter of streets in Stepney and Whitechapel. On other days, he journeyed down to the English county of Sussex to oversee the construction of dew ponds on the isolated bee-farm he had recently purchased.

My comrade's head appeared around the door, a Coutts cheque flapping in his hand.

He said in a most affable tone, "Courtesy of the mid-day post, the Duchess of Burwash has at last settled her account. Name any restaurant in the whole of London and allow me to invite you to dine there this weekend – I have obligations until then. What do you say to a fish-dinner? Shall we take a scow along the river to The Ship in Greenwich?"

The invitation came as a welcome surprise. When fortune smiles I am prepared to lay out two days' Army pension on partridge or an over-ripe pheasant at one of my clubs, or, for a special treat, Rother Rabbit with broccoli, followed by Lady Pettus' biscakes. Holmes, by contrast, even when he is the honoured guest of a wealthy client, has been known to call for a tin of his favourite over-salted Benitez corned beef.

"Holmes, I accept this rare invitation," I replied, adding emphatically, "with alacrity."

"And your choice of restaurant for our celebratory meal?" Holmes asked.

"If you really do mean any restaurant in the whole of London, I would opt for Simpson's Grand Cigar Divan."

"A fine decision," Holmes acknowledged cheerily.

I saw he was settling in for the day at a particularly noxious chemical experiment. I took my hat and strolled to the heronry in Regents Park, followed by a two mile walk to deliver the manuscript to my publishers.

The weekend approached. I stood at the sitting-room window, staring down at the bustling street. A diligence pulled by a team of Boulonnais mares was commencing its long journey, destination Glasgow and Scotland's ports to the Western Isles. The invaluable little Street Arabs, known to Holmes and me as the Baker Street Irregulars, bowled home-made hoops along the paving. Their ragged gang-leader, young Simpson, ran to the diligence's side, begging for a coin or fruit from well-dressed passengers. I spotted a tall figure ambling towards our front-door in a collarless cotton shirt and corduroy trousers, sporting a high, soft hat with a pipe stuck in the side of it, and a waistcoat reaching down almost to his knees. It was Holmes, in a disguise new to me. With a quick sideways dart he came in.

The morning post had come and gone without intrusion into our world, but a rat-tat-tat at the front door indicated a special delivery. Mrs. Hudson came up the stairs with a letter for Holmes. He read it and was about to place it in his notebook when he caught sight of my expectant face. He tossed the page across with a laugh.

The letter was from Inspector Lestrade, the Scotland Yard policeman Holmes first encountered in a case years before.

Lestrade's note read:

Dear Mr. Holmes,

I'm told you've been hanging around the London Docks disguised as a common Irish labourer. I wonder what mischief you're getting up to now? When you've settled back in your digs and have a moment to spare, we at the Yard would appreciate your cooperation in a pretty little mystery. Please give our cordial good wishes to Dr. Watson.

G. Lestrade.

There was a lengthy postscript.

I almost forgot. You will by now have seen the news your friend, Colonel Sebastian Moran, was released from Newgate Prison. So far, he seems to be conforming to the terms of good behaviour for obtaining his freedom early. There has been no sign of him at the Anglo-Indian, the Bagatelle Card Club, or the Tankerville. We believe we've traced him to a lonely and isolated farmhouse on the Haddiscoe Marshes, on the borders of Suffolk and Essex. An elderly man described as thin, with a projecting nose, high bald forehead, cruel blue eyes, and a huge grizzled moustache, has taken a short lease on the place, near some abandoned Maltings. He sports a red and black silk cravat, Moran's old neckwear. Superstition, no doubt. Magical thinking gives half the world's criminals away. The man surrounds his land in every direction with "DANGER KEEP OUT" signs. He may not plan to stay there for long. According to the village woman who "does" for him, the house is only sparsely furnished. He has a pair of commonplace ceramic dogs, a postcard of the Sussex cricketer, K.S. Ranjitsinhji, on the mantelpiece, a few pieces of old-fashioned china, and a couple of rickety chairs.

I read in Police Review *you have bought a farm in Sussex and are the owner of several hives of bees, with plans to write an opus on the meadow-flower in Mesolithic honey cultures. By a strange coincidence, Moran's taken up bee-keeping himself. The postman reported several deliveries of bees, though not the patriotic British bee. The Colonel's arrived from East Africa. What's odd is the way he's housing them. Instead of proper wooden-frame hives, he had an old skepper make up the baskets from coils of grass with a single entrance at the bottom, the way my grandfather used to. I say "odd," because I'm told these skeps have serious disadvantages compared to proper hives. Skeps are lighter in weight and easier to transport, but you can't inspect the comb for pests and diseases, and you may have to destroy the bee colony (and the skep) to remove the honey.*

I was relieved by the information that Moran, formerly so obsessed with seeking Holmes's death, had been tracked to a lair on the border of Suffolk and Essex, a good distance from Holmes's own isolated bee-farm on the Sussex Downs.

Moran's capture and imprisonment and our part in it flooded back. It took place at midnight in an empty house across the street from our lodgings, a setting with an unhampered view of our sitting-room. Moran planned to shoot Holmes through our window with the same remarkable weapon he used to murder his former whist partner, the Honourable Ronald Adair. Unfortunately for Moran, Holmes was one step ahead of him.

I can do no better than to repeat my description in "The Adventure of the Empty House":

A low, stealthy sound came to my ears, not from the direction of Baker Street, but from the back of the very house in which we lay concealed. A door opened and shut. An instant later steps crept down the passage-steps which were meant to be silent, but which reverberated harshly through the empty house. Holmes crouched back against the wall, and I did the same, my hand closing upon the handle of my revolver.

Peering through the gloom, I saw the vague outline of a man, a shade blacker than the blackness of the open door. He stood for an instant, and then he crept forward, crouching,

299

menacing, into the room. He was within three yards of us, this sinister figure, and I had braced myself to meet his spring, before I realized that he had no idea of our presence. He passed close beside us, stole over to the window, and softly and noiselessly raised it for half a foot. As he sank to the level of this opening, the light of the street, no longer dimmed by the dusty glass, fell full upon his face.

The man seemed to be beside himself with excitement. His eyes shone like stars, and his features were working convulsively. An opera hat was pushed to the back of his head, and an evening dress shirt-front gleamed out through his open overcoat. His face was gaunt and swarthy, scored with deep, savage lines. In his hand he carried what appeared to be a stick, but as he laid it down upon the floor it gave a metallic clang. Then from the pocket of his overcoat he drew a bulky object, and he busied himself in some task which ended with a loud, sharp click, as if a spring or bolt had fallen into its place.

Still kneeling upon the floor he bent forward and threw all his weight and strength upon some lever, with the result that there came a long, whirling, grinding noise, ending once more in a powerful click. He straightened himself then, and I saw that what he held in his hand was a sort of gun, with a curiously misshapen butt. He opened it at the breech, put something in, and snapped the breech-lock. I heard a little sigh of satisfaction as he cuddled the butt into his shoulder. For an instant he was rigid and motionless. Then his finger tightened on the trigger.

There was a strange, loud whiz and a long, silvery tinkle of broken glass across the street. At that instant Holmes sprang like a tiger on to the marksman's back, and hurled him flat upon his face. The man was up again in a moment, and with convulsive strength seized Holmes by the throat, but I struck him on the head with the butt of my revolver, and he dropped again upon the floor. There was the clatter of running feet upon the pavement, and two policemen in uniform, with one plain-clothes detective, rushed through the front entrance and into the room. Moran's eyes fixed upon Holmes's face with an expression in which hatred and amazement were equally blended. "You fiend!" he kept on muttering. "You clever, clever fiend!" – adding, "I shall break free from gaol, I can assure you, Holmes. And then I shall come and get you."

The evening arrived for the celebratory meal at Simpson's Grand Cigar Divan. The head waiter led us to a table overlooking the Strand. We ordered sherry at an extravagant 1/- the glass. Over the years, famous authors and politicians had sat at the same table, including William Gladstone. Each Feast of All Souls, Charles Dickens booked this same table with fellow members of the Everlasting Club to discuss the occult, Egyptian magic, and second sight.

The window commanded a fine sweep of the Adelphi Theatre. I felt satisfaction as I watched a line of velvet-gowned women and tail-coated men awaiting entry to see my new play. A case of ours had been adapted as a popular piece. One theatre critic said, "All London shivers . . . ." *The Sunday Times* pronounced, "A Corker! The audience was spellbound. Dr. John Watson's delightful play raises questions which should rally and startle all sincere students of the deductive arts."

We commenced our meal with a white soup of chicken, almonds, and lashings of cream, and waited for the main course. After a suitable time, the Chef appeared. Walking behind him was a lesser mortal pushing a silver dinner wagon. The Chef served Holmes's slices of beef with a heavy portion of fat, carved from a large, succulent joint. I opted for the smoked salmon at a price well beyond my own pocket. For dessert, we chose the treacle sponge, with a dressing of Madagascan vanilla custard.

Holmes's mood became pensive. I enquired why. With a wistful look, he replied, "I rather hope Colonel Moran won't keep the promises he made to gain his early release. I missed matching my wits against him while he was locked away. I quite like it when he gets up to his tricks. Some definite villainy in the blood passes down in his ancestry. From the point of view of the criminal expert, England has become a singularly uninteresting country since the extinction of his boss, the most dangerous and capable criminal in Europe. While Professor Moriarty was in the field, every morning my gazette presented infinite possibilities."

When Moriarty had been "in the field," Holmes had described him without a hint of hyperbole as "the organizer of half that is evil and nearly all that is undetected in this great city. He is a genius, a philosopher, an abstract thinker."

I threw down my napkin with an incredulous smile.

"Holmes, my dear chap! Surely you don't suffer from a lack of excitement? Almost weekly we catch the froufrou of Cabinet Ministers' and political dukes' frock-coats as they clamber up our stairs to seek your assistance. Why, take our most recent case . . . ."

"Watson," came the wry reply, "the crisis once over, the actors pass out of our lives forever. I value your effort to console me with my

301

notoriety, but I insist that every morning one must win a victory and every evening we must fight the good fight to retain our place, or else I must seek early retirement."

I was about to console him with, "I have no doubt that very soon Inspector Lestrade will bang on our door to summon us to the scene of another baffling crime," when we became aware a small tureen had appeared on our table, sitting apart from the magnificent silverware. I summoned the waiter. No, he replied. Absolutely not. He knew nothing about it.

Holmes pulled the vessel towards him and cautiously raised the lid. Inside lay an envelope marked "Sherlock Holmes, Esq." He flicked it to me. It contained a single sheet of Trafalgar blue note-paper, upon which, in a scribbled hand, were written the words:

"Dear Holmes, I know you will welcome me back into the world of the living. I have given considerable thought to the person who put me in Dante's Inferno (Seventh Circle) in the first place. I do not wish to put that person to great inconvenience but I wonder if he and I might arrange an encounter?"

My heart missed a beat. I had no need to read the initials at the bottom of the note. It was from the viperous Colonel Sebastian Moran, once the right-hand man of arch-criminal Professor Moriarty, whose criminal network had stretched from the Bentinck Street corner of Welbeck Street to the Daubensee above the Gemmi Pass.

Moran's letter was a reminder how often he had sought revenge for the death of his erstwhile Paymaster.

He wrote, *"It's been far too long since we met and decided certain things. Three years before, I was consigned to gaol you thwarted me on the 4th and 23rd of January. Two years before my incarceration, you thwarted me in the middle of February. In my last year of freedom you were good enough to wait until the end of March. You will understand why I felt it necessary to launch an attack on you. For too long, Professor Moriarty allowed you, through your continual persecution, to place him in positive danger of losing life or liberty, with results we know well."*

Wittily, Moran penned, *"Your compulsive urge to interfere in my life presents a hereditary tendency of the most diabolical kind."*

Holmes had sent Professor Moriarty plummeting to his doom in the Reichenbach Falls. With a deliberate reference to the rushing waters, Moran went on, "Given our mutual interest in cascades, I suggest we get together at the Old Roar Waterfall above Hastings, conveniently near your bee-farm in Sussex. I have looked in my memorandum-book for a date. Shall we say around two o'clock on the afternoon of the first

Monday of the coming month? I shall await your attendance for the final discussion of those questions which formerly lay between you and Professor Moriarty, which now, in his enforced absence, lie between you and me."

The Colonel signed off with a sardonic *"Pray give my greetings to your Sancho Panza, Dr. Watson. The Doctor and his antique Service revolver will be most welcome to join us."*

The jibes were followed with an impudent, *"Believe me to be, my dear chap, very sincerely yours, S.M."*

I folded Moran's letter. A murderous rage took control of my senses. Colonel, I thought, this time you will meet your quietus. My comrade, or better still his Sancho Panza, shall rid this world of you once and for all.

The rage subsided. Soon Holmes and I would be seated in a train on our way to Hastings, my trusty Service revolver in a pocket, a great adventure in the air. My heart began to sing. The Old Roar Waterfall it shall be – on the first Monday of the coming month!

A reflective note is in order here. Over the years I have come to realise the gods (more so the goddesses) play a remarkable role in our lives. During my military service in our Indian possessions, I often heard and repeated the word *kismet* in Urdu and Hindi, interpreted as *Fate* or *Providence*. Three "ifs," both providential and fateful, led to my years as Sherlock Holmes's chronicler, the happiest and most fulfilling period of my life. If the doctor in the village of my upbringing had not regaled me with stories of his time as a field surgeon in the Eastern War, serving with French and British armies at Sevastopol, I may never have had the ambition to become an Army doctor myself. If a ricocheting bullet from a hostile Afghan tribesman had missed me by an inch rather than thudding into my flesh (to stay there the rest of my life,) whereupon the Army left me, I would have served out my time on The Grim rather than being forced to return to England, with hardly more than a wound-stripe and a pile of Service chevrons to my name. And if I had had any family members in England other than a dissolute brother, I may not have found myself alone in London in 1881 in urgent need of diggings. In which case I would never have mentioned my search for accommodation to Stamford, my old dresser from Barts Hospital. He introduced me that same day to a young man also in need of bachelors' quarters, bearing the unusual Old English Christian name of *Sherlock*.

Now, all these years later, a further "If" was about to intervene.

The first Monday of the month approached. My "antique" Service revolver was oiled and ready. Holmes and I planned our trek in every detail. Old Roar Waterfall was known to me only through a sketch a century earlier by the landscape painter, J.M.W. Turner, now at the Tate Gallery. The chalk and graphite depiction portrayed a wild gully set in a deeply cut, narrow, wooded valley above the isolated fishing village of Hastings. The gully enjoyed the clime and dense plant life of a tropical jungle, home to rare orchids, bird and insect species. There was only one path to the falls, through terrain ideal for an ambuscade. Our foe, as author of *Heavy Game of the Western Himalayas* and *Three Months in the Jungle*, was no stranger to ambuscades. A hunter of iron nerve, he had once crawled down a drain after a wounded man-eating tiger.

Perhaps because we faced the possibility of death at the hands of a merciless assassin, there was considerable jocularity between Holmes and me as we discussed our plans. In "The Adventure of the Empty House", Holmes lured the Colonel to his capture and incarceration by substituting himself with a remarkably life-like wax effigy, executed by Monsieur Oscar Meunier of Grenoble. The bust was placed in full view in our Baker Street window. Once in every quarter of an hour, our obliging landlady crawled in below window level to twist and turn the figure. Holmes now proposed I borrow the full-size wax figure of himself from Madame Tussaud's to place like a ventriloquist's dummy among the orchids and ferns at Old Roar Waterfall. The wax figure and I would sit where Turner sat, squatting up to our nostrils in ferns. I could, Holmes suggested, for the sake of *auld lang syne*, wear my "Shikar", a favourite solar topee purchased at the Army & Navy Stores at a hefty 13/6d.

Holmes didn't laugh often, but when he did it boded ill for a foe. After we had done chuckling, we turned our attention to the serious matter at hand. The Colonel would apply the expertise gained in his years hunting the Bengal tiger. He would carve out a *machan* among the ferns, mosses, and liverworts of the wet dead wood to pick us off before we as much as caught sight of him. We planned to play him at his own game – construct our own machans ahead of him and wait silently for our human tiger through the night and into the following morning.

The stakes were high. Moran notoriously never played by the Englishman's unspoken rule of giving the other side a sporting chance. This time, neither would we. We would follow the diktat of natural justice. Colonel Sebastian Moran would soon trouble this world no more.

So engrossed were we with our preparations that it did not strike us for an instant that Moran's challenge was a hoodwink. The stinging use of Sancho Panza, rather than chronicler, had made my blood boil. Ditto the deliberate mockery of my trusty Service revolver. There was the goading tone, the almost nostalgic choice of setting, echoing the far mightier, more majestic Reichenbach in the Swiss Alps. But Moran had no intention of facing us at Old Roar Waterfall. He was putting in place a plan as devilish as human wit could devise.

When Lestrade of the Yard apprised us of Sebastian Moran's hideaway, he mentioned *en passant* how the Colonel had taken up raising bees. I dismissed this curious fact as mere coincidence and forgot all about it. *Kismet* was once more to intervene. If I had not retreated to a comfortable arm-chair after a decent lunch and a bottle of Albariño at the Junior United Service Club . . . .

I left the Club's handsome dining-room for the reading-room and was drifting into a nap behind a copy of *The Times* when an apparition from my long-gone days in Afghanistan appeared at my elbow.

"Why, it's Watson, isn't it?" a voice exclaimed. "Blow me down! Do you recognise me?"

For a moment I struggled to determine whether the figure was real or a figment of a reverie, until he leaned forward and clapped me on the shoulder. How could I forget! Surgeon-Major Alexander Preston had been with me in the thick of the Battle of Maiwand. His experience, gained through an earlier stint in The Crimea, served the Regiment well. Throughout the battle he bore himself with the traditional nonchalance of a British surgeon in a tight place, while around him our men were going down to a humiliating defeat.

Preston explained he was in London just for a day or two, restocking his supply of medicines. We reminisced about old times. He recounted the events after I was wounded and removed from the field. Ayub Khan's officer corps had been strengthened by the large number of Sepoys who fled to his side after the failure of the Indian Rebellion. Nevertheless, Preston sensed the enemy was losing morale, despite their superior numbers, until the day was saved for Ayub by a young woman by the name of Malalai. Alarmed by her side's mounting despair, she seized the Afghan flag and shouted: "*Young love! If you do not fall in the battle of Maiwand, by God, someone is saving you as a symbol of shame!*" Her cry rallied the Pashtuns to victory.

We reminisced further for a good while before I turned to the present and asked Preston where he was now practicing medicine.

"You say you're in London only briefly," I said. "Which means what? Where do you live now?"

Using the Sanskrit for the Hindu Kush, he replied, "Not in the *Pāriyātra Parvata*, I can tell you! I'm in the deepest English countryside.

Miles from anywhere. After my time in Army Medical Service, life in the most primitive village in England suits me completely. A few cottages huddled around the tiny church of the Blessed Virgin and St. John the Baptist. No telegraph office. Just the one telephone, at the Railway Arms. Not much else. I deliver a few peasant women's babies, treat the occasional marsh fever, even take out an appendix once in a while. The quietest place you can imagine."

The Surgeon-Major paused.

"Mark you, something did happen only a few days ago . . . never seen anything like it. There's nothing in the medical records nor anything on apiculture that I can find."

I raised my eyebrows.

"Apiculture?" I queried.

"Yes, bees, hives, that sort of thing."

"I know the word," I returned, "but what has that to do with your medical practice?"

He recounted how two sturdy walkers had decided to trek across remote marshes three or four miles from his surgery. Holding that signs in the countryside did not apply to visitors from London, they ignored the "Keep Out" boards.

"Then something very curious and inexplicable took place, Watson," Preston said. "The hikers were passing a cluster of abandoned Maltings when a witness said a swarm of bees poured out like a sudden dark rain-cloud. Most bees are quite polite if you don't disturb their nests. They don't usually chase you for over half a mile if you're rushing away as fast as your legs can take you. These bees did. Their ferocity was terrible. They attacked the two poor blighters relentlessly. In appearance, there was nothing exceptional about the bees. Possibly they were even slightly smaller than our familiar black honeybee. I estimate they inflicted two thousand stings on each of their victims. A bee stinger is barbed, like a harpoon. When you consider a human can die with just a hundred stings . . . ."

My narrator threw up his hands.

"By the time the local farmer came to fetch me, there was nothing I could do. Both men died within minutes."

He added, "The owner of the skeps must have worried the authorities would bring a charge of criminal negligence against him – as they should. That same night he upped sticks and disappeared, taking his bees with him."

I sprang to my feet.

"Tell me, Preston," I demanded, "where exactly do you have your practice? You say deepest countryside. Did this by any chance take place along the Stour, near a village by the name of Haddiscoe?"

My old Army comrade looked stunned.

"Why, my old friend!" he exclaimed, "You seem to have developed psychic powers! Heavens above, you'll be excreting ectoplasm next. That's exactly where the incident took place."

My blood chilled. All was now clear. The invitation to a showdown at the Old Roar Waterfall was a red herring, designed to engineer Holmes's absence from his orderly rows of hives. From his Stour Valley remoteness, our enemy had hatched the most cunning, deadly plot ever devised against us. While we crept our way through the undergrowth to the waterfall, Moran would be on the Downs preparing a deadly trap for us. He would switch Holmes's tractable *apis mellifera mellifera*, at home in Britain since the last Ice Age, for the breed of hideously dangerous African bees, which stung the unfortunate London visitors to death. Holmes was known to walk between his rows of hives without veil or gloves. The moment we returned from our futile trek to the waterfall, we would suffer the same fate as the hikers on the Suffolk marshes. The postcard of the Sussex cricketer, K.S. Ranjitsinhji, in the farmhouse indicated Moran had already reconnoitred the area. At this very moment, he and his deadly skeps might be within striking distance of Holmes's own bee-yard, tucked away in secondary woodland which had quickly recolonized my comrade's sheep-free land.

I said a rapid goodbye to my Regimental friend and hurried to the telephone. "Moran, you cunning, cunning fiend!" I repeated time after time.

Although Inspector Lestrade was often out of his depth and chronically lacked imagination, on this occasion he became a man of action and authority. He pointed out that Moran would have his henchmen watching our every move. The Colonel would unfold his plot only if he was assured we were well away from the bee-farm. One glimpse of our presence on Holmes's bee-farm on the day, and the effort to catch Moran *in flagrante delicto* and kill or return him to gaol would fail. In no uncertain terms, we were ordered to continue with our established plan. Lestrade telegraphed Tobias Gregson, the policeman who was keeping an eye on Holmes's bee-farm, to ask him to make rapid enquiries. Gregson replied the same day. Mysterious lights, more often seen over graveyards, had been spotted at Holmes's Hodcombe Farm, resulting in rumours of will-o'-the-wisps. Locals were giving the spot a wide berth.

By now the deadly skeps would be on their wooden bases for ease of transport, the entrances filled with loose grass to allow the bees to breath but prevent their exit. Reluctantly, we agreed to make our way to Old Roar Waterfall. Our departure for Hastings should be as conspicuous as possible. While Lestrade had logic and sense on his side, it was a bitter blow to know we would not have a direct hand in our adversary's fate.

In the meantime, Lestrade, Gregson, and a dozen armed police set up their ambuscade. They would lie in wait on the Downs. If Moran surrendered, our foe would be returned to gaol to serve out the remainder of his sentence. If he resisted . . . every one of Lestrade's squad was a marksman.

On the Monday, Holmes and I took the train to Hastings. We made our way to Old Roar Waterfall on foot and set about constructing two hides in the heavy undergrowth. Two p.m., the appointed time for our dénouement with Moran, came and went. We set off on the return journey to the bee-farm, eager to learn the outcome. Several police marksmen lay at ease, spread-eagled among the bushes. Lestrade was pacing up and down on Holmes's veranda, staring out across the Downs. There was no sign of a captive or corpse. It was clear from the Inspector's demeanour he was not relishing our return. Something had gone badly wrong.

We were a cricket pitch's length from the house when a shaken Lestrade turned and came hurrying towards us, ashen-faced. He stopped short, calling out, "It's no good your scowling, Mr. Holmes. We did our best. This time Moran was just too tricky for us."

With a heavy shudder he cried, "He was there, right in front of us, and then he wasn't. It was as though he possessed some supernatural power!"

It was to remain forever an unfathomable mystical experience in Lestrade's mind. Like the Cheshire Cat, our prey had appeared and disappeared, leaving nothing behind but a baleful snarl and an Italian revolver dropped in his hurry. Was the normally stolid Inspector right to believe he had come up against some supernatural power invested in Moran from his tiger-hunting days or – more likely – was it mere bungling? Had some sixth-sense warned the Colonel at the very last minute, even as he approached Holmes's hives? Or was one of Scotland Yard's marksmen now lolling on the grass a surviving member of Professor Moriarty's old guard?

Bitterly disappointed, I turned to console my comrade. What the beleaguered Scotland Yard Inspector had taken to be a scowl was nothing of the sort. There *was* a strange gleam in Holmes's eye, but it was not one of disapproval. It was a gleam of intense satisfaction.

When Lestrade's men returned from their fruitless chase, they discovered a skep within a hundred yards of Holmes's farm. Five more were found in Friston Bottom, less than a mile away, containing enough Africanized killer bees to colonise and terrorise the whole of Sussex and nearby Kent. An Army flame-thrower platoon, replete with triple-layer mesh bee suits, rid England of the terrible creatures. Once the flamethrowers had done their work, the keen-eyed Tobias Gregson discovered a note attached to a nearby tree. It read, *"My dear Holmes and Watson, you must forgive my handwriting, but I am in somewhat of a hurry. You have foiled me this time, but I can assure you the matters between us still stand and indeed intensify. You may take it I shall be in touch. Yrs ever, SM."*

There was a postscript: *"Niagara or Victoria Falls?"*

At a nearby Channel port, a man sporting a red and black silk cravat was observed boarding a Continental ferry in a great hurry.

Postscript

To be entirely safe, Holmes embarked on the total replacement of his stock with *Apis mellifera ligustica*, a mild-mannered Italian subspecies of the western honeybee. At Inspector Lestrade's request, the Suffolk Constabulary conducted a search of the farmhouse in the Stour Valley, which Moran was obliged to quit in such a hurry. They uncovered an exchange of letters between Moran and the British Beekeepers Association. Using a pseudonym, Moran claimed he wanted advice on cross-breeding bees to increase honey production. Were there any bees he should avoid? The answer came, *"You must at all costs avoid A. m. scutellata, the deadly hybrid of the Western honey bee, known as the* Tanganyikan *or* Killer Bee. *Do not allow even a single African killer bee queen into the hive. She hatches about two days before our British bee queens. She then proceeds to sting all the other queens to death, thus ensuring that her traits of aggressiveness are strengthened in her children."*

It was the information he needed.

The Opera Thief
by Larry Millett

Now that Sherlock Holmes has made known his retirement from the active pursuit of criminal affairs, I feel free to present a case which may shed some measure of light on his fateful decision. Holmes himself has offered no public explanation as to why he retired, at so young an age, from his work as the world's foremost consulting detective. Yet I am inclined to believe that in the end it was a deep weariness of spirit, above all else, which caused him to seek the solitude of Sussex.

Holmes, of course, has never been a stranger to the bleaker strains of existence, and over the years he occasionally succumbed to bouts of despondency. Fortunately, these episodes were always short-lived, for once he found an interesting case to chew upon, he instantly recovered his appetite for life. I cannot say exactly when Holmes began to display signs of a more pervasive melancholia, but the darkening of his mood became especially evident in the months before his sudden retirement. I remember in particular a remark he made one morning as we prepared to investigate the case (about which I have yet to write) of a missing wife and her lover in Lewisham. "But is not all life pathetic and futile?" Holmes asked me that day. "We reach. We grasp. And what is left in our hands at the end? A shadow. Or worse than a shadow – misery."

But it was another case – in faraway Minnesota – which seemed to affect him even more deeply. Curiously, it was case which, at first glance, appeared to involve a mere trifle. Its conclusion, however, was most remarkable, and it was not long thereafter, upon our return to London, that Holmes startled the world by announcing his retirement.

The case of the opera thief, as I have chosen to call it, may fairly be said to have begun with my gallbladder. Throughout much of 1903, I had been suffering from a series of painful episodes related to a buildup of gallstones. After one particularly agonizing attack in late November, I was persuaded by my physician that only surgery could afford the possibility of lasting relief. As it so happened, I had only recently read of new techniques pioneered by two surgeons in Minnesota, Charles and William Mayo. I believed – and Holmes agreed – that my best hope for a cure would be to put myself in the capable hands of the Mayo brothers.

Of course, Holmes and I were quite familiar with Minnesota, having visited the state on several occasions in connection with investigations, beginning in 1894 with the singular case of the Red Demon. Naturally, I told Holmes that he had no need to accompany me on such a long journey, but he would not hear of my going alone. "Doctors," he reminded me, "are well known to be the worst of all patients, and I fear you will be quite impossible unless I am at your side." Holmes also pointed out that a trip to Minnesota would provide a welcome opportunity to see our old friend Shadwell Rafferty, a detective and saloonkeeper possessed of extraordinary skills in both lines of work.

Rafferty was in fact on hand to greet us at the Union Depot in St. Paul when we reached that city in early January of 1904. By then, my condition was growing acute, and so we had time for only a brief conversation before Holmes and I continued on to Rochester, the small town in the southern Minnesota that is home to the Mayo brothers. I will not burden readers with an account of my surgery, other than to say that it was a resounding success and that by the end of January I was all but fully recovered.

By then, Holmes had already discovered a matter to occupy his attention. It concerned Adelaide Strongwood, an extraordinary young woman whose murder trial in Minneapolis was much trumpeted in the American press. Working with Rafferty, Holmes played a decisive role in Miss Strongwood's case, but as it does not bear upon the story of the opera thief, I will say no more about it.

Upon the conclusion of Miss Strongwood's trial in early February, I was well enough at last to travel, and so Holmes and I made plans to return to London. The morning of Saturday, February 6, found us in a comfortable suite at the Ryan Hotel in St. Paul. The night before, we had bid farewell to Rafferty at his saloon, which is part of the hotel. He was preparing to embark on a trip to visit friends in Canada, and we had sent him off with perhaps a few too many rounds of his favorite Irish whiskey. We were about to leave St. Paul as well, as I had already secured two tickets for the Burlington Railroad's afternoon express train to Chicago. From there, we would go New York, and then by steamer back to England.

The day was bitterly cold, as most winter days in Minnesota are, and I was content to sit before a fire that blazed in our hearth, reading the St. Paul newspapers. Holmes had already gone through all three of the city's dailies with his usual thoroughness. Now, he stood by the tall window in our room, staring outside with the glum, anxious countenance of a lost child.

"Did you find anything of interest in the newspapers?" I inquired, hoping that some conversation might help lift Holmes from his doldrums.

"There was one small matter of not inconsiderable interest," Holmes said, walking over and picking up the copy of the *St. Paul Pioneer Press* I had been reading. "Here it is, on page two."

The story, which I had hardly looked at before, read as follows: "*A curious incident has occurred at the Metropolitan Opera House, where a flute used as a prop in the Mozart opera now in performance there disappeared Thursday night. Mrs. Electa Snyder, the impresario who brought the Chicago Opera Company's touring production of The Magic Flute to St. Paul, said the prop was stolen from a locked storage room. The thief, however, left numerous other items of greater worth undisturbed. Mrs. Snyder called the theft 'an outrage,' although she acknowledged that the missing object has 'very little' monetary value. Chief of Detectives O'Connor, not known to be an avid opera-goer, is said to be on the case.*"

"My God," I said, recalling our encounters with O'Connor during the infamous ice palace murders of 1896, "I am astonished that so corrupt and vicious a man has been allowed to remain on the police force."

"I care not one whit about O'Connor," Holmes replied tartly. "It is the theft itself which intrigues me. Why would someone break into an apparently well secured storeroom to steal something of such little value?"

"Well, perhaps it has some value to the thief which we do not understand."

"Precisely," Holmes said, "and yet – "

He was interrupted by a firm series of knocks at the door to our suite.

"Are you expecting someone?" I asked.

"No, but our visitor is a woman and she is obviously in a hurry."

"And just how to you know it is a woman?"

"Because I listen, Watson. You, on the other hand, are content merely to hear."

Before I could respond to this provocation, Holmes had opened the door. A woman swept in past him with the force of a tidal surge. She was full-figured, about forty years of age, and she wore a flowing sea-green dress that all but enveloped her in an oceanic swirl of fabric. Her eyes were also sea green, and as I was soon to discover, unrelenting in their gaze.

I began to rise from my chair, but she said, in a commanding voice, "Don't bother with silly formalities, Dr. Watson. Stay right where you are and I'll have a seat by the fire so that we can talk. Please join us, Mr. Holmes."

Appearing quite bemused, Holmes pulled up a chair beside our visitor. He said, "It is a pleasure to meet you, Mrs. Snyder."

"Ah, so I am already the beneficiary of one of your famous deductions. I would ask you how you accomplished this feat, but – "

"I believe Mr. Holmes read the name tag pinned to your dress," I said. "As you know, he is renowned for his powers of observation."

Holmes gave me a withering look as Mrs. Snyder glanced down at the name tag on her bosom. She gave no evidence, however, that she found any humor in my remark. Instead, she began excavating a hole in my forehead with her piercing eyes. "Yes, I was just at a breakfast here at the hotel with the society women who support the opera. But that is of no consequence, is it?" Then she turned to Holmes and said, "I suppose you know why I have come."

Holmes nodded. "You would like me to find your missing flute."

"Exactly! I must say I could not believe my good fortune when I learned that you were here in St. Paul. Mr. Rafferty told me you are just the man I need."

"How kind of him," Holmes murmured.

"Yes, Shadwell is a dear friend. Now then, when can you start?"

I must confess that I was rather put off by the woman's presumptuous manner, as she seemed to believe that Holmes could not help but leap at the opportunity to investigate the disappearance of an inconsequential stage prop.

"Mr. Holmes and I will be departing later today for London," I noted, "so I do not think – "

Holmes broke in. "Dr. Watson, as you can tell, is most eager to leave St. Paul, and I doubt he gives much weight to the matter you have brought before us. I am not necessarily of the same mind. Indeed, I have always found that small crimes in their own way can be as interesting as affairs of state. However, if today's newspapers are to be believed, the police are already investigating the theft. I am sure they are very able."

"Ha!" said Mrs. Snyder. "Ha and ha and ha, ha, ha! The police have had a full day to investigate this brazen crime and they are already at wits' end, which in their case could not have been a very long journey. No, Mr. Holmes, you are the man I desperately need. I don't read detective stories myself – who has the time? – but I have heard all about you and your grand adventures. And, of course, Shadwell has often sung your praises. Naturally, I will pay you for your time. What is your fee, if I may ask?"

Holmes smiled. "There is no need to talk of money at the moment. But I am intrigued by the matter of your purloined flute. Pray tell us more about the circumstances of the theft."

313

Mrs. Snyder paused for a moment, her eyes fixed on Holmes, and said, "Unfortunately, there is not a great deal I can tell you, other than that it must have been what the police call an 'inside job.'"

"What makes you so sure of that?"

"The Metropolitan Opera House is a very secure venue, Mr. Holmes, and there is a watchman on duty every night, so it is unlikely anyone could have broken in after hours. The flute and other props are kept in a locked storeroom in the basement. Only the stage manager has the key, but I have been told that he sometimes leaves it in his office during performances. I am entirely convinced, therefore, that someone from the opera company or one of the stagehands did the deed."

"Your suspicions may be well founded, Mrs. Snyder. However, I must ask why the theft of a mere stage prop is of such great consequence to you. I take it from the newspapers that the flute has little monetary value."

"You are correct. It's just an ordinary flute that some prop man years ago painted gold. I doubt it would fetch fifty cents at a pawnshop. But money is not the measure of all things, Mr. Holmes. This particular flute has been used in performances of *The Magic Flute* around the world. It stands for the opera. It is Mozart in your hand, and it summons forth all the majesty of his music. To possess it to have a thing beyond the tawdry reach of the dollar."

Holmes seemed curiously moved by Mrs. Snyder's brief speech. He said, "I understand you perfectly, Mrs. Snyder. You wish me to retrieve a magic wand."

"Yes," she said, almost ecstatically, "that is what I wish."

"Very well. Dr. Watson and I will investigate."

"Surely you cannot be serious, Holmes," I said with some asperity. "We have train tickets for today and we must be in New York by Tuesday afternoon, when the *Lucania* sails for Southampton. I do not see – "

"We will take the train tomorrow," Holmes said. "One extra night in St. Paul will do us no harm. Besides, I believe there is a performance of *The Magic Flute* this evening. I assume you can secure tickets and backstage passes for us, Mrs. Snyder?"

"Certainly. I will also instruct all of the performers and stagehands to cooperate fully with your investigation."

"Good. Now, I must ask if you know of any member of the cast or stage crew who might have particularly coveted the flute?"

"The tenor, Mr. Schiele, is in my opinion a most a suspicious character."

314

"Most tenors are," Holmes said. "But do you have any evidence to suggest he is indeed the thief?"

"No. Finding evidence will be your job, Mr. Holmes. By the way, have you ever seen *The Magic Flute*? Some consider it to be Mozart's greatest opera."

"Yes, I have seen it, and I agree it is quite magnificent."

Mrs. Snyder stood up to leave. "Well, there is no more to be said then. I wish you good luck this evening, Mr. Holmes. I will await your report in the morning."

Once she was gone, I could only sigh. Holmes had disrupted our travel plans for what I considered to be an utterly trivial matter. Even worse, I would now be forced to spend a night at the opera.

We arrived at the Metropolitan Opera House, located less than a block from our hotel, well before the scheduled performance of *The Magic Flute*. The opera house was a tall building of rather grim appearance, its lower walls composed of massive blocks of gray granite. Once inside, however, we found a handsome auditorium displaying all the wonders of the plasterer's art in rich tones of ivory and gold. We immediately went backstage. There, amid a forest of sets and rigging inhabited by a busy crew of workers, we looked for the stage manager, who possessed the key to the storeroom from which the flute had been stolen.

A stagehand soon pointed us in the direction of the manager's office, located in the basement. After negotiating a tangle of steep stairs and narrow corridors, we found ourselves in a large subterranean room outfitted with traps, lifts, counterweights, and all the other devices required to sustain the artifice of the stage. As we approached the manager's office, a tall woman in a long black gown decorated with glittering stars intercepted us.

"Sherlock Holmes and Dr. Watson, I presume?" said the woman, whose large gray eyes sparkled with amusement. "I understand Mrs. Snyder has hired you to find her lost flute. How quaint! You know, of course, that it is just an old thing all painted up in gold. But how it has traveled! New York, Chicago, San Francisco, even Vienna, or so I've been told. I suppose it's a lucky charm of sorts. Oh dear, I haven't properly introduced myself. Very rude of me. I am Barbara Majors."

"Miss Majors, it is a pleasure," Holmes said with a slight bow. "You must be the Queen of Night this evening."

"Ah, so you know the opera," she said. "Yes, I am the Queen, or, more precisely, Astrofiammante. A peculiar name, really. But then what isn't peculiar about *Die Zauberflote*? In fact, the whole thing is perfectly

315

ridiculous, not to mention terribly hard on my voice. Oh, those dreadful high *C*'s! Mozart was the very devil as far as I'm concerned. Of course, there are people who consider it the most beautiful opera there ever was or ever will be. I have seen grown men in the audience weep over it."

I could not imagine that her last statement was true, but Holmes, to my surprise, confirmed that he, too, had witnessed manly tears during performances of the opera. "It does indeed seem to have a strange effect," he said, "even on the most hardened of souls. Now, Miss Majors, I wonder if you have any theories as to who might have absconded with the flute?"

Her response took me by surprise. "I think it would a sad person," she said.

Before Holmes could react to this unexpected observation, a stagehand rushed up. "You are needed at once in your dressing room, Miss Majors. It can't wait."

The singer nodded. "Well, good luck to you, gentlemen," she said. "I hope you will find the flute. I really do miss it."

We watched her vanish around a corner just as a little popinjay of a man in a brown suit came down the hallway. "Who are you?" he demanded. "Visitors are not allowed here. You must leave at once!"

"I think not," Holmes replied coolly. "We have business here. I am Sherlock Holmes, and this is Dr. John Watson."

The man's manner instantly changed from threatening to obsequious. "Oh yes, yes. My humblest apologies. I forgot for a moment that Mrs. Snyder said you would be coming tonight. It is an honor, sir, a genuine honor, to meet the great Sherlock Holmes. And of course, Dr. Watson as well. I am Peter Moore, the stage manager. I would be most pleased to assist you in any way I can."

"Yes, I imagine you would," Holmes said. "You may begin by showing us to your office."

Moore's office turned out to be not much bigger than a closet. It held a cluttered rolltop desk, a chair, and a few shelves. There was hardly room for three people inside, so we stood outside the door while Holmes questioned Moore about the missing flute.

"Tell us, if you would, Mr. Moore, when you first discovered that the flute had been taken."

"It was before last night's performance. I sent one of the stagehands down to fetch it from the storeroom, and he came back to tell me it was gone. Stagehands can hardly be relied upon, as I'm sure you know. I thought the fool simply hadn't bothered to look for it in the right place, so I went down myself. But the flute was gone all right. Well, we were in a bit of a panic then. Had to borrow a flute from one of the musicians to use for the performance."

"I see. And I take it you are certain the flute was in fact placed in the storeroom after Thursday night's performance?"

The little stage manager looked nervously at Holmes. "Well, I didn't put it there myself, if that's what you mean. Not my job. But I assume it was put there. That's the usual procedure."

"Ah, Mr. Moore, I have found during my long tenure as a detective that assumptions are, as often as not, merely a form of hope. But let me, for the moment, endorse your assumption that the flute was indeed returned to its proper place on Thursday night, and that the storeroom was locked thereafter. I am then led to consider the matter of the key to the storeroom. Do you carry it on your person at all times, or is it kept in some other place?"

A brief flash of alarm appeared in Moore's unpleasant, bulging eyes. "Well now, Mr. Holmes, in a theater as large as this one is, a great many keys are needed, and it would be very difficult for any man to keep them all on his person. I'm sure you can understand – "

"I understand only that you have not answered my question, Mr. Moore," Holmes said. Without another word, he stepped into the stage manager's office and gave it a quick but thorough inspection. Then he stepped back outside and said, "I imagine, Mr. Moore, that you keep the key in your office, on one of the small wall hooks above your desk. Which means, I take it, that anyone who works backstage would have access to it. Is that correct?"

"No, I wouldn't say so," Moore replied. "Everyone here knows that they are not to enter my office unless I am present."

A slight smile creased Holmes's lips. "My dear Mr. Moore, if people always did as they were told, I should have no work."

It required but a few more questions for Holmes to establish several other essential facts. Moore's office was not locked during performances. On the night of the theft, fifteen stagehands were in the theater, as were a like number of the opera's cast. Virtually all of the stagehands routinely used the key to retrieve or return props. Moore himself had never noticed that the key was missing. Nor could he identify any suspects among the stage crew or cast.

"I will tell you that it is a complete mystery to me, Mr. Holmes. I am at a loss to explain – "

Holmes put one finger to his lips in a gesture of silence. "I have heard quite enough, Mr. Moore. Kindly give me the key, and Dr. Watson and I shall examine the storeroom."

317

Located in the subbasement, the storeroom was, as expected, an unkempt gathering of theatrical paraphernalia, arranged on shelves, atop tables, and in miscellaneous piles rising from the floor. This clutter yielded no obvious clues. Before we left, Holmes bent down to examine the lock on the room's only door. He was soon shaking his head. "Well, Watson, this room is hardly well secured, as Mrs. Snyder suggested to us. The lock is of the flimsiest sort. I should think a reasonably dexterous child with a hairpin could open it with little effort."

"So I take it you are saying the thief may not even have needed to steal the key."

"Precisely. And I fear, Watson, that we are now in what the Americans like to call a 'pickle.' We have a theft that no one witnessed, a theft which could easily have been accomplished by any of thirty or more people, a theft which occurred at an unknown time, and a theft for which there is no obvious motive. Bah, I have been a fool, Watson, a fool to become involved in this matter!"

"Then perhaps we should simply tell Mrs. Snyder that the case is beyond any immediate hope of a solution," I suggested. "I am sure she would understand."

"Perhaps you are right," Holmes said in a quiet voice. I noticed now that same look of melancholy I had seen on his face earlier in the day.

"Then let us return to our hotel," I said. "You could use some rest, Holmes. We will have a long journey tomorrow."

Holmes consulted his pocket watch. "No, Watson, since we are here we might as well enjoy the consolations of Mozart. The performance will begin shortly."

We climbed out of the subbasement and reached the back of the stage, where there was a welter of last-minute activity. Someone shouted "five minutes," and we stepped off to the side, waiting for the curtain to rise.

To my utter surprise, I found the opera quite delightful. Although it was sung in German, a language with which I have little acquaintance, I was able follow the plot as Pamina pined and Tamino acted heroically, Papageno searched for true love with Papagena, and the Queen of Night sent her voice into the realm of the angels. Holmes, meanwhile, stood silently beside me, completely absorbed in the spectacle, and his melancholy gave way to a look of profound pleasure.

As the opera neared its end, however, there was a peculiar incident. The mighty chorus sang its last notes, the orchestra raced to its conclusion, and then – nothing! The curtain inexplicably failed to drop. After a period of awkward silence, the heavyset basso playing the role of

318

Sarastro looked backstage and began bobbing his head in dramatic fashion to indicate that the curtain should come down.

Moore, who was standing near us, raced over and grabbed the curtain ropes from a stagehand who seemed unable to move.

"For God's sake, Harold, what's the matter with you?" Moore hissed. "Pull man, pull."

The stagehand came out of his trance and helped bring down the curtain at last.

Moore was furious. "Harold, that's the second time this week you've turned into a damn statue. What's the matter with you?"

"I'm sorry," the stagehand said, still appearing quite distracted. "I just get caught up listening, that's all. I can't help myself, I guess. It won't let it happen again."

"No, it won't," Moore said. "You're done here, you idiot. Go on, get out."

"Mr. Moore, I – "

"Out," Moore repeated. "I don't want to ever see you again."

The stagehand slunk away, tears welling in his eyes. Holmes, I noticed, watched the scene with great interest. He went over to Moore, who seemed proud of himself for banishing the stagehand.

"Who is that man you just dismissed?" Holmes asked.

"It doesn't matter. He's just an idiot who doesn't know how to do his job."

Holmes repeated his question, only this time with such force in his voice that Moore looked as though he had just been struck by a powerful gust of wind.

"Skimpton," he blurted out. "Harold Skimpton."

"I should like to talk with him immediately. Where can I find him?"

A small circle of stagehands began to gather around us, presumably awaiting orders from Moore, who was becoming exasperated by Holmes's ceaseless inquisition. "Now, how in blazes would I know where to find him?" Moore asked irritably. "He's gone, and good riddance to him. I have work to do, if you don't mind. Besides, you're the great Sherlock Holmes. Go find him yourself."

For a moment, I thought Holmes might thrash the petulant little man, but instead he turned away and said to me, "We are wasting precious moments. Let us see if we can get our hands on Mr. Skimpton before he leaves the theater."

It was not to be. Skimpton, we learned from a guard stationed at the stage door, had left immediately after his painful public dismissal.

The guard, a lanky man with a pronounced Nordic accent, ("Swedish," Holmes later informed me, "and undoubtedly from the

Småland region of that nation.") proved to be in possession of one other valuable piece of information: he knew where Skimpton lived.

"Oh, *ja*, he told me once he was in that old rooming house on Eleventh, right next to the church there on Robert Street. You can't miss it."

"How far away is this rooming house?" Holmes asked.

"Not far. You could walk there in fifteen minutes, I'd say."

Holmes thanked the guard and gave him a silver dollar for his trouble.

"I suppose you intend to talk with this Skimpton fellow," I said as we stepped out into the frigid night. "Do you believe he is the man who stole the flute?"

"I have no doubt of that," Holmes said. "What I wish to know is why he did it."

It was quarter to eleven by the time we reached Skimpton's rooming house, which stood in a decrepit part of the city as far removed from the wondrous world of *The Magic Flute* as any place could be. The house, an irregular pile of dark bricks crowned by a pair of steep gables, was from the previous century, when it had doubtlessly been built by one of St. Paul's many merchant princes. Its grandeur, however, had long since faded, and it looked gloomy and forlorn in the wintry darkness. I had begun to shiver, for the wind was an icy dagger against which even our heavy fur coats offered no sure protection.

We went up to the front porch, where rows of wooden balusters had rotted away like bad teeth, and knocked on the door. A plump middle-aged woman dressed in a ragged housecoat eventually came to the door. She looked at us warily, as though we might be robbers, or worse.

"Visiting hours are over," she said.

"We are indeed sorry, madam, to disturb you at such a late hour," Holmes said. "However, it is imperative that we see one of your residents, Mr. Skimpton."

"And what would you be wanting of him at almost eleven o'clock at night? He never has visitors anyway."

Holmes responded by fishing two silver dollars out of his coat pocket and pressing them into the woman's hand. "I am sure he will want to talk with us. As I said, it is a most urgent matter. Now, please show us to his room."

"Come in then," the woman said, quickly slipping the coins into her coat pocket. "Just don't disturb the other residents. I run a respectable house, you know."

We followed her up a broad staircase to the second floor, and then up a much narrower set of steps to the attic, where a single gas jet struggled to illuminate a long hallway. "He's in number ten," she said, "way in the back."

Skimpton was still wearing his work clothes from the theater when he responded to our knock. "My God," he said, clearly stunned. "What are you doing here?"

He was, I guessed, in his early forties, tall and bony, with patches of thin hair gone largely to silver clinging to his head. His sad brown eyes were set in a face so narrow that it looked to have been shaped by a vise.

"I see there is no need for introductions," Holmes replied as he stepped uninvited into the apartment. I followed. "You know why we are here, Mr. Skimpton. It is about the missing flute."

"I don't know what you mean," Skimpton said, a slight quaver in his voice. "You had better leave."

"No, I think we will shall stay for a while," Holmes replied, his voracious eyes taking in every detail of Skimpton's quarters.

The stagehand's room was dim, threadbare, and cold. A paint-flaked radiator in one corner hissed at the chill. Above it hideous patterned wallpaper had started to peel away from patches of bare, water-stained plaster. The furnishings – a table, a few chairs, a sagging bed, a battered steamer trunk – were meager. There could be no doubt Skimpton was a poor man, alone and without prospects.

Holmes and I took seats at the table and persuaded Skimpton to join us. Propped up on the table was a large photograph showing Skimpton with a woman in a gingham dress. The woman's face was gaunt, yet she managed a broad smile. Skimpton looked equally happy.

"This photograph must be of great importance to you," Holmes said. "Your wife perhaps?"

Skimpton nodded. "Dead," he said in a monotone. "Last September. Consumption. She was my life. But what do you care? What does anyone care? All I ask is that you leave me alone."

"I understand," Holmes said in an uncharacteristically soft voice. I noticed as well that he had begun to look strangely uncomfortable, and was breathing heavily. "You may be assured that Dr. Watson and I have no wish to cause you any great difficulties," he now told Skimpton. "Yet, as you must know, Mrs. Snyder wishes to have the flute returned to the opera. May I ask why you took it? I have been informed it has little value."

Holmes, I knew, had no real evidence that Skimpton was the thief. Indeed, his certainty in the matter, as far as I could determine, was based solely on the fact that Skimpton, in a moment of distraction, had failed to pull down the stage curtain. But as I studied Skimpton's cheerless eyes, I could not help but think Holmes was right.

"I have nothing to say to you," Skimpton announced.

"Very well," Holmes said. Then he abruptly stood up, went over to the large steamer trunk that appeared to be the room's only hidden place of storage, and began to open it.

"No, don't do that," Skimpton cried out, and started toward Holmes. I immediately blocked his way.

Moments later, Holmes had the flute in his hand. It was, as Mrs. Snyder had readily admitted, not much to look at, just a battered old instrument covered in cheap gold paint.

Skimpton slumped back into his chair, looking as desolate as any man I have ever seen. When Holmes returned to the table, he said, "You haven't answered my question, Mr. Skimpton. Why did you take the flute?"

Tears welled up in the stagehand's eyes. The words that followed came in a whisper. "Don't you see, Mr. Holmes, I felt I could not live anymore, and I had to have it. It's all there is now for me and all there ever will be."

He put his head down before breaking out in loud sobs of the most anguished kind. It was a heart-wrenching scene, yet I was at loss to explain how or why Skimpton had become so deeply attached to a stage prop. Holmes, meanwhile, appeared to be growing agitated, as though some unseen force was acting upon him. To my surprise, he reached across the table and patted Skimpton on the shoulder. "It will be all right," he said. "I assure you, Mr. Skimpton, it will be all right."

Holmes rose from his chair and said, "Come along, Watson. I must leave this room. It has become too much for me. I wish you the best of luck, Mr. Skimpton."

The stagehand had by now regained his composure. He said to Holmes, "I suppose you will have to tell the police."

"The police? What would I have to tell them?'"

Skimpton was puzzled. "You know, about the flute."

"I know nothing about a flute, Mr. Skimpton." Holmes turned to me. "Watson, do you know anything about a flute?"

There was nothing I could say except, "No."

As we walked back to our hotel in the deep chill of the night, I pressed Holmes to explain his curious behavior in Skimpton's room. At first, he brushed aside all of my questions. But when we reached our suite at the Ryan and found there the welcome gifts of warmth and light,

Holmes became more talkative. While we thawed our stiff hands by the fireplace, I again asked Holmes why he had left the flute with Skimpton.

He turned to me, and in those probing gray eyes, so alive with the vital force of life, I saw a kind of resignation. "Have you never felt it, Watson, that old dark tide which creeps in upon a man in the depths of the night? It was there, in Skimpton's miserable little room, and it was so powerful that it all but took the air from my lungs."

"Holmes, whatever are you talking about? I felt no unusual sensations in that room."

"Ah, my dear Watson, you are indeed the most fortunate of men, for you never lose sight of the light of the world." Holmes rose and walked over to the window. Gazing out into the darkness, he said, "I did not tell you that when I retrieved the flute from Skimpton's trunk, it was resting upon a short length of rope with a noose tied at one end."

"Do you mean to say he was intending to do away with himself?"

"I know of no other way to interpret the evidence. Skimpton placed the flute atop the noose so as to remind himself that there are wondrous and beautiful things in the world. Had he not stolen the flute, I believe he would be dead by now. And that is why I could not take it from him. He has far greater need of it than Mrs. Snyder does."

"My God, Holmes, you have saved a man's life tonight!"

"Perhaps. But I do not know how long the flute will work its magic for poor Skimpton. He has fallen far into a chasm as gloomy as that of the Reichenbach, and in the end there may be no escape for him."

Holmes turned away from the window and said, "The hour is growing late, Watson, and I suggest you retire for the night. We shall have a long day of travel tomorrow."

I was indeed feeling quite tired. "By the way, what will you tell Mrs. Snyder in the morning when she comes to ask about the flute?"

"I will tell her the truth, which is that there are mysteries in this world without solution."

"She will not be happy to hear that."

"Nor will I be happy to say it," Holmes said as he walked toward his bedroom. "Goodnight, Watson."

I went to my room and soon fell fast asleep. Hours later, I awoke to the sound of Holmes's violin. He was playing one of Papageno's songs from *The Magic Flute*, and he kept at it until the first morning light.

Blood Brothers
by Kim Krisco

13 December, 1913

> *London – the center of the civilized world, mother port,*
> *colonial throne . . . proud empress whose decadence and*
> *disenchantment spills out, beyond the poor districts and*
> *back alleys, into once noble households.*

B ENJIE was mesmerized by the silver florin spinning in the
gentleman's fingers.

"My boy, this is yours for a few minutes work."

"What d'ya want?"

"A small thing really, Benjie. I'm . . . a doctor of sorts. I need a tiny
vial of your blood for a patient."

Benjie's body recoiled.

"Just a thimbleful, is all."

Benjie nodded, hesitantly. "For two bob, then."

"Good boy. Let's tell the dustman outside that he need not wait for
you, shall we?"

The angular man put his arm around the twelve-year-old boy's
shoulder and led him out to the street where Tux, a flying dustman, was
waiting to collect the ash, rubbish and *debris*.

"What's this then?" Tux asked, as Benjie approached, empty
handed, toward the waiting horse and cart.

The doctor held out a shilling. "I have a small task for the lad. I'm
sure you can do without him for the rest of the day." He pressed the coin
into Tux's palm.

The ageing dustman looked askance at Benjie, who nodded.

"Very good, guv'nor," Tux agreed. "Ya can find yer way home,
can't ya, Benjie?"

"Sure, Tux."

The dirty refuse collector shrugged his shoulders and, grumbling
under his breath, grabbed the reins of his nag and urged it onward.

Benjie was led back into the doctor's elegant home, and soon found
himself lying on his back atop a narrow padded table.

"I'm going to prick your arm with a needle. Hold it still and steady. Close your eyes."

Benjie shut his eyes; but they suddenly flew open when the doctor's hand clamped his arm against the tabletop.

"Ow!" Benjie yelped, as the needle struck his vein.

"Quiet. This will only take a moment."

The sting in Benjie's arm lessened, and his body relaxed.

"There," said the Doctor.

As the needle was pulled out, Benjie watched a bead of blood cut a scarlet track across his forearm.

"Wait here. I have to see to this blood now. I'll be back directly."

"Wiv two bob," Benjie added.

"Yes . . . with your money."

A short time later, the doctor returned to find Benjie sitting on the edge of the table. He twisted a silver coin before the youngster's eyes, and then placed it in his outstretched hand.

"You are a singular boy, Benjie. I have a friend who is looking for a lad just like you. She would pay you well for your help."

"'Ow much?"

"A half-crown per day."

The boy's eyes widened as if the gates of El Dorado were opening before him. "Yer 'avin' me on now, ain't ya, sir?"

"Not at all, Benjie. Would you be willing to go with me to see my friend? She is presently some distance away. I could have you back just after nightfall."

"Before nightfall, sir. Mi' muvver will worry if I'm late."

****

SHERLOCK HOLMES and I had just returned from Africa. Our recent adventure made it clear that Holmes's gentrified retirement in the Sussex Downs had come to an untimely end. Fortunately, my flat on Sheen Lane offered a similar hospitality to that which we had enjoyed, for so many years, on Baker Street.

As we made our way from Marylebone, the elegant brick and stone façades in Kensington peered at us through the December fog, creating an ethereal effect. The mist thickened, and an acerbic scent announced that we were approaching the Thames. The hansom offered a ghostly view of a waterman conducting a clumsy barge down the silent highway beneath Hammersmith Bridge.

Holmes had suggested that we gather some newspapers along the way. So, when I heard the distant cry of someone shouting headlines, I rapped on the roof. The cab slowed down, and an adolescent boy began to materialize before me.

As the lad hurried to the carriage, I pulled a penny from my pocket. A recognizable voice piped up.

"Dr. Watson . . . Mr. 'Olmes."

"Ah," I said, "it is good to see you so well, Archie."

Archie is the leader of a gang of street Arabs whom Holmes calls the "Irregulars." He employs this urban tribe from time to time to aid in his investigations. For many years, Archie has filled the shoes of his older cousin, Wiggins, as leader of this back-street brigade.

"Dr. Watson and I have been away," Holmes said.

"Yes, sir, I've noticed. Mi' muvver and me 'ave bin lookin' for ya." Archie baulked.

"Something's wrong then, Archie?" I asked.

"Aye, sir. It's mi' bruvver, Benjie. 'E's gone missin'. Can't find him nowhere, sir."

"If *you* cannot find him," I said with surprise, "then he is surely lost!"

Holmes cocked his head and leaned closer to Archie. "Give the good Doctor and me time to get settled, and come by. It appears you know the address."

"I surely do, sir. Can I bring mi' muvver? It'd be a comfort to 'er to know as you might 'elp us."

"By all means," Holmes answered. "Your mother is most welcome."

Archie handed me the newspaper, and stepped back from the curb. "Thanks, sir."

Holmes and I were off. The clip-clop of the horse's hooves on the cobbles was the only sound for some time . . . then, Holmes spoke: "It is important that we look after our urchin army, since we have been absent from our command, Watson. It would be only sensible to keep an eye on them, you know."

"Holmes! A bit of compassion bubbles up in you, and you relegate it to pragmatism."

As we drove to my flat, I leafed through the *Daily Mail* that I had recently purchased.

"Anything of interest?"

"Let me see . . . here's one for you, Holmes: *Mona Lisa Recovered. Thief in Custody. Vengeance his Motive.* Ha! What do you make of that?"

"More than two years ago, I wrote to François Calchas, in Paris, suggesting he seek out any Italian custodian, or guard, that had worked in the Louvre. It appears that my advice has only recently been heeded. What do you find on page three?"

I turned the page and scanned the columns with my finger.

"*King of Cottonopolis Missing*, it says here. Sir William Hyde Gregston, whose family sits prominently on the board of the Royal Cotton Exchange, has gone missing. It seems as though his twin brother is suspected of foul play, and has been questioned by the police, who continue to search for Sir William. And, over here we have . . . well, it appears the Panama Canal is nearly complete. Roosevelt should be pleased."

Then, an all too familiar story: "The body of a young boy was found in the Irwell River. Authorities are seeking information as to his identity."

Holmes nodded. "There is a mystery there to be sure, but one which is not likely ever to be solved."

My review of the *Daily Mail* was halted by our arrival at Sheen Lane. Within minutes, our driver delivered our trunks, marking the end to the adventure of *The Kongo Nkisi Spirit Train*.

However, there was little time for rest, for many of the troubles that unceasingly bubble up from London's melting-pot take the form of a knock upon our door.

"That must be Archie," I said, in response to the banging downstairs.

"That is not Archie's knock," Holmes observed. And of course, when I opened the door, Holmes's words proved correct.

A footman stood on my porch. As I caught his eye, he nodded toward a carriage at the curb. An immense gentleman stepped onto the pavement, and steadied himself. He stood like a portrait by Sargent, looming over everything around him. The Victorian fussiness of his dress, however, could not conceal an anxiety that worked its way through the twitching features of his face. The footman bolted down the stairs to take the gentleman's arm, stabilizing the corpulent body during its sluggish journey to my door.

When he arrived on my threshold, he lifted a multiplicity of chins. "Sir George Talbot Gregston to see Mr. Sherlock Holmes." A card was presented.

I ushered the distinguished guest into the parlour, where we found Holmes sitting at my desk, hunched over the newspaper.

"Holmes, Sir George Talbot Gregston to see you."

"Yes, yes . . . Sir George." Holmes looked up. "A fair trip from Manchester! But I expect that you have a house in London as well."

"Yes, Mr. Holmes – and in Paris, Zurich, and Cadiz."

327

"I suppose great riches are difficult to contain in only one home."

The man smiled. "I am uncertain as to how to take your remark, Mr. Holmes. I was told you were inscrutable – and so you seem to be." The man removed his topper and placed it on the table near the door.

"Please have a chair, Sir George," I said, as Holmes arose from the desk to take a place near the hearth.

Once seated, our visitor spoke in quiet, measured words. "I am here . . . to seek your aid . . . in finding my brother, William Gregston. His recent disappearance has found its way into the newspapers. So, I suspect that you may have already heard about it."

"Only minutes ago, as a matter of fact," Holmes replied. "The *Daily Mail* had him as *Sir* William Gregston."

"Ah, yes, Mr. Holmes. The contributions of my brother and I to British industry were recently recognized."

"No doubt your contributions to coffers of the Conservative Party were recognized as well," Holmes remarked.

Gregston's scowl was barely concealed by a feigned look of amusement.

"Mr. Holmes, it seems to me that it behoves us to graciously accept honours that others might bestow upon us. But, I digress."

"At the risk of digressing further, I have, for some time now, felt that the honour of which you speak has been debased." Holmes paused and leaned back in his chair. "But, I suppose this honour has whatever meaning one may wish to attribute to it."

Our guest remained stone-faced for a moment as he took in the full measure of the man sitting across from him.

Holmes continued. "And, as you say, we digress. May I assume the efforts of the police are proving unsatisfactory?"

"Nicely put. They are not satisfactory. As you might suppose, their efforts are being directed by my sister-in-law, whose goals run counter to my own."

I took up a place on the nearby *settee*. "Surely, you both share a concern for your brother's well-being?"

"My concern is *about* my brother's well-being – not necessarily *for* it." He withdrew a handkerchief from his coat pocket, and dabbed the corner of his mouth where some spittle had accumulated.

"There is ill-will between you, then," Holmes surmised.

"Exactly, sir. Our fraternal relationship was, I fear, destined to be oppositional from the start. Our father accumulated the great wealth that my brother and I now enjoy. We tend to the business, but that requires little genius, and only modest effort on our parts. The great mechanical looms grind on day and night with little active attention from us."

The man shifted forward to the edge of his chair, and stretched himself upward in a prideful manner. "My brother and I are twins – fraternal – born minutes apart. Remarkably, during a difficult birthing process that led to our mother's death, those in attendance did not make note of which of us was the first-born. And, Samuel Hyde Gregston's staunch religious beliefs precluded his simply declaring an heir."

"Most unusual, but one might think the matter would have been sorted out by now," I said.

"Quite so. However, our father died at the age of eighty-three – when my brother and I were fifty-one years old. His singular last will and testament stipulated that we should have equal shares in the mills and related enterprises. However, the great bulk of his personal wealth, which is scattered over the globe, was to be held in trust for the son that survives the longest . . . with one stipulation." The gentleman's grim gaze turned inward as his mind grasped at some chiselled memory. "If my brother and I should both live to our eighty-third birthdays, the remainder of our father's estate will be divided into equal parts between us."

"May I wager a guess as to your current age?" Holmes followed.

"Exactly so, Mr. Holmes. My eighty-third birthday, and that of my brother, is on December the twenty-first – eight days hence."

"Your brother has disappeared at a most inopportune time for you," I noted.

"But . . . a most *opportune* time, for Lady William Hyde Gregston," our guest observed.

His innuendo created an ill-omened pause before Gregston continued: "My brother has fallen into ill health recently. Liver difficulties, I am led to believe. He's looked yellowish for some time, and has been losing weight in recent months."

"You believe, then, that your brother is ill, dying . . . or already dead," I said in summary, as I jotted in my notebook.

Our guest smirked and raised his brows. "I will pay you handsomely, Mr. Holmes, if you can report the whereabouts and condition of my brother to me before the twenty-first of December."

Holmes clasped his hands together in front of him, and stretched back in his chair.

"I'm afraid your case falls outside my scope," Holmes declared.

"How much would it cost for it to fall *within* your scope, Mr. Holmes?"

"As remarkable as it might seem, more money than you possess."

Gregston grimaced. "A pity! I shall not waste any more of my time . . . nor yours."

And with that, the pompous gentleman rose, retrieved his hat, and left the apartment.

As I watched Gregston's carriage depart from the parlour window, I commented to Holmes: "So much for brotherly love!"

"Yes, they are hardly Castor and Pollux, are they?"

"No indeed, Holmes. With some, when they succeed in this world, all that they possess is money."

Then, as if to emphasize the extremes of our social circle, Archie and his mother arrived, as the dust from Sir George's carriage settled in the street.

Archie's mother wore a mouse-coloured dress and a dingy white apron. As she tidied her salt and pepper hair behind her head, I noticed that her rough hands were corded with blue veins. She wore the indelible stamp of a woman stooped under the weight of a hard life.

"Mr. Holmes, and Dr. Watson . . . I'm most beholdin' as you're takin' the time for the likes of us," Archie's mother began. "It's Benjie, sir. 'E's gone missin'."

"We're worried, sir," Archie added. "Scoured the city, we did – me and the rest."

Holmes studied the unassuming woman. "We took you from your work," Holmes observed. "It must have been a particularly difficult stain that you were cleaning."

The woman's eyes widened. She glanced at her son Archie, who was nodding. "As I told ya, muvver, Mr. 'Olmes can see what ain't there."

"Smelling the lingering scent of ammonia, and knowing that you hail from St. Giles, I surmised that you were cleaning and patching old clothing to sell," Holmes explained. "No mystery there! When did you last see Benjie?"

Archie chimed in again, "About two days ago, Benjie took up with one of the last flyin' dustmen – a fella by the name o' Tux. The old codger 'urt 'is self, and needed 'elp wiv 'is collections."

"All seemed good, sir," the woman said. "My boy was grateful t'ave a few pennies to share. So proud as 'e could 'elp to put food on the table. But, at the end of the day, it weren't Benjie coming home, but Tux – the grimy old geezer, telling us as a gentleman 'ad offered Benjie a fine bit of work along the way."

The woman's eyes brimmed with tears. "We waited for Benjie . . . but 'e never came, sir. I'm frightful worried. There's bin a couple o' young boys gone missin' lately from the Dials, and thereabouts."

"You went to this gentleman's home?"

"That very evenin', Doctor," Archie assured us. "To the *front* door. Told 'em as I was lookin' for my bruvver, and wanted to talk to the gentleman of the 'ouse."

"But he never came," Holmes surmised.

"Right again, Mr. 'Olmes!"

Holmes's alarm was revealed only by the insistent tapping of his forefinger on the arm of his chair. "I think it is important that we make further inquiries." Then, turning to Archie's mother: "At the moment, it may be best for you to return to your home. If you have no objection, I should like Archie to accompany us. He will be able to make a report."

"Oh, Bless ya, Mr. 'Olmes! Yer words 'ave given me new 'ope."

****

BENJIE stared out the train window as the asphalt streets of London dissolved into muddy roads. The doctor's face was buried in his newspaper during most of the long journey from London to Manchester. The boy's uneasiness increased when he was told that there would be a carriage ride from Manchester-Piccadilly Station. He was moving further and further from home.

"So, yer friend is not in Manchester?" Benjie asked, as the train pulled into the station.

"She is waiting just a short drive away."

Upon arrival, they walked to a trap that was waiting for them outside the station. The lad started when the steam-whistle blew its farewell. As the train moved out, Benjie had the unfamiliar feeling of being utterly alone in the world.

As the doctor stepped onboard, he gave an order to the driver: "To the lodge, Brodie."

The carriage moved at a swift pace. Benjie's eyes flashed side to side as the factory-dotted horizon of Manchester disappeared into empty rolling hills. The sky blackened with clouds. A slight drizzle added an increasing chill to the air.

Thirty minutes later, the carriage slowed as it came upon a stately white, two-storey house some distance from the road. "Braunmoss House," the doctor said, as the boy peered at the ivy-covered hunting lodge.

The carriage moved into the driveway, then lurched to a stop before a large green door flanked with shutters. As the door opened, a tall, angular woman in an austere black gown emerged, and walked to the edge of the steps overlooking the driveway. Her murky eyes were set deep into her loose-skinned face. A grim delight was barely concealed in her features.

As Benjie and the doctor climbed the stairs to the porch, the gaunt woman held out a gnarled hand. "So this is Benjie!" she said, almost to herself.

Her hand, suspended in the air, reached out toward Benjie and twisted, palm up, as if she were envisioning the boy's head in her hand. "We have some cakes waiting in the dining room. You must be hungry," she cooed.

The doctor whisked Benjie toward the sombre lady. "This is Lady Gregston, Benjie."

The lad nodded, and touched the brim of his cap, "Ma'am."

Her leathery hand pointed toward the house. Benjie obediently walked into the gaping doorway. As he crossed the threshold, Lady Gregston's smile vanished. She turned to the doctor. "And, he is what we've been seeking, you say?"

The man nodded. "A perfect match."

"What of the others?"

"Their usefulness is limited, as you know. That is why we need Benjie."

"Yes, of course. And, you will take care of the others . . . as you have before?

The doctor paused in mid-stride.

"For an additional fee, of course," Lady Gregston hastened to add. "Whatever you require."

Upon hearing this, Benjie turned to see the two forms silhouetted in the dimming grey light of the day. His smouldering fears ignited. His first thought went to his older brother.

"Archie!" Benjie gasped, *sotto voce.*

The door slammed shut.

****

SHERLOCK HOLMES, Archie, and I departed almost immediately for 11A Aubrey Walk, the home where Tux reported last seeing Benjie. *En route*, Holmes shared his plan.

"Watson, you will go to the front door, with Archie in hand, and make a forceful inquiry. Keep the person who answers at the door as long as possible. When your inquiry is rejected, as I suspect it will be, raise your voice in a shrill manner as a signal."

Archie and I parted ways with Holmes, and we made our way to an enormous black enamel door. Centered on the door was an ornate

332

knocker – a gryphon clawing its way inside. A maidservant answered our raps.

"I wish to see the master of the house," I announced, presenting my card. "I am Dr. John Watson."

The maid bent over Archie. "Ya've been told. Yer brother's not 'ere."

"I insist upon seeing your master," I stated. "Our business is with him."

"He is not at 'ome," the woman replied.

"Where has he gone?"

"I have no particulars, sir."

I interrupted the closing of the door with an insistent cry: "Please . . . I am a colleague. I must know of his whereabouts!"

The woman cocked her head and squinted. "As I say, I don't know, sir. I'll give him yer card when he returns."

As the door moved again, I raised my voice. "Look here, my good lady, I must leave a message. Bring me a pencil and paper at once!"

This masquerade continued for some time as I waited for the notepaper, and methodically scribbled a cryptic note. Then, from the corner of my eye, I spied Holmes stepping from the path beside the home onto Aubrey Walk.

"Thank you," I said. "I will wait for further word."

Once settled in my flat, Holmes retrieved paper and pencil, and made a hasty sketch. "Look at this, Watson. What are your thoughts concerning this apparatus, which I noticed at Aubrey Walk?"

I studied his drawing. "How big is it?"

"The India-rubber hose is approximately five feet long. I believe that the three-inch tubes at either end are silver. The black bulb in the middle of the hose is a pump of some kind."

"Yes . . . yes. This apparatus is a medical device. It can be used in a variety of ways, but primarily for transferring blood from one individual to another."

"As I suspected!" Holmes exclaimed.

"The fellow is a doctor, then?"

"Not a physician," Holmes remarked. "Medical research, it would appear from his laboratory. Are you acquainted with an individual called Rueben Rottenberg?" Holmes asked, holding a card to my eyes. "I found his box of cards in a desk drawer."

"No. However, a trip to the Royal College of Surgeons may tell us something."

"Excellent, Watson! I should appreciate it if you would explore that avenue."

Turning to Archie, Holmes gave further orders: "I suggest you put three of your lads on Aubrey Walk. Ask them to report here if the man in residence returns. And, of course, follow him if he leaves again." As Archie waved off, Holmes added, "When your sentries are in place, Archie, return here. We must find Tux. Hurry!"

The adolescent turned a worried face to Holmes. "You fear for me bruvver, don't you, Mr. Holmes?"

"I do, Archie."

****

"BENJIE, it is time to earn that half-crown we talked about," his furtive benefactor said. "Enjoy the cakes in the dining room. I will come for you soon."

Lady Gregston swooped in behind Benjie, prodding him toward a long mahogany table bearing plates of cakes and confections. Benjie's stomach growled. It had been nearly seven hours since he had eaten.

"Young boys like milk, don't they?" Lady Gregston asked, pouring a glass full.

"And ale," Benjie replied.

"Milk will do, for now. You must be strong and healthy if you wish to help Sir William and me. Eat your fill, Benjie."

Dark passions swept over her face as she watched Benjie consume the pastries. She nudged a plate of delicacies closer.

"None for you, ma'am?" Benjie asked.

"No, Benjie, I will dine later."

"Where has the doctor gone?"

"He is preparing the room for you and my husband."

"Then, my work is for yer husband?"

"Work? Not really, Benjie. We simply need some of your . . . ."

Benjie turned. "Blood?"

There was no reply.

Benjie moved back in his seat. "I don't want this work, ma'am," Benjie said, pushing his chair back.

The lady remained motionless.

Benjie stood, grabbed one more cake, and strode toward the hallway – immediately colliding with the doctor.

"Benjie, Benjie, slow down – there's nothing to fear here. Come along." The cake dropped to the floor as the doctor's hand grasped Benjie's neck and steered him into the hallway toward a wide oak staircase. The colourless daylight forced its way through a stained glass window above the stairs. The muted crystalline tableau depicted a fair-haired knight with his foot upon the throat of a dying dragon. The hero's sword had pierced the neck of the beast, and blood poured from the wound.

The man and the boy were soon padding silently down a dark corridor toward a room at the end of the second floor hall. The door was open. Someone was waiting.

Benjie's feet did not obey his mind that told him to flee. Like the ticking of a clock, his measured steps mechanically brought him toward the waiting chamber. A putrid smell permeated the air. In a dim corner, an old man lay under a canopied bed. His eyes were closed and his breathing was laboured. A long, narrow table stood next to the bed.

The doctor cleared his throat. "Sir William, this is Benjie."

With one last shove from behind, Benjie stumbled to the bedside. The old man's eyes opened narrowly. He raised his right hand, and beckoned.

Benjie moved closer.

Suddenly, the old man's hand struck out and grabbed the boy's forearm. The vice-like grip belied the man's seeming frailty. The youngster attempted to break the grip with his other hand, but could not. Benjie pulled away, but the bony hand, like that of death itself, held firm.

The old man's lips trembled as he spoke in a dry, hoarse tone: "Hmmm, So young!"

The doctor came forward and touched the old man's arm. His hand relaxed, and Benjie jerked free.

The man pressed a half-crown into Benjie's hand. "Here. Now, as you did before, I want you to lie on this table. There will be a small prick again. You must be quiet and still for a while longer this time."

A muddled feeling overtook Benjie. It was as if he were in a dream – watching himself climb onto the table. It was someone else's arm being strapped to the tabletop – not his. It must be another's eyes staring at the water-stained ceiling above.

The doctor opened a black bag resting on a nearby dresser, and extracted a hose with shiny needles on both ends.

"Close your eyes, Benjie," came the command.

Benjie braced himself for the stab. The puncture came once – then again, before his arm was released. The boy turned to see the doctor open a tiny valve at the other end of the hose, and slowly squeeze the black bulb. Blood spurted from the end of the tube, spattering across Benjie's face and lips. It tasted like wet pennies in his mouth.

SHERLOCK HOLMES was perusing a notebook he had taken from the Rottenberg home, and making notes, when I returned from my investigation at Lincoln's Inn Fields. Archie was quick upon my heels, having posted members of his urchin brigade around the house at Aubrey Walk.

"There may be a few threads in this expense ledger upon which we can pull, Archie, but Tux is our best compass. Let us find that antiquated dustman."

Then, he turned to me.

"Good hunting at the R.C.S., Watson?"

"Yes, the library offered some tasty morsels for us."

"Join Archie and me, if you will, and make your report while we search for Tux."

As our carriage departed, I shared what I had learned: "Rottenberg calls himself a haematologist. He's published several papers on the genotyping of blood. Are you familiar with the practice, Holmes?"

"Yes. An Austrian – Landsteiner – has recently classified blood into several types. Certainly, this process of identifying blood will be useful in future investigations."

"Indeed, as there are four types," I said. "In addition to genotyping, Rottenberg published an article in *The Lancet* with a rather novel and fantastic theory that new blood can revitalise degenerating organs in the human body."

"Fantastic, possibly, but the idea is far from novel. In the late sixteenth century, Pope Innocent VIII was said to have been given the world's first blood transfusion to keep him from aging."

"A legend, surely, Holmes!"

"One would hope so, for it was said that Innocent drank the blood of ten-year old boys."

My body froze in fear.

"Yes, Watson."

Holmes's eyes shot to Archie, who seemed lost in thought.

As Tux was an itinerant, finding him was no simple task. However, we were not surprised when the costermongers, and the Covent Garden flower women, pointed us to a public house set in the centre of Whitechapel Road. Sitting as it does, at the great east-to-west artery of the city, this ancient establishment served as a hub of dubious commerce.

As Archie, Holmes, and I approached, we saw a mixture of good and evil countenances lined up along the benches outside. Leaning against one corner of the public house stood a gentleman sporting a brilliant red scarf, and wearing a slouch hat. A steel hook protruded where his left hand should have been.

"'Ooky, we're lookin' for' Tux," said Archie. "'Ave ya seen'im?"

The man twisted himself around. "Yes, Archie – 'round the back. Is Benjie at 'ome?"

"No, Alf. That's why we need the old geezer."

We stepped around to the rear of the inn. There sat Tux, hunched over a mug of ale – foam dripping from the ginger-grey whiskers that wrapped around his jaw. His once white jacket was smudged, torn, and buttoned high upon his chest, as it was too small to enclose his great pear-shaped belly. When he saw Archie, he lowered his head and made himself small.

"Tux, these are my friends, Mr. 'Olmes and Dr. Watson. We need to talk to ya about Benjie."

Tux shook his head, and pushed away the mug. "Poor Benjie. I can tell ya, guv'nor, this 'ole business 'as knocked me off my perch."

Holmes and I took seats adjacent to the musty man. Archie stood behind us. "Tell me what you know about the house where you left Benjie."

Tux's head lifted, and his brows crunched together. "It wasn't me as left him, guv'nor. 'Twas Benjie's choice. Gotta respect a man's choices, Doctor."

"Benjie is a boy," Holmes said. "Nonetheless, what can you tell me about what you found at the house on Aubrey Walk?"

Tux settled back in his chair. "Not what ya might call fancy goods – but first-rate glass, fine cork from an old ice box one time, an' clo'es like new – soiled is all."

"Soiled how?"

Tux took on a look of confusion. "I dunno, guv'nor. Blood, could be."

"Blood!" Archie exclaimed. "Tux, if one drop of Benjie's blood gets spilled, ya old splodger, you'll find yourself in the chutes with th'other dust."

"Was it the blood then, or something else, that caused the householder to bring you, and not the parish dustman, to their home?" I asked.

"I can't say. I makes me own way in this world, guv'nor. I believe as what happens to a man's stuff before it goes into his dustbins is no business of mine."

Holmes leaned in. "I suggest you make it your business, or you may find the law coming down on you."

Tux screwed himself further down into his chair. "Among the dust, I often found empty bottles – for medicines, I believe."

"Did you ever notice anyone visiting the house?"

"Well, once, a carriage were outside whilst I gathered the dust. It 'ad a crest on it, as I recall."

"What was on the crest?" Holmes asked.

Tux's weathered face screwed up into a knot, and his eyes closed. "A shield of a kind – blue and yellow, it were, and . . . sitting atop it, a great silver 'elmet."

"Can you recall any words?"

"There was words written on it, but not so's I could read 'em."

Holmes cocked his head and squinted. "I have a proposition for you, Tux," Holmes said. "What would it cost me to rent your cart and horse, and borrow your jacket and hat?"

Tux chortled. "A bit long in the tooth to be takin' up in the streets, aren't ya, Mr. Holmes? I'm not sure as I can stand the competition." He laughed, obviously enjoying his rough jest more than we.

"My career will be less than a day in length, and I will make but one call," Holmes answered. "All will be returned to you to-morrow."

Tux assumed a serious look. "A good day can bring me as much as a pound, would ya believe?" he said, shaking his head side to side.

Holmes smiled. "You may be a good dustman, but you're a dreadful liar, Tux. You can have your pound – however, it will cost the loan of your trousers and shoes as well."

Tux's eyes flashed upwards, and his mouth hung open for a moment. "It's a bargain, sir," he said, holding out his grimy hand for a shake.

Holmes grasped it loosely, and sealed the deal.

Archie was sent to fetch Tux's garments to my flat, and the cart and horse to Holland Park, near Rottenberg's home. Holmes planned to masquerade as Tux to gain entry to the Aubrey Walk residence once again, and to put his own keen eyes on the dustbins therein. When we entered my lodgings to await Archie's return, Holmes bolted toward the bookshelves behind my desk.

"Do you have a book on heraldry, Watson?"

I pointed. Holmes retrieved it, and began leafing swiftly through the pages. He stopped, and poked his finger sharply into one of the pages. "Yes . . . yes, of course!"

****

BENJIE found himself emerging from a sombre gloom – dizzy and disoriented. He was lying down, but not in the bedroom. He heard a wee voice: "You'll be fine in time. They'll bring ya broth soon."

Benjie turned his head to find a pale face framed in the darkness. "I'm Jake. I've been 'ere a long while. What's the day – do ya know?"

Jake had a boy's body, but his face was wizened. The muscles of his cheeks were twitching, and his eyes blinked rapidly.

"They're takin' blood from all of us, ya know," Jake said.

"Us?"

Jake turned back. Huddled against the far wall of the dank room was another form.

"Tom and me. What do they call ya, eh?"

"Benjie. Where are we?"

"Manchester, or nearby . . . ."

"No," Benjie interrupted, "this room."

"Cellar . . . under the big 'ouse."

Benjie sat up. His head spun, and his eyes struggled to focus. "I'm thirsty."

"Yes, yes . . . we're always thirsty, aren't we Tom? Don't matter how much we drink. Always thirsty, we are."

"We have to get out of here."

"No way out, Benjie. One door – one window above it. That's all."

"The three of us can . . . ."

"No. Tom ran. They put the 'ound on 'im and dun him good," Jake said, pointing to Tom's feet.

Benjie's eyes had adjusted to the darkness, allowing him to see the skinny youth pressed against the far wall. Tom's legs were pulled up tight against his chest. His arms were clutched around his knobby knees. His bare feet were bleeding, black and blue. Raw flesh oozed where his toenails had dropped off.

"Beat 'is feet with a club. Tom can't walk now." Jake began to shake. "We're gonna die."

Benjie grabbed Jake by the shoulders. "Nobody's dyin'!"

****

SHERLOCK HOLMES had just shed Tux's grimy clothes, and was standing before a long mirror removing his false beard.

I used a broom to push the pile of tattered garments onto an open newspaper spread on the floor alongside the clothing. "I feel as though I should call the public disinfectors, Holmes. I don't know how you can tolerate having these horrid rags on your body."

339

"Soap and water is all the hygiene required," Holmes assured me. "Please be careful not to discard that sack there. Inside we may well find some pieces to this puzzle."

I put the kettle on and searched the cupboards for something to eat. A can of salmon, and three hard-boiled eggs, provided the makings for bachelor sandwiches. As I brought our dinner into the parlour, I saw that Holmes had already spread a newspaper on my desk, and was carefully placing objects from his dustman's sack thereon. He began poking each item with a pencil.

"Dustbins," he said, "write the most truthful biographies. The challenge here is to know which of these items might best put us on Benjie's trail."

He continued his incessant prodding, occasionally examining an object with his glass. Within five minutes he had put four of the objects to one side. "Here are the tell-tale clues, I believe."

I approached as a dutiful friend. For, while Holmes is a singular man in most regards, he shares a trait common to consummate craftsman and artisans. My friend requires an audience – not for adulation or approval, but in the way a magician enjoys revealing his sleight of hand to an apprentice.

"Object one," Holmes began: "blood stained cotton – fully in keeping with the work of a haematologist. Object two: an old railway timetable from Euston Station. And, related to this, there were three recent entries in his expense ledger for 16/6 under "train.""

Holmes reached back into the pile of previously discarded items, and retrieved a bit of old cheese in a torn wrapper. "Hm-m-m. This is not a local cheese. Let us add this to the mix."

Prodding several small pieces of badly soiled fabric, the size of a calling card, Holmes asked: "What do you make of these, Watson?"

I picked up one of the pieces, and held it to my nose. "Ah, yes, flannel patches used to clean a gun – a large bore. Most likely a shotgun."

"Exactly so," Holmes remarked. And then, pointing to each of the patches in turn, "This one had tow and oil on it . . . this one, turpentine . . . and this one, sperm oil, I believe. This might also explain the whistle I discovered in a canvas jacket hanging near the rear door."

"He hunts . . . the whistle calls the Herriers," I confirmed.

Then, Holmes stuck his pencil into the neck of an empty bottle, and held it up before me. "And, the real prize – a bottle that once held sodium citrate. What do you make of all this?"

I gazed upon the five objects. "The blood, we are agreed, relates to blood genotyping. The man is a hunter, most likely game fowl, and he recently cleaned his shotgun."

I picked up the bottle and smelled it. "Sodium citrate is a common alkalinizing agent. It's used to treat kidney stones."

"How might it be used with blood?"

"Possibly as a preservative . . . or an anti-clotting agent."

"Genius, Watson! And, what of the cheese – you are a gourmet, are you not?"

"I enjoy my cheese more than the next fellow, but I am not an expert."

I picked up the dried chunk of whitish cheese, along with a scrap of the wrapping. "A white cheese . . . semi-soft. As you say, the blue and green wrapping is not familiar to me."

"Exactly, Watson. It is not a common cheese in this city. I think we can put Archie and his band to work with regard to this cheese."

Within an hour, Archie returned with the last piece of the puzzle.

"Mr. Olmes, look 'ere." Archie held up a bright blue and green package in one hand. "Eden Glenn cheese."

"Made in Manchester?" Holmes queried.

"It's a witch you are," Archie replied. "Near Manchester, sir, in Leigh."

"A Leigh Toaster," I exclaimed. "Makes me rather peckish. What did that package of cheese cost you, Archie?"

Archie presented a sly smile. "Cost me sir?"

"Well then, what will it cost *me*?"

"A gift, sir," Archie said, as he presented the cheese.

"No time for dining, fellows," Holmes shouted. "We're off to Manchester!"

"Then you believe Benjie is in Manchester, Holmes?"

"Yes, likely near the Gregston Estate – the crest you know. You might check your wallet also. I am certain 16/6 is the fare from Euston to Manchester-Piccadilly. If your pistol is well oiled, I suggest you retrieve it, and grab a warm coat and hat."

Holmes put his hand on Archie's shoulder. "We need you here, Archie. If your lads report that Rottenberg has returned, you must wire us at Manchester-Piccadilly Station. Take these coins for a telegram. The extra money will help you make payment for the cheese."

****

BENJIE crouched on the narrow ledge of the window above the storeroom door.

"He's comin'," Jake whispered, "with the broth."

Benjie waved Jake away from the doorway, and put his finger to his lips. The lock clicked, and the hinges hummed as the door swung open. Jake and Tom shielded their eyes from the glaring lantern light splashing into the room.

A man's voice could be heard just outside the portal. "Benjie? Benjie? I have some broth for you. No need to hide from me."

Jake pointed to a dark corner. The man stepped inside, lantern in one hand, bowl in the other. He squinted into the darkness.

Benjie leaped from the ledge onto the back of the man. The bowl of broth shattered on the floor. Benjie gouged his fingers deep into the man's eyes. The devil screamed, twisted, and swung the lantern back and forth in an effort to dislodge the cat-like boy.

"A-a-agh, blast you, you bloody bastard!" he yelled. The man reached over his head and seized Benjie's neck, ripped him around, and cast him to the floor. Jake leaped forward to block the kicks being directed at Benjie.

"Get 'em, Jake!" Benjie screamed. The desperate man dropped the lantern, grabbed Jake by the collar, and tossed him against the wall. The lantern flickered out. In the darkness, the desperate man groped for the boy. Then came Benjie's foot – violently smashing into his face.

"Argh! My nose!" Blood gushed between the man's fingers, and streamed down his neck. A second kick caught the man in the groin. He dropped to his knees and rolled onto to his side moaning.

"Hurry, Jake, quick! Help me with Tom."

"Best ya go now, Benjie. Bring help."

The injured man struggled to his knees and made a feeble attempt to grasp his assailant. Benjie punched him hard, again in the nose. The man bellowed and collapsed on the floor.

Benjie rushed from the room. Scrambling up the wooden cellar stairs, he burst into the kitchen.

"What's all this!" a wiry cook woman said, as she poked her head around the pantry door. "You there . . . ."

Benjie ran toward the light of the rear door. He leaped into the garden with only one thought – run!

****

SHERLOCK HOLMES gazed through the train window at the weather-beaten moors that lay between London and Manchester. He had

342

wrapped himself in a tight silence for nearly an hour before he turned to me: "You are comfortable with silence, Watson, which makes you a rare and ideal companion."

Holmes's gaze turned back to the passing landscape. "There is something bestial and cruel at work in the human race – something I have never been able to fathom."

"Or accept, thank heaven. Don't worry, Holmes. We will find him . . . ."

"Find him, Watson? Benjie has less than eight pints of blood coursing through his young veins. The loss of more than three will put him at death's door."

"Rottenberg knows this."

"Yes, and that is what makes him such a hideous beast."

As soon as the train lurched to a stop, we rushed into the station. A governess cart pulled up to the curb as we emerged. As we opened the rear hatch, Holmes spied a large black motor-car waiting in the distance.

"The vulture circles, Watson."

"The motor-car?"

"Sir George Gregston, I am certain. Clever fellow! Waiting and watching us."

"He may have known all along, but kept himself free from suspicion whilst we did his dirty work."

Holmes addressed the carter: "We are looking for a cottage, or hunting lodge, in the countryside – near the Gregston Estate. The house of a Londoner."

"I imagine yer speakin' of Braunmoss House, sir. It's there you wish to go then?"

"We do," Holmes said.

As the cart splashed down the road, I pulled my collar up around my neck as a frosty drizzle began.

"There will be no place for subtlety or banter when we arrive, Watson. Have your revolver at the ready."

A little more than half-way into the journey, the driver pointed and remarked: "Most unusual sir."

He was referring to another set of wheel tracks in the mud ahead.

"Few travel this way in winter, sir."

This confirmed Holmes's deductions. Upon arriving, we paid the driver, and made the journey from the road to Braunmoss House on foot. Racing onto the front porch, we pounded on the door. No answer. Holmes thrust it open. We stood silently on the threshold – listening.

A woman, gowned in black lace, scurried into the hallway toward us. "How dare you!"

"Where's the boy?" Holmes demanded.

The woman stopped in her tracks. Holmes confronted her. "The boy, Benjie – where is he?"

She hung her head in resignation, and took a deep breath.

"Run away. The others are in the cellar."

"Others?" I exclaimed.

"Watson, to the cellar. I'll find Benjie!"

****

BENJIE knew a dog was hunting him when he heard it baying in the distance. Spying a hollow log, he ripped off his shirt, put it on a long stick, and poked it into the hollow. He grabbed nearby brush and jammed it into one end of the log. He frantically searched the area for something else to close the other end of his trap.

Holmes had heard the dog as well, and followed the retreating yelps into the woods. He came upon an ageing handler trotting well behind his Herrier. Holmes beckoned sharply. "Hello there!"

The man stopped, and turned toward the unfamiliar voice.

"Call your dog off, at once!" Holmes ordered.

The man grimaced. "And you'd be?"

"I'd be the man who is saving you from hanging at the Old Bailey."

The man paused but a moment before he blew two short blasts on a silver whistle slung around his neck. "Skyler! Skyler, come."

The yelping ceased, and the hound returned, panting heavily at the old man's side.

"Benjie! Benjie!" Holmes called out. "It's Mr. Holmes, Benjie."

After repeated calls, amid the rustle of brush, Benjie burst forth into the waiting arms of Sherlock Holmes.

"Mr. 'Olmes, bless ye sir," he said. "We must see to Jake and Tom."

"Dr. Watson is no doubt doing just that. Come along."

****

SHERLOCK HOLMES and Benjie returned to Braunmoss House again to find me in the parlour, nursing Jake and Tom.

"Good man, Watson. The boys are well then?"

"Alive, Holmes. Poor Tom here must go to hospital quickly."

"The Gregstons?"

"Upstairs."

344

"Rottenberg?"

"Secured in the cellar, a bit worst for the wear, thanks to Benjie, I believe."

Holmes ruffled the hair of the lad. "Well done, Benjie! Come along."

Holmes and Benjie hurried up the stairway, following the dreadful sobbing coming from above.

I heard the motorcar pull into the driveway, and waited for the twin to enter. Sir George Talbot Gregston appeared triumphant in the open doorway. He looked at the boys and me momentarily, then silently walked toward the mournful sounds of Mrs. Gregston above. As he climbed the stairs, I settled the boys down and followed him, patting the revolver in my pocket.

We reached the bedroom, which was plain, austere, and stripped of colour. Mrs. Gregston was on her knees, weeping at the bedside of her husband.

Sir George entered, pausing next to Holmes and Benjie, who were standing back a respectful distance.

"Is he alive?" the twin enquired.

With that, the dark woman's head swivelled. She arose and swept like a harpy to confront her brother-in-law. "You vile man! Leave my home!"

"I've come to pay my respects."

"Respects? Your brother still lives – no thanks to you. Your blood could save him."

"Save him from Hades? For what . . . another seven days? You cannot cheat death. And, really, what is the point? You will have little need of the Gregston fortune in Broadmoor."

The ghastly man then walked to the deathbed. He leaned over his brother, turning his head to better hear the gasping breaths. He retrieved a nearby chair and placed it next to the bed. Then, lowering himself onto the chair, he waited for his brother's life come to its blunt, and predictable, conclusion.

Holmes motioned Benjie and me toward the door.

The next morning, we took Benjie to his mother's shop in St. Giles. Archie was there as well. As we approached, Benjie pulled away from us. He stood silently on the threshold of the shop. His mother gasped with relief when she saw her son. Immediately, Benjie was crushed against the bosom of his mother in the tenderest regard. He bided there for some time.

When Benjie pulled away, he turned to Archie, who had been waiting off to the side. Tears welled up in their eyes as the brothers embraced.

Holmes and I stood as privileged interlopers.

"It takes more than blood to make a family, Holmes."

The Adventure of
The White Bird
by C. Edward Davis

Holmes and I had arrived in New York on Wednesday, 4 May 1927, in order to attend to some matters. We were both exhausted from the long sea voyage in rough weather, and a series of elaborate and thoroughly exhausting dinner parties sponsored by New York's mayor, Jimmy Walker, and the police commissioner, Joseph A. Warren, that occupied the rest of that week. Both of us were slowly ascending the ladder of time to old age: Holmes was 73 at the time, and I almost two years his senior.

Sunday, 8 May 1927, began sunny and mild. The sun had been up for several hours, but Holmes and I were behaving as tired old men, relaxing in our beds and enjoying some welcome solitude. Holmes was devouring the local newspapers, and I was reading the latest medical journal.

"Look at this, Watson," my friend exclaimed, slapping the newspaper with the fingers of his right hand. "The French have begun their adventure. Nungesser and Coli took off last night before midnight from Paris, bound for this very city. The paper says they took off at 5:17 a.m. Paris time. They are, let me see here," he said, as he adjusted his reading glasses, something he rarely wore in public, "I quote, 'expected to arrive at 2 p.m. tomorrow. They plan to land squarely in front of the Statue of Liberty.' How absolutely marvelous!"

My good friend had become infected with an interest in aviation ever since Louis Bleriot crossed the English Channel in 1909. He even took flying lessons the following year, much to his frustration. Since that year, and while it had never ascended to the lofty heights of his interest at beekeeping, he followed aeronautical matters with the restrained enthusiasm of a church deacon.

"And, of course," he continued, "some scoundrel, Monson, has taken a half-page advertisement demanding that 'true Americans and Patriots' constrain their enthusiasm and refuse to greet the, ahem, 'snail-eating bounders', should they succeed and land safely in New York Harbor. He goes on to wish *Corporal Nun-gasser* and *Monsieur Colitis* – my God, does the man have no decency? – the very worst of luck in their blighted journey. Ghastly man, that."

I barely glanced at my friend, finding a more absorbing bit of reading about the latest research into the Great Influenza Pandemic of 1918. "Yes," said I, "the man is rather difficult to swallow, isn't he. Made a great stink during the war with that silly nonsense of his, trying to sell a dog of an airplane to the French."

I spent that afternoon exploring that great American city, while Holmes remained at the hotel listening to the radio for the latest reports of the French flyers. I paid scant attention to the reports of Nungesser and Coli, but Holmes could barely restrain himself, running off to listen to the latest radio broadcast or read the latest headline of the plethora of newspapers available in America's greatest city.

Holmes said during dinner, "What say we make our way to Battery Park tomorrow afternoon and watch *The White Bird* alight in the harbor?" He made a reference to the name of Nungesser and Coli's white painted airplane, *L'Oiseau Blanc*, or *The White Bird*. He was positively giddy with excitement.

The following day, it was Monday the 9th, Holmes and I joined the throngs of well-wishers at Battery Park. It was foggy and raining lightly. Cold and damp, and I am to understand, quite typical for New York at that time of year. "The weather is quite dreadful, don't you think? We are not young men anymore, Holmes. This dampness and fog is not good for my old injuries."

"Posh!" said Holmes. "A little fog would do you wonders, old man! Loosen up those creaky lungs of yours, get the sinuses open, and all that."

The time of arrival of the intrepid French aviators came. The throngs that had gathered in Battery Park and other convenient places along the southern tip of Manhattan in anticipation of their arrival, and simultaneously snubbing that cur Monson, waited in the drizzle and fog. There was no sign of *The White Bird*. We waited another hour without sign of the French airplane. The weather was getting worse, and we made our way back to our hotel on Park Avenue. Holmes was obviously feeling the weather as well. He said "Well, then, you old curmudgeon. We shall at least listen to the great achievement on the radio. They have fuel enough to last them for another few hours. Probably weather forced to take a longer route. They shall be here before dinner." Holmes and I listened avidly to the radio reports in the comfort of our hotel room, warm and snug. We heard, over the radio, that *The White Bird* had been sighted near Portland, Maine, but no further sightings were reported. Surely they must be close to New York now.

Around 4:30, Holmes and I wandered up to the hotel roof to enjoy a before-dinner smoke, something Holmes inaugurated shortly after our arrival, and after several guests complained of the odor of Holmes's favorite tobacco. We chatted about the French fliers when, shortly before five o'clock, three large seaplanes roared overhead bound to the east. "I suspect that they have found the Frenchmen and are on their way to bring those brave men to the city," Holmes said with confidence. It proved to be unfounded.

Six o'clock passed – well past the time when their fuel would have been exhausted. Then seven and still no sign of *The White Bird*. When the clocks tolled nine, many began to give up hope and sullenly wandered to warmer and dryer accommodations. A kind of pall of worry had settled over the city. The Frenchmen were long overdue. But there were stalwarts who proclaimed that the duo had landed on Long Island or Cape Cod and would proceed to New York on the morrow. The Ortieg Prize had been won and the two French fliers would triumphantly enter the city tomorrow to collect their grand prize of $25,000.

Sadly, there were no reports of a successful landing. The following day, the 10th, Nungesser and Coli were officially declared missing. The searches began immediately; even Floyd Bennett, confined to a hospital after his earlier crash, began a search at the behest of a newspaper that would last for nine days, and prove fruitless. Several millionaires offered a total of $32,000 reward for the discovery of the missing flyers. Holmes was rather concerned and began to ponder, sometimes mumbling to himself, what could have happened. "There were storms near Newfoundland, Watson. Quite possible that they crashed somewhere on that island and are even now being cared for by the local inhabitants," he would say. His concern grew as the days passed. He paced incessantly, interrupting our evening meal to wander to the hotel bar and listen to the radio there. There wasn't a newspaper that he wouldn't buy to read of the latest searches.

No news, no sightings, no hope.

Our days passed in this now gloomy city with conferences with my publisher, and conferences and lectures at local police precincts, one as far out as Paterson in New Jersey. We endured stuffy luncheons with New York's influential and prosperous. All quite dull and, at times, excruciatingly tedious. I doubt that the continuing mystery of *The White Bird* was ever far from Holmes's consciousness. Indeed, I often caught him with that intense gaze, indicative of his mind wrestling with a difficult enigma. Already, Holmes was working on a solution.

We had made plans for an extended stay in America, at the behest of none other than Raymond Ortieg, the benefactor of the New York-to-Paris endeavor, who nervously pestered Holmes with questions. Ortieg gave me the impression that he would like us to investigate the matter, but was walking a tightrope between the press and the government. The government wanted to handle the search itself.

On the 19th, the Coast Guard found what they hoped was a piece of *The White Bird* in Fort Pond Bay, Long Island. It turned out to be from another Coast Guard plane that force landed earlier. So many false leads and rumors.

On the 20th of May, a Friday, we found ourselves enveloped in a chill mist and drizzle in the early morning hours at Roosevelt Field outside of the town of Mineola, Long Island. We waited for the latest entrant in the Ortieg Prize to begin his perilous journey.

Charles Lindbergh, whom we met very briefly just a few hours before, paced by his silver airplane, *The Spirit of St. Louis*, glancing nervously at the ominous skies to the east. Finally, a break in the weather occurred, and within minutes Lindbergh's little monoplane was roaring across the marshy field.

I know that I was holding my breath as the little, silver plane barely cleared the trees at the east end of the aerodrome. Once he had cleared the grove and was disappearing into the watery dawn, I heard Holmes beside me heave a great sigh of relief.

"An amazing and thrilling endeavor, eh, Watson?" said Sherlock Holmes, quite softly. There was a rousing cheer from the gathered throng, and I could barely hear him over the din. I turned and watched his aquiline profile as he stared after the diminishing flying machine. To me, it seemed rather appropriate that this hawk of deductive reasoning and thought should be so taken with the eagle of this new era.

Holmes turned and tapped me with his walking stick. "Shall we be off to luncheon, Watson? I understand that there is a café here where we can mingle with some of Mr. Lindbergh's colleagues and partake of that icon of American cuisine, the hamburger." I nodded distractedly, because I had noticed a striking young woman and a dapper young man slowly approaching us. The woman's attention was focused on the numerous puddles around her and she stepped daintily between them. The man stared directly at us and his stride was purposeful and proud.

We, too, were concentrating on keeping our boots dry, when they stopped before us. Confidently, and with a melodious voice that thrilled, the woman addressed us. "Mr. Holmes and Doctor Watson? I am Consuelo Hatmaker, Charles Nungesser's ex-wife. We should like to engage you to find my ex-husband." The young man then spoke. "And I am Robert Nungesser, Charles' half-brother. I, too, would like you to investigate my brother's disappearance."

Holmes and I were somewhat astounded by the beauty of this young woman, and by her confidence and presence. Her angelic face was, however, marred by an expression of extreme sorrow and despair.

Holmes took Miss Hatmaker's elbow and we all began walking slowly to the hangars, where numerous taxis and limousines awaited. "What makes you to assume that I can be of any service to you in this simple matter of an aviation tragedy, Miss Hatmaker, Mr. Nungesser? Surely you do not suspect foul play?" Holmes said.

Miss Hatmaker's face contorted in grief and anger. "But I do, Mr. Holmes, I do suspect that something terrible has happened. Someone did not want Charles to succeed, and particularly did not wish for Charles and me to re-marry. In that matter, I suspect my father, James R. Hatmaker. He despised Charles because he was a pilot." Her voice broke and tears flowed down her cheeks. "Charles wrote me a week before his flight that when he landed, he would stand in the cockpit and salute and search the crowd for me. He said that he would not smile until he saw my face. After his flight, we planned to re-marry. Charles would have the money to support me and, being an international hero, my father would have to respect him and accept him. Whether my father approved or not, we would marry."

Holmes observed the distraught woman closely, from the corners of his eyes. I saw him study her face, her posture, the way she dabbed a handkerchief at her eyes.

"Do you truly believe," I interjected, "that your father would do something to harm monsieurs Nungesser and Coli? Do you believe him to be that ruthless and black hearted, Miss Hatmaker?" She turned to me with sorrow in her eyes, pondering the question for just a few seconds. Then her head drooped and she seemed to sag before us. "Actually, Doctor, I do. My father did not approve of Charles and hated the fact that Charles and I were in love. He forced me to divorce Charles two years ago by threatening to terminate my allowance and write me out of his will. I never forgave him for that."

"Could your father have contracted with someone to sabotage the French aircraft?" asked Holmes. Miss Hatmaker's face paled.

Robert Nungesser said, "Yes. At first, we suspected that her father may have had someone tamper with Charles' airplane. There was a slight fire on the 3rd, but there was little damage. However, Mr. Hatmaker is a respectable business man. I may not like the man, but I have a difficult time believing that he would do such a thing."

"Still," said Holmes, "It is not entirely out of the question, is it?"

Both Miss Hatmaker and Mr. Nungesser looked taken aback. "No," said Miss Hatmaker, quite sheepishly. Holmes stood before the girl.

"Then why would you suspect your father? He must have given you reason. Did he not?"

"Well,' she stammered, "Well . . . ." Her voice trembled, and she could not go on. The expression on her face revealed to us that her suspicions were indeed the result of anger. She obviously failed to think the matter through entirely.

By this time, we had reached the hangars and the various limousines and taxis awaiting their fares for a return ride to Manhattan. We were only yards away from the little café Holmes had mentioned. The enticing aroma of grilling onions and beef mingled with the heady odor of strong coffee. My mouth watered and my shivers demanded something hot to drink.

"Miss Hatmaker," Sherlock Holmes began, ""I am sure that a man of your father's respectability and stature is not the suspect you imagine him to be. However, I do suspect, like you, that someone has contrived to prevent your beloved from attaining his goal, and that the disappearance is more than mechanical failure, nasty weather, or simply a tragic navigational error. We will look into it, though. Will you accompany us back to the city in our cab? We can then discuss the details of the case in relative comfort. Watson, would be so kind as to purchase some hot coffee for the four of us?"

The four of us rode back to Manhattan. On the ride back, Mr. Nungesser mentioned that the aeronautical entrepreneur, Monson, the very man who had published the vile newspaper advertisement, had once attended a lecture that Charles Nungesser had presented to the veterans of the Lafayette Escadrille, in which his half-brother had served during the Great War. Monson had interrupted the proceedings with ugly accusations of Nungesser's incompetence and his deliberate destruction of a scouting airplane Monson hoped to sell, and had to be escorted out. I considered this rather interesting and said so. Holmes agreed. We dropped the two at their respective homes and continued on to our hotel in silence. We adjourned to our room and unburdened ourselves of our damp coats and hats. Holmes called the front desk to have some sandwiches brought up and the latest newspapers as well. He was anxious to learn of Mr. Lindbergh's progress.

Immediately we finished our lunch, and after I had pestered Holmes about his promise of American hamburgers, my friend began his ritualistic pacing. "What do you make of it, Watson? Do you feel this Monson character a suspect? How about Mr. Hatmaker?" He turned to me and tapped his foot.

I was sitting by a window looking out at a wind and rain swept Park Avenue. I mulled the matter over in my mind. I had of late, been more assertive in my give and take with Holmes, no doubt a product of my advancing years. "It is surely justifiable to suspect some manner of treachery in this matter, particularly when one considers the amount of money to be made from a successful endeavor, and the amount of money a person could lose should they fail. I agree with you that foul weather, errors in navigation, or catastrophic mechanical failure are the most likely causes of this unfortunate state of affairs," said I. "But one cannot entirely rule out some criminal mischief, again considering the amount of the prize money. However, we have little evidence as to the nature of the plot, if one exists, or as to who could be responsible for the deed."

Holmes pinched the bridge of his nose and squeezed shut his eyes. He rubbed his face vigorously with both hands. He stepped to the windows and peered out intently. I knew from his fierce expression that his mind was miles away.

Almost to himself he said, "We may be correct in assuming a purely natural, but still tragic, conclusion to this matter. Yet the first successful crossing of the Atlantic represents a great advance in not just aeronautical technology and capability, but would result in the winning country reaping more than just simple prize money." He turned to me, his eyes serious and intense. "Think of the consequences of a successful flight, Watson. Men could make or lose huge fortunes! And let us not forget those of lower morals who would make bets on the outcome. There, too, you would have men, some of them of a very criminal nature, who stand to win or lose large sums of capital. There are those among them who would be very upset should someone borrow a large amount to make a wager, then not have the funds to repay the loan."

"Great rewards for great risk." I added.

As though he had not heard me, Sherlock Holmes continued, "I would like to speak with Mr. Raymond Ortieg again. See if there is anyone who stands out in his mind who could be involved. Someone who stands to gain a healthy sum for a victory."

"Holmes," said I, "you must be aware that Mr. Ortieg is a very busy man right now? He may not be able to indulge us at this time."

Holmes looked at me curiously. "Ah, never mind, we shall pay a visit to his offices and find someone who will speak to us about this."

I looked intensely at my friend. I knew that look only too well. "You already have someone in mind, don't you? Tell me who is on your list, Holmes. Let us compare lists!"

Holmes smiled at me as one would an intelligent, precocious child. He chuckled. "Yes, Watson, I do have someone in mind. Several suspects, in fact. But I wish to gather more information before I give voice to my suspicions. You will have to wait until later, I'm afraid."

I leapt to my feet, which may not have been a bright idea considering my sore knees and back. "It is that scabby Monson fellow, isn't it, Holmes! That Francophobe scoundrel who took out that despicable advertisement!" I cried.

But Sherlock Holmes had already left the room and was proceeding down the corridor.

I called after him, "At least have them send up one of those hamburgers to me, Holmes! Holmes?"

That night Holmes paced about the room, occasionally turning on the radio to listen for news of Lindbergh's progress.

The next day, as Lindbergh was plying the clouds over the Atlantic, Holmes and I went to the New York Public Library to read what we could find about Mr. Ortieg, Mr. James Hatmaker, and Mr. Monson. Mr. Ortieg and Mr. Hatmaker proved to be above reproach. We found nothing but glowing praises about their character and business practices. However, Monson proved to be cut of a different cloth. We discovered that he had been involved in several court cases for fraud and misappropriation of funds, even two cases in which he was acquitted of racketeering. Articles about his airplanes were less than favorable. One aeronautical expert, Mr. Gordon Page, wrote that Monson's airplanes were flying death traps. Lastly, we discovered that Monson's company was on the verge of bankruptcy, and that he owed several people, including some of rather disreputable character, large sums of money.

It proved to be an interesting day.

We were just beginning an early dinner when the news came that Lindbergh had safely made it to Paris. The dining room erupted in cheers and impromptu dancing. Even Holmes, very uncharacteristically for him, cheered and danced with a very young girl around our table. "Watson!" he shouted above the din, "Watson! A new age, Watson! Marvelous! Absolutely marvelous!" We did not get to bed until after midnight.

The next day was a Sunday, if I remember, the 22nd. There was nothing to get done, so Holmes and I stayed at the hotel and reviewed our case notes. Holmes sent for a large map of the Newfoundland area and of eastern Long Island, trying to trace a route that the Frenchman may have taken. He was still convinced, as many others were, that *The White Bird* was forced down in the wilderness somewhere and the pilots were desperately awaiting discovery and rescue.

Early the following morning, the 23rd, Holmes and I took a cab to Raymond Ortieg's offices downtown. Upon inquiring at the reception desk, we were informed that Mr. Ortieg was currently in Paris, on vacation with his wife. They had left the previous week.

Holmes smiled at the pretty dark-haired girl behind the ornate desk. He looked at the nameplate on her desk. "Yes, Miss Cannella is it?" She nodded. "Yes, my dear Miss Cannella, I am aware of where Mr. Ortieg is. You may have misunderstood my English accent. I wanted only to speak with someone on Mr. Ortieg's personal staff who is familiar with the entrants for the prize. Someone who is responsible for the daily operations of this grand endeavor. Do you see what I am asking now, Miss Cannella?"

Relief washed over the pretty girl's face. "Well, then let me see if Mr. Ortieg's aeronautical advisor, Mr. Page, is available." She buzzed an intercom and asked another young lady if Mr. Page was, indeed, available.

Our charming friend smiled at us. "Mr. Page is available, Mr. Holmes, and he will be out shortly." She motioned us to a luxurious divan in the waiting area. No sooner had we settled into the plush leather than an athletic looking man in a dark gray suit rushed through a double door and greeted us enthusiastically. He pumped our hands vigorously.

"It is indeed a pleasure to meet such a famous person as yourself, Mr. Holmes. It is an honor. And you also, Dr. Watson. May I say that I have read everything that you have written, and have enjoyed those stories a great deal? In fact, I read them to my daughters at least once a week." He indicated that we follow him through the great doors.

"My name is Gordon Page, and I am Mr. Ortieg's consulting aeronautical engineer." He guided us down a well-appointed hallway, with several doors leading to small offices, and on to his office at the end of the hall. This room was large and comfortable, and featured two great windows commanding imposing views of New York Harbor and the Statue of Liberty. Paintings of airplanes were spaced about the two remaining walls. A table against one wall was over-flowing with blueprints, maps, and a myriad of documents. After we had settled into some wooden chairs, we began our interview.

"As you may no doubt be aware, Mr. Page, Dr. Watson and I have been commissioned by Miss Consuelo Hatmaker and Mr. Robert Nungesser to investigate the unfortunate disappearance of Captain Nungesser and Francois Coli. Our clients, justified or not, suspect some nefarious motive behind this unfortunate event. Our intention here is to get a feel for the other American entrants and to deduce if there was anyone who had a motive to see the French fail," said Holmes.

Mr. Page shook his head in dismay. "I'm afraid that just about every entrant has motive to see the others fail, but no one had any particular grievance against the French team. $25,000 is quite an incentive, you can imagine. Not all the entrants are officially registered with us. Nungesser and Coli are technically outsiders, but eligible in any case."

Page tapped the blotter on his desk with his fingers. His fingers were those of a man well acquainted to using tools and getting dirty, a workingman's fingers. "As you may be aware, Mr. Holmes, several men have already perished in the attempt. Others are currently in the hospital. Now that Mr. Lindbergh has succeeded in his flight, I would absolve any of those of any wrong-doing." Page paused and glanced out the window. Clearly he was wrestling with a difficult issue.

"There was one man," he continued, "whom I would consider a prime suspect if any criminal activity were involved. Not because I have definitive proof, you understand. I would only suspect him because of his odious manners and unscrupulous business practices. His embarrassingly outspoken contempt for his fellow aviators is particularly abhorrent to me."

I broke in, "Can I conclude that you are speaking of this Monson person, the one who took out that charming advertisement in the papers earlier this month?"

Page looked at me with an expression of astonishment. He broke into a grin. "Exactly the man I was thinking of. William R. Monson. Possibly the most annoying and detestable person ever associated with aeronautics. Sorry for my odd reaction, Doctor, but it was like you were reading my mind and your sarcasm took me by surprise. Yes, Monson. How can one *not* suspect him?" Page smiled broadly and waggled an accusatory finger at me. "'Charming' indeed! You had me there, Doctor. That man would do anything, and I mean anything, to gain the upper hand on anyone, or anything, that stood in his way.

"You see, it is my duty to review each entrant's proposal. I had to examine their planned flight route, the aircraft they intended to use, fuel loads, safety equipment, and other minor details. And still, most of them failed in their attempts. Too many died. I would make some suggestions to the ones who appeared better prepared than others." He barked a laugh. "Why, we even had one man enter a Curtiss Jenny that was over twenty-years old and was falling apart as I watched!

"All submitted proposals. That is, except Monson. He was rude and secretive regarding his airplane, his experience, and his plans. Downright combative. Even before I had a chance to inform him that cooperation was in his best interest, he slapped ten $100 bills on my desk!" He tapped his blotter. "He said, 'These should be documents enough to prove my validity, Page.' Imagine that! A bribe! Well, I shoved the money back across the desk to him. 'Mr. Monson,' I said, 'This review is for your own safety. I am offended that you think me of such low caliber that I would consider any bribe. Please leave my office immediately.' I demanded. With that said, I stood to show him I meant business."

"And what did our esteemed Mr. Monson do after that?" asked Holmes, steepeling his fingers before his face.

Page laughed angrily. "The scoundrel glowered at me, scooped up the cash and stormed from the office. He said something at the door that caused me some concern."

Holmes raised an eyebrow and motioned with his forefinger for Page to continue.

"He said, 'This is not over, Page. Not by a longshot.' Then he left the building. I immediately informed Mr. Ortieg, and he assured me that I acted in the best interest of the prize commission. He would personally inform Mr. Monson, by letter, of his exclusion from the race."

"Did anything happen after that?"

"In fact, yes. There were some odd occurrences over the following weeks. I received unmarked, unaddressed letters in my mailbox, both at home and here, each containing ten $100 bills. I turned each one over to Mr. Ortieg."

Holmes had assumed his classical pose when interviewing a witness: fingers before his face, eyes closed, and his mouth set grimly. "And what did Mr. Ortieg make of this?"

"When I told Mr. Ortieg the whole story, he gave the money to some veterans' charities."

"Did Monson ever gain legitimate entry into the competition, say through another agent of Ortieg's?"

Page shook his head. "Monson never presented any aircraft, maps or flying logs. After the fiasco with me, he took to the newspapers, trying to pressure Mr. Ortieg and myself with public opinion. Claimed his 'secret' aircraft was so amazing that he would fly not just to Paris, but beyond. To Berlin or Cairo. He was unabashedly bragging. Nobody in the know bought any of his nonsense."

While Holmes was questioning Mr. Page, I had busied myself with rummaging through the stacks of engineering drawings, maps and legal documents. I turned back to Page. "Could somebody claim the prize if they were not officially entered in the competition?"

Page thought for just a few seconds. "Yes. Mr. Ortieg stated when Nungesser and Coli took off that whoever successfully made the flight first could claim the prize, regardless of the technicalities."

Holmes abruptly stood and paced to the window, his hands clasped behind his back. "Tell me, Mr. Page, did Mr. Monson ever attempt to bribe either Mr. Ortieg or any of the directors?"

Page answered without hesitation. "No! Absolutely not!"

"Then, in your educated opinion, would Mr. Monson attempt sabotaging either airman or aircraft?"

"Mr. Holmes," said Page, enunciating each word, "you have not heard all the facts of Mr. Monson's crooked business activities. The man is as ruthless and cunning as a pirate. And about as subtle. He is obsessed with winning at any cost, regardless of how large or small the reward. Regardless, even, of the consequences. I haven't anything solid to tell you that wouldn't sound like mean-spirited gossip, but the man has few friends and fewer people willing to do business with him. I, for one, have no idea how the bastard has stayed solvent for so long."

I asked, "Where could we speak to Mr. Monson? Get his take on the matter?"

"Monson's factory, if one could call it that, is located in Kingston, New York, on the Hudson River," replied Page.

Holmes turned from the window and extended his hand to Page. "Thank you for your time and your honesty, Mr. Page. We shan't bother you further." Holmes took up his hat and coat from the chair, then paused. With his face towards the floor, he peered at Page sidelong. "Would it be possible, Mr. Page, for Dr. Watson and I to obtain a copy of the entrants listing? Names and addresses and the like?"

"Certainly. I shall have Miss Cannella type a copy for you immediately. I can bring it to your hotel tomorrow morning, myself." He then offered to loan us his folder concerning Monson.

"Splendid," said Holmes. "Here is our hotel." He scribbled the address on a scrap of paper. "Thank you, Mr. Page, for your cooperation."

As Holmes and I left Page's office, he called after us.

"One other thing, Mr. Holmes. I almost forgot about it. Just before Lindbergh took off, a suspicious man was arrested snooping around Lindbergh's hangar. The Mineola Police have him in custody. They suspect that he was either trying to steal a souvenir from Slim or sabotage the aircraft. He had a knife, wire cutters, and a hand file on him. Does that give you any clues?"

Holmes and I exchanged surprised looks. "Why yes, Mr. Page. That may be a thread worth looking into. Good day."

As we reached the sidewalk, I said to Holmes, "Then we are off to Mineola, Holmes?"

"In due time, Doctor. In due time. I wish to see Monson's factory first."

We returned to our hotel and collected our thoughts. Mr. Page had given us his folder on Monson and his flight proposal. To be honest, both Holmes and I were out of our element with these aeronautical details. I checked with the front desk to inquire about trains running to Kingston. There was one at nine a.m. the following day. We planned on partaking of an early breakfast and taking the early train north.

The next morning, Tuesday the 24th, after a rather unpleasant train ride and a bumpy cab ride with a surly driver, we arrived at Monson's Kingston factory. To our surprise, while we expected a bustling center of aeronautical activity, the Monson factory was all but deserted. A lone security guard was on duty at the kiosk before the entrance, sullenly reading a newspaper.

We addressed him and inquired about speaking with Mr. Monson. He knew of no such man, only that he had to spend ten hours each day sitting in this run-down shack, turning away everyone seeking employment. When Holmes ensured the rummy guard that we were not seeking employment and wished to speak with someone in charge, he directed us to the main entrance and told us to ask for Mr. Sutton.

At the main entrance, we encountered another disheveled person of indeterminate age, sitting behind a wobbly wooden desk. He, too, was reading a newspaper and appeared to have no other function than to keep the unkempt lobby occupied. On his desk he had a single old telephone.

"Good morning, we should like to speak to a Mr. Sutton, please," said Holmes, as pleasantly as he was able. The old man looked at us with squinted eyes and an attitude of suspicion and contempt.

"Why?" he said.

"We have business with Mr. Sutton. That should be sufficient," replied Holmes.

The old man muttered something insulting under his breath and picked up the phone. He dialed a single number. After a second or two, he spoke. "Sutton? Two clowns here to see you. You comin' down to fetch them or you want me to send 'em up to you?" There was a pause. "Yeah," he said and hung up the phone abruptly. "He'll be down in a minute," and went back to his newspaper.

Holmes and I stepped away from the desk and examined the dilapidated surroundings. Paint and wallpaper pealing from the walls. Darker rectangles showed where once pictures hung. Magazines five years out of date littered a sagging coffee table, with no chairs or sofas to sit on. The room spoke of prosperous times long gone.

The echoes of footsteps caught our attention and we turned to watch a middle-aged gentleman, with graying hairs and sagging jowls, approach. He wore no jacket, no vest, but a dingy white shirt and stained dark slacks. His sleeves were rolled up and his tie was loosened and askew.

"Is that them, Ralph?" he said, addressing the guard.

"Who do you think? Sure it's not President Harding over there in the corner?" the guard replied. "Moron," he said, just loud enough to be heard. Sutton ignored him.

He walked over to where we stood. "Yeah? What can I do for you guys? Want to buy an airplane, go somewhere else."

"Mr. Sutton, I presume," said Holmes extending his hand. "I am Sherlock Holmes and this is my colleague, Doctor Watson. We would like to speak to you about Mr. Monson."

Sutton looked at Holmes's gloved hand as if it were a venomous reptile. Then he looked at both of us in turn, I felt as though the man had not seen another human being in ages.

"Monson? Yeah, I'd like to speak to him too. Haven't been paid in two weeks. I sit here day after day working on his damned blueprints and I can't get an answer to any of my calls, letters, or telegrams. Man's like ghost around here."

"May we talk in your office, Mr. Sutton?" asked Holmes. Sutton nodded, albeit reluctantly, and turned about to lead us down a dingy hallway. Dirty floor-to-ceiling windows along one side of the hall admitted a depressing, grayish light. Sutton turned into a large office, without a door or windows. Several drawing boards were scattered about, and piles of drawings and notebooks cluttered them all. A layer of dust indicated that the office hadn't been fully occupied in some time. Sutton swept some magazines off two creaky chairs and motioned for us to be seated. He took his seat behind a large drafting table, intertwined his fingers, and stared at us.

"What do you do for Mr. Monson, Mr. Sutton?" inquired Holmes. I looked around the room, noticing the same dilapidation as in the lobby. The whole place gave me the feeling of being lost in time.

Sutton did not smile. In fact, his face remained passive and his dark eyes fixed Holmes with a disgusted glare. "I'm his draftsman and designer. Not that there's much work to do, so I draw up houses for the local architect. I'd be broke if it weren't for him."

"Does Monson produce any airplanes here? This place looks like it has fallen on hard times," said I.

"Hah!" Sutton guffawed. "Hasn't been an airplane built here in months. Last ones were the two Amphibian Patrol Planes Monson was hoping to sell to Argentina. Now, they're gone. Don't ask me where, I don't know. You guys here to foreclose on us?"

Holmes and I glanced at each other. So the Monson Airplane factory was in financial difficulty. "No," said Holmes, "we wish to speak with Mr. Monson about some matters regarding missing airplanes."

"Ah! That French plane business, right? I knew that bastard had something to do with it. He's been ranting and raging about the Nungesser feller since April. Almost obsessed with him. Ever since Monson's own Trans-Atlantic plane crashed, he started going on and on about how it should be an American that wins, that the Frenchies had no business with airplanes, stuff like that. Made me real nervous, when he would go on about it like that. Would work himself up into real frenzy. Start talking about how America should invade France and put an end to them all. Real crazy stuff, you know?"

Holmes steepled his fingers and stared intensely at Sutton. "So Monson wanted to win the Ortieg Prize himself. When was the last time Mr. Monson spoke to you, personally?"

Sutton lit a cigarette as he thought. "Maybe a few weeks ago. Haven't seen him at least since the end of April. Doesn't answer his phone, either. Last time I called, the Operator said the line was disconnected. Can't get in touch with Mr. Woodhouse, either."

"Who is Mr. Woodhouse?"

"That's Mr. Monson's chief designer, test pilot, and right hand man. Haven't seen him or his wife since the first week in May."

Holmes rose from his chair. "Thank you, Mr. Sutton."

We hand the outside security guard call a cab for us, which he did with an outstretched hand. Holmes gave him a silver dollar. The cab deposited us at the train station.

On the train back to New York, Holmes spoke quietly. "We have an unusual case before us, Watson. Two missing people, two missing and probably deceased aviators, and a multitude of questions. Our main suspect has been revealed as a man with an intense hatred of all things French, and the owner of an airplane that has crashed and two others that are unaccounted for. His colleague and the colleague's wife are nowhere to be found. We shall need to speak with Mr. Page once more. See if he is aware of Monson and Woodhouse's whereabouts."

The train ride back to New York was concluded in silence as Holmes stared sullenly out the windows. I scribbled my notes and examined the list that Page had provided us. No other suspicious characters grabbed my attention. I was perplexed.

I slept fitfully that night, but I heard Holmes snoring loudly from the opposite bed. It was a long night.

On Wednesday, the 25th, we proceeded to take the train out to Mineola, where we met with Detective Raymond Detmer. The detective informed us that the suspect, Carter, had confessed to being hired by a local gangster named Feliciano to break into the Lindbergh hangar and loosen some screws on the plane. He was caught before he could jimmy the window open. Further questioning proved fruitless. Carter was merely a thief who had been paid for work that he was sure he would not carry out. He stated that he wanted to watch Lindbergh take off, and admitted that he could not do what Feliciano wanted. Holmes asked to see Carter.

When we were led to Carter's cell, Holmes simply stared at the man, who was clearly disconcerted by the hawkish man glaring at him. After several minutes of silence, Holmes spoke. "Why did Feliciano want you to sabotage Lindbergh's plane, Carter? Did he have some stake in the matter?"

Carter cowered upon his cot, trying to will himself deeper into the concrete corner. "Don't know, mister. When Mr. Feliciano asks you to do a job, you do it. Whether you want to or not. Paid me five dollars, though. Not a lot, but it bought a bottle of whiskey."

Holmes gestured for Detmer to hand him a photograph of Monson. He held it out for Carter to see. "Ever see this man before?"

Carter squinted at the picture. His eyes brightened with recognition. "Yeah! Saw that guy talkin' to Mr. Feliciano a few nights before the job. In a local bar here. Seemed like he was outta place, y'know? Nice coat and tie, fancy shoes. Looked like he knew Mr. Feliciano. They was talkin' like they was ol' friends." Carter turned to Detmer. There was near panic in his voice. "You promised you were gonna protect me if I flipped on Feliciano. You promised, Detmer."

"Yeah, Carter, we will. Just waiting for transportation is all. Nice place upstate." Detmer replied.

"May we speak privately, Mr. Holmes?" Detmer asked as he walked towards the stairs to the offices above. Holmes and I followed. Once we were in Detmer's office, Holmes paced to a window overlooking the street. Today, the sun shone and the air was warm and humid. I noticed that Detmer was perspiring and had loosened his cravat.

"Page and I spoke yesterday about Carter and his connection to organized crime. Let's just say that Page was more than upset about this getting into the press." Detmer said.

I was watching Holmes. "Why did you inform Page about this?" I asked.

Detmer was intent, watching Holmes stare outside. He said, "Mr. Page was to be informed about any illegal activities surrounding the competitors' hangars. It was a secret request originated by Raymond Ortieg. Matter of security and safety. We checked it all out. Page is on the up and up."

"Tell me, Detective Detmer, what do you make about this whole affair regarding the missing French flyers? Could Feliciano have had something to do with it?"

Detmer thought a minute, twiddling a pencil in his fingers. "To be honest, Mr. Holmes, I don't think Feliciano had much to do with it. Yeah, he's mobbed up, but his main business is running booze from Canada into Maine and Long Island. I doubt he cared who won as long as people celebrated with his booze."

"And where would you place Monson in all this?" asked Holmes.

"That's easy, sir. Monson and Feliciano grew up together, ran with the same crowd. Monson sometimes gave Feliciano a plane to get booze for some special customer, but we could never get enough evidence on that to indict him as an accessory. The plane always turned up missing. But Monson is cut of the same cloth as Feliciano, though I think Monson has a few more screws missing than that dago crook. Y'know what I mean?"

Holmes suddenly turned to Detmer. "May I use your telephone to make a call, Detective? I need to ask Mr. Page a few questions."

"Certainly, Mr. Holmes. I will connect you to our switchboard."

While Holmes was busy talking with Page in New York, I questioned Detmer on his knowledge of the Nungesser and Coli disappearance.

"As local police, Doctor, we are not privy to all the investigations that are undertaken outside our jurisdiction, but we were notified to contact the Coast Guard should anything arise in that matter. I can put you in touch with our contact at the Guard, if you choose."

"That would be splendid, Detective. Yes, I should like to discover if they have learned anything new."

Detmer lead me into an adjoining office and, while Holmes continued speaking to Page, I was connected to a Commander Belanger, who updated me on the search for the missing aviators. Belanger informed me that there were a dozen or more people in Newfoundland, all around the Harbor Grace and Saint Pierre Island area on the south coast of the island, who either heard or saw a white airplane pass overhead. He also informed me that a single witness in rural Maine claimed to have seen a white airplane pass over him and heard it crash in a lake on which he was canoeing. Belanger stated that he would be more than honored to assist "his hero, Mr. Holmes" in his search for *The White*

Bird. I told Belanger that we would contact him for more assistance shortly.

I rejoined Holmes in Detmer's office. "Well?" I inquired.

"Page said that Monson was facing bankruptcy. He had tried to fly a plane for the trans-Atlantic attempt, unregistered either to the Ortieg Foundation or to the federal authorities. The plane crashed for reasons undetermined killing all aboard. Monson, against all regulations, disposed of the wreckage before a full investigation could commence. He may also have 'stolen' his two patrol airplane prototypes to prevent them from being seized by the banks. Monson, he confirmed, hasn't been seen in public since late April. Page doesn't know anything about Feliciano, only that he's deeply involved with bootlegging. What about you? What did you learn from the Coast Guard?"

I consulted my little notebook. "I spoke to a Commander Belanger in Bangor, Maine. He has been assigned to coordinate the Coast Guard search with the Canadians. There are a dozen people in Newfoundland who claim to have seen *The White Bird* pass overhead. I think we should arrange to meet Belanger in Newfoundland and speak to these people. What say you, Holmes?"

"It seems to me, Watson," my friend said, "that we are about to get acquainted with the island of Newfoundland."

Holmes and I gathered a portfolio of pictures of *The White Bird* airplane, Nungesser and Coli, Monson, Woodhouse, Feliciano, and the Monson Amphibians, and proceeded to meet with Belanger at Harbor Grace, Newfoundland. Between then and the 30th, we interviewed eighteen witnesses, showed them all the pictures. Few recognized the pictures of Charles Nungesser and Francois Coli. None recognized Monson's picture, or Woodhouse's. Holmes grew frustrated that the witnesses identified both *The White Bird* and the Monson Amphibian as the airplane that flew overhead. There was a visual similarity to the two machines, but since none could differentiate between the two, we were left to concede that *The White Bird* could have flown overhead.

We were confronted with a similar situation with the few witnesses at Saint Pierre Island, about one-hundred-and-fifty miles west-southwest from Harbor Grace. Our efforts in Newfoundland came to naught, but Holmes was beginning to formulate the timeline of events in his head. As to the fate of *The White Bird*, he was still perplexed. I began to suspect that rum-runners may have shot down the plane by mistake near Saint Pierre Island, for two witnesses, both fishermen, claimed to have heard machine gun fire, but they could not attest to where or when.

Belanger offered to fly us in his Coast Guard amphibian to Machias, Maine, where we would interview the Round Lake witness. We stopped in Halifax, for fuel. While we waited, Belanger was informed that a strange white airplane was found abandoned in the vicinity of Lubec, Maine. What was more, there was a body in the cockpit. Immediately our plane was fueled, we flew to Lubec, as small town on the border between Maine and New Brunswick.

By the time we reached Lubec, the authorities had identified the body in the plane, dead for a while now, as one H. G. Woodhouse, Monson's right hand man and chief pilot. The police attempted to inform his widow, but she could not be found. The airplane was confirmed as one belonging to Monson. When we reached the site, the Coast Guard had already secured the airplane, which was partially submerged in a marshy area south of the city of Lubec. The airplane was armed with four Browning machine guns, the ammunition boxes were empty, and there were indications that the guns had been used. Woodhouse's autopsy revealed a single gunshot wound to the forehead.

We re-boarded Belanger's amphibian to make the short hop to Machias. Holmes sat beside Belanger in the cockpit for the take-off. The man was like a child in a toy store. After we had climbed to 5,000 feet and were set upon our course, Holmes came back into the cabin and sat beside me.

"Occasionally I still sometimes question whether Mr. Monson is truly deeply involved with the disappearance of Nungesser and Coli," said Holmes.

I said, "But why, Holmes?"

"Monson is the most obvious suspect, Watson, because of the fact that he has been so blatantly conspicuous in his hatred of Nungesser and his extreme nationalism. And that is the problem. Is he *too* obvious a suspect?"

I was thrown off my balance at this statement. "*Too* obvious? Holmes, do you suspect a conspiracy? What would be the ultimate motive?" I paused and regarded my friend. "If there was a conspiracy, then, to me, the obvious suspect would be that Feliciano fellow. A rum-runner and known murderer, ties to organized crime. Ah, but why would gangsters have motive to see the French fail?"

Belanger called from the cockpit, "Perhaps they had a tidy wager on the outcome and wished to ensure that they won?"

"Do you really believe such a thing, Holmes?" I said.

"Do you, Watson? Consider your hypothesis thoroughly."

Yes, I thought, it did seem rather petty. But who could the other suspects be? "Would Page have motive for murder, Holmes? What about Ortieg himself, or any of the other contenders?"

"No, Page would have no motive. He is a man above reproach. So is Raymond Ortieg. Neither man would benefit from having either an American or European win. The same holds true for the other contenders. Let us not forget the number of men who have already died in the attempts and so far, no one has gained anything from their sacrifice. No, Watson, the only person who would benefit from a French failure, indeed, *any* failure would be a man in similar straits as Monson.

"Consider the facts: Monson's company is in foreclosure with no contracts and no production. Therefore, financial motive." Holmes ticked the points off on his fingers. "Monson's colleague and pilot is found dead inside a plane that had disappeared from Monson's own factory, and found near an area where Monson owns property. Monson is known to have ties to organized crime; therefore he may owe substantial sums to gangsters. Monson, Feliciano and Mrs. Woodhouse are missing. Where are they and why? *The White Bird* appears to have overflown areas where Monson has connections. Belanger mentioned to us that Monson owned some property in Passamaquoddy Bay in New Brunswick, the area that *The White Bird* would have flown close to. No, Watson, to my thinking, while obvious, Monson can be the only suspect here. No others have his distaste for Nungesser and things French; he stands to gain from an American victory. In fact, he would stand to gain even more if it were he that won. But he is missing with the rest."

Holmes shook his head slowly. "I must say, Watson, that I do not like this case, and I find myself at odds as to suspects and motive. I say we return to New York at the earliest and inform Miss Hatmaker and Mr. Nungesser that we have little to offer them."

I had never heard my friend utter such a desolate opinion in any case. For him to even suggest retiring from an investigation was completely unlike him. Has he grown weary of the effort, the hunt? Perhaps he was merely tired and wished to withdraw gracefully. Again, it was unlike him. Holmes returned to the cockpit while my mind whirled. Could the Great Detective could be wearing down?

Our stop at Machias was brief and non-productive. The witness there, Andrew Berryman, turned out to be the owner of an illegal still and a well-known vagrant. He had been arrested on the 10th in downtown Machias for public drunkenness, and began boasting about seeing a white airplane fly over his head. Holmes and I could not get anything solid from the poor man's addled brain.

As we again boarded Belanger's plane for the final trip back to New York, and I prayed for no more flights, Holmes said, "Our case just grew more interesting. Commander Belanger here has just informed me that a gangster named Feliciano was found murdered last night in a flop house outside of Mineola."

I was stunned at the news. I turned to Belanger. "How did you find out?"

Belanger smiled. "Detective Detmer of the Mineola Police and I served together in France. We have kept in touch with each other over the years, and he knows that I am assisting with the case. He called my office in Bangor to inquire about my whereabouts, knowing that I was with you and Holmes. They radioed my amphibian to inform me that one of my suspects was now deceased. I got the message while you and Holmes were interviewing Berryman."

"You suspected Feliciano?" said I. "As the primary suspect?"

"Not on this case. He was under investigation for rum-running, but now I think he was involved somehow with Monson. Want to know what else I was informed, Doctor?"

I nodded my head and observed Holmes from the corner of my eye grin.

Belanger continued, "It seems that the late Mr. Woodhouse had some property on Long Island that he kept as a 'play house', if you will. Entertained young ladies there supplied by Mr. Feliciano. Seems that Mr. Monson used the house as well, for similar assignations. The house is in Mrs. Woodhouse's name, can you believe that?"

I looked to both men and their smiles annoyed me. They were keeping information from me, I felt it. Then it suddenly dawned on me: "Monson used the 'play house' to stage his planes!"

"No, Watson, but close. Mrs. Woodhouse was observed two nights ago shopping for medical supplies in South Jamesport. Commander Belanger has summoned the New York State Police to inspect the Woodhouse property near there," Holmes said. "We are heading for Long Island right now."

We flew first to Boston for more fuel, then directly to South Jamesport, Long Island, where Belanger landed his amphibian in the bay just to the west. We sailed up and onto the beach below a small white cottage, with dark shingled roof, and sea green shutters and trim. Aside from the three police vehicles on the side of the cottage, there were two others in the driveway; one a fancy roadster convertible, the other a black Ford that had seen better days. Detective Detmer met us on the beach. The four of use made our way up to the cottage, and Holmes made a bee-line for the roadster. The front seat was covered with blood, and an 1898

Broom-handled Mauser pistol was laying on the passenger's floor. Holmes bent close to examine the weapon. "Gentlemen, I believe that this is the weapon that killed Mr. Feliciano. It has been fired recently, you can smell the gunpowder, and the magazine is empty."

Holmes stood abruptly and strode into the cottage. Belanger and I followed. The cottage was small with only a living room, small kitchen and a single bedroom. In the living room, sprawled on the single couch, was Monson. Kneeling beside him on the floor, was a weeping woman, Mrs. Woodhouse. Monson's shirt was bloodied and the man was barely alive.

Holmes stepped past the grieving woman and stooped close to Monson. The dying man opened his eyes, focused on Holmes and said, "Nungesser. Did he make it?"

Holmes spoke softly. I heard him whisper, "No." Monson began whispering something else, but I could not hear from my position just inside the door. Holmes stooped lower to hear. Then he stood. "Mr. Monson is dead," he said matter-of-factly. Mrs. Woodhouse burst into wailing sobs.

"What did he say, Holmes?" Belanger asked.

Holmes pushed past me and walked onto the tiny porch. With his back to us, Holmes said, "'Damn. At least an American did it.'"

Holmes withdrew his pipe and lit it, puffing thoughtfully. "I believe that I can assemble a scenario that has just concluded. Monson has always held a hatred of the French and of Charles Nungesser in particular. I am sure that we can extract the exact details from Mrs. Woodhouse, whom I surmise, according to her presence here and her emotional reaction to Monson's passing, was having an illicit affair with Monson. Monson, on his part, did not wish to see Nungesser and Coli win the Ortieg Prize. Why, you may ask? Because any person who won the prize would have much to celebrate: prestige, personal appearances and endorsements, even increased sales of the airplane used to make the crossing. Monson's xenophobia would not permit such to happen. His pride, his ego would insist that not just any American plane win, but it must be his, piloted by himself.

"He tried last year, as Sutton told us, and the plane crashed. When Monson heard of Nungesser's declaration, he could not abide his hated rival to succeed. Since his own plane failed, and he was facing bankruptcy and the prospect of not being able to construct a new plane in time, then he would have to eliminate his rivals, starting with Nungesser.

"His connections to Feliciano, a known rum-runner and gangster, could mean that Monson hired Feliciano's associates to sabotage Nungesser's aircraft in France. However, because Nungesser and Coli took-off from Paris, we can assume that sabotage efforts there failed. Therefore, how could Monson stop Nungesser?

"I believe by this time, Monson's paranoia and his overinflated ego combined to rob the man of a certain degree of rational thought. He would, he concluded, have to physically destroy *The White Bird* in flight. He took his only assets that could accomplish the job, his two armed patrol amphibians, and stationed them along Nungesser's projected route. It is possible, considering Feliciano's business, that rum-running boats were used along the route to radio reports of *The White Bird's* progress. Somewhere around Passamaquoddy Bay, where if you will remember, Monson owned lake-side property, he waited for the French aircraft to pass."

"But there were two planes, Holmes," said Belanger.

"Correct, Commander. Monson and Woodhouse flew in one plane and two other men flew the other. On the fateful day, both planes would have been patrolling, waiting to catch Nungesser and Coli. The French aviators would be exhausted at this point and probably not very alert. Monson or Woodhouse spotted *The White Bird*, then swooped to attack. I am not an aerial combat expert, nor am I an expert pilot, but I will assume that one has only seconds to fire at another target. The weather that day was cloudy, according to Commander Belanger, foggy, rain, quite poor visibility. I will assume Monson made a single pass at Nungesser, but wounded or killed both men. I have spoken to several experts who flew in the Great War, and they said that the first thing an unarmed pilot would do was to seek refuge in the clouds. This I am sure Nungesser and Coli did. Monson, after his first attack, had lost sight of *The White Bird*, but suddenly saw another white airplane before him and, believing it to be his hated enemy, opened fire. Woodhouse, however, probably recognized the aircraft as Monson's other amphibian.

"With *The White Bird* destroyed, in Monson's mind, Woodhouse tried to convince Monson that he had just shot down his own men. Monson, not being a man who took criticism gently, possibly driven mad by all the financial pressures upon him, then murdered Woodhouse in a rage. He landed near Lubec, hoping that the plane would either drift out to sea or sink, with Woodhouse in the cockpit. He then made his way back to Mineola and sought out Feliciano."

Belanger looked puzzled. "Then where is *The White Bird*, Holmes? And what of the other Monson plane? Nobody had reported any crashes in that area."

"There were no crashes in that area, you are correct, Commander. *The White Bird* must have turned out to sea, with one man dead or wounded or the other barely conscious. I am told that some airplanes can fly for some distance without direction from a pilot. I believe that *The White Bird* flew on, essentially unmanned, and crashed in the Gulf of Maine."

"And the other plane?" I asked.

"Commander Belanger, I am positive that if you have some men investigate the Maine lake where that one gentleman claimed to have heard a crash – Round Lake, was it? – you will find the remains of Monson's other plane and the dead crew. It is only some fifty miles from Passamaquoddy Bay. A stable aircraft, and Sutton did say that Monson's amphibian was extraordinarily stable, could fly that distance."

Detective Detmer, who had met us when we landed, interjected, "What about Feliciano, then. Who shot him? What has this to do with *The White Bird*?"

"Ah, Mr. Feliciano was merely a minor player in this drama. He took Monson in when Monson had realized that he had just murdered five men. Even a personality such as Mr. Monson would find such a thing shattering. He most likely contacted Feliciano in the hopes that the gangster could supply him with a way of leaving the area, even the country, unnoticed. But they argued. Feliciano was found in one of his own flop-houses that were used by his prostitutes. Perhaps Monson made a nuisance of himself and Feliciano was forced to intervene and eject his friend from the premises. The argument deteriorated into a mutual gunfight that you Americans seem so fond of, and both men were mortally wounded. Feliciano died before he could be helped. Monson, wounded but conscious, drove out to the only other refuge he knew, Woodhouse's 'play house', and then, as the reality of his actions entered his mind, called his mistress, Mrs. Woodhouse, for solace. She may have already been at the house awaiting him."

"Then the guy lived for a while until we got to him. Anything else, Mr. Holmes?" said Detmer. "Any thoughts as to where we can find *The White Bird*?"

Holmes spoke without hesitation. "No, Detective. I am afraid that *The White Bird* shall forever remain a ghost. Ocean currents have most likely deposited the wreckage far out to sea. The question remains: shall we make our finding public or not?"

I looked at Holmes with furrowed brow. "Surely you do not suggest that we keep this all a secret, Holmes? The world must know what happened here. The French flyers made it all the way across to America. A despicable industrialist thwarted their success. We must tell the world."

Belanger looked from Holmes to me. He had a peculiar expression, a mixture of understanding and determination. "I think I know what Mr.

Holmes will say to that, Doctor." He shuffled his feet and looked at Holmes. Holmes nodded and mouthed the words *go on*.

"Look at the celebrations in New York, Doctor," he continued. "America is ecstatic over Lindbergh's achievement. America's aeronautical industry stands at the top of the world now. We cannot cast a pail of cold water on such pride. It would be better for all concerned that the world believe that Nungesser and Coli almost succeeded but that Lindbergh did. It would be counterproductive to reveal the events of May 9th. Agreed, Mr. Holmes?"

"Yes. I concur completely, Belanger. We shall inform Miss Hatmaker and Mr. Nungesser that the disappearance of their dear Charles was due to navigational error and dismal weather. We should spare them the grisly truth, as all who were responsible are now deceased. There would be no sense in complicating their suffering."

As Holmes and I walked back to the seaplane, I contemplated the implications. History would forever consider the disappearance of Charles Nungesser and Francois Coli, intrepid and brave aviators who sought only to advance aviation, as an enduring mystery. I convinced myself to record this investigation, one that I consider to be one of the most unsatisfying cases of my association with Sherlock Holmes, and store it away in a safe place until such time as the world became ready for such. Of Holmes, I worried that he was losing his touch, his enthusiasm for the relentless pursuit of truth and justice.

We stayed in America long enough to see Charles Lindbergh return in triumph to New York City on 11 June 1927. The following day, Holmes and I had a final dinner with Detmer and Belanger to say farewell. We left for home on the 14th.

On the trip home, Holmes continued reading the accounts of Mr. Lindbergh's incredible feat. His enthusiasm for aviation was growing. On the day before we were to dock in Southampton, Holmes and I were relaxing on deck, I reading a medical journal, Holmes the newspaper. Out of the blue, my friend said, "Amazing stuff this aviation business. Now there will be people clamoring for a flight to everywhere. Know what I think I shall do, Watson?" he did not wait for my response. "I shall make a small investment in the Imperial Airlines. I think they should do rather well, don't you think?"

I did not have it in me to tell Holmes what I thought – air travel is for the birds and they are welcome to it!

Epilogue

On the 18th of August I received a telegram from Commander Belanger informing me that some wreckage from a white colored airplane was recovered two-hundred miles east of New York City. He went on to say that the remains were too badly decomposed to identify what aircraft they came from. He hinted that Holmes was right and *The White Bird* rested on the sea floor. For now, the case was closed.

At the end of August, Holmes excitedly read of the disappearance of *The St. Raphael*, a Fokker tri-motor attempting to cross the Atlantic with Princess Anne Lowenstein-Westhern (or Lady Anne Saville) aboard. He was sure that he could solve that case too.

As long as there are no more airplane flights, I shall be happy.

The Adventure of the
Avaricious Bookkeeper
by Joel and Carolyn Senter

For many years, my visits with my old friend, Sherlock Holmes, had been both infrequent and brief. During The Great War, we were completely lost to one another. I was on frequent, sometimes almost constant call as a volunteer physician to provide medical attention to our wounded returning from France. The injuries to our soldiers were so numerous and so severe that I fear I more often found myself lamenting the failures than delighting in the successes of my attempts to heal those desperately mangled bodies. I had no direct knowledge of Holmes's activities during that appalling conflict. On two occasions, I travelled down to Sussex with the intention of not only assuring myself of his safety and well-being but, perhaps to visit with him, if only briefly. On the first occasion, I found the cottage empty; there was simply no one at all in residence. Enquiries in the neighborhood raised no information as to where Holmes might be, so I returned to my place of dwelling as uninformed about Holmes as I had been before my visit. On the second occasion, I was met by Holmes's housekeeper, who greeted me most warmly. She invited me in and set before me a most welcomed and elegant tea. We chatted for, perhaps, two hours about old times interspersed with a bit of local gossip, but whenever I made an enquiry about Holmes, I was told only that, "Mr. Holmes is away just now."

The very few visits we had enjoyed, after the long awaited armistice, occurred more by happenstance than by design. Occasionally, Holmes's interests and, perhaps, some business endeavors, brought him back to London. During such times, Holmes would, occasionally, honour me with a telephone call from his lodging place suggesting that we meet. Sometimes I would join him at his hotel for a meal and perhaps a leisurely stroll through the streets of London. One of his unheralded invitations bore the welcomed suggestion that we meet at Simpson's for dinner for old time's sake. I was delighted to be able to join him there once again. It was while we were enjoying our after dinner cigars that I broached the suggestion that we might actually plan a proper meeting for some future date – a meeting of longer duration than our "ships passing in the night" encounters, and one which we could both pleasantly anticipate. I suggested that a propitious occasion might be in celebration of his 75th birthday. He agreed without hesitation, to my surprise, and suggested, again to my surprise, that he would plan to devote a fortnight, perhaps a bit longer, to our visit.

Mrs. Hudson still owns the Baker Street property, but bless her, she is no longer physically able to manage it as of old. Her niece, Agnes, now occupies Mrs. Hudson's old flat on the ground floor. Over the years, Mrs. Hudson had garnered a substantial portion of her own income from continuing to let the flats at 221 Baker Street to some parade of new tenants. I had been in contact with both Mrs. Hudson and Agnes for several weeks and, as luck would have it, the "B" flat was to be vacant for the first month of the new year. I dipped into my savings and sent payment for the entire month's rent, even though it was unlikely that we would occupy the flat for that entire time. Being able to enjoy Holmes's company in our old digs would have been worth a great deal more to me.

Holmes arrived at our old Baker Street address first. Agnes provided him with a key, and he had already made himself at home by the time I arrived. The door was unlocked and I felt perfectly comfortable in turning the knob and walking into the sitting room as I had done thousands of times before. What an incredible delight it was to find Holmes ensconced in an easy chair, his legs stretched out toward the comfortable glowing coals in the fireplace, and smoking a bowl of shag in one of his more fetid old pipes.

Ever the perpetual stoic, Holmes simply said, "Hello there, Watson, nice to see you." Then he continued to puff clouds of blue-gray smoke which formed a vaporous halo around his slightly balding head.

"Happy birthday," I greeted him, sounding much less enthusiastic than I felt.

Holmes nodded an acknowledgement of my good wishes, took an exceptionally long puff on his pipe, exhaled at length and said, "Nice of you to remember, Watson, and to arrange for us to occupy our old digs. I suppose that that required a bit of doing. This chair isn't quite as comfortable as my old one, but wrapped in our familiar surrounds, it will certainly do." He resumed his fixed gaze on the glowing coals for several minutes. Then he looked at me for the first time since I entered the room, twitched his lips into as much of a smile as Holmes could ever muster, and said, "Really, very nice to see you, old friend."

I suppose that it might appear odd that two old friends, no matter how extensive their mutual history might have been, would spend the better part of a fortnight merely enjoying each other's company. We ventured out only for constitutionals, which were brief for the rain was incessant, or for partaking of some repast. We spent a great deal of our time chatting about our memories from our old days together. Of course, we shared information and confidences about each of our mutual experiences since that "most terrible August in the history of the world." My contributions to those moments of sharing were, I fear, remarkably dull. Save for my medical endeavors during The War, my life had been filled with those humdrum events that collect from an unremarkable and routine existence. I had continued to practice medicine now and then. I attended the theater from time to time. I was an occasional spectator at sporting events (some of which involved horses,) and otherwise, I had spent my days reading, chatting with neighbors, or indulging in whatever pastime as might present itself.

Holmes, on the other hand, could keep me fascinated for hours with the tales of his various adventures. The commonly accepted view that he had retired to the South Downs was far from true. He had moved to The Downs, but he had certainly in no way retired. I could fill volumes by recounting his personal adventures accumulated during the past decade. Perhaps, indeed, one day I shall undertake doing just that. It had been quite a while since I had touched pen to paper to tell the public about the remarkable adventures of Sherlock Holmes, and I have rather missed that.

Occasionally, he would make allusion to some fragment of information which gave me a glimpse of the activities in which he had engaged during The War. I never knew whether he did this purposefully or accidentally. Some of these brief glimpses revealed to me a hint of the invaluable services which he had rendered The Crown during that disastrous conflict. I felt quite uneasy even listening to his passing comments about some of his more clandestine activities. Suffice it to say that without Holmes's efforts, The War might well have continued for many more months. I learned that, for the past few years, Holmes had spent some time in France and had actually developed additional fluency in the French language. Not surprisingly, considering his wartime activities, he had also acquired a familiarity with the German language.

Upon coming down for breakfast one morning, I found Holmes standing at the bay window silently staring down into Baker Street.

"Good morning, Holmes," I bade him. "Have you already finished breakfast?"

"Yes, some time ago," he replied.

"Would you mind if I had mine now?"

"Of course not, not at all. Take your time. I think you'll find it quite delicious," he said, but he made no move to join me at breakfast table. He just remained fixed at the window.

I uncovered my tray to find the usual fare that Agnes was so thoughtful as to provide every morning: eggs, rashers, a muffin, a pot of still-steaming tea, with small bowls of marmalade, jam, and butter. Holmes was correct, the breakfast was delicious.

Just as I had finished my last sip of tea, Holmes turned away from the window and asked me, "Watson, the rain has stopped at last. Would you fancy a stroll in the great outdoors?"

I was a bit taken aback by this suggestion. True, the rain had stopped, but I thought that the January weather would still be a bit cool for a comfortable morning's constitutional. I hesitated a few seconds before answering him.

"Do you not think it a bit chilly for such an outing?" I asked.

"No, no, old fellow. Where is that old Watson spirit? We both have top coats, hats, and warm scarves. Come along. The freshly rain-washed air will be good for us," Holmes urged as he was donning his own scarf and coat. He adjusted his hat and waited by the door for me to follow suit and join him.

Holmes was, again correct. The weather was chilly but not unpleasant, and the air had been amazingly freshened by the fortnight of rain. Even on a chilly January day, Regent's Park seemed the best place in the environs to stretch our legs after many days of near isolation in Baker Street. It took but a few minutes for us to reach the park where we both concluded that a turn around the Outer Circle would be a bit demanding for two no-longer-young fellows, so we continued to the Inner Circle. As one might expect, very few other visitors to the park were in evidence on a January morning, but a woman pushing a man in a wheelchair came toward us shortly.

"Poor devil," I whispered to Holmes, "I don't know how many of his like still suffer from injuries received in that wretched war. I couldn't count the number of mutilated young bodies I saw." Just then the couple passed us continuing their counterclockwise circumnavigation of the Circle.

"Yes, of course, we both saw our share of the tragedies of that war, but I'd say that the young man in the wheelchair was neither a victim of, nor even a witness to, those tragedies," Holmes said.

"How so, Holmes?"

"Well, his age, first of all. I would have taken him to be no more than a year or two past his twentieth birthday. It is possible that he could have served in the military but not during The War. He had his left leg extended in a very rigid position. Although I could not actually see the cast on that limb, I think it likely that he was wearing one. The woman pushing the chair is not his nurse, but I'd say, rather, she is his wife. I believe that the young man was suffering from an injured leg, possibly a broken leg, from some fairly recent accident."

"How do you know that the woman was his wife?"

"The young woman was with child. I would venture to estimate that she was in her fourth month. I would have thought that such a matter would not have escaped the notice of a medical man."

"Well," I replied, more defensively than I intended, "I am not in the habit of staring at young women's abdomens."

"But consider, this pregnant young woman is pushing a young man, of approximately her same age, in a wheelchair. Would it be likely that that young man would be anyone other than her husband?" Holmes asked.

"It could be a brother or some other relative," I conjectured.

"That is certainly possible," Holmes admitted, "but the fact that they were wearing matching wedding bands speaks more loudly of their being husband and wife, don't you think?"

"Wedding rings! That's almost beneath you, Holmes. Why, even I could have . . . ."

Holmes just glanced at me with one of his knowing glances. I let the matter drop.

We continued our stroll around the Circle until a light drizzle caused us to quicken our pace.

"It is inconceivable to me, Holmes," I said, "that neither of us thought to bring an umbrella."

Holmes said, "Yes, the casual observer might take us for tourists unaccustomed to the London weather." We both chuckled and hurried back to our old digs where it was both dry and warm.

The next morning two odd things happened. First, I came down for breakfast to find that I had preceded Holmes. Our breakfasts lay upon the table under their covers, as usual, but the second unusual matter was the fact that Agnes, our temporary landlady, was still in the room puttering around with dusting, adjusting the furniture, and such. So far during our stay, we had seldom seen her and had been only aware of her presence by the temporary incursions into our quarters required by her serving our breakfast.

"Good morning, Agnes," I greeted her, "nice to see you. I hope all is well with you this morning."

"Oh yes, Dr. Watson, I am well, as I trust are you."

"As we medical folk are accustomed to saying, 'As well as can be expected.'"

I hesitated for a moment, resisting the temptation to launch into a description of my increasing infirmities of aging, but noticed that Agnes seemed somewhat distracted and unsettled. Finally, she asked, "Is Mr. Holmes not up yet?"

377

"I presume not. He almost always precedes me to the breakfast table. In fact, it is not unusual for him to have finished his morning repast by the time I join him. If you have not heard him go out, then I presume that he is still in his chambers."

"Do you think it would be unseemly of me to ask his advice on a somewhat personal matter?" she queried.

"Oh, I think not, Agnes. I'm sure that he will be glad to help in any way he might be able."

Since there was no way of knowing how long it would be before Holmes might present himself for breakfast, Agnes politely excused herself, saying, "I'll come back for the dishes later," and returned to her own quarters.

After a few moments, I heard behind me, "Sorry, Watson, I overslept," he explained, "I can't remember when I last stayed in bed longer than I intended. I am starved. I see that breakfast is ready."

The breakfast was excellent, as usual, and we consumed it with pleasure. Actually, I would say that Holmes consumed his with gusto. I had rarely seen him with such a vigorous appetite. I had not yet finished my tea when Agnes knocked on our door. This was most unusual, for she almost never came to clear away the breakfast dishes until we both were long finished.

"May I come in now, sirs?" came the muffled voice from the other side of the door.

"By all means, Agnes, do come in," Holmes replied brightly.

The door opened quietly, almost cautiously, and Agnes poked her head tentatively through the opening.

"Come in," Holmes invited, almost cheerily, "do come in, Agnes."

I could not help being taken by what a remarkably good humour Holmes was in that morning.

"I know that you are retired, Mr. Holmes," she began, "and I hope that you won't think me rude or out of my place asking you for the favor of your advice, but it is for my sister, Susan. She and her husband, Edward Stratton, have a flat not far from here, around the corner on Marylebone. She is concerned about her husband."

Holmes and I exchanged a quick glance. I thought, and assumed that Holmes shared the same thought, that surely, this woman does not expect Sherlock Holmes to engage himself in some sort of problem involving an errant husband!

Holmes most politely said, "Yes, Agnes, please continue. What seems to be the problem?"

"Well, Mr. Holmes," she went on to explain, "Susan's husband, Edward, has been behaving strangely for the past few days. She has told me of several odd things he has been doing."

Holmes and I exchanged quick glances again.

"But two evenings ago, he did something that she is at a complete loss to account for. Edward came home at about his usual time but rushed quickly by her with scarcely a greeting and went directly to his office, a small room which he keeps in the back of the flat and uses for business purposes. Susan heard him bumping about, opening and closing drawers, and just generally shuffling around for several minutes. Then he came out and greeted Susan more appropriately, but she said it was clear that there was something on his mind that was distracting him. They had dinner together and then he went, as he did about once a week, down to the local pub for a pint with some of his friends. While he was gone, Susan did something that I fear is weighing on her conscience. She went into his office, which she seldom did except to clean, and then she did something she had never done before. She searched through his desk! There, under a liner in the bottom of the topmost drawer she found," Agnes hesitated and took a deep breath before continuing, "a one hundred pound Bank of England note! Susan, of course, said nothing to Edward about it, for she didn't want him to know that she had been intruding in his private office."

Holmes and I both continued to look at Agnes in silence, as though expecting her to continue. Then, we took a long glance at each other.

Finally, I broke the silence and asked, "Now Agnes, just where does this present a problem? I had always thought that possessing a one hundred pound bank note was something to be highly desired."

"The problem does not lie in the bank note itself, but rather, I fancy, the question of how your brother-in-law came by it." Holmes suggested. Then added the query, "What does he do for a living, Agnes?"

"He is an accountant. Well, actually a bookkeeper at the Liberty store."

"Would you have any idea how much his salary might be?"

"Susan has never shared that knowledge with me, but whatever it is, it would never be enough for Edward to accumulate one hundred pounds all at once. It would have taken him quite some time to do that!"

Holmes peaked his fingers in his inimitable fashion, furrowed his brow, but before he could say anything, Agnes added, "But that's not all of it, Mr. Holmes. Last evening he came home in the same hurried way, went to his office, shuffled about and then came out for dinner, after which he, again, hurried out to the pub, which he seldom did two nights in a row.

Susan again ventured into Edward's office, peeked into his hiding place, and found that the hundred pound note was gone. Instead there were two fifty pound notes!"

"So, she told you that the two fifty pound notes were in Edward's hiding place instead of the original one hundred pound note, not in addition to the one hundred pound note?" Holmes asked.

"Yes sir, she was quite definite about that. She said that she took the time to look around to make certain." Agnes assured.

"What does your brother-in-law look like? Can you give us a description?" Holmes asked.

"He is a quite ordinary looking chap. Three, perhaps four inches taller than me. A bit of gray hair at the temples, otherwise dark brown hair, rather slim, I'd say not much over eleven stone. I've never seen him wear anything other than a gray suit to his work. He usually wears a bowler hat and never goes out without his umbrella." Agnes described.

"I wonder if our following him would tell us anything? What time does he usually leave for work?" Holmes queried further.

"Well, this time of year he usually takes the Tube. He would need to leave home no later than a quarter past eight."

"It is not quite 7:30 yet. Watson, shall we . . . ?"

"Holmes!" I said in astonishment, "Surely you aren't thinking . . . ."

"Why not, old man, there has been no game afoot at all for us in quite a while and I thought that any game might be an interesting use of what time we still have left of our visit. Besides, we could use the exercise. Except for our stroll in the park, we've been captive to the rain. Don your warm winter wear, Watson, and we'll be off! If he is going to take the Tube, we should be able to catch him at the Marylebone entrance. Come, Watson! Need I say more?"

We bade Agnes goodbye and went down the stairs, not nearly as quickly as we once had done, but we managed to get to the street level without incident. We crossed the street and took up positions outside the Tube entrance. I suppose we gave the appearance of quite commonplace loiterers. Soon, we spotted a chap who fit the description given us by Agnes. Just as he passed, Holmes did an odd but remarkably clever thing. He turned to me and, in a voice much louder than the circumstances required said, "And then, John, you wouldn't believe what Edward told me. He said . . ." and his voice trailed off. "I just wanted to see if that fellow would respond to hearing the name 'Edward.' He did turn his head when I said 'Edward,' so I think we have our man. Let us move along for, as you can see, he did not turn into the Tube station as we had expected."

380

I recall hoping, very earnestly, that he wasn't planning to walk to work. That could have been quite a march for a couple of no-longer-young chaps such as we. Edward Stratton crossed Baker Street and turned a short block to the corner bank. There he hesitated for a few seconds and then entered. Holmes and I were not far behind him. Without hesitation, Holmes entered the bank. I followed. We could not see Edward Stratton anywhere, so Holmes approached one of the tellers.

"Pardon me," he apologized, "I just saw my friend Edward Stratton come in here, but I don't see him anywhere. Would you know him?"

"Oh, certainly sir. He is a frequent customer here."

"Would you know where he went, or, perhaps, I was mistaken, and it was not Edward that I saw at all."

"You were not mistaken, sir, Mr. Stratton did come into the bank just a few minutes ago. He went over there to speak with our Mr. Carrington in his office."

"All right, thank you very much. I'll just wait until he comes out," Holmes said and turned away as if to go. At the last moment, though, he turned back to the teller and asked, "Is Mr. Carrington an official of the bank?"

"Yes, sir, I guess you could say so. He is our chief loan officer."

At this Holmes joined me where I waited, and we left the bank together.

"Curious," he said. "Why would a fellow whom we know to have at least one hundred, perhaps even two hundred pounds, need to chat with a bank's loan officer?"

"Perhaps he was going to use his pounds to pay a loan he already had," I suggested.

Holmes only said, "Perhaps."

Just then, Edward Stratton came out of the bank. He seemed to be in something of a hurry when he crossed Baker Street and approached the Underground entrance. This time he passed into it and descended to the platform below.

Since, in anticipation of Holmes's visit, I had purchased two monthly passes for the Underground, we had no difficulty in moving along with him into the train. We took seats such that Mr. Stratton was unlikely to catch sight of us, but from which we could clearly observe him.

"I never cared for the Underground," Holmes told me. "Since we will all, eventually, be spending eternity underground, it has always been my contention that we should spend as much of our times alive in the open air."

"I understand," I agreed. "You know, I've heard that when the Underground was first opened, it was commonly called 'the suicide hole.' Times change. People need to move more rapidly today, although I'm not sure why, and the Underground provides a rapid and inexpensive mode of transportation. People have taken to it and, I suppose, would be most inconvenienced without it now."

Holmes just nodded casual agreement and sat silently for several minutes. He then said, "You know what I miss most, Watson?"

"Tell me."

"The sound of the horses' hooves on the pavement," he said. "I suppose one can still catch a hansom once in a while."

"Oh, yes, I'm sure that one can, but I haven't actually seen an old hansom for some time. Today, people seem to go where they must either in the Tube or in one of those high top motor taxicabs." I said.

"Times change and we must change with them, no matter how reluctantly," Holmes sighed, and then added, "I suppose that it is for the better, eventually."

As we approached Oxford Circus, we shifted our positions in our seats in preparation for standing up and exiting the car. We had anticipated that Mr. Stratton would exit the train at Oxford Circus, since that was the station nearest to his workplace. Much to our surprise, Edward Stratton made no move to arise, but continued to peruse his newspaper. Holmes and I looked at each other quizzically.

The train was slowing for its stop at Charing Cross Station before Edward Stratton showed any signs of removing himself from his seat. Again, Holmes and I exchanged quizzical glances and awaited for Stratton to rise and prepare to exit the train before we moved. It was still very easy to keep him in view as we continued our tracking of Mr. Stratton to the surface. His route continued along the Strand for a few hundred yards. We were able to keep up with him. I was a bit out of breath when Edward Stratton finally turned into a small street, the name of which I didn't see. Just a few yards into this street, we saw a small cluster of men loitering around in front of what might have been an old residence, or a shop which now seemed abandoned. Stratton hailed someone in the cluster of men and he and perhaps six or so others gathered aside and engaged in some energetic conversation, while occasionally casting glances toward the building in front of which they were assembled. We kept a discrete distance, yet still close enough that we could easily continue to view the men.

Shortly, some of them started moving toward the building. We could see that they were, one at a time, approaching the door where each hesitated for a few seconds, after which the door opened briefly admitting one man. This procedure was repeated until only a dozen or so remained in the queue outside. Holmes abruptly got up from his seat on the bench beside me.

"Where are you going?" I asked.

Holmes answered with a single word, "Inside," and before I could catch his arm and discourage him from this rash action, he was on his way to mix with the men in the queue.

It was but a very short time before Holmes returned. "Problem?" I asked.

"Well, a pair of eyes appeared through a slit in the door and a most unwelcoming and gruff voice demanded 'password,'" he explained. "I had no password so I said 'Madagascar,' which was simply the first word that occurred to me."

"What happened?"

"The door on the peephole slammed shut. Listen, Watson, there are still some chaps straggling in, do you think you could step over there, loiter about and see if you can overhear whatever these fellows might be using for a password?"

"If you wish. I can but try."

I really had no faith in this sort of slipshod eavesdropping, but as a few stragglers hurried toward the problematic door, I strolled over and joined them, taking care to be last in the queue. As each man approached the door, the little trapdoor opened and someone inside snarled something after which I heard some muttered word. I listened to each and it was only on the fourth occurrence that I heard anything that sounded like a real word. I simply walked away, with the fellow inside the door probably being unaware that I was ever in the queue, and returned to Holmes with what information I had gleaned, such as it was.

"I really couldn't hear very well, but from what I could piece together from listening to four different chaps gaining entry, it sounded to me to be something like, '*hostina*.'"

"*Hostina*?" Holmes asked. "What an odd password."

"Do you know what it means?"

"No idea."

"Do you think it is an English word?" I asked.

Holmes's only response was, "Hmmmm!"

We continued to sit on our bench and, as far as I could tell, do nothing. Eventually, the occupants of the old building started streaming out onto the street. Holmes said, "Here come the fellows back. Let us watch and see what we can learn."

I watched. I saw Edward Stratton come out with a group of five or six other men with whom he seemed to be talking in a most animated

383

fashion. Other than that, I only saw some men dissolving from a larger group and going their various ways.

"What did you see?" Holmes asked me.

"Well, I saw Edward Stratton chatting with some chaps, and some other chaps milling around and, eventually, going their separate ways."

"We shall return here tomorrow and continue our observation," Holmes advised.

"How do you know that they will be here tomorrow?" I asked.

"The energy and activity level today did not bespeak of men who had concluded business and received a closure to whatever enterprise they might have been pursuing, but rather, of men still engaged and impatient to get on with it," Holmes explained.

"I see," was the best response I could muster.

"Besides," Holmes continued, "I overheard one fellow say to another, after bidding him farewell, 'See you back here tomorrow, Gus.'"

"I see."

What I really did see was another instance in which one of Sherlock Holmes's deductions was not quite as mysterious as it might have appeared. As we rose from our bench, I saw Holmes's brow furrow and he became pensive and silent.

We passed the journey back to Baker Street in almost total silence. Holmes sat with furrowed brow, staring at the floor of the car and only occasionally muttering something unintelligible. Once or twice I could make out a whispered, "You could be right." From time to time Holmes shifted his weight in his seat in a nervous and agitated way. He kept looking out of the car's window, leaning forward as though he were trying to push the car ahead with his own weight. When I asked him if there might be something wrong, he simply shook his head and returned to whatever deep thoughts he was thinking.

When we arrived at the station, Holmes virtually sprang from his seat and hurried out of the car without as much as a glance toward me. He almost dashed up to the surface. I wasn't able to keep up with him, and he reached our flat well ahead of me. When I arrived, he was already engaged in a brisk telephone conversation. I heard him say, ". . . yes, that's right. I think it should be on the shelf. Yes, it is one of the scrapbooks. Good, thank you. Can you find the 'L' volume? Yes, I know, but not so large as the 'M's,' as you can see. Sorry, I know it is a great imposition, but it is important. Thank you. Now, if you would, just browse through some pages from the beginning and read to me the first few lines of each page."

From there on, his side of the conversation consisted of grunts, a few rather irritated "no, no," a number of "yes, go on," then, "Right!

Right! Now, if you would read that entire page to me," followed by a lengthy silence during which Holmes jotted a few notes on a scrap of paper which he had rescued from his pocket. Once he said, "Would you spell that please?" At that, he jotted another line on his paper scrap.

When the telephone conversation ended, Holmes's demeanor underwent a complete change. He was smiling, as much as Holmes ever smiled, and he was even humming to himself quietly.

"What was the telephone conversation about?" I asked.

"Oh, nothing, nothing. It is an inconvenience not to have one's reference books at hand, so I imposed on that sweet lady who keeps my cottage in order, to gather some information for me. By the by, she asked me to give you her best regards."

"How lovely. I appreciate her remembrance to me. Did she find what you wanted?"

"Oh, yes, quite admirably, although I can't say that she did it with enthusiasm."

"Can't blame her," I said thinking of how daunting a task it must have been for her to wade through, and decipher, Holmes's scribblings, "I heard you mention 'scrapbook.' Have you continued to keep your formidable scrapbooks up to date all these years?"

"Well, 'up to date' would not be fully accurate, but I do record new material very frequently even now. Years ago, it became a habit, perhaps even a compulsion, of mine. I still find it interesting and it fills my time," he explained, then added, "We must arise and leave early tomorrow. I know that those whom we wish to observe will be assembling tomorrow, but I do not know at what hour they will do so. We will need to make every effort to be in place when the action begins. I am a bit hungry. Would you care to stroll down to the pub for a bite and, perhaps, a glass of wine?"

It was scarcely past dawn the next morning when Holmes shook me awake. He was, of course, dressed and ready to go. I shaved and dressed as quickly as I could. My breakfast consisted of a cup of tea, which Holmes had somehow persuaded Agnes to provide at that early hour. I managed to sip it while I was shaving.

As we were leaving the flat, Holmes took a few minutes to stuff various items from valise to pocket. That seemed to me to be a waste of time, for I couldn't imagine what he might need on that day. When I asked him about it, he merely said, "Better to have and not need than to need and not have. Don't forget your coat and hat. It is still quite chilly."

In deference to Holmes's distaste of the Underground, we hailed a high top taxicab, which we were fortunate to have been able to do at that hour of the morning. We instructed the driver to take us to Charing

Cross. We could walk to our destination from there. During the trip, Holmes occasionally commented about various landmarks that had not changed over the years, those that had changed, and particularly about those that were no longer there at all. Once he leaned over to speak directly into my ear and said, "Know what I miss most, Watson?"

"I think so, you mentioned it yesterday. The sound of the horses' hooves against the pavement."

A whisper of a smile crossed Holmes's lips. He settled back in his seat, closed his eyes and was silent for the remainder of the trip.

When we arrived, ready to set up our observation post, it became apparent that our mere presence in that neighborhood at that hour made us conspicuous, so we spent two hours just strolling here and there, down to the River, back across from the Underground station, around the monuments, and wherever we felt we could spend time but never be away from our proposed point of observation for more than fifteen minutes. We never knew when the action might begin, and we had no intention of missing it.

By midmorning, there seemed to be enough people in evidence so that two old fellows sitting on a bench trying to warm themselves in the winter sun would not have seemed odd to the casual observer. At last, Holmes thought it all right for us to take our seat, so we did so. I must say that it was a most welcomed event for me. I had found the morning's walks to be a bit tiring. It turned out to be a long morning indeed, for it was about half past noon before anyone began to assemble at the mysterious door. Edward Stratton and some of his friends arrived early. Other men began to assemble; yet it was more than half an hour before their numbers began to approach the size of the group we had observed on the previous day.

It was shortly after one o'clock in the afternoon when the men started to move toward the door through which they had passed the previous day. One at a time they each approached the door, hesitated as they were scrutinized, presented the identifying password, and, ultimately disappeared through the doorway.

Holmes leaned over to me and said, "Go."

I looked at him with surprise and asked, "Go where?"

He directed, "Down there. Go with those fellows. We need to see what is afoot in that building and I could be easily recognized as the bloke who tried to use 'Madagascar' as the password. You'll have to go. If anyone in there has seen you at all, it would have been only briefly. Now, go! Use the password you learned yesterday and hope that they haven't changed it. This is important. Go!"

I rose with the utmost reluctance. "Why am I doing this?" I asked myself. "Because Holmes said it was important," I answered myself. I started to cross the grassy ground between our observation post and the building, then, quickly turned back as it hit me that I had forgotten the password!

"Holmes," I said, "I've forgotten the password."

Holmes smiled an indulgent smile, shook his head disapprovingly and reminded me, "'*Hostina*.' You are the one that heard it. Go!"

I glanced back but once on my short sally across the grassy area. Holmes had arisen and was walking back toward the street. I certainly hoped that he wasn't going to abandon me to whatever this mission might turn out to be.

When I arrived, the queue had dwindled to about six men. I took my place at the end of the line and waited until it was my turn to approach the door. The little trapdoor opened and a gruff voice demanded, "Password."

I cleared my throat and, with as much steadiness as I could muster, pronounced, "*Hostina*."

There was a moment's hesitation, which concerned me. Had I been detected? The little peephole closed and the door opened.

I entered to see a medium sized room fitted with long, wooden benches, upon which perhaps twenty-five men sat, mostly in small groups. It was easy to identify Edward Stratton, and those I supposed to be his friends, seated on the second bench removed from what appeared to be a low wooden stage at the front of the room. I took a seat beside the Edward Stratton group, hoping to be taken as one of their number. Any attention I drew was casual and fleeting. Just as I was seating myself, I heard the door open and close one more time. I glanced around, but the room was gloomy, and I could discern but a vague human form.

The attention of the group was fully focused on something positioned on the stage. It was, perhaps, three to three-and-a-half feet tall, and about that equal in the other dimensions, and covered with some sort of dingy cloth. There was one bulky fellow standing alongside who seemed to be guarding the object. I sat in anticipation, but only heard the quiet buzzing of conversation which is always associated with a collection of people who are idly waiting together. There was a slight movement behind a curtain which was hung across the back of the stage. The conversational buzzing quieted.

A man of medium height came from behind the curtain, and the audience's buzzing silenced completely. If this man had ever entered one of my consulting rooms, I would have been immediately concerned for his health. He was exceedingly thin, and his skin had an unhealthy gray pallor about it. He moved with great effort, as though in constant pain. He drew himself to the center of the stage, put his hand on the concealed object, and faced his small audience. He started to speak haltingly, in a weak but audible voice with the trace of a foreign, as it turned out, Germanic, accent.

He began, "Most of you know me, for we have met in this place previously. I do see some new faces in the audience, though. Please know that you are most welcome here. For the benefit of the newcomers, I am Professor Werner Leitz, and I have spent most of my life in Vienna at the University. I am a physical scientist, both by persuasion and education, and I have devoted my life to the creation of the machine you see before you. The Provider."

At this point he removed the cover from the hidden object on stage, and as he did, an audible gasp arose from the audience, and a few of the men actually rose to their feet. Removal of the cover revealed, atop a table, a device not unlike the mangles often attached to those new mechanical clothes washing machines. This device, however, was quite a bit larger, and was contained in a polished wooden box. It consisted of two large rollers lying horizontally, one above the other, and in contact with one another. The box within which the rollers were housed had affixed unto it coils of wire and various small metal boxes with some sort of electrical attachments. I could see, in the rear of the apparatus, a cranking device.

Professor Leitz continued, "Most of you have already seen at least one demonstration of the most desirable products which The Provider can produce; some of you have seen more than one. However, for newcomers, I will consent to demonstrate just one more time."

With this, he reached behind the curtain which draped over the back of the stage and brought out a small box. He withdrew a small paper rectangle, raised it and turned it over; it was blank on both sides. He approached the machine, adjusted a few dials, activated a switch, and the device responded with a buzzing sound. The Professor very carefully placed the paper rectangle between the rollers and, very slowly, started to turn the cranking mechanism. In response to the cranking, the paper rectangle moved forward as it was squeezed between the rollers. Immediately one could see the paper start to emerge from the other side of the rollers. Perhaps five minutes passed as the paper slid between the rollers and emerged on the other side. As soon as the transfer was completed, the Professor tugged the remaining fraction of the paper, still wedged between the rollers, loose and held the paper up for the audience to see. It now had printing on it.

The Professor waved the paper about freely and asked if anyone in the audience would care to examine it. Among a few others, I raised my hand. An assistant took the paper from the Professor and chose me, among the others wishing to have a close look, to examine it first. I was truly amazed! In retrospect, as I am writing this account, I am now quite embarrassed by that amazement, but at the time the effect was most dramatic. I held in my hand a one hundred pound Bank of England note. I turned it over and examined it from all angles; it appeared to be quite genuine. It would have been ideal to have been able to compare this note with one I knew to be genuine, but alas, I didn't own a one hundred pound note. The assistant took the note from me and gave it to one of the other fellows who had shown interest in examining the paper. One burly chap sitting in the row in front of me took a long look at it and said, "So, what good is a counterfeit bank note? A fellow is sure to get caught trying to pass bad bills."

The Professor seemed to be offended by this challenge and responded with a tinge of anger in his voice. "Sir," he protested, "I am insulted to know that you think that I, Professor Werner Leitz, would present you, or anyone, with a machine that produces counterfeit currency. The note you hold in your hand is counterfeit only in the respect that it was not produced and circulated by The Bank of England. In all other respects, it is identical to those bank issued notes." The Professor seemed to get control of his indignation and continued, "several of you have previously been given samples of The Provider's products to take with you and test as you might have wished." Three members of the audience indicated that they had received such samples.

"And what did you do with your samples?" the Professor asked.

"I took mine to my bank and asked it to be changed into two fifty pound notes. My bank did so without the slightest question," Edward Stratton testified.

"Ah ha," I thought to myself, "that explains the change of bank notes in Stratton's desk."

Another fellow reported, "I took mine to a bank and asked them, directly, to examine it to determine if it was either counterfeit or genuine. Several people in the bank occupied themselves for a good fifteen minutes in examining the note, and reported to me that it was unquestionably genuine. They also asked me why I might question that the note was real. I told them that I had found the note on the street and was certain that I couldn't have been so lucky as to find a real hundred pounds."

A chuckle passed through the room.

The Professor faced his accuser in the audience and raised his eyebrows in a quizzical fashion, "Well," said the skeptical fellow from the audience, "how do I know that you didn't pay these fellows to say what they did?"

There was a mutter of protest from the audience.

"I can think of no way to prove to you that I have done no such thing, I can only offer the solemn word of these good men."

The men who had received the samples nodded affirmation and grumbled a bit at having their honour challenged. Edward Stratton said, with an undisguised note of annoyance, "Please, Professor, can we get on with it?"

"All right, we shall begin with the auction," the Professor announced.

"Just a minute. If you have a money printing machine, why would you ever sell it?"

I had to admit that that question had most certainly crossed my mind, too.

The Professor sighed a sigh of great weariness, "I have answered that question several times before in these meetings. I say again, reluctantly, for I don't like to share my problems in public. My doctors have told me that I have but a few weeks to live. The Provider has served me well, and I have used it judiciously only for my true needs. I have no heirs. What will happen to The Provider when I die? God only knows what hands it might fall into and what economic destruction could arise from its misuse. I have given thought to destroying it, but could never bring myself actually to do so. It is my life's work. I wanted The Provider to pass on to someone who would truly value it, and I could think of no better way to judge a person's value for the machine than to ask that the next owner make a personal commitment, a personal sacrifice, a token of their appreciation for my life's work, in the form of their hard earned cash. I never intended to keep the receipts from this auction. I shall donate all of it to charity. In a few weeks, money will be completely useless to me. Some of you already know that there is an additional requirement for the new owner. He must sign a sacred and legal oath that he will never abuse the use of The Provider. It can assure its owner of a very comfortable income for life, but if greed and avarice should rear their heads, great grief can descend on the owner and his loved ones."

"All right, Professor, can we get on with it now?" Edward Stratton had jumped to his feet in anger.

"Let's get right down to the business at hand, Professor," Stratton continued. "Me and my friends have begged and borrowed every cent we can and we'll go together and just bid, right now, twenty-nine thousand pounds." Stratton turned to the audience and continued, "That's our bid. If anybody else here wishes to top it, go ahead, and me and my chums will just put our money back in our pockets and go home, and God bless you!"

A groan of disappointment arose from the audience.

Stratton waited, tensely, but there was no challenge to his bid.

The Professor shook his head disapprovingly and warned, "Very well, but I must say that I have always discouraged joint ownership of any financial endeavor. Sharing ownership of The Provider will lead to conflict and strife, and will certainly destroy your friendship and, perhaps your lives. Would you care to reconsider?"

"No!" said Stratton almost shouting it, "we can handle all that!"

"Very well, if you insist," the Professor acquiesced. He surveyed the audience and asked, "Do we have bids higher than twenty-nine thousand pounds?"

There was silence for a moment, then the Professor continued, "Going once for twenty-nine thousand pounds."

Silence.

"Going twice for twenty-nine thousand pounds."

Silence.

"And going . . . ." the Professor began.

Suddenly, I heard someone arise behind me so abruptly that the bench was knocked over with a loud clatter.

"Sir, do you wish to increase the bid?" the Professor asked.

"No, sir, I do not! I wish to see to it that you are arrested and sent to prison. You are no Professor Leitz or any other kind of professor. You are Viktor Lustig, international swindler, and your Provider is a fraud!"

"Sir!" the Professor shouted indignantly.

There was the sound of a police whistle and I turned just in time to see Sherlock Holmes tearing off the white wig and false beard that had gained him admittance to the auction. There was a great smashing noise at the door and a squad of constables came rushing into the room. The man who introduced himself as The Professor bounded from the stage, with remarkable agility for a sick man near death, and disappeared behind the curtain with constables in quick pursuit. Other constables surrounded The Provider. The members of the audience stood in silent shock, shifting their gazes from the stage to each other and back again.

Holmes, now free of his disguise, slapped me on the back and said, "Good show, Watson! You will make an excellent witness for the prosecution."

391

Since we were in the near neighborhood, we thought that dinner at Simpson's might be pleasant. It was only after we had finished an unusually palatable and filling meal that Holmes seemed in the mood to discuss the Edward Stratton matter. Even though I had satisfied myself that I understood the basic workings of the money printing machine, I enjoyed listening to Holmes's explanation of the details, which he began just as we lit our after dinner pipes.

"You see, Watson," he began, "the rollers between which Lustig placed the blank piece of paper weren't actually rollers, in the usual sense. The cylinders concealed a conveyor belt made of some pliable cloth material. Before presenting any demonstration of the machine, Lustig loaded onto the belt some number of real bank notes. These were, then, rolled up out of sight, inside the belt. Now, when the machine was demonstrated to a potential customer, Lustig placed a blank rectangle of paper, with the same dimensions as the bank note, such that when the rollers were rotated, the paper was drawn into and concealed within the cloth belt while, at the same time, one of the actual bank notes previously loaded into the belt was dispensed on the other side of the rollers. When effected as expertly as Lustig could do it, it gave the perfect illusion that the blank piece of paper was being printed with the likeness of the bank note. For the gullible and greedy, this machine gave the promise of endless riches. What would a few thousand pounds be in exchange for a lifetime with a machine offering an endless source of perfect banknotes? A very enticing prospect, I'd say."

"What was the first thing that led you to think that something nefarious was afoot?" I asked.

Holmes puffed his pipe thoughtfully, "Well, old fellow, in the beginning, I honestly thought that the matter was nothing more than another errant husband off on a tryst. The first matter that caused me to wrinkle my brow was the report of Stratton's apparently having exchanged his one hundred pound for two fifty pound notes. I had surmised, at the time, that Stratton's hundred pound note was the fruit of some ill-got gain. One can see why he might want to exchange the hundred pound note for notes of smaller denomination. One could not expect to walk into the local tobacconist's shop, order an ounce of shag, and present a one hundred pound note in payment without raising a few eyebrows. But, if that had been his motivation, he would have wanted to acquire notes, perhaps even coins, of denominations commonly exchanged in every day commerce. Why two fifty pound notes? This was, indeed, puzzling for me. Of course, as you eventually found out, all he wanted to do was to see if the bank would accept, as genuine, a note printed by The Provider. The bank did accept it, for it was genuine."

Holmes puffed again, then continued, "Then it was curious that a man in possession of a hundred pounds, not an inconsiderable amount, would be seeking the services of a loan officer at a bank. He might have been repaying a loan, but he would probably have just done that at a teller's window, rather than seeking audience with a loan official. He needed more money. My thought was immediately, for what? Hence, our pursuit of him to the mysterious building near the river."

"But, something must have alerted you to some criminal activity going on in that building, else you would not have arranged for the police to arrive in such a timely manner." It was both a surmise on my part and a request for information.

"Actually, Watson, you gave me the first clue," Holmes said.

"I?" I was astounded. I had done nothing.

"It was the password." Holmes said.

"The password? What was it? Oh, yes, '*hostina*,'" I recalled.

"You know, we did puzzle ourselves over that word and, you might recall, you asked if it were an English word. That set my brain awhirl. I couldn't bring to mind any such English word, so I began to sort through my knowledge of foreign words that might sound like '*hostina*.' Lustig was born in Hostinne, Austria. 'Hostina,' spoken by an Englishman, can certainly pass for the German '*Hostinne*.' Lustig had used the name of the town of his birth as the password. Then, you may recall, I telephoned my housekeeper at my cottage and asked her to look in my scrapbook for information on Viktor Lustig. A few years ago, I had recorded something of his history of deceit and deception and committed those notes to the pages of my scrap-book."

"Holmes, how could you possibly know that Viktor Lustig was born in Hostinne, Austria?" I asked with a scarcely concealed note of incredulity in my tone.

"I was in Paris in 1925."

"So?"

"In Paris in 1925, Viktor Lustig was known as 'the man who sold the Eiffel Tower'."

"What?"

"I thought that you might have heard of that escapade," Holmes said. "There was some notoriety associated with it. It seems that some officials in Paris had been bemoaning the cost of upkeep of the Tower, you know, maintenance, removing rust, painting, and so forth. That concern was noted in the press. Well, Lustig, ever the one to seize opportunity, through the use of counterfeit and forged documents, was able to pass himself off as an official of the city government in charge of demolishing the Tower. He held what appeared to have been an official meeting with various scrap dealers in the city. He told them that the Tower was to be demolished, and that the resulting huge residue of metal would be sold to the highest bidder. The whole issue was, of course, an absolute fraud, but he received bids on the scrap and absconded with the money before the scrap dealer found out that the Tower wasn't going to be demolished at all. Someplace in my reading of the records of this event, I just encountered the fact that Lustig was born in Hostinne, Austria, and that just stuck in my mind, as such things sometimes do. We had, here, a series of fortunate vicissitudes which led to saving Edward Stratton and his friends from disaster and," Holmes added with a chuckle, "actually, he is the better for all of it, for he will get to keep the hundred pounds which Lustig gave him as bait for his nefarious swindle."

Holmes stopped to recharge his pipe. He looked at me and said, "Watson, old friend, I think I shall return to Sussex tomorrow. I grow concerned about the well-being of my bees. I don't like to leave them for so long. You and I have had a marvelous visit with something of an exciting end to it."

"I will regret seeing you go, Holmes," I said, "but I certainly understand."

We took a taxicab back to Baker Street. Agnes had retired by the time Holmes and I returned, but I left a note, briefly explaining how all had been favorably resolved, and telling her that we would be vacating the flat next morning.

I had not asked for anything special, but the very grateful Agnes had outdone herself for our goodbye breakfast. We had our usual rashers and eggs, coffee and tea, but on this date she added kippers, and some excellent fresh-baked scones, along with ample servings of butter and marmalade. We enjoyed the meal, mostly in silence, save for a few comments about the excellence of the food. I noticed Holmes's eyes wandering around the room and hesitating here and there as, I suppose, he reflected, as I did, on the memories of all the interesting people who had crossed our threshold over the years, and all the fascinating adventures they had brought to us. We were both absorbed in our private reveries when Holmes finally rose from the table and said, "It is time to go now, Watson. I have a train to catch."

I arose, reluctantly, fetched his hat and coat. He had already packed his few belongings in a valise, so as soon as he donned his coat, and I mine, we were through the door and down the stairs. I stopped by Agnes's flat to deliver the key and to tell her that Holmes and I would be going now, and that I would send for my things later. Her eyes glistened with tears, as I admit, did my own, as we said goodbye.

By the time I joined Holmes at the curbside, his taxicab had already arrived. We shook hands with both of us prolonging our grasps longer than necessary.

"Holmes, I hope you won't mind if I don't accompany you to the station. To tell you the truth, I am a bit washed out and not really feeling quite as chipper as I'd like. I guess that with all the excitement . . . ."

"Certainly, old friend," he said, "neither of us is as young as we once were. Go home and take a good rest. I can certainly find my way to the station after all these years. I have to admit that goodbyes are not my *forte*. I never know quite what to say. I think, though, that 'farewell' might be just the right thing."

"Yes, knowing just what to say is never easy for me, either, but I've heard the Yanks use an expression that I think most suitable, 'I'll be seeing you.'" I said.

He smiled and nodded agreement.

"Perhaps next year?" I offered.

"Perhaps," he agreed. One final handshake and he was away in his taxi.

I hailed my own taxi. Holmes's voice and the word "perhaps" continued to linger in my mind all the way home.

About the Contributors

The following authors appear in this volume
The MX Book of New Sherlock Holmes Stories
Part III – 1896-1929

Mark Alberstat, BSI, has been a Sherlockian based in Nova Scotia since his early teens, when he began reading the stories from his father's two-volume Doubleday edition. When he discovered the wider world of Sherlock Holmes, he was fortunate enough to become a regular correspondent with American John Bennett Shaw, who encouraged Mark to start a local club, which he did while still in high school. That club, *The Spence Munros*, continues to meet and is the Sherlockian achievement of which Mark is most proud. In addition, Mark, and his wife, JoAnn, edit *Canadian Holmes*, the quarterly journal published by *The Bootmakers of Toronto*. At the January 2014 Baker Street Irregulars dinner, Mark was given the investiture name of *Halifax*.

Peter K. Andersson is a Swedish historian specialising in urban culture in the late nineteenth century. He has previously published a collection of Sherlock Holmes stories, *The Cotswolds Werewolf and Other Stories of Sherlock Holmes*.

Claire Bartlett is a writer and journalist who has worked extensively in comics and magazines. With her regular writing partner, Iain McLaughlin, she has worked on several radio and audio series, including *Doctor Who* and *UNIT* for Big Finish Productions and Imagination Theater's horror anthology series, and *Kerides the Thinker*, which she co-created and co-writes with McLaughlin. They have also written novels for Big Finish Productions, Telos Publishing, and Thebes Publishing. She is currently working on a non-fiction book for publication in 2015. Claire lives in Dundee, Scotland.

Bob Byrne was a columnist for *Sherlock Magazine* and has contributed to *Sherlock Holmes Mystery Magazine* and the Sherlock Holmes short story collection *Curious Incidents*. He publishes two free online newsletters: *Baker Street Essays* and *The Solar Pons Gazette*, both of which can be found at *www.SolarPons.com*, the only website dedicated to August Derleth's successor to the great detective. Bob's column, *The Public Life of Sherlock Holmes*, appears every Monday morning at *www.BlackGate.com* and explores Holmes, hard boiled, and other mystery matters, and whatever other topics come to mind by the deadline. His mystery-themed blog is *Almost Holmes*.

Leslie F.E. Coombs is a true polymath whose interests include the writings and work of Conan Doyle, and he is a Holmes devotee. He has a keen interest in the social and technical history of Victorian Britain, and has extensive knowledge of military weaponry and ergonomics, and of naval, military, aviation and transport technologies. In addition to his writing of books and articles for magazines, he has written extensively on aviation and steam locomotion, and he is an editor and publisher's reader. Leslie Coombs's fictional writing has already produced two collections of Holmes short stories, and "The Royal Arsenal Affair" is one of a number of short stories which will appear in his third collection, to be published shortly.

David Stuart Davies BSI is a long time Sherlockian. He is a member of *Sherlock Holmes Society of London* and an invested *Baker Street Irregular*. He is a writer and editor and author of six Sherlock Holmes novels – the latest being *Sherlock Holmes: The Devil's Promise* (Titan), and two books on the films of the Great Detective. He has also penned two plays about Holmes and *Bending the Willow*, a volume about Jeremy Brett playing Sherlock. David is a member of the national committee of the *Crime Writer's Association* and edits their monthly magazine, *Red Herrings*. He has edited various collections of mystery & supernatural fiction and is the author of two crime series: one set in the Second World War featuring the detective Johnny One Eye, and another based in Yorkshire in the 1980's with DI Paul Snow. The latest novel in this series is *Innocent Blood* (Mystery Press).

C. Edward "Chuck" Davis was born and raised in New Jersey, and has lived in Colorado since 1993. He worked for over forty years as a draftsman and technical illustrator for AT&T, Sikorsky Aircraft, Exxon Engineering and Research, and Lockheed-Martin/Federal Aviation Administration. Additionally, he provided research, editing, illustrations, and technical advisory services for a number of publications, and is currently working on several projects, including *The Lunarnauts: The Rescue of Professor Cavor* (A sequel to the 1901 H. G. Wells novel *The First Men in the Moon*), *The Years of Infamy: The Japanese Invasion of Hawaii*, and *The Lion of the Sea (Il Leone di Mare)*, a historical fictional novel based upon the experiences of his late father-in-law who served in the Italian Navy during World War II.

Stuart Douglas runs Obverse Books *www.obversebooks.co.uk*, a small genre publisher. He has written short stories for many imprints, and his debut novel, *Sherlock Holmes: The Albino's Treasure* has just been released by Titan Books.

Sir Arthur Conan Doyle (1859-1930) *Holmes Chronicler Emeritus*. If not for him, this anthology would not exist. Author, physician, patriot, sportsman, spiritualist, husband and father, and advocate for the oppressed. He is remembered and honored for the purposes of this collection by being the man who introduced Sherlock Holmes to the world. Through fifty-six Holmes short stories, four novels, and additional Apocryphal entries, Doyle revolutionized mystery stories and also greatly influenced and improved police forensic methods and techniques for the betterment of all. *Steel True Blade Straight*

Séamas Duffy lives and works in Glasgow. His areas of interest are crime fiction, historical fiction, social history, and London writing. He has contributed articles to the London Fictions website and to the *Baker Street Journal*, and wrote the Foreword for *The Aggravations of Minnie Ashe* by Cyril Kersh, published by Valancourt Books in January 2014. His first collection *Sherlock Holmes In Paris* was published Black Coat Press in February 2013, and in May 2015 *Sherlock Holmes and The Four Corners of Hell* was published by Robert Hale of London. A third novel *The Tenants of Cinnamon Street* will be published in autumn 2015. This is historical crime fiction set in 1811, centred on Aaron Graham – a real Bow Street Magistrate – who investigated the Ratcliff Highway Murders. Séamas Duffy is also a musician and composer with an interest in Irish Language and History, and has produced *Tairngreacht Na nDraoideann* ("A Druid's Prophecy") in Irish and *Ó Ghartan Go Ghlaschú: Odaisé Colm Cille* ("From Gartan to Glasgow: Odyssey of Colm Cille") in Irish and Scottish Gaelic – both suites of Celtic music and song celebrating aspects of early Celtic culture, the latter emphasising the shared cultural heritage of Scottish and Irish Gaels.

Matthew J. Elliott is the author of *Lost in Time and Space: An Unofficial Guide to the Uncharted Journeys of Doctor Who*, *Sherlock Holmes on the Air* (2012), *Sherlock Holmes in Pursuit* (2013), *The Immortals: An Unauthorized Guide to* Sherlock *and* Elementary (2013), and *The Throne Eternal* (2014). His articles, fiction and reviews have appeared in the magazines *Scarlet Street*, *Total DVD*, *SHERLOCK*, and *Sherlock Holmes Mystery Magazine*, and the collections *The Game's Afoot*, *Curious Incidents 2*, *Gaslight Grimoire*, and *The Mammoth Book of Best British Crime 8*. He has scripted over 260 radio plays, including episodes of *The Further Adventures of Sherlock Holmes*, *The Classic Adventures of Sherlock Holmes*, *Doctor Who*, *The Twilight Zone*, *The New Adventures of Mickey Spillane's Mike Hammer*, *Fangoria's Dreadtime Stories*, and award-winning adaptations of *The Hound of the Baskervilles* and *The War of the Worlds*. Matthew is a writer and performer on *RiffTrax.com*, the online comedy experience from the creators of cult sci-fi TV series *Mystery Science Theater 3000* (*MST3K* to the initiated). He's also written a few comic books.

Steve Emecz's main field is technology, in which he has been working for about twenty years. Following multiple senior roles at Xerox, where he grew their European eCommerce from $6m to $200m, Steve joined platform provider Venda, and moved across to Powa Technologies in 2010. Steve is a regular trade show speaker on the subject of mobile commerce, and his time at Powa has taken him to more than forty countries – so he's no stranger to planes and airports. He wrote two novels (one bestseller) in the 1990's and a screenplay in 2001. Shortly after he set up MX Publishing, specialising in NLP books. In 2008, MX published its first Sherlock Holmes book, and MX has gone on to become the largest specialist Holmes publisher in the world, with around one hundred authors and over two hundred books. Profits from MX go towards his second passion – a children's rescue project in Nairobi, Kenya, where he and his wife, Sharon, spend every Christmas at the rescue centre in Kasarani. In 2014, they wrote a short book about the project, *The Happy Life Story*.

James R. "Jim" French became a morning DJ on KIRO (AM) in Seattle in 1959. He later founded *Imagination Theatre*, a syndicated program that is now broadcast on over 120 stations in the U.S. and Canada, and also heard on the XM Satellite Radio system all over North America. Actors in French's dramas have included John Patrick Lowrie, Larry Albert, Patty Duke, Russell Johnson, Tom Smothers, Keenan Wynn, Roddy MacDowall, Ruta Lee, John Astin, Cynthia Lauren Tewes, and Richard Sanders. Mr. French states, "To me, the characters of Sherlock Holmes and Doctor Watson always seemed to be figures Doyle created as a challenge to lesser writers. He gave us two interesting characters – different from each other in their histories, talents and experience but complimentary as a team – who have been applied to a variety of situations and plots far beyond the times and places in the Canon. In the hands of different writers, Holmes and Watson have lent their identities to different times, ages, and even genders. But I wanted to break no new ground. I feel Sir Arthur provided us with enough references to locations, landmarks, and the social conditions of his time, to give a pretty large canvas on which to paint our own images and actions to animate Holmes and Watson."

Mark A. Gagen BSI is co-founder of Wessex Press, sponsor of the popular *From Gillette to Brett* conferences, and publisher of *The Sherlock Holmes Reference Library* and many other fine Sherlockian titles. A life-long Holmes enthusiast, he is a member of *The Baker Street Irregulars* and *The Illustrious Clients of Indianapolis*. A graphic artist by profession, his work is often seen on the covers of *The Baker Street Journal* and various BSI books.

Bob Gibson, graphic designer, is the Director at Staunch Design, located in Oxford, England. In addition to designing the covers for MX Book publications, Staunch also provides identity design and brand development for small and medium sized companies through print and web for a wide range of clients, including independent schools, retail, financial services and the health sector. *www.staunch.com*

Paul D. Gilbert was born in 1954 and has lived in and around Lindon all of his life. He has been married to Jackie for thirty-eight years, and she is a Holmes expert who keeps him on the straight and narrow! He has two sons, one of whom now lives in Spain. His interests include literature, ancient history, all religions, most sports, and movies. He is currently employed full-time as a funeral director. His books so far include *The Lost Files of Sherlock Holmes* (2007), *The Chronicles of Sherlock Holmes* (2008), *Sherlock Holmes and the Giant Rat of Sumatra* (2010), *The Annals of Sherlock Holmes* (2012), and *Sherlock Holmes and the Unholy Trinity* (2015). He has just started work on *Sherlock Holmes: The Four Handed Game.*

John Atkinson Grimshaw (1836-1893) was born in Leeds, England. His amazing paintings, usually featuring twilight or night scenes illuminated by gas-lamps or moonlight, are easily recognizable, and are often used on the covers of books about the Great Detective to set the mood, as shadowy figures move in the distance through misty mysterious settings and over rain-slicked streets.

Phil Growick has been a Sherlock Holmes fan since he watched a black and white Basil Rathbone and Nigel Bruce on his grandparents' TV when he was five. His first Holmes novel was *The Secret Journal of Dr. Watson.* It has a surprise ending that no one, as yet, expected, and left everyone demanding to know what happened to all the major characters; primarily, of course, Holmes. Ergo, he wrote the sequel, *The Revenge of Sherlock Holmes,* which answered all the questions the readers of the first book were asking. His greatest joys are his wife, his sons, his daughters-in-law, and his grandsons.

Roger Johnson BSI is a retired librarian, now working as a volunteer assistant at Essex Police Museum. In his spare time he is commissioning editor of *The Sherlock Holmes Journal*, an occasional lecturer, and a frequent contributor to the Writings About the Writings. His sole work of Holmesian pastiche was published in 1997 in Mike Ashley's anthology *The Mammoth Book of New Sherlock Holmes Adventures*, and he has the greatest respect for the many authors who have contributed new tales to the present mighty trilogy. Like his wife, Jean Upton, he is a member of both *The Baker Street Irregulars* and *The Adventuresses of Sherlock Holmes.*

Kim Krisco, author of three books on leadership, now follows in the footsteps of the master storyteller Sir Arthur Conan Doyle by adding five totally new Sherlock Holmes adventures to the canon with the recently released *Sherlock Holmes – The Golden Years.* He captures the voice and style of Doyle, as Holmes and Watson find themselves unraveling mysteries in America, Africa and around turn-of-the-century London that, as Holmes puts it, "appears to have taken on an unsavory European influence." Meticulously researched, all of Krisco's stories read as mini historical novels. Indeed, he traveled to the UK and Scotland in May of 2013 to do research for his most recent book. The five novellas all take place after Holmes and Watson were supposed to have retired. *Sherlock Holmes – The Golden Years* breathes new life into the beloved "odd couple," revealing deeper insights into their protean friendship that has become richer with age . . . and a bit puckish. Krisco's diverse career fashioned a circuitous route to his becoming a full-time writer. He has taught college, written and directed TV and films, and served in corporate communications. He has two writing desks: one in a travel trailer on a river in the Rocky Mountains of Colorado, and the other in a *pequeña casa* on an estuary in La Penta, Mexico.

Andrew Lane is a British writer with thirty-odd books to his credit, a mixture of fiction & non-fiction, Adult & Young Adult, and books under his own name and ghost-written works. Most recently he has written eight books in a series (sold in translation to more than twenty countries at the last count) imagining what Sherlock Holmes would have been like when he was fourteen years old. The third of these books, *Black Ice*, is referenced in passing in his story for this anthology. *A Study in Scarlet* was the first book that Andrew Lane bought with his own pocket money. He was nine years old at the time, and the purchase warped his life from that moment on.

James Lovegrove is the author of more than fifty books, including *The Hope, Days, Untied Kingdom, Provender Gleed*, the *New York Times* bestselling *Pantheon* series, the *Redlaw* novels, and the *Dev Harmer Missions*. He has produced three Sherlock Holmes novels, with a Holmes/Cthulhu mashup trilogy in the works. He has also sold well over forty short stories and published two collections, *Imagined Slights* and *Diversifications*. He has produced a dozen short books for readers with reading difficulties, and a four-volume fantasy saga for teenagers, *The Clouded World*, under the pseudonym Jay Amory. James has been shortlisted for numerous awards, including the Arthur C. Clarke Award, the John W. Campbell Memorial Award, the Bram Stoker Award, the British Fantasy Society Award, and the Manchester Book Award. His short story "Carry The Moon In My Pocket" won the 2011 Seiun Award in Japan for Best Translated Short Story. His work has been translated into over a dozen languages, and his journalism has appeared in periodicals as diverse as *Literary Review, Interzone* and *BBC MindGames*. He reviews fiction regularly for the *Financial Times*. He lives with his wife, two sons, cat, and tiny dog in Eastbourne, not far from the site of the "small farm upon the South Downs" to which Sherlock Holmes retired.

Bonnie MacBird has loved Sherlock Holmes since breathlessly devouring the Canon at ten. She has degrees in music and film from Stanford, is the original writer of the movie *TRON*, won three Emmys for documentary film, studied Shakespearean acting at Oxford, and divides her time between her home in Los Angeles and a hotel room in Baker Street. She runs *The Sherlock Breakfast Club* and a playreading series in Los Angeles, where she also teaches writing at UCLA Extension. Her first novel, *Art in the Blood* (HarperCollins 2015) features a kidnapping, murder, and an art theft, and challenges Holmes's artistic nature and his friendship with Watson to the limits.

David Marcum first discovered Sherlock Holmes in 1975, at the age of ten, when he received an abridged version of *The Adventures* during a trade. Since that time, David has collected literally thousands of traditional Holmes pastiches in the form of novels, short stories, radio and television episodes, movies and scripts, comics, fan-fiction, and unpublished manuscripts. He is the author of *The Papers of Sherlock Holmes Vol.'s I* and *II* (2011, 2013), *Sherlock Holmes and A Quantity of Debt* (2013) and *Sherlock Holmes – Tangled Skeins* (2015). Additionally, he is the editor of the three-volume set *Sherlock Holmes in Montague Street* (2014, recasting Arthur Morrison's Martin Hewitt stories as early Holmes adventures,) and most recently this current collection, *The MX Book of New Sherlock Holmes Stories* (2015). He has contributed essays to the *Baker Street Journal* and *The Gazette*, the journal of the Nero Wolfe *Wolfe Pack*. He began his adult work life as a Federal Investigator for an obscure U.S. Government agency, before the organization was eliminated. He returned to school for a second degree, and is now a licensed Civil Engineer, living in Tennessee with his wife and son. He is a member of *The Sherlock Holmes Society of London*, *The John H. Watson Society* ("Marker"), *The Praed Street Irregulars* ("The Obrisset Snuff Box"), *The Solar Pons Society of London*, and *The Diogenes Club West (East Tennessee Annex)*, a curious and unofficial Scion of one. Since the age of nineteen, he has worn a deerstalker as his regular-and-only hat from autumn to spring. In 2013, he and his deerstalker were finally able make a trip-of-a-lifetime Holmes Pilgrimage to England, where you may have spotted him. If you ever run into him and his deerstalker out and about, feel free to say hello!

Lyn McConchie began writing professionally in 1990. Since then, she has seen thirty-two of her books published, and almost three hundred of her short stories appear. Her work has been published to date in nine countries and four languages, which she says isn't bad for an elderly, crippled, female farmer. Lyn lives on her farm in the North island of New Zealand where she breeds coloured sheep, and has free-range geese and hens. She shares her 19th century farmhouse with her Ocicat, Thunder, 7,469 books by other authors, and says that she plans to write forever or die trying.

Iain McLaughlin has been writing for a living since 1985. He has worked on numerous comics in the UK, and was editor of the *Beano* for a time. He has written novels, short stories, radio plays, and some TV episodes, often working with regular writing partner Claire Bartlett. He wrote several stories in the "Doctor Who" universe, beginning with 2001's *The Eye of the Scorpion*, which introduced the character of Erimem. He has also written audios for *Blake's 7*, and radio plays of legendary sleuth Sherlock Holmes. Additionally, he has written numerous horror radio plays, and created and wrote every episode of Imagination Theater's *Kerides The Thinker* radio series. His *noir* novel, *Movie Star*, was released by Thebes Publishing in 2015. He was born and still lives in Dundee on the east coast of Scotland.

Larry Millett worked for thirty years as a newspaper reporter in St. Paul, where he lives, while building a parallel career as a mystery novelist and architectural historian. He has written seven mysteries featuring Sherlock Holmes, all but one of them set in Minnesota. His first novel, *Sherlock Holmes and the Red Demon*, appeared in 1996. His second novel, *Sherlock Holmes and the Ice Palace Murders*, was adapted in 2015 into a play that performed to full houses at a theater in St. Paul. He is now working on a new mystery featuring Holmes that will be published in 2016 by the University of Minnesota Press.

Sidney Paget (1860-1908), a few of whose illustrations are used within this anthology, was born in London, and like his two older brothers, became a famed illustrator and painter. He completed over three-hundred-and-fifty drawings for the Sherlock Holmes stories first published in *The Strand* magazine, defining Holmes's image forever after in the public mind.

GC Rosenquist was born in Chicago, Illinois, and has been writing since he was ten years old. His interests are very eclectic. His eleven previously published books include literary fiction, horror, poetry, a comedic memoir, and lots of science fiction. His latest published work for MX Books is *Sherlock Holmes: The Pearl of Death and Other Stories* (2015). He works professionally as a graphic artist. He has studied writing and poetry at the College of Lake County in Grayslake, Illinois, and currently resides in Lindenhurst,

Illinois. For more information on GC Rosenquist, you can go to his website at *www.gcrosenquist.com.*

Geri Schear is a novelist and short story writer. Her work has been published in literary journals in the U.S. and Ireland. Her first novel, *A Biased Judgement: The Diaries of Sherlock Holmes 1897* was released to critical acclaim in 2014. The sequel, *Sherlock Holmes and the Other Woman,* will be released by MX Publishing in November 2015. She lives in Kells, Ireland.

Carolyn and Joel Senter ("Those Sherlock Holmes People in Cincinnati") were the founders of *Classic Specialties,* which they operated for more than a quarter century, as "North America's leading purveyor of items appertaining to Mr. Sherlock Holmes and His Times." After retiring *Classic Specialties* in 2014, the Senters have maintained their contact with The Sherlockian Community via membership in several scions and Sherlockian societies, continued participation in numerous Sherlockian gatherings and, primarily, through their monthly (almost) internet newsletter, *The Sherlockian E-Times.* Their previous contributions to the world of Sherlockian printed literature have included the compiling and editing of *The Formidable Scrap-Book of Baker Street,* the publication of three full-length Sherlockian books, and the authoring of articles for various Sherlockian periodicals.

Tim Symonds was born in London. He grew up in Somerset, Dorset, and Guernsey. After several years in East and Central Africa, he settled in California and graduated Phi Beta Kappa in Political Science from UCLA. He is a Fellow of the *Royal Geographical Society.* He writes his novels in the woods and hidden valleys surrounding his home in the High Weald of East Sussex. Dr. Watson knew the untamed region well. In "The Adventure of Black Peter", Watson wrote, "the Weald was once part of that great forest which for so long held the Saxon invaders at bay." Tim's novels are published by MX Publishing. His latest is titled *Sherlock Holmes and The Sword Of Osman.* Previous novels include *Sherlock Holmes and The Mystery of Einstein's Daughter, Sherlock Holmes and The Dead Boer At Scotney Castle,* and *Sherlock Holmes and The Case of The Bulgarian Codex.*

The following contributors appear in
The MX Book of New Sherlock Holmes Stories
Part I – 1881-1889 *and* Part II – 1890-1895

Hugh Ashton was born in the UK, and moved to Japan in 1988, where he has remained since then, living with his wife Yoshiko in the historic city of Kamakura, a little to the south of Yokohama. In the past, he has worked in the technology and financial services industries, which have provided him with material for some of his books set in the 21st century. He currently works as a writer: novelist, copywriter (his work for large Japanese corporations appears in international business journals), and journalist, as well as producing industry reports on various aspects of the financial services industry. Recently, however, his lifelong interest in Sherlock Holmes has developed into an acclaimed series of adventures featuring the world's most famous detective, written in the style of the originals, and published by Inknbeans Press. In addition to these, he has also published historical and alternate historical novels, short stories, and thrillers. Together with artist Andy Boerger, he has produced the *Sherlock Ferret* series of stories for children, featuring the world's cutest detective.

Deanna Baran lives in a remote part of Texas where cowboys may still be seen in their natural habitat. A librarian and former museum curator, she writes in between cups of tea, playing *Go*, and trading postcards with people around the world. This is her first venture into the foggy streets of gaslit London.

Kevin David Barratt became a fan of Sherlock Holmes whilst at school. He is an active member of the *The Scandalous Bohemians*, a group who meet regularly in Leeds and for whom Kevin has contributed an essay on *Sherlock Holmes and Drugs* (which can be read at *www.scandalousbohemians.com*). Kevin is also a member of *The Sherlock Holmes Society of London*. He is married with two grown-up children and lives in Yorkshire.

Derrick Belanger is an author and educator most noted for his books and lectures on Sherlock Holmes and Sir Arthur Conan Doyle, as well as his writing for the blog *I Hear of Sherlock Everywhere*. Both volumes of his two-volume anthology, *A Study in Terror: Sir Arthur Conan Doyle's Revolutionary Stories of Fear and the Supernatural* were #1 best sellers on the Amazon.com UK Sherlock Holmes book list, and his *MacDougall Twins with Sherlock Holmes* chapter book, *Attack of the Violet Vampire!* was also a #1 best selling new release in the UK. His novella, *Sherlock Holmes and the Adventure of the Peculiar Provenance*, is forthcoming from Endeavour Press. Mr. Belanger's academic work has been published in *The Colorado Reading Journal* and *Gifted Child Today*. Find him at *www.belangerbooks.com*.

Matthew Booth is the author of *Sherlock Holmes and the Giant's Hand*, a collection of Sherlock Holmes short stories published by Breese Books. He is a scriptwriter for the American radio network *Imagination Theatre*, syndicated by Jim French Productions, contributing particularly to their series, *The Further Adventures of Sherlock Holmes*. Matthew has contributed two original stories to *The Game Is Afoot*, a collection of Sherlock Holmes short stories published in 2008 by Wordsworth Editions. His contributions are "The Tragedy of Saxon's Gate" and "The Dragon of Lea Lane". He has provided an original story entitled "A Darkness Discovered", featuring his own creation, Manchester-based private detective John Dakin, for the short story collection *Crime Scenes*, also published by Wordsworth Editions in 2008. Matthew is currently working on a supernatural novel called *The Ravenfirth Horror*.

Peter Calamai, BSI, a resident of Ottawa, was a reporter, editor and foreign correspondent with major Canadian newspapers since 1966. For half those years he has worked five minutes' walk from the Rideau Canal and the Commissariat Building. When editor of the Ottawa Citizen's editorial pages, Calamai had the good fortune to spend an afternoon interviewing canal historian Robert Legget. He has been an active Sherlockian since the mid-1990's, concentrating on Holmes and the Victorian press. Honours include designation as a Master Bootmaker by Canada's leading Sherlockian society and investiture in the *Baker Street Irregulars* as "The Leeds Mercury", a name taken from *The Hound of the Baskervilles*.

J.R. Campbell is a Calgary-based writer who always enjoys setting problems before the Great Detective. Along with his steadfast friend Charles Prepolec, he has co-edited the Sherlock Holmes anthologies *Curious Incidents, Curious Incidents 2, Gaslight Grimoire: Fantastic Tales of Sherlock Holmes, Gaslight Grotesque: Nightmare Takes of Sherlock Holmes*, and *Gaslight Arcanum: Uncanny Tales of Sherlock Holmes*. He has also contributed stories to Imagination Theater's Radio Drama *The Further Adventures of*

Sherlock Holmes, and the anthologies *A Study in Lavender: Queering Sherlock Holmes* and *Challenger Unbound*. At the time of writing, his next project, again with Charles Prepolec, is the anthology *Professor Challenger: New Worlds, Lost Places*.

Catherine Cooke BSI is a Librarian with Westminster Libraries who divides her time between maintaining and developing the Libraries' computer systems and the Sherlock Holmes Collection. She is a Fellow of the *Chartered Institute of Library and Information Professionals*, Joint Honorary Secretary of the *Sherlock Holmes Society of London*, a member of the *Baker Street Irregulars*, and of the *Adventuresses of Sherlock Holmes*. She won the Baker Street Irregulars' *Morley-Montgomery Award* for 2005 and the Sherlock Holmes Society of London's *Tony Howlett Award* in 2014.

Bert Coules wandered through a succession of jobs from fringe opera company manager to BBC radio drama producer-director before becoming a full-time writer at the beginning of 1989. Bert works in a wide range of genres, including science fiction, horror, comedy, romance and action-adventure but he is especially associated with crime and detective stories: he was the head writer on the BBC's unique project to dramatise the entire Sherlock Holmes canon, and went on to script four further series of original Holmes and Watson mysteries. As well as radio, he also writes for TV and the stage.

Bill Crider is a former college English teacher, and is the author of more than fifty published novels and an equal number of short stories. He's won two *Anthony* awards and a *Derringer* Award, and he's been nominated for the *Shamus* and the *Edgar* awards. His latest novel in the Sheriff Dan Rhodes series is *Between the Living and the Dead*. Check out his homepage at *www.billcrider.com*, or take a look at his peculiar blog at *http://billcrider.blogspot.com*.

Carole Nelson Douglas is the author of sixty New-York-published novels, and the first woman to write a Sherlock Holmes spin-off series using the first woman protagonist, Irene Adler. *Good Night, Mr. Holmes* debuted as a *New York Times* Notable Book of the Year. Holmes and Watson have been Douglas' "go-to guys" since childhood, appearing in a high school skit and her weekly newspaper column. Seeing only one pseudonymous woman in print with Holmes derivations, she based her Irene Adler on how Conan Doyle presented her: a talented, compassionate, independent, and audacious woman, in eight acclaimed novels. ("Readers will doff their deerstalkers." – *Publishers Weekly*) Those readers pine in vain for a film version of the truly substantial and fascinating Irene Adler that Holmes and Sir Arthur Conan Doyle admired as "The Woman." Now indie publishing, Douglas plans to make more of her Irene Adler stories available in print and eBook. *www.carolenelsondouglas.com*

C.H. Dye first discovered Sherlock Holmes when she was eleven, in a collection that ended at Reichenbach Falls. It was another six months before she discovered *The Hound of the Baskervilles*, and two weeks after that before a librarian handed her *The Return*. She has loved the stories ever since. She has written fanfiction, but this is her first published pastiche.

Lyndsay Faye, BSI, grew up in the Pacific Northwest, graduating from Notre Dame de Namur University. She worked as a professional actress throughout the Bay Area for several years before moving to New York. Her first novel was the critically acclaimed pastiche *Dust and Shadow: An Account of the Ripper Killings by Dr. John H Watson*. Faye's love of her adopted city led her to research the origins of the New York City

Police Department, as related in the *Edgar*-nominated Timothy Wilde trilogy. She is a frequent writer for the *Strand Magazine* and the Eisner-nominated comic *Watson and Holmes.* Lyndsay and her husband, Gabriel Lehner, live in Queens with their cats, Grendel and Prufrock. She is a very proud member of the *Baker Street Babes, Actor's Equity Association, Mystery Writers of America, The Adventuresses of Sherlock Holmes,* and *The Baker Street Irregulars.* Her works have currently been translated into fourteen languages

Wendy C. Fries is the author of *Sherlock Holmes and John Watson: The Day They Met* and also writes under the name Atlin Merrick. Wendy is fascinated with London theatre, scriptwriting, and lattes. Website: *wendycfries.com.*

Jayantika Ganguly is the General Secretary and Editor of the *Sherlock Holmes Society of India,* a member of the *Sherlock Holmes Society of London,* and the *Czech Sherlock Holmes Society.* She is the author of *The Holmes Sutra* (MX 2014). She is a corporate lawyer working with one of the Big Six law firms.

Dick Gillman is a Yorkshire-man in his mid-sixties. He retired from teaching Science in 2005 and moved to Brittany, France in 2008 with his wife Alex, Truffle the Black Labrador, and two cats. He still has strong family links with the UK, where he visits his two grown up children and his grandchildren. Dick is a prolific writer, and during his retirement he has written fourteen Sherlock Holmes short stories and a Sci-Fi novella. His latest short story, "Sherlock Holmes and The Man on Westminster Bridge" was completed in July 2015, and is published for the first time in this anthology.

Jack Grochot is a retired investigative newspaper journalist and a former federal law enforcement agent specializing in mail fraud cases. He lives on a small farm in southwestern Pennsylvania, USA, where he writes and cares for five boarded horses. His fiction work includes stories in *Sherlock Holmes Mystery Magazine, The Sherlock Holmes Megapack* (an e-book), as well as the book *Come, Watson! Quickly!,* a collection of five Sherlock Holmes pastiches. The author, an active member of *Mystery Writers of America,* can be contacted by e-mail at *grochot@comcast.net.*

Dr. John Hall has written widely on Holmes. His books includes *Sidelights on Holmes,* a commentary on the Canon, *The Abominable Wife,* on the unrecorded cases, *Unexplored Possibilities,* a study of Dr. John H. Watson, and a monograph on Professor Moriarty, "The Dynamics of a Falling Star". (Most of these are now out of print.) His novels include *Sherlock Holmes and the Adler Papers, The Travels of Sherlock Holmes, Sherlock Holmes and the Boulevard Assassin, Sherlock Holmes and the Disgraced Inspector, Sherlock Holmes and the Telephone Mystery, Sherlock Holmes and the Hammerford Will, Sherlock Holmes and the Abbey School Mystery,* and *Sherlock Holmes at the Raffles Hotel.* John is a member of the *International Pipe-smoker's Hall of Fame,* and lives in Yorkshire, England.

Carl L. Heifetz Over thirty years of inquiry as a research microbiologist have prepared Carl Heifetz to explore new horizons in science. As an author, he has published numerous articles and short stories for fan magazines and other publications. In 2013 he published a book entitled *Voyage of the Blue Carbuncle* that is based on the works of Sir Arthur Conan Doyle and Gene Roddenberry. *Voyage of the Blue Carbuncle* is a fun and exciting spoof, sure to please science fiction fans as well as those who love the stories of Sherlock

Holmes and *Star Trek*. Carl and his wife have two grown children and live in Trinity, Florida.

John Heywood (not the author's real name) was born in Gloucestershire in 1951, and educated at Katharine Lady Berkeley's Grammar School and Jesus College, Cambridge. After graduating, he supported himself in many different ways, including teaching, decorating, house-sitting, laboring, and mowing graveyards, while at the same time making paintings, prints and drawings. He continues to make art, and his work is now in collections in Europe and America, and is regularly exhibited. He currently lives in Brixton, South London, and works as a painter and as a teacher of art and English in adult education. In 2014, his first book, *The Investigations of Sherlock Holmes*, was published by MX Publishing. It was enthusiastically received by the critics, and has recently been issued in India.

Mike Hogan writes mostly historical novels and short stories, many set in Victorian London and featuring Sherlock Holmes and Doctor Watson. He read the Conan Doyle stories at school with great enjoyment, but hadn't thought much about Sherlock Holmes until, having missed the Granada/Jeremy Brett TV series when it was originally shown in the eighties, he came across a box set of videos in a street market and was hooked on Holmes again. He started writing Sherlock Holmes pastiches about four years ago, having great fun re-imagining situations for the Conan Doyle characters to act in. The relationship between Holmes and Watson fascinates him as one of the great literary friendships. (He's also a huge admirer of Patrick O'Brian's Aubrey-Maturin novels). Like Captain Aubrey and Doctor Maturin, Holmes and Watson are an odd couple, differing in almost every facet of their characters, but sharing a common sense of decency and a common humanity. Living with Sherlock Holmes can't have been easy, and Mike enjoys adding a stronger vein of "pawky humour" into the Conan Doyle mix, even letting Watson have the second-to-last word on occasions. Mike is British, and he lives in Italy. His books include *Sherlock Holmes and the Scottish Question*; *The Gory Season – Sherlock Holmes, Jack the Ripper and the Thames Torso Murders* and the Sherlock Holmes & Young Winston 1887 Trilogy (*The Deadwood Stage*; *The Jubilee Plot*; and *The Giant Moles*), He has also written the following short story collections: *Sherlock Holmes: Murder at the Savoy and Other Stories, Sherlock Holmes: The Skull of Kohada Koheiji and Other Stories*, and *Sherlock Holmes: Murder on the Brighton Line and Other Stories*. *www.mikehoganbooks.com*

Jeremy Holstein first discovered Sherlock Holmes at age five when he became convinced that the Hound of the Baskervilles lived in his bedroom closet. A life long enthusiast of radio dramas, Jeremy is currently the lead dramatist and director for the Post Meridian Radio Players adaptations of Sherlock Holmes, where he has adapted *The Hound of the Baskervilles*, *The Sign of Four*, and "Jack the Harlot Killer" (retitled "The Whitechapel Murders") from William S. Baring-Gould's *Sherlock Holmes of Baker Street* for the company. He is currently in production with an adaptation of "Charles Augustus Milverton". Jeremy has also written Sherlock Holmes scripts for Jim French's *Imagination Theatre*. He lives with his wife and daughter in the Boston, MA area.

In the year 1998 **Craig Janacek** took his degree of Doctor of Medicine at Vanderbilt University, and proceeded to Stanford to go through the training prescribed for pediatricians in practice. Having completed his studies there, he was duly attached to the University of California, San Francisco as Associate Professor. The author of over seventy medical monographs upon a variety of obscure lesions, his travel-worn and battered tin dispatch-box is crammed with papers, nearly all of which are records of his fictional works. To date, these have been published solely in electronic format, including two non-Holmes novels (*The Oxford Deception* and *The Anger of Achilles Peterson*), the trio of holiday adventures collected as *The Midwinter Mysteries of Sherlock Holmes*, and a Watsonian novel entitled *The Isle of Devils*. His next project is the short trilogy *The Assassination of Sherlock Holmes*. Craig Janacek is a *nom de plume*.

Leslie S. Klinger BSI is the editor of *The New Annotated Sherlock Holmes* and many other books on Holmes, Watson, and the Victorian age.

Luke Benjamen Kuhns is a crime writer who lives in London. He has authored several Sherlock Holmes collections including *The Untold Adventures of Sherlock Holmes* (published in India & Italy), *Sherlock Holmes Studies in Legacy*, and the graphic novel *Sherlock Holmes and the Horror of Frankenstein*. He has written and spoken on the various forms of pastiche writing, which can be found in the *Fan Phenomena Series: Sherlock Holmes*.

Michael Kurland has written over thirty novels and a melange of short stories, articles, and other stuff, and has been nominated for two Edgars and the American Book Award. His books have appeared in Chinese, Czech, French, Italian, German, Japanese, Polish, Portuguese, Spanish, Swedish, and some alphabet full of little pothooks and curlicues. He lives in a Secular Humanist Hermitage in a secluded bay north of San Francisco, California, where he kills and skins his own vegetables. He may be communicated with through his website, *michaelkurland.com*.

Ann Margaret Lewis attended Michigan State University, where she received her Bachelor's Degree in English Literature. She began her writing career writing tie-in children's books and short stories for DC Comics. She then published two editions of the book *Star Wars: The New Essential Guide to Alien Species* for Random House. She is the author of the award-winning *Murder in the Vatican: The Church Mysteries of Sherlock Holmes* (Wessex Press), and her most recent book is a Holmes novel entitled *The Watson Chronicles: A Sherlock Holmes Novel in Stories* (Wessex Press).

Daniel McGachey Outside of his day job – which, over the past quarter century has seen him write extensively for comics, newspapers, magazines, digital media, and animation – Scottish writer Daniel McGachey's stories first appeared in several volumes of *The BHF Book of Horror Stories* and *Black Book of Horror* anthology series, and *Filthy Creations* magazine. In 2009, Dark Regions Press published his first ghost story collection, *They That Dwell in Dark Places*, dedicated in part to M.R. James, whose works inspired the creation of the collected stories. Since 2005, he has reviewed television and radio adaptations of James's stories for *The Ghosts and Scholars M.R. James Newsletter*, while his sequels to several of James's original tales appeared as the Haunted Library publication *Ex Libris: Lufford* in 2012. Moving from M.R. James to his other lifelong literary hero, his 2010 Dark Regions Press collection pitted Sir Arthur Conan Doyle's rational detective against the irrational forces of the supernatural in *Sherlock Holmes: The Impossible Cases*. His radio plays have been broadcast since 2005 as part of the mystery and suspense series *Imagination Theater*, including entries in its long-running strand of new Holmesian mysteries, *The Further Adventures of Sherlock Holmes*. He is working on a new "impossible case" for Sherlock Holmes and Dr. Watson in the novel, *The Devil's Crown*.

William Patrick Maynard was born and raised in Cleveland, Ohio. His passion for writing began in childhood and was fueled by early love of detective and thriller fiction. He was licensed by the Sax Rohmer Literary Estate to continue the Fu Manchu thrillers for Black Coat Press. *The Terror of Fu Manchu* was published in 2009 and was followed by *The Destiny of Fu Manchu* in 2012 and *The Triumph of Fu Manchu* in 2015. His previous Sherlock Holmes stories appeared in *Gaslight Grotesque* (2009/EDGE Publishing) and *Further Encounters of Sherlock Holmes* (2014/Titan Books). He currently resides in Northeast Ohio with his wife and family.

Adrian Middleton is a Staffordshire born independent publisher. The son of a real-world detective, he is a former civil servant and policy adviser who now writes and edits science fiction, fantasy, and a popular series of steampunked Sherlock Holmes stories.

Steve Mountain is a "born and bred" native of Portsmouth in the UK. Married with two grown-up children, he works for a local Council as a civil engineer, trying to retro-fit cycle riding facilities into roads not originally built for the purpose. This is usually, but not always, successful. Seeing his name in print is nothing new, although to date this has been mostly in articles in the local newspaper complaining about the effect of said cycle facilities on other road users. Having helped his daughter solve a problem with one of her Holmes pastiches, he caught the fiction writing bug himself. He has self-published one of his early stories with *Lulu*.

Mark Mower is a crime writer and historian and a member of the Crime Writers' Association. His books include *Bloody British History: Norwich* (The History Press, 2014) and *Suffolk Murders* (The History Press, 2011). His first book, *Suffolk Tales of Mystery & Murder* (Countryside Books, 2006), contained a potent blend of tales from the seamier side of country life – described by the East Anglian Daily Times *Suffolk* magazine as ". . . a good serving of grisliness, a strong flavour of the unusual, a seasoning of ghoulishness and just a hint of the unexpected . . . ." Alongside his writing, Mark lectures on crime history and runs a murder mystery business.

Summer Perkins is a film student who lives in Portland, Oregon, and has been a fan of the various incarnations of Sherlock Holmes for many years. Though no stranger to writing in the world of Holmes, this is Summer's first published piece. In addition to writing, Summer can be found reading, watching films, and studying various eras in history.

Chris Redmond, BSI, is editor of the website *Sherlockian.Net*, and the author of *A Sherlock Holmes Handbook*, *In Bed with Sherlock Holmes*, and other books, as well as many Sherlockian articles. He is a member of the *Baker Street Irregulars, The Bootmakers of Toronto, The Adventuresses of Sherlock Holmes*, and other societies. He lives in Waterloo, Ontario, Canada.

Martin Rosenstock studied English, American, and German literature. In 2008, he received a Ph.D. from the University of California, Santa Barbara for looking into what happens when things go badly – as they do from time to time – for detectives in German-language literature. After job hopping around the colder latitudes of the U.S. for three years, he decided to return to warmer climes. In 2011, he took a job at Gulf University for Science and Technology in Kuwait, where he currently teaches. When not brooding over plot twists, he spends too much time and money traveling the Indian Ocean littoral. There is a novel somewhere there, he feels sure.

Shane Simmons is a multi-award-winning screenwriter and graphic novelist whose work has appeared in international film festivals, museums and lectures about design and structure. His best-known piece of fiction, *The Long and Unlearned Life of Roland Gethers*, has been discussed in multiple books and academic journals about sequential art, and his short stories have been printed in critically praised anthologies of history, crime and horror. He lives in Montreal with his wife and too many cats. Follow him at eyestrainproductions.com and @Shane_Eyestrain

Denis O. Smith's first published story of Sherlock Holmes and Doctor Watson, "The Adventure of The Purple Hand", appeared in 1982. Since then, numerous other such accounts have been published in magazines and anthologies both in the U.K. and the U.S. In the 1990's, four volumes of his stories were published under the general title of *The Chronicles of Sherlock Holmes*, and, more recently, a dozen of his stories, most not previously published in book form, appeared as *The Lost Chronicles of Sherlock Holmes* (2014), and he wrote a new story for the anthology, *Sherlock Holmes Abroad* (2015). Born in Yorkshire, in the north of England, Denis Smith has lived and worked in various parts of the country, including London, and has now been resident in Norfolk for many years. His interests range widely, but apart from his dedication to the career of Sherlock Holmes, he has a passion for historical mysteries of all kinds, the railways of Britain and the history of London.

Robert V. Stapleton was born and brought up in Leeds, Yorkshire, England, and studied at Durham University. After working in various parts of the country as an Anglican parish priest, he is now retired and lives with his wife in North Yorkshire. As a member of his local writing group, he now has time to develop his other life as a writer of adventure stories. He has recently had a number of short stories published, and he is hoping to have a couple of completed novels published at some time in the future.

Amy Thomas is a member of the *Baker Street Babes* Podcast, and the author of *The Detective and The Woman* mystery novels featuring Sherlock Holmes and Irene Adler. She blogs at *girlmeetssherlock.wordpress.com*, and she writes and edits professionally from her home in Fort Myers, Florida.

Will Thomas is the author of seven books in the Barker and Llewelyn Victorian mystery series, including *Some Danger Involved, Fatal Enquiry*, and *Anatomy of Evil*. He was nominated for a *Barry* and a *Shamus*, and is a two time winner of the Oklahoma Book Award. He lives in Broken Arrow, Oklahoma, where he studies Victorian martial arts and models British railways.

Daniel D. Victor, a Ph.D. in American literature, is a retired high school English teacher who taught in the Los Angeles Unified School District for forty-six years. His doctoral dissertation on little-known American author, David Graham Phillips, led to the creation of Victor's first Sherlock Holmes pastiche, *The Seventh Bullet*, in which Holmes investigates Phillips' actual murder. Victor's second novel, *A Study in Synchronicity,* is a two-stranded murder mystery, which features a Sherlock Holmes-like private eye. He is currently completing a trilogy called *Sherlock Holmes and the American Literati*. Each novel introduces Holmes to a different American author who actually passed through London at the turn of the century. In *The Final Page of Baker Street*, Holmes meets Raymond Chandler; in *The Baron of Brede Place*, Stephen Crane; in *Seventeen Minutes* *to Baker Street*, Mark Twain. Victor, who is also writing a novel about his early years as a teacher, lives with his wife in Los Angeles, California. They have two adult sons.

Stephen Wade has a special interest in crime history, having published widely on regional crime. His book, *The Girl who Lived on Air* (Seren) was a Welsh Book of the Month for Waterstones last year. He was formerly a lecturer in English, and also worked as a writer in prisons for six years. His latest book is a short story collection, *Uncle Albert* (Priory Press). The current fiction project is a collection of crime stories featuring Lestrade.

Sam Wiebe's debut novel *Last of the Independents* was published by Dundurn Press. An alternative private detective novel set in the Pacific Northwest, *Last of the Independents*, won the 2012 Arthur Ellis Award for Best Unpublished First Novel. Sam's short fiction has been published in *Thuglit, Spinetingler, Subterrain,* and *Criminal Element,* among others. Follow him at @sam_wiebe and at *samwiebe.com*.

Marcia Wilson is a freelance researcher and illustrator who likes to work in a style compatible for the color blind and visually impaired. She is Canon-centric and her first MX offering, *You Buy Bones*, uses the point-of-view of Scotland Yard to show the unique talents of Dr. Watson. She can be contacted at *gravelgirty.deviantart.com*

Vincent W. Wright has been a Sherlockian and member of *The Illustrious Clients of Indianapolis* since 1997. He is the creator of a blog, *Historical Sherlock*, which is dedicated to the chronology of The Canon, and has written a column on that subject for his home scion's newsletter since 2005. He lives in Indiana, and works for the federal government. This is his first pastiche.

MX Publishing

MX Publishing is the world's largest specialist Sherlock Holmes publisher, with several hundred titles and over a hundred authors creating the latest in Sherlock Holmes fiction and non-fiction.

From traditional short stories and novels to travel guides and quiz books, MX Publishing caters to all Holmes fans.

The collection includes leading titles such as *Benedict Cumberbatch In Transition* and *The Norwood Author* which won the 2011 *Tony Howlett Award* (Sherlock Holmes Book of the Year).

MX Publishing also has one of the largest communities of Holmes fans on *Facebook*, with regular contributions from dozens of authors.

www.mxpublishing.co.uk (UK) and *www.mxpublishing.com* (USA).

Lightning Source UK Ltd.
Milton Keynes UK
UKOW02f0357030816

279835UK00001B/82/P